Innocent Passions

BRENDA HIATT

Innocent Passions

AVON BOOKS

An Imprint of HarperCollinsPublishers

This is a work of fiction. Names, characters, places, and incidents are products of the author's imagination or are used fictitiously and are not to be construed as real. Any resemblance to actual events, locales, organizations, or persons, living or dead, is entirely coincidental.

AVON BOOKS
An Imprint of HarperCollins*Publishers*
10 East 53rd Street
New York, New York 10022-5299

Printed in the U.S.A.

For INDYWITTS,
my wonderful critique group.
Thank you for all of your help!

Chapter 1

August 1816

"**W**e'll be murdered in our beds, miss, just see if we won't."

Rowena Riverstone smiled indulgently at her maid, though in truth she was rather overwhelmed herself by the teeming streets of London on this, her first visit to the metropolis.

"Nonsense, Matthilda. My brother's house is in the nicer part of Town and quite secure. As long as we refrain from wandering the streets alone and at night, we should be perfectly safe."

But Matthilda shook her head and continued to mutter dire predictions for their visit. "The sooner we can return to River Chase, the happier I'll be."

"Especially since that will mean returning to your Jeb," Rowena said, chuckling at the maid's blush. "Very well, I won't tease any more."

In fact it was partly for the sake of Jeb's future that

Rowena had felt it necessary to come to Town, his future and that of other tenants like him. As for her own future . . .

Rowena stifled a sigh. After twenty-one years immured in the country, her future was all too easy to predict: year after year of spinsterhood, perhaps to be enlivened one day by the role of maiden aunt, should her brother Nelson ever marry and have children.

She refused to give in to regrets, however. She led a full life, what with her studies, the management of Nelson's country household and the writing of her political essays—essays that would become more timely once she was established in London.

She smiled a secret smile, for not even Matthilda had any clue that Rowena was the mysterious MRR, regular—and controversial—contributor to William Cobbett's *Political Register*. If she stayed in London long enough, she might meet Mr. Cobbett himself, as well as some of the other men whose views she admired, such as essayist Leigh Hunt and her idol, the fiery Spencean reformer Lester Richards.

She had actually corresponded with the latter early in the year—not that he was likely to remember, of course. Still, she cherished his two letters, and had all but committed them to memory. To meet him face to face would be—

"This be Hay Street, miss," the coachman called down to them. "What number did you say?"

"Number twelve," Rowena replied, adjusting her spectacles and leaning forward to peer out of the window.

Her father had maintained this Town residence for fifteen years and her brother for two, but this would be her first glimpse of it, as neither of them had ever allowed her to visit London. Now that she was mistress of her own funds, however, her brother could no longer prevent her doing as she wished.

"I hope Nelson is in," she remarked to Matthilda. "And that he has room for us."

The maid stared at her in horror. "Is he not expecting you, miss? But you said—"

"I said I was needed in London—but not by my brother."

Matthilda sputtered her dismay as the coach pulled to a halt, but Rowena ignored her to stare with interest at the tall, narrow house, virtually identical to all of the other tall, narrow houses on Hay Street.

"I can't say it looks like much," she commented as the coachman lowered the steps and assisted her from the coach.

"Shall I knock, miss?" he asked.

"Please." Head high, trailed by her maid, Rowena mounted the steps to the door, trying to look as though she'd done so every day of her life.

A portly butler answered the knock. Regarding the young lady on the doorstep without recognition, he raised a supercilious eyebrow but Rowena refused to be cowed by a mere retainer when she had fiercer dragons to face.

"Pray inform Sir Nelson that his sister, Miss Riverstone, has come to visit." She rather enjoyed the blank astonishment that replaced the butler's original haughtiness.

"Of . . . of course, miss." He stood aside so that she and her maid could enter. "If you'll wait in the parlor while I inform Sir Nelson, I can have tea brought."

"That would be lovely," Rowena said graciously. She directed the coachman to have her trunk brought in, sent Matthilda off to the servants' hall, then followed the butler across the wooden parquet floor of the front hall to the indicated room.

The small, pleasant parlor was furnished in ruby and cream—favorite colors, she recalled, of her mother, who had died seven years earlier. No doubt she'd had a hand in decorating the house when her father had first taken it for his extended stays in London, where he had held a position of some importance in the Home Office.

"Rubbish!" came a familiar voice from the hall. "My sister never comes to Town. It must be some supplicant pretending—" Entering the parlor, he broke off, sandy eyebrows ascending into carefully disordered sandy hair as he spotted her. "Ro? What the devil are you doing here?"

"Good afternoon, Nelson," she responded calmly to the stocky young man some three years her senior. "I am delighted to see you, too."

His brows now drew down to a frown. "You didn't answer my question. Nor did you send word you were coming."

"If I had, you would have forbidden it." She glanced at the listening butler, who, catching her eye, suddenly seemed to realize he was needed elsewhere and hurried off.

"With good reason." Sir Nelson's frown deepened to a scowl. "You and your radical ideas." Belatedly, he glanced behind him.

Seeing no listening servants, he closed the parlor door. "I won't have you spouting your seditious theories here in London, Ro. It could do irreparable damage to my position. The politics at Whitehall are dicey right now. Besides—"

"You've been saying that for two years, and Father for years before that," she reminded him. "And my theories are *not* seditious. They are mere common sense, if you'd only—"

He held up a hand. "Not another word. If you can't promise to hold your Whiggish tongue on such matters, I'll pack you straight back to River Chase in the morning."

That had always been the sticking point. Their father had demanded just such a promise as a condition of Rowena visiting London and she had never been willing to give it. After all, what would have been the point in coming to the seat of England's power if she had to compromise her principles to get there?

Now, however, she smiled. "Perhaps you have forgotten that I celebrated a birthday five days since. If you are unwilling to house me, I am quite capable of setting up an establishment of my own—nor can you prevent me doing so."

Nelson stared. "Devil take it, I *had* forgotten." He ran a hand through his hair in agitation.

"Don't worry, Nelson. I haven't come here with the express purpose of embarrassing you. I simply wish to see London."

Her brother frowned again, clearly disbelieving. "I know you better than that, Ro. That time Lord Sidmouth came to the Chase to see Father while he was ill—you hadn't been in the room with him ten minutes before you started talking about the plight of the soldiers released from service after the Treaty of Paris."

"I remember. But it was important that—" At her brother's alarmed expression, she stopped. "I'm older and wiser now, Nelson, and I can't stay buried in the country forever."

Though he still looked skeptical, her brother shrugged. "I suppose it's only fair you should have your chance before you're permanently on the shelf," he said grudgingly.

Rowena ignored the hurt and resentment his words produced, focusing instead on her real goal. "I'm glad you understand." She was pleased with the evenness of her voice.

A tap on the door heralded the arrival of tea.

"If you're going to stay here, you'll need a companion," said Sir Nelson, his expression softening slightly. "I'll order a room made up while you have a bite to eat."

"Thank you," she said, "but I may not need it. I mean to send a note round to Lady Pearl directly, telling her I'm here. She has frequently invited me to stay with her—and I'm sure she can give me pointers on how to behave properly, as well."

Her brother brightened noticeably. "That would be capital!" Then he pulled out his pocket watch and consulted it. "I'm expected at Whitehall," he said. "You can tell me this evening what your plans are."

When he had gone, Rowena carried her cup and a plate of biscuits to the writing desk near the window and proceeded to write her note to Lady Pearl—now Lady Hardwyck—her best friend in the world.

She and Pearl had practically grown up together, as River Chase bordered the main estate of the imposing Duke of Oakshire, Pearl's father. She and Pearl had shared many interests as well as a strong bond of friendship, and the disparity in their social stations had never mattered to anyone except Pearl's stepmother.

Now, however, Rowena's pen hesitated. That was in the country. Here in London, where Pearl was not only daughter to a duke but also a countess, wife of one of the wealthiest men in England . . . Would it be terribly forward of her to write?

"Nonsense," she told herself sternly. "This is Pearl. Besides, when have you ever cared about other people's opinions?" She wrote quickly, then rang for a footman to deliver the note before she could reconsider.

Noel Paxton signed his report, set his pen down on the battered oak writing desk, and sighed. This had become the most frustrating investigation of his career, and not because he'd failed to apprehend the notorious Saint of Seven Dials. In fact, the legendary thief would be in prison now, had Noel chosen it, but that would have brought him no closer to his true goal—a goal his "superiors" at Bow Street knew nothing about.

"Will you be wanting anything else, sir?" Kemp, Noel's aide, manservant, and confidante, refilled the empty teacup on the corner of the desk.

"A clue, Kemp. A clue. I can't help feeling we're missing something obvious."

Abandoning his proper servant pose, the wiry young man leaned against the mantelpiece, balancing the chipped teapot between his hands, handle in one, spout in the other. "Can't see how, sir. You've picked up on things Runners, with years of experience, missed. Had the Saint in the palm of your hand."

Noel wished he could share his henchman's unswerving faith in his abilities. "At least I've verified that the Saint—Saints, I should say—and the Bishop are not the same man. Which means those anonymous essays are again my only lead."

It was damnably frustrating. He'd been so certain the author of those essays was the Saint, as well as the soulless Black Bishop, that vile traitor who had cost so many English lives during the recent war.

Who had killed at least two men Noel had called friend.

Posing as a British agent in France, the Black Bishop had in fact sold information to Napoleon. His treason had endangered more than one true agent, including Noel himself. Twice, fellow agents had come close to identifying the man and both of those agents had died violently before revealing what they'd learned.

Based on certain evidence found on the battlefield, the Foreign Office had believed the Bishop perished at Waterloo. Noel reluctantly retired to his Derbyshire estate, his services as Puss in Boots, the Foreign Office's top spy, no longer required. He had finally accepted that the Bishop was beyond justice—until portions of a certain essay in the *Political Register* had struck him as eerily familiar.

Noel told the Foreign Office of his suspicion that the Bishop was in fact alive and in England, only to learn that his superiors had already come to the same conclusion. Another agent, investigating the disappearance of certain documents from the Home Office pertaining to the Bishop, had recently died in an all-too-convenient accident. Noel was recalled to service to hunt down the traitor, a task he was more than willing to resume.

A visit to the offices of the *Political Register* revealed that the essay which had aroused Noel's suspicions had been posted from Oakshire—and that the handwriting of the original bore striking similarities to the Bishop's letters to the Foreign Office during the war.

"Mr. R," the anonymous essayist, was so passionate in his defense of the Saint of Seven Dials that Noel had postulated a link. With the approval of the Foreign Office, he offered his services to Bow Street to help apprehend the thief—an offer the magistrate eagerly accepted.

At first, it had appeared he was on the right track. Bow Street's primary suspect seemed to fit everything Noel knew of the Black Bishop. Going by the names of Luke St. Clair, Lucio di Santo, and now the Earl of Hardwyck, the man possessed a genius for disguise, a Continental background, and even an Oakshire connection, through his wife.

But further investigation revealed that Hardwyck had never been in France, had never left England, in fact. His supposed Continental ties were fictitious, invented to allow him to fit in at Oxford and, later, in Society, to further his larcenous ends. Nor had he written those essays.

Frustrated as he was, Noel couldn't find it in him to condemn Lord Hardwyck, nor his successor as Saint,

Lord Marcus Northrup. Both had given the lion's share of their booty to London's poor, and had stolen only from the most undeserving of the *ton*. No, he'd prefer not to be known as the man who brought Robin Hood to justice.

"I don't fancy myself a modern-day Sheriff of Nottingham, Kemp," he said aloud. "The Saint is free to continue his work—not that it sounds as though he plans to do so."

Lord Hardwyck had given up the role upon his marriage two months since, and it appeared that Lord Marcus, also recently wed, had now done the same. Which presented Noel with a definite problem.

"London won't be the same without the Saint of Seven Dials," said Kemp, echoing his thoughts. "Lots of folks count on him, from what I hear. And didn't the bloke gather evidence against real criminals, as well? Useful, that."

Noel nodded. "Useful indeed." Lord Marcus had given him enough evidence to break up a ring of crimps—men profiting from the kidnapping and selling of young boys into service aboard ships—and to put three of them in prison. A valuable resource gone, along with Noel's ostensible reason for nosing about London.

Without the cover of hunting down the Saint, how was he to track down the Black Bishop without giving himself away to his crafty nemesis? Discovery would likely mean the same fate as the last agent— not that fear of death would stop him. His pursuit of the Bishop had long passed from the patriotic to the personal.

"You're right, Kemp," he said slowly, thinking

hard. "London needs the Saint of Seven Dials—and so do I."

If Lord Marcus was unwilling to take up that mantle again, perhaps the answer was to do so himself. As the Saint, surely he could ferret out the real identity of the essayist Mr. R, now his only link to the Black Bishop. With the Saint still active, he could continue his public investigation, which would allow him to pursue his covert one as well.

His decision made, Noel stood. "I'll be back in a few hours," he told his manservant.

The next Saint of Seven Dials would need more information from his predecessors before he could step fully into their shoes.

Rowena finished her tea. No doubt Matthilda was getting something to eat in the kitchens, but perhaps she should—

No, this was London, where the division between mistress and servant would be more rigidly enforced. She must remember that, as well as countless other items of protocol, if she was to remain long enough to further her goals.

Should she have sent that note to Pearl? She recalled how grand her friend had looked at her wedding earlier that summer. They'd scarcely had a chance to do more than nod at each other amid the festivities at Oakshire. What if she had changed?

But even as she wondered whether it was too late to call the footman back, a knock came at the door and a moment later she heard Pearl's own voice in the hall, demanding to see her. Rowena sprang to her feet and hurried out to greet her friend.

"Rowena!" Pearl exclaimed before she could speak. "You've come at last. I must say it's about time. Oh, I've missed you so!"

Laughing with relief and delight, Rowena returned her embrace, then ushered her into the parlor and called for more tea. "Surely with a new husband you haven't had much time to miss old friends?" she asked with a grin.

Pearl blushed slightly. "Well, perhaps not . . ." Then she smiled again, and she was the same Pearl as always.

"But what has brought you to Town?" she asked. "Never tell me it's simply to sightsee, or even to make your come-out during the autumn Season, for I won't believe it. Knowing you, there must be some ulterior motive."

Rowena had to chuckle. Pearl knew her so well. "I thought it was time I saw something of the world beyond Oakshire," she explained. "You above all should understand that all of one's education can't come from books."

"Very true. And I *am* delighted you are here. You can't imagine how insipid the conversation of most Society ladies is. Clothes, gossip, which entertainments to attend—never a word on serious topics. And heaven forbid I should introduce them myself. I'm considered enough of an oddity already."

Rowena gazed at her friend's violet-blue eyes, golden ringlets and classically beautiful face, such a contrast to her own bespectacled gray eyes, straight, coppery tresses, and unremarkable features. Pearl, an oddity? "Then I fear I'll never manage to fit in at all."

"Fitting in is overrated," Pearl declared. "Why, if I

hadn't been willing to ignore Society's rules, I'd never have met Luke, or found out—But that's a story for another time. Please tell me you'll stay at Hardwyck Hall. Luke is so busy lately, it would be wonderful to have someone around I can talk to—really talk to."

Though she had hoped for the invitation, Rowena hesitated. Her own life seemed so far removed from Pearl's now. But at her friend's pleading look, she nodded. She had never been able to deny Pearl anything.

"I'd love to. Will tomorrow be all right?"

"Certainly—as early as you can come. Luke has meetings all day, I believe, and this will give me the perfect excuse to avoid taking tea at Lady Mountheath's."

"If you're sure . . ."

Pearl rose to embrace her. "I'm absolutely determined on it, and you know how stubborn I can be. I'm due for a fitting, so I must run, but we'll talk more tomorrow. And welcome to London, Rowena. Trust me, you're going to love it here."

A moment later Pearl was gone, and Rowena was left to consider the likelihood of that parting prediction. While Pearl had been a zealous reformer in her own right before her marriage, Rowena had been the one to bring issues to her attention. More than once, Pearl had talked her out of taking radical steps to further their aims—steps that Rowena had to admit could have landed them both in serious trouble.

What would Pearl say if she knew about Rowena's political essays and the comments they occasioned? she wondered with a smile. Though she'd told her brother she had changed, she knew she hadn't. It only seemed that way because she had lately diverted her reformist energies into her writings.

Again seating herself at the writing desk, she began to jot down the thoughts that had occurred to her during her journey, for inclusion in her next essay for the *Political Register*.

At the appointed time, Noel knocked at the imposing front door of Hardwyck Hall. While Lord Marcus had been relatively easy to talk to, Lord Hardwyck had proved more elusive—due, no doubt, to the constant demands on a man of his wealth and importance. Noel had had to arrange an appointment through Hardwyck's secretary for an interview.

If he ever took up the title of Earl Ellsdon, for which he was heir presumptive, he would not be so self-important, Noel promised himself.

The door was opened by Hardwyck's surprisingly young butler. "Ah, Mr. Paxton. His lordship awaits you in the library."

Just as in his previous two meetings with Lord Hardwyck, Noel felt slightly defensive—as though he had kept the man waiting, when in fact he was a minute or two early. No doubt just what Hardwyck intended.

The earl rose to greet him as he entered the large, well-stocked library. "Good afternoon, Mr. Paxton. I must say, I was surprised to hear you wished for yet another interview. At our last, you implied you had put the case of the Saint behind you."

Noel seated himself on an expensively upholstered chair as the butler retreated and closed the door behind him. "I've given up trying to put a stop to his activities, yes," he said carefully.

"As they appear to have stopped of their own accord, that would seem a reasonable course." As before, Lord Hardwyck admitted nothing, though Noel knew full well he had been the original Saint—and Hardwyck knew that he knew it.

"So, your interest now is purely academic?" Hardwyck prompted, when Noel remained silent, trying to diplomatically phrase his first question.

"Not purely, no. One might say that it's of a more—practical nature." When Lord Hardwyck did not respond, Noel went straight to the point. "I'm looking for the sort of information a man might need to carry on as Saint of Seven Dials."

His host's brows rose. "Indeed. You have a candidate for the post, then?"

Noel met Lord Hardwyck's gaze squarely. "I do. Myself."

"Why?"

Having already decided that only the truth would do, Noel recounted the details of his own career as a spy during the war—first unofficial, then, once he had proved himself, under the direction of the Foreign Office. His work had necessitated constant and numerous disguises, as well as a fair amount of breaking and entering, to obtain the information the Foreign Office required to counter Napoleon's plans.

"So you are the fabled Puss in Boots," said Lord Hardwyck wonderingly, shaking his head with a smile. "You are well qualified, then, but I still do not understand your motive for wishing to become the next Saint."

Grimly, Noel explained about the Black Bishop— how he had pursued the murderous traitor in France until it was believed he was dead, and that he had now resumed that pursuit on English soil. To under-score the importance of his quest, he told Lord Hard-wyck about his cohorts who had met their deaths at the hands of the Bishop, including the latest, right here in London.

"So while I do intend to carry on the Saint's work of providing for the poor, I also mean to use that guise to gather the information I need to bring the Bishop to justice—much as Lord Marcus gathered the informa-tion on those crimps," he finally concluded. "Will you help me?"

There was a long, tense silence, during which the earl stared at Noel, dark eyes narrowed, as though he would bore a hole in his brain. Finally, he leaned back in his chair and smiled.

"Call me Luke," he said. "It appears we are des-tined to get to know each other quite well, so we may as well begin on a first-name basis."

Chapter 2

"**A**re you certain you won't let Francesca attempt something with your hair?" Pearl asked, as she and Rowena prepared to go downstairs for dinner. "And I know you've never cared two pins for fashion, but a new gown or two wouldn't hurt."

Rowena smiled, but shook her head at her friend. "Would that not be hypocritical of me, after all the lectures I've given you over the years about conforming yourself to the expectations of a patriarchal Society?"

"You make me seem so frivolous. But we'll see if you feel the same after a few days in Town."

Rowena smiled again, but doubted she would change her mind—or that it would make any difference if she did. She was no beauty, after all.

"Oh, I forgot to mention, Luke sent up word that we are to have another guest for dinner tonight," Pearl said as they approached the dining room. "Some official acquaintance or other, I believe."

The ladies entered the long, elegantly appointed

room, where Lord Hardwyck and another gentleman awaited them. Rowena gazed about in appreciation at the rich but tasteful decor. Though her own home was far more simply furnished, she had spent enough time at the duke's manor in Oakshire to become accustomed to—and to appreciate—such surroundings.

"My dear, you have heard me mention Mr. Paxton, I believe. Noel, this is my wife, Lady Hardwyck," said Lord Hardwyck, by way of introduction. "And Miss Riverstone, who is staying with my wife," he added, almost as an afterthought. Rowena suspected he had momentarily forgotten her name.

"Lady Hardwyck, Miss Riverstone," Mr. Paxton murmured. He barely glanced at Rowena, before turning his attention to his hostess—not that Rowena could blame him. Pearl looked particularly beautiful tonight in lilac satin, while she herself all but faded into the woodwork in her plain brown cambric.

"I hear you are quite the philanthropist, my lady," said Mr. Paxton as they took their seats. "I would love to hear about some of your projects."

Rowena's attention was caught, and though he continued to ignore her, she examined Mr. Paxton with interest. Physically, at least, he certainly merited a closer look. He was tall, broad-shouldered and most definitely handsome, with curling chestnut hair and classic features. But it was the intelligence in his hazel eyes that gave him a deeper appeal for her.

Suddenly embarrassed, she looked away before anyone realized she was staring at the man and tried to pick up the thread of conversation.

". . . conditions at Newgate and other prisons," Pearl was saying.

"There is considerable room for improvement," Mr. Paxton agreed. Rowena couldn't help noticing that his voice was deep, firm, and rather pleasant. "If you'd like, I can pass along your concerns to my superiors at Bow Street."

"Bow Street? You are a Runner then, Mr. Paxton?" Rowena asked, startled. He didn't seem to fit what she had read of that elite group of law enforcers.

But he shook his head. "Not a Runner, no. I'm acting in a semi-official capacity, at the behest of Sir Nathaniel Conant, chief magistrate at Bow Street."

"Yes," added Lord Hardwyck with a curious smile. "He's to catch the Saint of Seven Dials for them, as he has managed to elude the regular Runners thus far."

Rowena stared, dismayed. She had read enough about the Saint to have developed a great admiration for the anonymous thief, and had praised his work in more than one of her essays.

"That seems an unworthy goal, sir," she said, "given how few true champions the common people can claim in these difficult times."

Noel had already turned to his host again, but now he looked back across the table at Miss Riverstone, really seeing her for the first time. Drab, old-fashioned gown, brownish hair scraped into a tight bun, spectacles—she appeared to be acting in the capacity of companion to Lady Hardwyck, and he had therefore dismissed her. Unworthily, it appeared.

"Surely a true champion should not find it necessary to break the laws of the land?" he said, repeating what he'd told more than one lady who had tried to talk him out of his pursuit of the legendary thief. "I would prefer to rely on Parliament to give relief to the deserving poor rather than the whims of some mysterious house-breaker."

"Parliament!" Clearly, Miss Riverstone did not hold that august body in great esteem. "Why, even now they are discussing yet more oppressive corn laws. Unless wages are raised to compensate, we shall soon have even more starving and homeless people to consider."

"Therefore we should give free reign to a thief like the Saint of Seven Dials to alleviate their problems—no doubt while lining his own pockets in the process?" Noel had all he could do not to chuckle at her outraged expression.

"At least he is doing *something*," she responded, waving her fork for emphasis. "Legislation, even if introduced, moves so slowly that people will starve waiting for it. In fact—"

She broke off, setting down her fork and glancing guiltily at Lady Hardwyck, but Noel was intrigued. Miss Riverstone clearly stayed abreast of political issues and held strong opinions on them. This did not seem the proper forum to pursue them, however, as he did not wish to get her into trouble with her mistress.

"Doubtless such matters are under discussion by Parliament," he said mildly. Despite her spectacles, severe hairstyle, and the scatter of freckles across her nose, Miss Riverstone was not unattractive, he suddenly realized. "Lady Hardwyck, you were discussing your ideas for prison reform, I believe?"

With a glance at her companion which, to Noel's relief, held more amusement than condemnation, Lady Hardwyck turned back to him. "Yes. If the overcrowding could be alleviated, several other problems would be solved as well."

As she continued to expound on her ideas, Noel's attention strayed back to Miss Riverstone, who now ate in silence. Though she appeared subdued, he suspected this was not her normal aspect. Her gray eyes had sparkled with spirit and intelligence when she had spoken before. What might she look like when she smiled?

He realized he very much wished to find out.

Rowena's pride was still smarting when she and Pearl left the gentlemen to their brandy and retired to the parlor. "I can't say I care much for Mr. Paxton," she said as soon as they were out of earshot. "Self-righteous, legalistic, toadying—"

"What?" Pearl cut her off laughingly. "I found him none of those things, though I confess I rather expected to." She paused while a maid brought tea, watching Rowena's face closely.

"Oh, I see," Pearl continued as soon as they were alone again. "You're irked that he didn't wish to discuss corn laws and Parliamentary reform with you."

"No, it's just—" Rowena broke off with a sigh. "Oh, Nelson was right. I can't spend half an hour in Society without spouting off my political opinions. I'm sorry if I embarrassed you, Pearl."

But her friend only smiled. "I thought you knew me better than that. I'll allow it was a bit rude of Mr. Paxton to change the subject so abruptly, but perhaps he didn't feel he could hold his own in such a discussion. He's not a member of Parliament, after all, and may not follow such issues closely."

"Perhaps." But Rowena didn't believe it. He had quite pointedly turned the conversation back to Pearl, whose views on reform had seemed to hold his attention quite well. But why should that surprise—or bother—her? Men had always behaved thus.

"What say you to a game of chess to pass the time?" she asked, to distract herself.

Pearl grimaced. "You're sure to win as you always do, but very well. The practice will be good for me." She rang for the chess set, and by the time the gentlemen joined them, they were well into their second game.

Rowena barely glanced up when Lord Hardwyck and Mr. Paxton entered, her mind filled with strategy for several moves to come. She had beaten Pearl handily the first game, but the second was proving more of a challenge—perhaps because her thoughts persisted in wandering far from the chessmen before her.

"Shall I call for another board, or would cards suit you better?" Lord Hardwyck asked his guest after the two of them had watched the game in silence for some minutes.

"I was going to offer to play the winner," Mr. Paxton replied. "Unless you would care for cards yourself?"

"Not at all. I quite enjoy watching a good game of chess."

Rowena felt a distinct thrill of anticipation mingled with alarm, though she was careful to let neither show in her expression. She expected to beat Pearl in four more moves and it might be interesting to discover whether the handsome Mr. Paxton was a worthy opponent.

"Checkmate," she said a few minutes later.

Pearl shook her head and rose. "I never even saw that coming. You're every bit as good as I remember. Mr. Paxton, you wish to try your luck? I warn you, Rowena is quite adept."

Rowena dared a glance at the gentleman, to find him regarding her appraisingly. Their eyes met for a long moment and she felt a quiver in her midsection that was unlike anything she had experienced before.

"With two skilled opponents, there is no luck involved," he said, taking the chair Pearl had vacated.

Refusing to let him fluster her, Rowena began placing the pieces back into position for another game, glad of the excuse to break away from his oddly intent gaze. Was this part of his strategy? If so, it certainly wouldn't work on *her*.

"I was going to offer to play black," he continued, "but if you feel I need an advantage, I am willing to take it, after Lady Hardwyck's warning."

Rowena had unthinkingly set up the board as it had been before, as by tacit agreement she always gave Pearl the first move. Traditionally, of course, a lady played white against a gentleman.

"I have no idea whether you need an advantage or not, sir," she said stiffly, to hide her embarrassment. "We can reverse the board if you prefer."

In response, he moved a pawn forward two spaces. "At the risk of taking unfair advantage of a lady, I will leave it as it is."

She regarded him uncertainly. Was he . . . he couldn't be *flirting* with her? No, doubtless he was simply smoothing over an awkward moment—an awkwardness of her own making. She moved a pawn herself, then watched the board as he made his next move, trying to concentrate on the pieces rather than the long, strong fingers manipulating them.

An hour later, Rowena realized she was pitted against the best opponent she had ever faced. After watching for some time, Pearl and Lord Hardwyck had retired to conversation in another corner while Rowena and Mr. Paxton continued to focus on the game.

Few words had been exchanged between them thus far, but now he said, "I've only seen that defense deployed once before, in Austria. However did you learn of it, Miss Riverstone?"

Rowena shook free of her strategizing for a moment. "I, ah, I have read about many famous matches over the years. You have been to Austria then, Mr. Paxton?"

The game had distracted her for a time from his unsettling effect upon her, but the warm timbre of his voice, so deep, so masculine, caused a renewal of that delicious quiver in her midsection.

"Yes, briefly, a year and a half ago." He moved a knight, blocking the line between her bishop and his queen.

"Were you involved in the Congress of Vienna, then?" she asked with sudden interest. She had assumed his background was in local law enforcement.

"Not directly involved, no. I had a small role to play, winter before last." He smiled into her eyes, making her breath unaccountably quicken. "Your move, Miss Riverstone."

With a start, Rowena looked down to discover she

had lost the thread of the game. What had she planned to do after circumventing his knight? Frowning, she moved her bishop two squares, hoping the next two obvious moves would nudge her memory for the third.

"And what of you?" he asked then, surprising her by moving his knight again instead of the pawn she had expected. "Have you been in London long, or did you become so adept at chess elsewhere?"

Revising her strategy, she took the unmoved pawn with her remaining rook, flattered in spite of herself by his words. "I arrived but yesterday. This is the first time I've left Oakshire, actually."

"Oakshire?" He regarded her keenly. "Then you are a . . . relative of Lady Hardwyck's?"

She wondered what he'd almost said. "No, a neighbor. I live next to the main Oakshire estate. Pearl, er, Lady Hardwyck and I have known each other all our lives."

"Ah." His tone implied he had solved some mystery, but she couldn't imagine what it might be.

Before she could ask, he reached forward to take her rook with his knight. *Blast!* How had she missed that? She stared at the board, her strategy in shambles. He had left his queen open, however. Seeing little else to do, she took it.

"You sound as though my history explained something to you, sir. How so?" She was still scanning the board as she spoke, and saw too late the trap into which she had just fallen.

"I was wondering how such an intelligent and obviously well-educated woman came to be hired as

Lady Hardwyck's companion," he replied, moving his knight again. "Checkmate."

Rowena wasn't sure whether she was more stunned by his assumption that she was a servant, or by losing so abruptly and disastrously. She stared at the board, then at him, totally at a loss for words. His eyebrows rose questioningly.

"Congratulations," she said, belatedly gathering her wits.

"Another game?"

Shaken by her first loss in years—since old Mr. Winston, the vicar, had died, in fact—she shook her head. "I believe Lord Hardwyck expressed an interest in playing the winner."

She knew she should correct his misconception about her place in the Hardwyck household but couldn't think how, without being rude. *How dare you assume I'm merely Pearl's companion?* No. *Do you assume any plain woman must be a servant?* Still worse.

Seeing the game was at an end, Pearl and Lord Hardwyck came forward. "Never say you beat her, Mr. Paxton?" Pearl exclaimed. "You must tell me how you managed it, for I never have."

"I fear I distracted her with personal questions," Mr. Paxton confessed with a smile. "Unsporting of me, but I was growing desperate."

"Do not discredit yourself, sir," said Rowena, stung. "Nor need you patronize me. I am not so easily flustered, I assure you, and know when I have been fairly beaten."

Even as she spoke, however, she knew her words

were false. He *had* distracted her, not only with conversation but with his very presence. She would far rather proclaim him a superior player than admit to such weakness, however. Especially since it now seemed clear he was merely being kind to Pearl's poor "companion."

"As you wish, Miss Riverstone." The glint in his hazel eyes told her he understood all too well.

Hastily, she turned away. "I believe I will go up to bed, if you will all excuse me. I have not yet become accustomed to Town hours."

"Of course, dear," said Pearl. "I will see you upstairs and make certain you do not lack for anything. Gentlemen, if you will excuse us? I will return in a moment."

Lord Hardwyck and Mr. Paxton bid Rowena good night, then settled down to the chessboard as the ladies left the parlor.

"Poor Luke doesn't stand a chance," Pearl confided as they climbed the staircase. "I have beaten him the few times we have played. He didn't have many chances to—that is—" She broke off.

Rowena scarcely noticed, her mind still on the scene below. "Did you know that Mr. Paxton thinks I am your companion? Your *paid* companion?" She was still outraged.

"No, really? How absurd!" Pearl exclaimed with a laugh. "What did he say when you corrected him?"

"I, er, didn't," Rowena confessed. "I didn't wish to seem rude, you see—"

"So instead you accused him of patronizing you." Pearl still seemed amused. "Really, dear, his mistake was understandable, seeing how you are dressed. Perhaps now you'll be willing to take my advice and buy a few new gowns?"

For the first time, Rowena considered Pearl's question seriously. She had always maintained that men who focused on such externals—nearly all men, in her experience—were not worth regretting. Now, however, she realized that there might be a more important issue at stake.

Men, after all, were the shapers of England's laws, much as she might wish otherwise. To influence those laws, she would have to influence those men. Pearl, clearly, was able to do so more effectively than she herself, no doubt due partly to her appearance. Could she, just possibly, increase her own influence by taking a page from Pearl's book?

Rowena nodded. "Yes, I believe I will."

"Splendid! We'll go shopping tomorrow," Pearl promised as they reached the upper hallway.

For a moment Rowena allowed herself to imagine Mr. Paxton's expression should he see her again, dressed as Pearl was. In such a guise, would she be able to distract him into losing a game of chess? She almost grinned at the thought, but then the pleasant fantasy dissipated.

A new gown and hairstyle would never turn her into a beauty, and there were still her spectacles. All she could really hope to do was fit in, so that she could meet men of influence—and perhaps become a person of some small influence herself.

"I shall rely on your guidance to help me look my best," she told Pearl as they reached her room.

Her friend seemed so delighted at the prospect that

Rowena wasn't sure whether to be pleased or concerned—or even insulted. Pearl directed a maid to see to Rowena's comfort, then kissed her cheek. "Good night, dear. I *am* so glad you're here, and I'm quite looking forward to tomorrow."

"So am I," Rowena echoed, and realized to her surprise that it was true.

As Pearl had predicted, Noel was finding Luke a far less challenging opponent than Miss Riverstone. By the time Lady Hardwyck returned to the parlor, the outcome was assured. Five minutes later, Luke conceded the game.

"Perhaps you can tutor me in chess while I tutor you in larceny," Luke suggested without rancor as he stood.

Noel glanced at Lady Hardwyck in alarm, but she appeared merely surprised, not shocked. She regarded her husband with an upraised brow.

"You've told him, then?"

Luke shrugged. "He already knew. We were both merely pretending otherwise. Now that Marcus has retired, Noel is interested in taking over himself—for various reasons."

"And you've agreed to help him." The look she sent Noel was less than approving.

"Only with advice, my lady," he assured her. "Lord Hardwyck will be in no danger from the law."

She glanced at her husband, seeking reassurance, and apparently received it, for her expression softened to a smile. "As you *are* the law in this case, Mr. Paxton, I suppose you can be trusted to know."

"The irony has not escaped me," he said with an

answering smile. "I suppose, in conscience, I should turn the investigation over to someone else to avoid a conflict of interest, but as that investigation is my ostensible reason for being in Town, I'll simply have to work very hard at catching myself."

They all laughed, but then Noel became serious. "You said there are people I will need to meet, if I am to take up the Saint's mantle," he reminded Luke.

The earl nodded. "You've already met one of them—the young footman who refilled the glasses at dinner. He used to go by the name of Squint when he lived on the streets, though now we call him Steven."

"Then he was one of the youths who used to help the Saint?" During his investigation, Noel had been thwarted more than once by that loyal regiment of street urchins.

"It would be fairer to say that the Saint helped him," Lady Hardwyck said, putting a hand on her husband's shoulder. "Most of our servants have been rescued from the streets."

Noel nodded, beginning to understand. "So your goals never changed—merely your methods. I salute you, my lord, my lady. However, your former methods are what I need to master now."

"And for that you will need the trust of those you would help," Luke said. "Where are you staying?"

"I have lodgings on Long Acre, near Bow Street."

"Convenient placement—only two streets away from Seven Dials. But for the next few days, I'd like to invite you to stay here as my guest. It will . . . simplify things."

This caught Noel by surprise, though it made sense. Frequent visits here might be noticed, while an extended visit would require but one explanation. "What will we give out as the reason for my stay?" he asked, suspecting Lord Hardwyck had already concocted one.

"My wife and I have decided to have a house party before everyone returns to their country seats. Have we not, my love?"

Though it was clear that this was the first Lady Hardwyck had heard of such a scheme, her eyes lit at once. "Indeed we have. We may even induce some of those who have already left Town to return for a week or two. It will be just the thing for Rowena, now that I think on it."

Confused, Noel asked, "Miss Riverstone, you mean? Your companion?" He wondered how he would keep his secret from that very intelligent lady while under this roof.

To his surprise, Lady Hardwyck laughed. "She is my friend, Mr. Paxton, not my companion. Her brother keeps a house on Hay Street, but I induced her to stay with me so that we could spend more time together."

With a start, Noel realized that Miss Riverstone's brother must be Sir Nelson Riverstone, a senior clerk at the Home Office and son of the late Sir Nelson, who had been a powerful political figure before his death. No wonder she'd been upset when he had all but called her a servant to her face. He'd thought she was merely irritated at losing a hard-fought game of chess.

"Pray convey my apologies to Miss Riverstone," he said to Lady Hardwyck. "I fear I implied—"

"An understandable mistake. I've told her for years

she should pay more attention to her appearance. But I'll tell her."

"I presume you'll want to send for a few things?" Luke asked Noel then. "You may as well stay the night, so that we can get started first thing tomorrow. Once other guests arrive, we may find it more difficult to be private."

Noel blinked, pulling his thoughts away from the intriguing Miss Riverstone. "Yes, of course. I'll have Kemp, my manservant, bring what I'll need." He quickly scrawled a note and sent it with a footman— the one Luke had called Squint, in fact.

"Now then," said Luke once that was done. "How are you at picking locks?"

Even as Noel explained his experience in that area, acquired during his years spying on some of Napoleon's highest officials, his thoughts strayed again to Miss Riverstone.

She might be the very link he needed to the Home Office. The Bishop was obtaining information from someone there, he was certain. Perhaps her brother, Sir Nelson Riverstone . . .

Sudden excitement gripped him. *Mr. R?* He couldn't go about suspecting every man with a surname beginning with that letter, of course, but Riverstone's estate was in Oakshire—Miss Riverstone had said so. Oakshire, where at least one of those mysterious essays had originated. And he worked at the Home Office, from which certain documents had been stolen—

"Mr. Paxton?" Lady Hardwyck recalled him to his surroundings.

"I'm sorry, my lady. I was recalling a particularly harrowing experience on the outskirts of Paris." He told of the time he had nearly been caught meeting his contact, during the months he had spent disguised as a servant in Fouché's own household.

Not until Lord and Lady Hardwyck began speaking again did he pursue this new train of thought.

He must get to know Miss Riverstone better, he decided—much better. If he could win her trust and liking, she might be able to tell him all he needed to know about her brother, and perhaps even introduce him to his newest suspect. As a potential suitor?

Noel smiled to himself. He rather doubted Miss Riverstone had had many suitors. It should not be difficult to turn her head with compliments and discover everything he needed to know.

Though deadly serious, this investigation might prove to have its charms. Along the way, he could look forward to many more stimulating chess matches, at the very least. And perhaps to other, even more enjoyable diversions—all in the name of duty.

Chapter 3

Rowena was surprised to hear male voices in the dining room when she descended to breakfast the next morning—and even more surprised to discover Mr. Paxton helping himself from the sideboard.

"Good morning, Rowena," Pearl said brightly from the table, before she could speak. "I expected you to be up before any of us, but then I remembered that you would still be tired from your two-day journey. I hope you slept well?"

Flustered by being the focus of three pairs of eyes—and particularly by one intense pair of hazel eyes—Rowena nodded. "Yes, I, ah, slept perfectly well, thank you."

"Good, because you'll need your energy for our shopping expedition today. I've decided to throw a house party, so I'll want to buy a few things for myself, as well."

Rowena regarded Pearl suspiciously. "A house

party? In London? I thought those were country affairs."

"I've never been one to bow to convention, you know that. We haven't had so much as a real dinner party since our return to Town, so this will be a way to welcome all of our acquaintances to Hardwyck Hall and chase away old ghosts, as it were." She and Lord Hardwyck exchanged amused glances.

Mr. Paxton had finished filling his plate, so Rowena moved to the sideboard as he took his place at the table. "I see," she said, though she did not really see at all. "Shall I return to my brother's house? You will be terribly crowded here."

"Certainly not. I'm counting on you to help me. I will send out invitations today for a ball Friday, which will open the party. Most of the guests will undoubtedly prefer to sleep at their own houses and come only for the activities, so I don't foresee a shortage of rooms."

"Activities?" Rowena asked weakly.

"She's been planning since daybreak," Lord Hardwyck said with a chuckle. "Picnics, group excursions to the 'Change, whist tournaments—what else, my dear?"

Pearl cheerfully listed off half a dozen other amusements while Rowena listened in dismay, forgetting the fragrant sausages and pastries before her. So many opportunities for her to embarrass herself—and Pearl as well.

During the litany she glanced over at Mr. Paxton and saw that he looked nearly as bemused as she felt. It heartened her a bit, especially when he caught her eye and sent her a rueful grin and slight shrug.

"I told you, did I not, that I intended to make sure you enjoy your stay in London," Pearl concluded. "This way, you'll see everything it has to offer, over the course of a week or two."

It seemed last night's resolve to enter Society was to be put to an immediate test.

"Yes, I . . . suppose I will. Thank you." She would not appear ungrateful, not when Pearl was going to so much trouble. She only hoped that both of them would not live to regret it.

Belatedly remembering her breakfast, she filled a plate and took the same seat she had occupied at dinner, across from Mr. Paxton. Their earlier shared glance of sympathy made it less awkward than she had expected, though her pulse still quickened.

He looked up from his plate as she sat down, his expression now serious. "Miss Riverstone, pray allow me to apologize. It appears I did you a disservice last night."

Rowena shot a quick glance at Pearl, who must have set him straight, but she was speaking with her husband. "A simple misunderstanding, sir. Pray think no more of it." His mistaking her for a paid companion still rankled somewhat, however.

He appeared to realize it. "I leaped to an assumption based on mere appearances—something I learned long ago is a dangerous thing to do."

Was this meant for her? She'd made her own assumptions about Mr. Paxton, she realized, while in truth knowing little about him. "I must agree, sir, though I fear it is a common human failing, from my own experience." Certainly she herself had been

judged by her appearance for as long as she could remember.

His eyes were disconcertingly knowing, seeming to
probe her very thoughts. "And from my own, as
well—though I confess that I have used that failing to
my advantage on occasion. Still, I apologize for
falling victim to it myself, in your case."

"You are forgiven, Mr. Paxton." What else could
she say? And in truth, she no longer felt any anger toward him. There was something about those eyes,
that deep, warm voice . . .

"Thank you." He sounded sincere, still holding her
gaze with his own. "I hope that we can start over and,
in time, become friends."

"Of . . . of course," she responded, even more flustered than she'd been last night.

The idea of becoming friends with this handsome,
intelligent man held an undeniable appeal, even
though what little she knew of him was hardly to his
credit. A supporter of Parliament, employed by Bow
Street to catch the heroic Saint of Seven Dials—but he
had played some role in Vienna, as well. Who *was* this
man, really?

Besides the best chess player she had ever met.

Though she very much wanted to dig beneath the
surface, to avoid judging by externals as he admitted
he had done, she couldn't think how to ask questions
without sounding impertinent. Wordplay with handsome men was something entirely outside her experience, alas.

As she was still trying to frame her next comment,
Lord Hardwyck and Mr. Paxton rose. "We have busi-

ness to attend, my dear," said her host, "but we will see you at dinner."

"If not before," Mr. Paxton added, his eyes still on Rowena.

All she could do was nod like a simpleton as they took their leave. Later, Rowena promised herself. Perhaps the transformation Pearl promised would give her the courage she lacked.

"Let me do the talking at first," Luke advised as he and Noel approached a crumbling three-story building in Seven Dials.

Noel nodded. Both gentlemen had changed into nondescript fustian coats in the coach. He was reminded of Miss Riverstone and her drab clothing, and wondered again about the woman beneath. She was undoubtedly more than she appeared, just as he and Luke were now. Perhaps even—

"Ah, we're in luck," Luke said, breaking into his thoughts as a tall, thin boy peered out of the doorway they were nearing. "Stilt—a word with you, lad."

Though he frowned suspiciously from Luke to Noel and back, the boy came forward. "Can't say I expected to see you in these parts, milord," he said as he reached them. "Thought you'd given up all to do with Seven Dials."

"I may not be playing the Saint anymore," Luke said, "but I've not given up my interest in those who live here."

"Aye, and your gifts have been much appreciated, milord." Again, the boy glanced frowningly at Noel.

"This is Mr. Paxton," Luke said, putting a hand on Noel's shoulder. "He's interested in helping, and I'm here to introduce him to some of the lads. You can trust him, Stilt—he's a friend of mine."

The boy relaxed visibly. "Then he's a friend of ours. But there ain't that many lads left from the group you knew, milord. You took in Flute and Squint, then his other lordship hired away Gobby and his sister, along with Renny. Tig wouldn't go, though—he's still hereabouts, and me and Skeet."

"Still working for Twitchell, are you?" Luke was frowning now, and Noel couldn't blame him. During his investigation of the Saint, he'd discovered how vicious Twitchell and his rival thief-masters could be to their young apprentices.

Stilt shrugged. "It's a living. And if we'd all gone to work in fine houses, who'd be left to help the Saint and his friends?" He flashed a sudden grin that lit up his lean face.

Luke laughed. "A hit, indeed. Now, take us to Tig, Skeet and any others you think trustworthy enough to help in our cause. If all goes well, it won't be long before the Saint of Seven Dials is back in business."

Bond Street, the heart of London's shopping district, was a novel experience for Rowena. She looked about with interest at the deep, narrow shops selling every conceivable ware, the raucous street vendors, and the bustling crowds of shoppers. Poor Matthilda was terrified.

"There must be cutthroats and pickpockets everywhere in a mob like this, miss!" she exclaimed as they descended from Pearl's opulent coach. "Can't we have the goods sent 'round instead?"

"And miss all this? Of course not. Buck up,

Matthilda," Rowena told her. "I'm sure it's not nearly as dangerous as all that." She turned to Pearl, who nodded.

"It's not dangerous at all. At this hour, it's mostly ladies and their maids and escorts. Hettie, reassure her, won't you?"

Pearl's own maid set about soothing Matthilda, pointing out objects of interest—*safe* objects of interest—as they proceeded to Madame Fanchot's establishment.

"The finest modiste in London, my dear," Pearl assured Rowena as they entered the shop. At once the proprietress hurried forward to greet them.

"Lady Hardwyck! How delightful to see you again." She turned shrewd eyes on Rowena. "A young friend from the country to outfit? Ah, great potential here, I think."

Rowena found herself warming to the modiste. At least *she* didn't assume she was Pearl's companion. That thought brought Mr. Paxton forcibly to mind, of course—not that he had been far from her thoughts all morning.

Pearl stepped forward with a smile. "I have in mind a complete makeover, Madame Fanchot. Once we've ordered a few suitable gowns, we'll discuss accessories and hairstyles. Francesca is itching to unpin that bun, as you may imagine."

"An excellent plan, my lady. This way, if you please." The modiste led them into her inner sanctum, a display room draped with swaths of beautiful fabrics, fashion magazines piled on elegant little tables.

"I've always detested pastels," Pearl confided, "but as a seventeen-year-old debutante, they were *de rigeur.* You, however, are old enough—and independent enough—to dispense with them. Nor are you an insipid blonde like me, lucky girl."

Madame Fanchot nodded vigorously. "Yes, your coloring demands stronger hues. That copper hair—rich greens, blues and yellows will set it off to admiration." So saying, she unrolled bolts of vibrant-hued silks, satins and muslins.

Rowena, who had always secretly envied Pearl her golden tresses, listened to them in amazement. No one had ever implied that her reddish-brown hair was an *asset* before. "If you're sure. It all seems so frivolous."

"But fun, you must admit," said Pearl with a wink.

And it was. Though a part of her recoiled at the cost of new gowns, another part reveled in pure, feminine pleasure. The money she was spending could feed a small village for months—but any guilt could wait until later, she decided, fingering a bolt of luscious turquoise blue satin.

An hour later they left the shop with the promise that the first gown would be delivered in two days.

"She must have an army of seamstresses," Rowena exclaimed.

Pearl nodded. "She can afford to, believe me—the very best seamstresses. Now, we must find gloves, stockings, slippers and ribbons to match those gowns."

When they finally left Bond Street, the carriage crammed with parcels, the number of ladies on the walkways had thinned considerably, to be replaced by gentlemen in top hats and tails.

"If we think of anything else, we can come back tomorrow," Pearl said, though Rowena couldn't imagine a single item they could have possibly forgotten. Guilt returned in full force when she mentally tallied up all of her purchases.

So much money, simply so that she could flutter along with the other Society butterflies, something she had always disdained. Was her goal of social reform really worth it? But then she thought of Mr. Paxton and felt it might just possibly be worthwhile after all.

On their return to Hardwyck Hall, they were informed that the gentlemen were not expected to return until evening.

"Just as well," Pearl said. "That gives us time to plan your transformation. This is Francesca's day off, so your hair, I fear, will have to wait."

Rowena stifled her disappointment. She had hoped to achieve that step, at least, before facing Mr. Paxton at dinner tonight.

Still, she thought with a spurt of amusement, it might be diverting to solidify Mr. Paxton's opinion of her as a drab nonentity before appearing in her new guise, that she might the better enjoy his surprise at her transformation.

"We'll have you ready by Friday's ball," Pearl promised, echoing her thoughts. "Then you can burst upon the scene in full splendor. In the meantime, we can work on other things."

"Other things?" Rowena asked almost fearfully.

Pearl frowned thoughtfully at her. "Just how badly do you really need those spectacles?"

Rowena put an involuntary hand to her face. "I'm quite nearsighted—you know that. You used to hide them from me for a prank when we were young."

"Oh yes, I remember. Without them you squint."
Pearl sighed.

Nettled by her friend's obvious disappointment,
Rowena said, "Anyone who can't see past my spectacles is not likely to be someone I care to impress. I
know the *ton* tends to focus on the externals, but are
they really so superficial as that?"

"Not all of them. In fact, you'll be pleased to know
that I have invited a number of London's leading literary lights to my little party. Robert Southey, Leigh
Hunt, and a few others you'll be interested to meet."

"Indeed I will," Rowena agreed, suddenly feeling a
flutter of enthusiasm for the coming ordeal. "Who
else?"

But Pearl shook her head. "I don't wish to raise
your hopes too high. Most of these men eschew such
things as balls and card parties, and some are doubtless gone from Town by now. However, if any do attend, I will be certain to introduce you."

So the very men she would most like to meet were
the ones least likely to come—not that she could
blame them, as she shared their aversion to such frivolous pursuits. Some might attend, however, giving
her the chance to implement her plan.

Meanwhile, another game or two of chess with
Mr. Paxton might serve to sharpen her wits for the
challenges ahead.

When the ladies entered the dining room that evening, Noel's gaze went at once to Miss Riverstone,
despite his hostess's blond beauty. As before, she was
dressed almost as a servant, this time in puritanical

gray and white. The lack of color in her dress only served to emphasize the bright shimmer of her hair, however. At least, what little he could see of it, in that bun.

It was as though she used her severe appearance as armor, keeping any man from seeing the woman within, he mused. Perhaps it had worked on the country gents she'd encountered thus far, but he prided himself on digging beneath the surface. That thought brought forth a fascinating—and distinctly inappropriate—image, so he quickly turned his attention to his host.

"You were going to tell me more about the concerns some in Parliament have expressed on the relief efforts," he reminded Luke as they took their seats. Out of the corner of his eye he saw Miss Riverstone's head turn toward him, her interest evidently caught— as he had hoped.

Luke nodded. "Yes, there are those who fear nothing less than the disintegration of the social order, should commoners be given control of even the smallest pieces of land. Absurd, of course, but the notion of land ownership and power going hand in hand is very deeply entrenched."

"And power in the hands of commoners is anathema, my lord?" Miss Riverstone interjected before Noel could respond.

Luke appeared startled, but answered readily enough. "To some, certainly, though not to all."

Her intelligent gaze swung from Luke to Noel and back. "And to those present?"

"Anathema would be too strong a word in my

case," Luke said rather evasively, motioning for the hovering footman to commence serving the soup.

"And in mine," Noel echoed. "I can understand the concerns of those who worry that sudden acquisition of land by those not trained to the management of it might result in abuses. However, a gradual, reasoned approach that includes the requisite training would seem to be a viable solution."

Miss Riverstone fixed clear gray eyes upon him. Lovely eyes, really, beneath the spectacles, fringed with thick, dark lashes. "So if change is inevitable, it should be embraced as slowly as possible?"

Noel pulled himself from contemplation of her eyes to respond. "Abrupt change without thoughtful preparation rarely serves anyone well."

"An excuse all too easily taken to extremes, precluding any change at all," she pointed out.

He tended to agree, but was enjoying their sparring too much to say so. "Better that than a headlong rush into changes that could prove disastrous for all sides, taking years or even generations to repair."

"I perceive you must have a vested interest in the status quo, Mr. Paxton," she said, finally picking up her spoon. "Who, pray, are your antecedents?"

The question bordered on rude, but it did not occur to Noel to take offense. Distracted by the motion of her spoon to her nicely shaped lips, he debated how much to tell her. "My father was a younger son to an earl, it is true," he confessed, "though his own estate was quite modest."

"An estate that is now yours, I presume?"

He nodded. "In Derbyshire."

"Not so very far from Oakshire," she commented. "And have you a mother? Siblings?" She seemed to suddenly realize she was watching him intently and turned her attention back to her soup dish.

"A mother and two sisters," he said, smiling at her confusion. "The eldest lives with my mother in Derbyshire. The younger is married, and currently in Yorkshire with her husband."

She seemed disinclined for more questions, apparently perceiving that she had overstepped the bounds of politeness. Noel was just as glad. Telling her that his twin sister's husband was in line to be the next Duke of Wickburn would do his case no good at all, he suspected.

Lord and Lady Hardwyck took over the conversation at that point, discussing plans for their coming house party. Noel found himself paying closer attention to what Miss Riverstone ate than to what his hosts said, however. Behind those lovely lips lay white, even teeth and a darting pink tongue that made him think of things she might do with it beyond talking and eating.

All too soon, the ladies excused themselves to the parlor. Eager for another chess match, Noel waved away the offer of a cigar and accepted only a small measure of brandy.

"You seem rather taken with Miss Riverstone," Luke observed with a grin once the footman had left them alone.

Oops. Noel hadn't meant to be so obvious. "Intrigued, at least. She seems quite an original." Though the word was generally not used as a compliment, Noel considered it as such.

"She is that," Luke agreed with a chuckle. "Not that I'd expect anything less of a girl my wife claims as a lifelong friend. But tell me, have you thought further about your plans, now that you've met some of the lads you'd be working with?"

They fell then to discussing the denizens of Seven Dials and the smoothest way to effect a transition to Noel as the next Saint. Lord Marcus would have to be advised, they both agreed.

"We'll be inviting him and his new bride to our house party, of course, but I'll try to have a private word with him beforehand," Luke said. "Now, what say you we join the ladies in the parlor?"

Noel was startled by the sudden lift in his spirits at these words. He had always enjoyed a challenging game of chess, he reminded himself. And Miss River-stone was proving a challenge of a different sort, as well.

He could not afford any sort of emotional entanglement, of course, but winning her confidence was essential to his mission. Sheltered as she'd apparently been, she would no doubt be susceptible to a flirtation. At any rate, he would enjoy trying.

He and Luke entered the parlor to find the two women deep in conversation—a conversation that broke off abruptly at their appearance. Lady Hard-wyck rose.

"Chess again, or would you prefer cards tonight, Mr. Paxton?"

Glancing at Miss Riverstone, Noel found her gaze averted, whether from confusion or some other reason, he couldn't say. As she offered no input, he made the decision himself.

"I confess I've quite looked forward to another match with Miss Riverstone. Besides, I owe her a chance to revenge herself for my win last night."

The lady in question did meet his eye then, and there was nothing of confusion in her bright gaze. "That's very sporting of you, sir. I accept the challenge."

Two boards were produced, and a few moments later he and Miss Riverstone faced each other across one while Lord and Lady Hardwyck matched their respective skills at the other.

"Given my pitiful performance last night, I'll not accuse you of arrogance for adhering to tradition this time," Miss Riverstone remarked when he set up the board so that she had the white pieces and subsequent first move.

"Pitiful? Hardly that," he replied with perfect honesty. "You're the best opponent I've faced in some time. I was quite sincere when I said I've looked forward to another match."

She smiled then, for the first time since he'd met her, and it transformed her face into something sweet and distinctly pretty, the impact hitting him like a blow. Had he actually thought her plain before? The smile was all too brief, but its effect on him lingered as she spoke.

"I can say the same for you, Mr. Paxton, though I've undoubtedly had far fewer opponents for comparison, which makes your compliment the greater. I thank you." Then, turning her gaze to the board, she moved her king's pawn two spaces forward.

For several minutes they played in silence, while Noel tried to rein in the effect her combined intelligence and attractiveness had upon him. He was contemplating how best to broach the subject of her brother when Miss Riverstone spoke again.

"You mentioned last night that you had played some small role at the Congress of Vienna, Mr. Paxton. I would be interested to hear what it was."

He glanced up, but her attention remained on the board between them. "I was merely a minor aide of sorts to Wellington," he said carefully. In fact, he had been the duke's eyes and ears in places a more prominent man could not venture without danger and suspicion.

Miss Riverstone did look up now. "You actually met the Duke of Wellington? Worked with him? What is he like?" Her face was alight, eager, and disturbingly alluring.

Noel forced himself to study the board for a moment, making his next move before replying.

"Physically, he is an imposing man, though perhaps not classically handsome. Mentally, he is even more impressive. He has an awesome intellect, particularly in matters of strategy. You would enjoy engaging him in chess, I assure you."

As he'd hoped, she smiled again. Though he might have expected a less dramatic effect upon him this time, the opposite was the case.

"I'm certain I would. I had hoped to meet him while in London, but I understand his visit here is to be a brief one, and that he returns soon to Paris."

"He might possibly accept Lady Hardwyck's invitation before leaving," Noel replied, startled to discover he didn't share her hope. Wellington was a notorious womanizer—not that Miss Riverstone was at all in his usual style, of course. Still . . .

"May I trouble you for an introduction, then, should he attend?" Even as she spoke, she took his rook with her knight. Damn! That hadn't been part of his strategy.

"Of course," he said vaguely, trying to concentrate on the game again. He'd planned to use that rook to draw out her queen. Now he'd have to extricate his other rook for that maneuver. Would Wellington be as intrigued by Miss Riverstone's intelligence as he was? Dash it all, he mustn't let it matter.

Shaking his head slightly, he moved the pawn that blocked the path of his remaining rook. He barely knew this girl, after all. Certainly, he had no business becoming protective of her. She had a brother for that. His goal was simply to win her confidence and liking so that he could learn more about that brother.

"What did you do before you went to Austria?" she asked then, taking his pawn just as he'd intended. "Were you in the army?"

"I, ah, worked *with* the army, in a civilian capacity." He knew it sounded evasive, but he could hardly tell her he'd spent nearly three years as a spy in France.

She blocked his rook with a bishop. "What sort of capacity?"

"I was a courier of sorts," he said, using the cover story he'd maintained for years. "First in Upper Canada, during the second war with America, and later traveling to various parts of the Continent."

"Canada?" The chessboard apparently forgotten for the moment, her eyes shone. "Is it as wild and expansive as I've read? Did you meet any savages there?"

In truth, Noel had never set foot in Canada, but he'd made a point of learning about it so that he could answer just such questions as these.

"The forests are so thick one can scarcely see through them, and extend for hundreds of miles, interrupted only by pristine, frigid lakes. A beautiful, if rugged, country. There were no savages near our outpost, however, so I know only what I was told of them."

"And what of the Continent? Where did you travel?"

Her expression was rapt as she soaked up every bit of information he revealed. The girl definitely had the mind of a scholar. And the face and body of . . . With an effort, he pulled his gaze away, to focus again on the board. His inattention had taken its toll, forcing him to again modify his strategy.

"Germany, Prussia, Italy—wherever messages were being sent," he replied absently, moving his rook three spaces to the left to circumvent her bishop. He could only hope she had been equally distracted from the game.

Apparently not. Her next move revealed that he had fallen into a carefully prepared trap from which he could see no easy escape.

"How I should like to travel," she said as he moved his rook back to its starting point. "That has long been one of my dreams."

"What other dreams do you have, Miss Riverstone?" he asked in an unworthy attempt to rattle her.

He had clearly managed it the night before, but now she seemed more resistant.

She moved her queen one space to the right before responding, tightening the noose around his remaining pieces. "To set the world to rights, of course. To effect justice for all, rich and poor, titled and base."

"A humble goal." He laughed, despite his dire position in the game. "So you would wipe out all crime and poverty—and war as well, no doubt?" He took her bishop with his rook.

"Of course, had I the means to do so. I have long maintained that if women ruled the world, it would be a far more peaceful and prosperous place." She slid her remaining bishop to the opposite corner of the board, exposing his king to her queen while blocking its escape. "Checkmate."

He'd seen it coming, of course, but losing was still a shock. "Well played, Miss Riverstone," he said sincerely, though he was hard pressed not to frown.

What on earth was the matter with him? He had played—and beaten—some of the best, most devious minds of Europe, while simutaneously ferreting out their deepest secrets. It was precisely what he'd planned to do tonight, but instead she had managed to distract him. He must be losing his edge.

Noel forced a smile. "Another match? I'm willing to play white this time, as it appears I need the advantage."

That elicited another smile, one that set his heart pounding. Merely pretty, he had thought her? He realized now that she was in fact one of the loveliest women he'd met, her beauty uncluttered by frivolous ringlets or fancy clothes, the pure curves of her face only slightly concealed by her spectacles, with no art-ful tresses to obscure them.

"I'm far less tired than I was last night," she said, her voice flowing over him like fine wine. "I'd enjoy another game, yes."

Taking white as promised, he began with a gambit he'd used successfully on many occasions. It appeared to be one with which she was unfamiliar, to judge by her level of concentration. He was just as glad to be spared more probing questions. It felt more wrong somehow to lie to Miss Riverstone than to all of the exalted dignitaries and officials he had deceived over the years.

Determined not to let his focus waver, Noel spoke not a word for half an hour. Then, feeling he had es-tablished a sufficient advantage, he launched another attempt at flirtation, aiming his flattery at her skill rather than her appearance. She would suspect the latter as flummery, he was certain.

"You are an audacious and unconventional player, Miss Riverstone. I continue to be amazed that you have achieved this level of skill immured in the country."

"I subscribe to a wide variety of newspapers and periodicals, some of which recount famous matches in great detail. In addition, I had the advantage of an accomplished master in our late vicar, Mr. Winston, a man whose intellect I fear few besides myself appreci-ated during his lifetime."

Again, Noel felt himself becoming caught up in cu-riosity about Miss Riverstone, to the detriment of his attention to the game. What was his next move to be?

She reached forward to counter his move with her

knight, and he noticed how long and slender her fingers were. He'd thought her plump on first meeting her last night, but now realized she was almost perfectly proportioned, though her frumpy dresses obscured her figure.

Sternly, he recalled his thoughts and made his next move, which should force her to withdraw her knight so that he could advance on her queen. Instead, she surprised him by taking his white bishop, sacrificing said knight.

"I've never been able to bear being funneled into a particular course of action," she commented, a twinkle in her gray eyes. "My tendency to rebel cost me more than one match with Mr. Winston, but he rarely beat me in the same method as he had planned, which I regarded as a sort of victory."

And so it transpired. Though Noel was eventually able to win the game, he was forced to alter his strategy numerous times in order to do so.

"Again, my compliments, Miss Riverstone," he said when he had finally checkmated her. "You kept me on my toes the entire time. I must say, you are a formidable opponent."

He realized his words were true in more ways than one.

Chapter 4

Rowena smiled sunnily, aware that she had acquitted herself well and feeling that she fully merited Mr. Paxton's praise. She had been determined not to let her ridiculous attraction to the man distract her tonight and was pleased by her success, though it had taken a surprising degree of concentration.

"I thank you, sir. I would suggest yet another match, but I perceive that it is nearly midnight."

Indeed, Pearl and her husband had long ago given up their own play, and were all but dozing on the sofa, leaning cozily against each other. They stood now and came forward to inquire about the match just ended.

"I fear I lack the patience for so long a game myself," Pearl confessed. "So you beat him tonight, did you, Rowena? Brava! A point for the so-called weaker sex."

Rowena glanced at Mr. Paxton and thought he looked slightly nettled. "I was able to rally for our second match," he said. "I won't deny, however, that your Miss Riverstone plays far better than I'd have believed a woman could. I flatter myself that she is far from typical of your sex."

Rowena wasn't certain whether he meant that as a compliment or an insult, but could not prevent herself from retorting, "I suspect I am more typical than you imagine, sir—simply less practiced than most at concealing my abilities."

Mr. Paxton's brows rose, but it was Lord Hardwyck who spoke first. "What a terrifying thought," he exclaimed. Then, to Pearl, "Never say you possess talents you have not yet revealed, my dear?"

"I can only hope so," Pearl replied with a grin. "But now, I think we terrifying creatures must bid you good night."

After taking polite leave of the gentlemen, Rowena accompanied Pearl out of the room, still irked by Mr. Paxton's remark. Not that she *wanted* to be thought typical, of course . . .

"Now I'll have to reassure Luke that I haven't been keeping secrets," Pearl said laughingly as they climbed the stairs. "Luckily for me, he seems to find my intelligence attractive rather than intimidating."

Rowena thought she understood the underlying message. "But most men are not so enlightened?"

"You scarcely need me to tell you that, after all of your study on such matters."

"Surely you are not suggesting that I should have let him win that first match?" Rowena asked in surprise.

"No, no, of course not." But Pearl's voice lacked conviction.

Mr. Paxton had seemed rather distracted, Rowena

recalled. It would have been an easy thing to play a shade below her best—but that would be a species of dishonesty she despised. She admitted that she had hoped for his friendship, but what sort of friendship would it be, if she could not be herself?

"Would you have done so?" she challenged her friend.

Pearl thought for a moment, then smiled ruefully. "No, I confess I would not have let him win either. After all, I do not let Luke beat me, and he would not wish me to. But he is a gem, in that way as in so many others."

Pearl's obvious adoration of her husband, clearly reciprocated, created a small ache somewhere in the vicinity of Rowena's heart. What must it be like to experience such love, such trust? It seemed unlikely that she, plain and too intelligent for a "proper" woman, would ever know.

"Your Miss Riverstone is rather a quiz, my dear," Luke said as he and Pearl prepared for bed. "Are you certain attempting to launch her into Society is a good idea?"

Pearl laughed. "You sound like her father used to. Rowena is my oldest, dearest friend, and has helped me through more than one rough spot in the past. I feel I owe her this much. Never say you are afraid she'll embarrass us?"

"Us? No. Perhaps herself. She seems to speak without thinking, for all she appears uncommonly intelligent."

"Uncommon indeed. I consider myself one of the best educated women in England, but Rowena casts me in the shade when it comes to intellectual pursuits. I doubt there is a book on her brother's estate—or my father's for that matter—that she hasn't read. Newspapers and magazines, as well."

Pulling Pearl down onto the bed next to him, Luke nodded. "I surmised that. She seems exceptionally well informed on current events."

"Indeed, if she weren't a woman, I've no doubt she'd stand for Parliament—not that we haven't had more than one discussion on the unfairness of a system that prevents women from doing just that," Pearl said with a chuckle.

Luke raised his hands in mock horror. "We men must preserve some small portion of leadership to ourselves, or your sex would ride roughshod over us all. No doubt she'll manage to scrape along in Society if she is so well informed as that, however."

Pearl frowned. "I hope so. But for all her reading, she's had precious little experience with the real world. I fear she may be . . . susceptible."

"To men, do you mean? She's hardly likely to draw the sort of masculine attention you do, my dear," he said teasingly.

Pearl grinned, but regarded him speculatively. "Do you think her so plain, then? I believe she merely hides her light under a bushel. I'd say something disparaging about male observational powers if I hadn't noticed the way your Mr. Paxton was watching her tonight."

Luke's brows rose. "Not matchmaking, are you, love?"

"Certainly not. In fact, I'd thought to warn her

away from him, as his prospects seem rather poor. Besides, will he not disappear once he's caught this spy you say he is after? I'd not have Rowena's heart broken over him."

Rather than reply, Luke gathered his wife to him for a kiss. Noel's prospects were far better than Pearl knew, but that was not Luke's confidence to divulge. And whatever might spark between Noel and Miss Riverstone was best left to burn or fizzle without Pearl's interference.

"With your shepherding, I'm sure your friend will do quite well," he murmured into her hair. "I have no doubt you can make her ready for Society in two days' time. I only hope Society is ready for Miss Riverstone."

The next morning Rowena was the first downstairs for breakfast. The *Times* and *Morning Chronicle* had been placed on the sideboard to await Lord and Lady Hardwyck's pleasure, along with that week's *Political Register*, which Rowena had not yet read.

She rather doubted that most of the great houses in Mayfair received that publication, but it didn't surprise her that Pearl's would. Surely her friend wouldn't mind if she took a peek.

Rowena was deep in her reading, coffee and toast having been supplied by an unobtrusive footman, when Mr. Paxton appeared. Flustered, she put down the *Register,* tucking it facedown under her saucer to hide the name of the controversial circular.

"Good morning, Miss Riverstone," he greeted her cheerfully. "I see Lady Hardwyck was right about your usual habits."

"I—I beg your pardon?" Rowena shot a guilty glance at the folded paper at her elbow.

"Rising early," he clarified. "I tend to keep country hours myself, being a relative newcomer to London."

She looked at him in surprise. "You do not strike me as a rustic, sir. In fact, quite the opposite." For a moment, her gaze became tangled with his and she was struck again by the perceptiveness of his complex hazel eyes.

"I've traveled a bit, yes," he conceded. "But until a few weeks ago I was buried in Derbyshire."

"On your estate." She knew her tone was disapproving, and regretted it at once. He could not help having inherited, after all.

His smile held a trace of mockery. "While you have lived . . . in the cottage of your brother's poorest tenant?"

She could feel the color rising to her cheeks. "No, of course not—and I apologize. I have grown up privileged as well." Then, lifting her chin, she met his eyes again. "However, I *am* trying to make some reparation for that."

"By stirring up sympathy for the common man—or by criticizing every landowner you meet?"

He had scored another hit but Rowena refused to acknowledge it, nettled by his obvious amusement. "The former, of course."

"How admirable." His expression softened to something she could not decipher, though it quickened her heartbeat. "And how—"

"Good morning, early risers!" exclaimed Pearl, breezing into the dining room and interrupting whatever Mr. Paxton had been about to say. She looked fresh and vibrant in blue-sprigged muslin, making Rowena feel dowdier than ever.

Mr. Paxton rose to bow in greeting. "Good morning, my lady. May I say that you look lovely today."

Rowena stifled a sigh. He had directed no such compliments her way—not that she merited them, of course. Still—

"I'm glad to find you both here," Pearl continued after thanking him. "I have realized that as this is Rowena's first visit to Town, she may need a few pointers in order to feel comfortable at her first Society function. I'd like to enlist your aid, Mr. Paxton."

"Honored to oblige, of course," he responded politely, but Rowena thought she detected a flicker of alarm in his eyes.

As for herself, she wished she could disappear through the floor. Pearl made her sound like a charity case, a poor country bumpkin with no idea of how to go on in civilized society.

Turning, Pearl caught her reproachful glance and came forward to hug her. "I'm sorry, dear, I shouldn't have phrased it so. I only meant that you've had few opportunities to practice your social skills in Oakshire. How long has it been since you danced, for instance?"

Rowena fought down a sudden stab of panic. "Ah, quite some time, actually." Not since her last lesson with the dancing master, some four years since, in fact. "But surely there will be no need for me to do so?"

"No need to dance—at a ball?" Pearl's delicate eyebrows arched in amusement. "It is the whole point. I won't have you playing the wallflower or disappearing into a corner to discuss politics. Not at your very first ball."

Swallowing, Rowena nodded, though she had hoped to do just that. "Then I suppose you are right that I will need a bit of practice first. I don't wish to embarrass you, after all." She was acutely aware of Mr. Paxton witnessing this humiliating exchange.

"I have no fear of that whatsoever," Pearl assured her warmly. "It's settled, then. We'll start directly after breakfast. I believe we should run over some of the more popular card games as well, as I've planned a card party for Saturday."

Lord Hardwyck joined them then, and Rowena was glad to no longer be the focus of attention. As the others talked, she was aware of a rebellious thrill at the thought of Mr. Paxton standing up to dance with her. His hand would touch hers, she would look into his eyes . . .

And then step on his foot. Oh, this was going to be terrible! She sat in barely concealed agitation while Lord Hardwyck and Mr. Paxton discussed the unusually cool weather.

As soon as all had eaten, Pearl directed them to the ballroom. Servants were already polishing sconces and hanging brackets for the flowers for tomorrow night's event.

"We will make do with humming for music for now," Pearl said after a quick check of the preparations. "If you will oblige me, my lord, I thought we might model a waltz."

"Very well, my love, one waltz," Lord Hardwyck replied. "But then I must leave you to your protégée's lessons. I have several appointments today."

Pearl pouted prettily, but nodded. "All right,

Rowena, watch how I place my hands. The style has changed slightly since last year."

"Not that that matters, as I never learned to waltz at all," Rowena muttered to herself, watching the effortless way Pearl and her husband moved about the floor.

"It's not as hard as it looks," came an answering murmur from just behind her. She hadn't realized Mr. Paxton was standing so close. "We'll have you waltzing beautifully in no time."

She half turned, to look up at him gratefully. "I'm sure this wasn't what you had planned for this morning, sir. I appreciate your sacrificing your time on my behalf. And I do hope you're right, though I take leave to doubt it."

"You've clearly spent your time on more useful pursuits than dancing and flirting. You shouldn't be penalized for that," he responded with a warmth that startled her. "My plans were not so urgent that they can't wait for such a cause."

He understood! Rowena started to thank him again, but found herself caught in his gaze, his eyes darkening to a deep green as they seemed to probe hers for secrets.

"Rowena, you're not watching!" came Pearl's admonishing voice, snapping her back to her surroundings.

Embarrassed by the direction her thoughts had been tending, she quickly swung back around. "I . . . I have been," she stammered. "But I fear I'll have to begin at a more basic level. You've committed to more than you know, Pearl, with your insistence on making me fit for a ball by tomorrow night."

Though Rowena was quite serious, Pearl only laughed. "You know how I love a challenge, dear. But I'm convinced you only need some pointers. I know from experience what a quick study you are."

Rowena was spared from replying by Lord Hardwyck, who took his leave of them then. With a glance at Mr. Paxton that might have been pitying, he said, "I'll see you this afternoon at White's, as we discussed?"

Mr. Paxton nodded. "I'm quite looking forward to it."

"Don't plan on us for dinner then, my love," Lord Hardwyck said to Pearl. He gave her a quick but undeniably passionate kiss, then was gone.

Pearl turned back to the others, her cheeks a bit pink. "Now, where were we? Mr. Paxton, if you are willing, I will play a simple waltz on the pianoforte and you may partner Rowena. Half-time, to start."

Accordingly, she moved to the instrument in the corner of the large room and struck up a tune at a dirgelike pace. Rowena, her heart hammering wildly, turned to face Mr. Paxton.

"You really don't have to—"

"Nonsense. We have our instructions." With a smile that soothed one set of fears while creating another, he held out his hand.

Tentatively, she placed her own in it, while he set his other hand at her waist. He was even taller than she'd realized, her face on a level with his shirtfront. "I . . . I'll try not to tread on your feet," she promised breathlessly.

"No matter if you do. My shoes are quite sturdy. Now." Slowly, in time with the music, he moved her across the floor. "A waltz is simply a count of three, repeated. *One*, two, three, *one*, two, three. No, the other foot. That's right."

Though his touch was hugely distracting, Rowena concentrated with all her might on his words and his feet, trying to match her steps to his. All the while he spoke calmly, patiently, correcting her in gentle, matter-of-fact tones whenever she made a mistake.

Gradually, she was able to relax. As she became less stiff, her mistakes grew fewer, and by the end of the piece, she felt she had the basic movements fairly well mastered. Her partner reinforced her satisfaction.

"I told you it wasn't hard," he said. "You're doing excellently. Another, I think, Lady Hardwyck, this time at full tempo."

Pearl began another waltz at twice the speed as the last, and Rowena had to concentrate all over again. This time her progress was faster, partly because Mr. Paxton seemed adept at anticipating her errors and correcting them in advance.

The music ended with a flourish and Rowena, flush with her success, tried a small flourish of her own. Unfortunately, her left foot came down squarely on Mr. Paxton's right.

"Oops!" she exclaimed, quickly taking her weight off that foot. Too quickly. She lost her balance, and was saved from falling only by his superior reflexes.

"I'm . . . I'm terribly sorry." The feel of his arms around her, like warm, supple steel bands, made it hard to think. She hadn't realized he would be so strong.

Gently, he set her upright. "No harm done. Shall we try the minuet? Balls traditionally open with that one."

Rowena nodded mutely, still exceedingly flustered.

Pearl obliged with a sprightly minuet. Without the disturbing distraction of constant contact, Rowena was able to think again. Automatically, she went through the motions of the familiar, old-fashioned dance—not perfectly, but at least no one's feet were endangered by her occasional missteps.

She had already recognized Mr. Paxton's superior intelligence, but now she had to credit him with an unusual degree of kindness, as well. She repeatedly caught herself staring at him as they danced, the line of his jaw fascinating her with its masculine strength.

"Without more people, we cannot attempt any of the country dances or the quadrille," Pearl commented at the close of the minuet. "You know enough of those to get by, do you not, Rowena?"

"I hope so," she replied doubtfully. She now regretted never practicing once her dancing lessons had ended when she was seventeen. At the time, she had seen it as a blessed release from weekly hours of torture.

"We will watch out for you, Miss Riverstone, and come to your rescue should you find yourself out of your depth," Mr. Paxton said with a smile that served to make him even more handsome.

Though she felt herself pinkening with embarrassment that such measures should be necessary, she thanked him. "I fear I shall never be proficient, but I do feel less nervous now than I did when we began."

"Good!" Pearl's tone was bracing. "I have no doubt you will do quite well. You need not dance every dance, after all. And you, sir," she said to Mr. Paxton, her eyes twinkling, "had best not promise her too many dances yourself, or it will give rise to expectations among those assembled."

Rowena turned away quickly to hide her mortification, but not before she saw the startled look in Mr. Paxton's eyes. Why must Pearl tease so? She was greatly relieved when the butler chose that moment to interrupt them to announce morning callers.

Noel watched Miss Riverstone as he followed the two ladies to the parlor where the visitors awaited. Not only did the girl have one of the sharpest minds he'd encountered, she possessed a humorous awareness of her own limitations that he found quite appealing. Too appealing.

There was courage there as well, for it was clear she was dreading tomorrow night's ball but meant to see it through anyway. He presumed an unwillingness to disappoint Pearl was her primary motivation, and that spoke well of her loyalty, too.

That same loyalty would likely make it more difficult to get to her brother through her, but he had no choice. He'd noticed her choice of reading material at breakfast, though he hadn't let on. That she read the *Political Register* was one more bit of evidence that her brother might be the mysterious essayist.

At first opportunity, he would have to deftly question her about her brother, to see if he fit the profile of the Black Bishop. He would create such an opportunity soon—for of course that must be his only real interest in Miss Riverstone.

"Lady Mountheath, how good to see you," Pearl exclaimed as she entered the parlor. "I apologize again that I was unable to come for tea on Tuesday.

This is Miss Riverstone, the friend I mentioned. Rowena, Mr. Paxton, may I present Lady Mountheath and her daughters, Miss Lucy Mountheath and Miss Fanny Mountheath."

All of the proper greetings were exchanged. Noel moved to sit next to Miss Riverstone, thinking to put his plan into effect at once, but was forestalled by the younger Miss Mountheath, who beckoned him to sit by her.

"Lucy and I met you at Lady Jeller's Venetian breakfast two weeks ago," she reminded him with a giggle. "I'm delighted to find you are still in Town, Mr. Paxton, it has become so thin of late." She giggled again.

Noel smiled blandly, remembering all too well the tedious half hour he had spent with the sisters on that occasion. Again he was trapped, listening to their fatuous chatter while his hope of more interesting conversation, Miss Riverstone, was out of reach on the far side of their gimlet-eyed mother.

It was a distinct relief when more callers were announced. He rose and greeted Mr. Galloway, Mr. Orrin and Lady Minerva Chatham with enthusiasm. The newcomers dispersed themselves about the room and he took that opportunity to move closer to Miss Riverstone.

"I just received the invitation to your house party, and I am so distraught," Lady Minerva was saying to Lady Hardwyck. "Mother and I leave tomorrow to join Father in the country, so we will not be able to attend. It sounds like such fun."

"I'm sorry to give so little notice, Minnie. It was one of my starts, thrown together at the last moment.

You've heard me mention my friend, Rowena River-stone?" Lady Hardwyck made the introductions.

While Lady Minerva greeted Miss Riverstone pleasantly, Noel noticed that the two gentlemen gave her only the most cursory nod before turning their attention back to the other ladies present. He frowned at their rudeness, surprised that Lady Hardwyck did not call them to task for it—then realized he had reacted precisely the same way on first meeting Miss Riverstone.

What a difference a few hours in her company had made! Now he scarcely noticed her nondescript attire and unfashionable hairstyle, knowing the keen intelligence and wry humor that lurked beneath.

"So you are Bow Street's new hope to catch the Saint, are you, Mr. Paxton?" Lady Minerva interrupted his thoughts. "I can't say I wish you success, but I should love to hear any stories you know of our local hero."

Noel had to smile at her eagerness. "Most of what there is to tell has already found its way into the papers. It seems he is a master of disguise, able to act the nobleman as easily as the servant, making him quite difficult to track."

Miss Riverstone turned to listen, as did Lady Mountheath. The latter said, "I do hope you will manage it, however, Mr. Paxton. The villain stole jewels and plate from my home some months since, and they were never recovered. The Runners surmised that he masqueraded as a footman, hired on for the evening."

"A risky practice, hiring men off the street, Lady Mountheath," Lady Minerva commented. "I should be afraid to do so myself, much as I might like to have the Saint in my own house." She winked at the other ladies, drawing a general chuckle.

Miss Riverstone spoke for the first time since entering the parlor. "If everyone shared your caution, Lady Minerva, think how much harder it would be for those in difficult straits to earn enough to feed their families."

Lady Mountheath sniffed audibly, cutting off any reply Lady Minerva might have made. "Such men work cheaply, so will always find those willing to hire them. For my part, I now make certain that any chance hires are closely supervised, and carefully searched before leaving my employ."

Miss Riverstone frowned and opened her mouth, no doubt to protest such demeaning treatment.

"A wise precaution, my lady," said Noel quickly, before Miss Riverstone could draw the censure of the others. "I'd recommend requesting references as well, whenever possible."

All but Miss Riverstone murmured their agreement. The conversation moved on to the topic of Lady Hardwyck's upcoming house party, the Misses Mountheath and the two gentlemen clearly looking forward to such a novel amusement so late in the Season.

Noel glanced at Miss Riverstone to find her frowning at him, no doubt irritated by his implicit agreement with Lady Mountheath's methods. Though he could not explain, he smiled and shrugged to show he understood. He could not afford to lose her good opinion—not yet.

She raised one brow, as though trying to decipher

his meaning, then looked away. Lady Hardwyck caught his eye then and smiled approvingly. She, at least, realized what he had done for her friend.

The Mountheath ladies took their leave and other callers arrived. Over the next hour, it seemed that half the important personages still in London stopped by to congratulate Lady Hardwyck on her clever idea.

Lady Hardwyck dutifully introduced Miss Riverstone to each visitor, and almost without exception they greeted, then ignored her. Miss Riverstone appeared not to care, but Noel couldn't quite suppress his own irritation, hypocritical though it was.

He made a point of exchanging a few words with each visitor, memorizing names and mentally placing each one in relation to those he wished to cultivate. The groundwork for his investigation was being laid nicely.

When the last callers finally took their leave, Lady Hardwyck rose with a sigh. "Dear me, what a lot of curious people remain in Town! But it bodes well for tomorrow night's attendance. Dare I hope you will remember any names, Rowena?"

Miss Riverstone nodded. "I made a point of it, as it seemed one of the few things that might help me show to advantage. People are flattered to be remembered."

"Very true," Lady Hardwyck agreed with a laugh. "I suppose if you can plan a chess strategy ten moves in advance, a few dozen names should present little challenge. But now, let us continue our lessons. I thought we would move on to card games, as few people are likely to want to play chess."

Accordingly, she rang for decks of cards and the

three of them sat down to go over the rules of whist, faro, piquet and *vingt-un*. Not at all to Noel's surprise, Miss Riverstone proved a quick study, particularly in those games involving more strategy than luck.

"You should have no trouble holding your own in this arena," Lady Hardwyck declared after less than an hour. "How are you with a fan?"

Miss Riverstone stared at her, reminding Noel forcibly of a deer cornered by a hound. "A fan? Gesturing or, ah, flirting with one, do you mean?" She shot a quick, alarmed glance at Noel, then quickly looked away, her cheeks pinkening.

He stifled a smile. "Will that really be necessary, Lady Hardwyck?" he asked.

Somehow he couldn't imagine direct, unadorned Miss Riverstone intentionally flirting, fan or no fan. Flirting smacked of intrigue—one reason he'd made a point of learning to do it well himself—and her honesty was one of her more attractive traits.

"Only the basics, for now," Lady Hardwyck assured them. "Let me ring for a fan."

Noel hastily stood. "I'm certain you won't need me for this enterprise. Surely these are mysteries of which my sex is supposed to remain ignorant? Besides, it's getting late and I did promise to meet Lord Hardwyck."

"Coward," Lady Hardwyck teased. "Very well, run along then. You've been most patient and helpful, and I do thank you."

"As do I," echoed Miss Riverstone. "Without your help—both of you—I'd have been sure to embarrass myself. Now, perhaps, there is less certainty of that."

Again, Noel was charmed by her subtle, self-deprecating humor. "Fitting in is simply a matter of following the lead of those around you, Miss Riverstone," he said with a reassuring smile. "I have no doubt you will do splendidly. Ladies."

Bowing, he took his leave of them, trying not to notice the lingering anxiety in Miss Riverstone's eyes, or the effect that anxiety had upon him. She was simply a means to an end. He had no business feeling protective of her.

Perhaps it was just as well other gentlemen tended to overlook her. He had a vague suspicion he might not react particularly well should they do otherwise. Thankfully, her unfashionable appearance made it unlikely he would be put to any such test.

Chapter 5

"**R**inglets? Are you certain? They seem so . . . frivolous." Rowena frowned at the sketch Pearl's coiffeuse showed her.

After a disastrous hour playing with fans, Pearl had given up on teaching her that particular skill and had led her upstairs to begin her transformation.

Francesca nodded vigorously. "See how your hair wishes to curl of itself? A natural curl, when released from its bondage, one many women would envy. And the color, so rich, now that one can see it. You will wish for that richness about your face, no?"

Rowena glanced questioningly at Pearl, who echoed the woman's nod. "I've learned to trust Francesca in such matters," she said.

"Very well," Rowena agreed. "At least she's not proposing to cut too much of the length, so if I don't like it, I can still put it back into its bun." She was only half teasing, still determined to go through with it. What did she have to lose, after all?

Only her integrity, a small voice whispered.

"It's as well the men will not be here for dinner," Pearl was saying. "You must take breakfast in your room tomorrow as well. We will wait until your transformation is complete before springing you upon the world tomorrow night at the ball. I can scarcely wait to see Luke's face, or Mr. Paxton's."

Rowena had thought the same, but now her feelings swung from one extreme to the other. Suppose she looked ridiculous in her new trappings, like an ape playing dress up? She didn't think she could bear for Mr. Paxton to regard her as a figure of fun.

"Now then." Removing Rowena's spectacles, Francesca plied her scissors. At the first sound of her hair being shorn, Rowena closed her eyes. Pearl was her friend. She would never make her a laughing-stock, she told herself desperately.

Still, she was just as glad she was unable to watch as the coiffeuse fluttered about her head with scissors, pins and hot tongs. Pearl made no sound at all, which Rowena considered ominous. Finally, Francesca removed the cloth she had draped about Rowena's shoulders and backed away.

"Voila!" she cried. "A glass, my lady, if you please."

Rowena opened her eyes to see Pearl approaching with a hand mirror and a smile. "See what you think," she said, handing her the mirror.

Hesitantly, she lifted the glass. And gasped. How could a mere hairstyle effect such a change? But it had. Framed by coppery ringlets, her face looked softer, more feminine. Prettier. She darted a questioning glance at Pearl.

"I always told you that you were not so plain as

you believed," her friend reminded her with a smug expression. "Now you must confess that I was right."

Rowena looked again at the image in the mirror, not quite able to believe what she saw there. "My spectacles?" Pearl handed them to her and she donned them for a better look.

Now she looked a bit more like herself, her eyes less pronounced, the curve of her cheek somewhat disguised.

"Are you sure you don't want to try doing without them?" Pearl asked. "You could carry them with you, of course, to use if absolutely necessary."

For a long moment, Rowena hesitated. Dispensing with her spectacles would be pure vanity, and would make her feel more vulnerable, besides. But if she kept them handy . . .

Her goal, she reminded herself, was to become the sort of woman who might influence those in power to bring about necessary change. Slowly, she took off her eyeglasses and looked again at the mirror. Perhaps it would not be so impossible as she had thought.

"Very well," she said. "I will try."

"You're certain the family is away?" Noel surveyed the rear of the fashionable town house on Mount Street, noting that every window on the main floors was dark.

Stilt, the tall urchin lad, nodded. "Aye, guv. Lots of swells and their families are gone this time o' year, off to the country for whatever it is they do there."

Noel smiled at the boy's baffled tone. Clearly he couldn't imagine anything that would lure someone away from London. For a moment, he thought longingly of Tidebourne, his small estate in Derbyshire. And the grander estate of Ellsdon Abbey, where he had spent a few summers as a boy, and which he seemed likely to inherit on his uncle's death.

"Good," he said. "I'll try not to give the servants any reason to leave the attics." He started across the alleyway leading from the mews.

Stilt followed him. "Nowt but two of 'em anyway, from what we've been able to tell. An old couple, housekeeper and butler, most like."

In other words, no one to pose any threat, Noel thought. Still, he would do his best to get in and out undetected.

His goal tonight was simply to acquire enough booty to feed and house three Seven Dials families— and to brush up his housebreaking skills. Luke had told him about those families at their meeting earlier, suggesting he use this free evening for his first foray as the Saint.

Moving to a good vantage point just outside the back gate, he waited until the attic went dark, then cautiously moved forward. The gate was locked, but it was the work of a moment to climb it. As he'd expected, the back door and windows were also fastened securely. This would be the first test of his skills.

Luke had offered him the use of his set of lock-picks, but Noel preferred to use his own. They had served him well during his career as Puss in Boots in France, getting him into various locked offices and desk drawers.

Sliding a thin, curved piece of metal into the key-hole, he expertly turned it until the latch released. Then, pulling a tiny bottle from his breast pocket, he oiled the hinges before pushing the door silently open.

"Wait here," he cautioned Stilt, who had stood watching with obvious approval. The one thing that had motivated him to continue pursuit of the Saint, once he'd learned the Black Bishop wasn't involved, was the mistaken belief that the Saint was recruiting boys to help in his housebreaking. Noel certainly wasn't going to involve them himself, any more than necessary.

The back hallway was almost entirely dark, the only light coming from a fanlight above the front door at the far end, which let in some faint illumination from a nearby street lamp. Noel moved in that direction, peering into each of the four doors on that level as he went.

With the owners away, the plate would be securely locked up, probably in a closet belowstairs. He decided to check the dining room first, pulling a large sack from his waistband as he entered to examine the sideboard. The only dishes appeared to be pewter in the feeble light from the long front window, and the pair of candlesticks on top were undoubtedly silver plate. Still, they'd fetch something. Wrapping them in the cloths he'd brought, he stuffed them into his sack.

On his way back to the stairs, he slipped into the study for a quick look around. An ornate clock on the mantelpiece joined the candlesticks, and then he turned his attention to the desk.

Sir Randolph Olney was known to have strong connections to the Sussex smugglers, though no charges had ever been brought against him. It was one of the reasons Noel had targeted this house. He felt few qualms about stealing from a man whose wealth was largely ill-gotten.

The desk at first revealed nothing beyond a few letters, impossible to read in the dark. Reaching to the back of the smallest drawer, however, Noel discovered a handful of coins that, by their size and heft, he deduced must be gold guineas. Smiling, he pocketed them. No trip to the plate closet would be necessary now.

From the same breast pocket where he kept his phial of oil and his lockpicks, he pulled one of the cards Luke had given him, etched with the Saint's trademark sign: a black numeral seven surmounted by a golden halo. He tucked the card into the drawer from which he'd removed the guineas, then, with a last glance about, left the room and, a moment later, the house.

Rejoining Stilt in the small garden, he felt his first foray as Saint of Seven Dials had been rather anticlimactic. But then, he'd expected it to be easy, compared to most of his exploits in France. Even if he were caught—an unlikely event, considering he himself was Bow Street's prime weapon against the Saint—he'd face a more merciful fate than the French would have granted him.

"Care to have another go, guv?" asked Stilt as they regained the alleyway behind the garden. "House two doors down is empty as well. Skeet checked it out."

But Noel shook his head. He didn't know who lived in the other house, and he was determined to steal only from those he felt deserved it in some way— or who might yield some information about the Black Bishop.

"Not tonight, Stilt, but thank Skeet for his intelligence. We may attempt that one a different time," he added, hoping thereby to prevent the boys from trying a housebreaking on their own.

Unwrapping the candlesticks, he handed them to Stilt, along with the guineas. "Here's tonight's haul. This should take care of the O'Malleys, the Fabrizios and old Mrs. Fenniwick, as well as your cut for Twitchell."

"Aye, this'll do 'em for a good bit," Stilt agreed, rewrapping the candlesticks and pocketing the coins.

"You know how to contact me, if something else arises?"

The lad nodded. "Tig'll slip a note to Squint, who'll see you gets it."

"Right. Now, you boys keep your noses clean, and your ears to the ground in the meantime. We'll meet again in a few days."

Though he'd have liked to bring all of the boys back with him that very night, Noel knew they wouldn't come. Besides, they were useful on the streets. In addition to keeping an eye on the poorest denizens of Seven Dials, he'd told Stilt just enough about the Black Bishop that he was confident the lad would notify him if he heard anything.

Returning to Hardwyck Hall half an hour later, he was glad he planned no similar excursions over the next few days. Already he found himself missing Miss Riverstone and her quick wits. Perhaps he could manage a chess game with her before Lady Hardwyck's ball. It would be a good way to keep his own wits sharpened, and might afford him the opportunity he needed to ask about her brother.

Whether he had any other motive, he refused to contemplate.

The next morning, Noel was up early, despite a poor night's sleep. Thoughts of the intriguing Miss Riverstone had repeatedly interfered with the plans he needed to make, plans for the eventual unmasking and capture of the Black Bishop.

He could no longer deny that he found Miss Riverstone dangerously attractive. Her intelligence, curiosity and innocence all combined to form a potent allure that threatened to distract him from his real goal—a vital goal, he reminded himself. One that would likely alienate her forever, should he achieve it.

"Your blue coat, sir?" Kemp asked, opening the carved oaken wardrobe.

Noel shook his head. "Too flashy. Save that for tonight. The brown today, I think. I've an early appointment at Bow Street that's likely to last some time, then I plan to spend the afternoon and evening catching up with the word on the streets in the usual haunts. I've been out of circulation too long."

And starting tonight, he was unlikely to have a chance to approach his usual informants for some days, trapped here by Lady Hardwyck's house party. He was determined to use that opportunity to gather a different sort of information, however. If his suspicions were correct, it would be the only information he would need.

"Thank you, Kemp," he said as his manservant helped him into the brown coat. "Nip down to the kitchens and bring up a roll or two and some coffee, and then we'll be off."

Not knowing what stratum of Society the Black Bishop inhabited in England, Noel had begun with the lowest and worked his way up. Only in the past few weeks had he made real forays into the upper echelons of Society, and he had spent most of that time pursuing the false lead of the Saint.

He wondered if he should publicize the fact that his sister was so highly placed in Society, play up his grandfather's title. Neither fact would remain secret for long, anyway. But then Miss Riverstone's face rose before him.

No, he would wait. For the moment, he preferred she think him a mere son of a younger son. It would make her more likely to tell him what he needed to know.

"Luncheon as well?" Rowena asked in dismay when Pearl appeared in her bedchamber at two o'clock, followed by a maid bearing a covered tray. She had spent the morning writing a draft of her new essay for the *Political Register*. Now she had nothing to do— or even to read.

"I told you, I don't want anyone to see you before our grand unveiling tonight. Guests will begin arriving around six," Pearl continued, joining Rowena at a small table to partake of the tea and sandwiches. "Your gown should arrive by four. What fun it will be to put your toilette together!"

Rowena frowned at her friend. "I'm beginning to feel like a large doll, here for your amusement. I warn you, I won't go down at all if you make me ridiculous."

"Ridiculous?" Pearl's lovely eyes went wide and innocent, which Rowena found not at all reassuring. "Have you no more faith in me than that? You will be stunning, my dear—the belle of the evening. You must trust me."

Rowena nodded. Though she knew that her friend had unrealistic expectations, she could trust her to make certain Rowena's appearance would not be an embarrassment to either of them. It would be up to Rowena to make certain the same was true of her behavior.

Rowena's dress arrived on schedule. Matthilda lifted the emerald silk ballgown from the elegant box and gasped with delight. "Oh, miss!" she exclaimed in hushed tones. "The drawing at the modiste's didn't do it justice."

"No. No, it didn't." Rowena gazed at the shimmering gown in mingled awe and delight.

"Let's see how it looks on, shall we?" Pearl suggested.

Matthilda laced her into her best corset and dropped the silken folds over Rowena's head.

"Oh, Rowena, it's simply scrumptious," Pearl declared. "I wish I could wear such a color. No, don't turn around. Not yet."

Feeling more than ever like a large doll, Rowena stood passively while Matthilda and Pearl fussed about her, her frustration at not being able to see the result growing by the minute. Pins and ribbons were placed just so, with twitches at shoulders and waist to improve the fit of the gown.

"Now the hair. No, not yet, Rowena!" Pearl admonished as she tried to peek over her shoulder at the pier glass. "Francesca must put the finishing touches to you first. Promise not to look." She sent Matthilda to fetch her coiffeuse and a pot of tea.

The moment she arrived, Francesca set to work, murmuring to herself in French and English. "This curl, so. *Ceci aussi.* A ribbon through the top cluster. *Et voila!*" After what seemed an eternity, she stepped back, beaming at her handiwork.

Rowena glanced questioningly at Pearl, who was smiling as broadly as her hairdresser was. "Yes, you can look now."

Almost fearfully, Rowena turned around to see the stranger in the glass—for stranger it certainly appeared to be. Surely, this vision could not be herself?

The emerald green silk brightened the copper of her hair until it nearly glowed. Tied tight under her ample breasts with a darker green ribbon, cut low, but not too low, the gown emphasized her curves, skimming her narrow waist and the generous flare of her hips, making her look voluptuous rather than simply plump.

"Your spectacles, remember?" Pearl prompted as Rowena stared transfixed at her image. She handed her the green silk reticule that had come with the gown.

"Yes. Yes, of course." Still unable to look away from her reflection, Rowena removed her spectacles—and the reflection blurred.

"No squinting," Pearl reminded her as Rowena instinctively squeezed her eyes into better focus. "Here's your reticule. You can keep your spectacles there—in case of emergency."

Rowena glanced at Pearl in vague alarm, but even without seeing her expression clearly, she could tell that her friend was teasing. "Yes, we wouldn't want me to pick up a candlestick instead of a glass of ratafia, or a carnation instead of a canape, would we?"

"Now, now. I know you're not as blind as all that and it's not as though you'll do any reading at a ball. Have you a fan?"

"Yes, right here." Rowena displayed the green silk fan figured in gold that she'd purchased to go with the dress.

Pearl stepped back to take one more good look—an ability Rowena now envied—and nodded her approval. "Excellent. Now, wait here while I get ready myself—it won't take me more than half an hour, I promise."

She bustled off, Francesca in tow, and Rowena sighed. If only she shared Pearl's confidence. Now that her first evening in Society was less than an hour away, she realized afresh how unprepared she really was.

Oh, she looked well enough—far better than she'd ever imagined she could, in fact—but what of the woman beneath the trappings? She had no gift for small talk, for conversing upon trivialities while ignoring the larger issues.

And what would she do, she wondered in sudden panic, if some gentleman were to *flirt* with her? She would be completely out of her element. She'd do far better to remain in her room, where she would be unable to embarrass either Pearl or herself.

Matthilda, returning just then with the tea tray, gasped with delight. "Oh, miss, who'd have ever thought it? You're as beautiful as any fine lady ever was, and that's the truth."

Rowena shook her head, both irritated and flattered by her maid's overblown admiration. "Hardly that, but I do confess the gown suits me well. Have I not taught you by now not to focus on appearances, however?"

"I already know what's underneath," Matthilda replied saucily, setting down the tray. "And that won't have changed, will it? Where's the harm in saying how well you look?"

More than a bit shaken at her maid's so closely echoing her own thoughts, Rowena didn't answer, but moved to pour out the tea instead. She was relieved to discover she could do so without the benefit of her spectacles. Perhaps she could manage this after all, she thought, taking a fortifying sip of the hot liquid.

True to her word, Pearl reappeared not twenty minutes later, resplendent in pale blue satin and snowy Mechlin lace. "Ah, pour me a cup as well, Rowena, do. We still have a few minutes before we need to go down."

This time, conscious of her friend's watchful eye, Rowena spilled a few drops while pouring. Though it was surely due to nervousness rather than nearsightedness, she said, "See what comes of taking away my spectacles? You are fortunate I've sullied only the tray and not your gown."

"Pish! I do that all the time, and my eyes are perfectly fine. You've promised me to go through with our experiment," Pearl, reminded her severely. "Don't you dare cry craven now."

Though she felt a strong inclination to do just that, Rowena shook her head. "No, I'll go through with it."

Pearl laughed. "You needn't make it sound as though you are going to your own execution. Please,

Rowena, do *try* to enjoy yourself tonight. I've invited only a small, select crowd, so you should not be overwhelmed. Let's go down, shall we? The guests will be arriving soon."

Trying her hardest to look cheerful for Pearl's sake, Rowena rose. "Very well. And I will do my best, I promise. It's the least I can do, after all your effort on my behalf."

"That's the spirit! Come, we'll treat it as a military campaign, with you well armed to breach the defenses of whatever forces you meet."

Despite herself, Rowena's spirits rose at the metaphor. Yes, she would pretend the evening was merely an elaborate chess match, where each move by her opponents—the other guests—must be matched by a strategic move of her own. Absurd, of course, but oddly comforting.

They descended the stairs together, to find Lord Hardwyck waiting for them at the bottom. His eyes widened when he caught sight of Rowena, and he glanced questioningly at Pearl, then back at Rowena with an amazement that might have been insulting if she had not reacted the same way to her own changed appearance.

"My dear, you have outdone yourself," he said to his wife. "Miss Riverstone, I scarcely recognized you. You are quite stunning."

Though it came from her friend's husband, it was the first compliment upon her appearance Rowena had received from a man and it flustered her badly. "I, er, thank you, my lord. The credit all goes to Pearl, however."

"I see we need to work on your response to compliments," Pearl admonished her. "You're sure to receive many, and you can't refer them all to me. A simple thank you will suffice, if you do not feel bold enough to return the compliment or playfully accuse the gentleman in question of flattery—also acceptable responses."

Rowena felt her color rising with embarrassment. "I told you I was not ready for this."

"All you need is a bit of practice," Pearl assured her. "That's what tonight is for. Come, you can help me look over the buffet tables to be certain all is as it should be."

Rowena followed obediently, wondering where Mr. Paxton might be. Would she dither as badly when he spoke to her? Undoubtedly. Much as she hoped to see admiration in his eyes, at the moment she felt she'd prefer not to see him at all.

Pearl had just declared adequate the assorted dainties that were to serve in lieu of dinner when the sound of the door knocker reached the ballroom.

"Ah! Our first guests. No, you come with me, Rowena. You needn't greet the guests as they come in, but I'm not giving you an opportunity to hide, either."

Again Rowena followed her friend, this time with gathering dread. *Treat it as a chess match,* she reminded herself firmly. Lifting her chin, she took a position just inside the ballroom, only a few yards from Pearl and her husband.

To her surprise, the first guest was her brother. She had not known Pearl had invited him, though of course it made sense that she had. He completed the pleasantries with his hosts, then turned to the ballroom, only to see Rowena standing there.

Sir Nelson stared, blinked, then stared again. "Gadslife! Ro?" he finally said.

Suddenly struck by the absurdity of the situation, Rowena dropped into a curtsey. "How pleasant to see you again, Nelson," she replied in well-modulated tones. "I'm glad you could come."

"So am I. You look a treat, Ro." Her brother still looked disbelieving. "Lady Hardwyck must be some sort of sorceress to have pulled off such a change."

Both touched and irritated, Rowena clung to her smile. "Merely a new gown and hairstyle—but Pearl can be quite determined when she sets her mind on a project."

As they talked, more guests filtered in and before Rowena knew it, the room was quite crowded. Her earlier panic revived. She glanced at Pearl to find her urgently beckoning to her.

"I want you to meet Lord and Lady Marcus Northrup," Pearl said as Rowena came forward. "Lord Marcus is one of Luke's oldest friends, and his wife is also relatively new to London. You two should get along famously."

The couple greeted Rowena cordially, and she realized that it was easier to meet people who had no idea of the change that had been wrought in her. "Pearl tells me you two were but recently married?" she asked after greetings were exchanged.

"Yes, scarcely three weeks since," replied the diminutive Lady Marcus in a distinctly American accent. "And please, call me Quinn. I'm still not used to my new designation, and am determined to dispense with it when among friends."

Rowena warmed to the young woman at once, put

at ease by her casual air. She was quite different from the simpering, gossiping ladies Rowena met yesterday. They chatted about their impressions of London, while Lord Marcus moved away to speak to two other gentlemen.

"Were you as afraid of breaking some unwritten Society rule as I am?" Rowena asked the charming American.

"Oh, gracious, yes!" Quinn exclaimed. "I still am, in fact. Perhaps we should compare notes and combine our knowledge, to our mutual benefit."

Rowena laughingly agreed that this was a good scheme. Glancing at Pearl again, she saw her greeting an imposing man with a large, hooked nose who looked vaguely familiar. Squinting slightly in an effort to determine where she'd seen him before, she brought someone else into focus, someone who made her heart do a funny little flip.

Mr. Paxton, staring at her in blank astonishment.

Chapter 6

With an effort, Noel pulled his gaze away from Miss Riverstone to answer Luke's question. "No great successes today, but some small progress, or so I hope."

He had already related last night's events to Luke. He had spent the morning at Bow Street, and the afternoon visiting certain taverns and gaming hells, casting for information that might lead to the Bishop. He intended to follow up one lead about a group of radicals said to meet at the Crown and Horn.

"Good, good. We'll talk later," said Luke. "Go on and enjoy yourself. The crab puffs are excellent, I hear."

Noel nodded absently, his attention straying to Miss Riverstone again. What on earth had she done to herself? Her hair ... that gown ... and where were her spectacles? Slowly moving in her direction, he was almost surprised he had recognized her so quickly. She looked so different from the mousy chess master he knew and liked.

Before he could reach her side, he was accosted by Lord Marcus.

"Evening, Paxton," he said. "Luke mentioned you were to attend tonight. We'll have to talk later." His expression made it clear that Luke had explained Noel's new mission to Lord Marcus, the last Saint of Seven Dials. "You've met my brother, Lord Peter, and Mr. Thatcher, haven't you?"

Noel greeted all three gentlemen. "Yes, we all met in Vienna, winter before last," he said, regarding the yellow-waistcoated Lord Peter a bit warily. At that time, Lord Marcus's elder brother had considered Noel a bad influence on his friend, laughable as that was considering Harry Thatcher's own propensity for debauchery.

Lord Peter smiled cordially enough now, though his gaze was piercing. "Good to see you again, Paxton. Harry told me you were in Town. Something to do with thief-catching?"

"Yes, I've been working with Bow Street, helping them to run the Saint of Seven Dials to ground. Damnably elusive fellow, I must say," he added with a perfectly straight face. He found it hard to concentrate on the conversation with Miss Riverstone standing only a few feet away, just beyond Lord Peter's shoulder.

The change in her was both startling and disturbing: frilled, flounced and ringleted like every other lady present. Such fripperies seemed out of character. And her spectacles—how well could she see without them? Had she noticed him yet?

"—connection to Lord Ellsdon?" Lord Peter was

saying, snapping Noel's attention back. "In fact, it occurs to me—"

"Yes, you're right," Noel cut him off. Moving a step or two further from Miss Riverstone and Lady Marcus, he continued softly, "As you are no doubt about to surmise, the fact that my aging uncle has only daughters makes me his heir presumptive—something I've been careful not to publicize."

Peter's brows rose, while Marcus and Harry stared at him in evident surprise. "Indeed? The better to move unnoticed among the criminal class, I presume?"

As he had in Vienna, Noel marveled that someone of such dandified appearance as Lord Peter could possess such rapier intellect. "Precisely. If anonymity can help me to track down the slippery Saint—" He broke off. Did Peter know about his brother's involvement?

If so, he gave no sign of it. "Of course. Society won't learn the truth from me—or from any of us. Right, Harry? Marcus?"

The others nodded. "Can't say I blame you," Harry remarked, reaching for a glass of wine with his remaining arm. His left had been lost in the recent war. "Bloody nuisances, titles, from all I've seen. Even courtesy ones." He grinned at Lord Marcus. "Make you do idiot things like get married."

"The title had nothing—" Marcus began, then broke off with a shake of his head, perceiving that Harry was bamming him. "I'd say Peter had better watch out, then."

Lord Peter shrugged. "I'm willing enough, should the proper lady come along. Now Harry, here—if ever a man could benefit by matrimony—"

Harry Thatcher snorted and made an extremely rude reply, but Noel's attention had wandered back to Miss Riverstone, who now seemed to have attracted several male admirers. Damn it.

"If you'll excuse me?" he murmured to the arguing trio and moved away without waiting for a reply. Innocent as she was, someone should definitely warn Miss Riverstone away from such questionable personages as Mr. Galloway, a known fortune hunter, and Lord Fernworth, a complete fribble—both of whom appeared to be ogling her in a most improper manner.

"Well met, Miss Riverstone," he greeted her with forced heartiness, making the whole group around her swing around to face him. "Dare I hope to engage you in another chess match later?"

Galloway's brows rose and he regarded Miss Riverstone curiously, while Fernworth actually took a step away from her. Noel took advantage of the opportunity to move closer.

"This scarcely seems the setting, Mr. Paxton," she replied with a look he couldn't quite decipher.

Rowena had been achingly aware of Mr. Paxton's slow approach, but now that he had reached her, she felt more irritated than pleased. Beyond that first surprised glance, he showed no indication he even noticed the dramatic change in her appearance—not that she wanted his flattery, of course. Still . . .

"So you play chess, Miss Riverstone?" asked Mr. Galloway. "I'd like a match as well, sometime. I'm quite fond of the game."

She regarded the too-charming redheaded man with some amusement. When he had called on Pearl yesterday, he'd completely ignored her, but now he was overflowing with compliments.

Five minutes' conversation with him had only rein-forced her low opinion of gentlemen's perceptiveness—though he did seem more intelligent than Lord Fernworth.

"Certainly, sir, should the opportunity arise."

Mr. Paxton had the effrontery to chuckle. "I should like to watch that match, I think. Shall I ask Lady Hardwyck to provide a board and a suitable corner somewhere?"

"Now?" Rowena asked in surprise. Not that she wasn't sorely tempted to retreat from this alien milieu to a more familiar one—

"Don't be absurd, Paxton," Lord Fernworth ex-claimed. "Chess at a ball? You may be the biggest stick-in-the-mud in London, but there's no need to drag Miss Riverstone into your dull pursuits when so many more amusing ones offer."

Lady Marcus nodded. "I fear he's right, Mr. Pax-ton. This is Miss Riverstone's first Society function, after all. It would be a shame for her to miss any of it."

Rowena stifled a sigh. They were right, of course. And much as she enjoyed chess, she had to admit the experience of being admired by handsome gentlemen was a rather enjoyable novelty.

"Indeed, Lady Hardwyck gave me strict orders to meet as many people as possible tonight," she said. "As kind as she has been, I wish to be obedient."

"I was jesting, of course," Mr. Paxton said with a smile she thought looked rather forced. "I believe Lady Hardwyck said something about a card party tomorrow. That will be a far more suitable venue."

Was the man so determined to prove her win two nights since had been an anomaly? It was unlikely he simply wished to spend time with her, oblivious as he seemed to her appearance tonight. More nettled than she cared to admit by his indifference, she turned to Mr. Galloway with a smile.

"Will you be attending tomorrow as well, sir?"

He bowed gallantly. "I wouldn't miss another evening in your company for the world, Miss Riverstone."

Lord Fernworth snorted. "Won't miss a chance at cards, he means. If you can lure him away from *vingt-un* I'll be amazed."

"Prepare to be amazed, then," Mr. Galloway retorted, with a wink at Rowena. Flustered, she made no response.

"I'll stick to cards myself," Lord Fernworth said, missing the byplay. "Never been much for chess."

Mr. Paxton watched her rather knowingly. "I'm sure Miss Riverstone will oblige you both with a hand or two of whist."

That was the card game Rowena found to rely most on skill—and therefore the one at which she most excelled. Mr. Paxton must dislike these two gentlemen intensely to be so eager to see her best them at something.

"Or perhaps I'll try my hand at *vingt-un*," she said with a warning glance at Mr. Paxton. She would not be a tool for any male posturing.

Vingt-un relied far more on luck than did whist, but Pearl had warned her that most gentlemen were put off by a lady who exceeded their own skills. If she wished to make her mark in Society, she must strive to suppress her competitive tendencies—at least until she was established.

"Dare I hope you still have a dance or two free?" Mr. Paxton asked then, obediently dropping the topic of cards.

The question revived all of Rowena's earlier nervousness. "Mr. Galloway has asked for the first set, but I am free after that."

"The second set, then? And perhaps a waltz?" Those penetrating hazel eyes soothed her with unspoken reassurance.

She relaxed marginally, though her senses tingled with his nearness. "Very well, sir." She didn't dare waltz with anyone else, in fact, as unschooled as she yet was at the new dance. But she could trust Mr. Paxton to overlook her inevitable errors.

"Third set to me, then?" Lord Fernworth asked.

As Rowena assented, Lord Marcus approached to introduce his brother and Mr. Thatcher, each of whom also claimed a dance. More people joined their circle, and soon Rowena was bespoken for most of the evening.

Amazement warred with both fear and delight. Pearl had been quite correct, it seemed. She only hoped she could get through the evening without committing any monumental gaffes.

While guests continued to stream into Pearl's "select" gathering, the orchestra started tuning its instruments.

"The dancing will begin in a few minutes," Mr. Paxton commented. "Would you care to visit the buffet tables beforehand?"

Suppressing a small thrill at his attentiveness, Rowena agreed, gingerly placing a hand on the crooked arm he held out to her. He looked far more handsome in his formal attire than she'd expected, making her nervous in his presence despite the rapport they'd achieved previously.

"See that man there, between the pillar and the potted palm?" He pointed. "That's the Duke of Wellington. I'll introduce you to him later."

Rowena looked eagerly in the indicated direction, but saw only a blurred figure of a tall man on the opposite side of the ballroom. With an impatient exclamation, she opened her reticule to retrieve her spectacles, but then noticed Mr. Galloway on her other side, watching her.

Guiltily, she dropped the reticule, mentally chiding herself for vanity. "Thank you," she said to Mr. Paxton. "I will look forward to that."

He rather transparently smothered a grin, letting her know that he'd noticed her dilemma. "Up close, you'll understand how he acquired the affectionate nickname of Old Nosey among his men."

"Up close?" Mr. Galloway laughed. "Why, you can see the fellow's proboscis from here."

Rowena realized he must be the man she had noticed earlier, greeting Pearl. She looked his way again and nodded, ignoring Mr. Paxton's amusement at her plight. She had promised Pearl to do without her spectacles as much as possible. This was not vanity—she was merely keeping her word.

"The duke's abilities must surely make up for any deficiencies of appearance," she said. "By all accounts, he is a brilliant military strategist."

Both gentlemen agreed, and fell to discussing one of his more famous campaigns. Rowena refrained from asking questions about the specifics, though she listened avidly.

"I am reliably informed that the crab puffs are excellent," said Mr. Paxton, dropping the military topic as they reached the buffet tables. "Perhaps some orgeat to drink as well?"

Rowena scanned the table, remembering not to squint, but before she could identify the crab puffs, Mr. Galloway had placed two upon a plate and handed them to her.

"Thank you." Relief gave her words added warmth, which he appeared to misinterpret, judging by his wide smile and the sudden sparkle in his blue eyes.

"Anything for a lovely lady," he said, and there was no denying the suggestiveness in his tone.

Suddenly uncomfortable, Rowena took a bite of crab puff, coughing when she swallowed too quickly. Her eyes watered and she tried desperately to get her breath back.

"Your orgeat." Mr. Paxton was at her elbow, offering a glass, concern in his eyes.

Rowena gulped gratefully, her eyes conveying her thanks until she could speak. "I—I didn't realize the puffs would be so flaky," she finally said by way of explanation. "I've never tasted one before."

"Really?" asked Mr. Galloway in evident surprise. "They're a staple at such dos here in Town. Do they not serve them at country balls?"

"Perhaps Miss Riverstone has had better things to do in the country than attend balls," Mr. Paxton suggested before she could answer.

Though he was perfectly right, she shot him an annoyed glance. Did he *want* her to appear a bookish rustic? She was likely enough to do so without his help. Just then, the orchestra struck up the opening chords to a minuet.

"This is our dance, is it not, Mr. Galloway?" she said sweetly, handing plate and empty glass to Mr. Paxton. She barely had time to see him raise one brow as she turned away.

Mr. Galloway led her to the floor with alacrity and she took her place opposite him. He bowed, she curtsied, and the dance began. For the first few minutes Rowena concentrated on her steps but it was a dance she'd known since childhood, and soon she felt secure enough to pay attention to those around her.

"I confess, I'm racking my brains to think what you might have done in the country that could be more enjoyable than a ball," Mr. Galloway said when the movement of the dance brought them together again.

Rowena decided it was safest to blend truth with convention. "I have been in charge of my brother's household for the past few years," she said, "and I see to the needs of our tenants. Not more enjoyable, perhaps, but necessary."

"But surely that leaves you some time for more pleasurable pursuits?" He waggled his sandy eyebrows. "Lusty country squires? Novels, perhaps?"

"I do read, yes," she admitted. Luckily, the dance moved them apart before she could add that her reading choices rarely encompassed anything so light as novels. No, better not to elaborate on that, or on her lack of beaux in the country.

When next they came together, her partner related tidbits of gossip about two or three of their fellow guests, identifying them with nods as he spoke. Rowena smiled and obediently looked in the indicated directions, though none were close enough to see clearly.

Just as well. She did not care to have her opinions clouded by such trivialities.

By the end of the dance, she had regretfully concluded that Mr. Galloway had no depth to his personality, flattering as his compliments might be. She hoped all of her partners would not prove the same.

"I thank you for an enjoyable dance, Miss Riverstone," he said, bowing gallantly. "Dare I hope you will favor me with another later on?"

She smiled politely, but noncommittally. "Perhaps. Thank you, Mr. Galloway."

It occurred to her that at least *one* of her partners promised interesting conversation. Her spirits rose, recalling that she was promised to Mr. Paxton for the next set. She was easily able to pick him out of the crowd as he approached.

When he was close enough for her to decipher the expression on his face, she was reminded that she had all but snubbed him at the buffet tables—even though he had been perfectly correct.

"Are you still willing to partner me?" she asked as soon as Mr. Galloway moved out of earshot. "I was rather rude to you, I fear."

To her relief, he grinned. "And I was baiting you, so I certainly deserved it. Unworthy of me, I know."

The orchestra struck up a waltz then, and his grin turned to mock dismay. "Unfair!" he exclaimed. "I had hoped for this dance *and* a waltz, and now I find the two are one."

Rowena felt a distinct surge of pleasure at this evidence that he enjoyed her company. He was, after all, the handsomest man she had seen here tonight, and could presumably claim dances with any lady present.

"Suppose I promise you the next waltz as well, should there be another?" she asked shyly as he took her gloved hand in his. "*You* already know how little I excel at this dance, but I would prefer that not become common knowledge."

She realized too late that her words might be construed as either flirtation or an insult, but he appeared to take them as neither, smiling warmly down at her. "Your secret is safe with me," he promised.

Where Mr. Galloway's closeness had made her uncomfortable, Mr. Paxton's caused tendrils of pleasure to curl through her midsection. Still, remembering what he'd said earlier, she felt obliged to ask, "And what of my other secrets?"

"I do apologize," he said, only the tiniest flicker of amusement in his eyes. "It is simply that I find the real you more interesting than this pattern card of propriety you are attempting to emulate tonight. I hate seeing you hide your light under a bushel—even such an exceedingly attractive bushel."

She felt herself blushing. Pearl had said something similar, but with far different meaning, regarding her usual plain appearance as the disguise. No wonder she felt so comfortable with this man—if "comfortable" was the right word.

The dance began and she followed his lead, belatedly grateful for her practice session yesterday. Without it, she'd have been forced to sit out any waltzes tonight. Earlier she had thought dancing would be torture, but now she was quite—pleased—to be able to participate in this particular dance.

"You are doing splendidly," Mr. Paxton commented after giving her a few moments to settle into the movements of the waltz. "I must be a better teacher than I realized."

Rowena smiled up at him, trying to ignore her pleasure at his words. "How like a man, to take the credit for a woman's achievement."

His brows rose, acknowledging the hit, but then she missed her step and he quickly adjusted his own to compensate before anyone watching could have noticed her mistake.

"Very well, I'll give you credit for that one," she said.

He laughed aloud, drawing glances from those around them. Quickly, he lowered his voice, though his eyes still danced. "You are a true original, Miss Riverstone. And I mean that as a compliment of the highest order."

Rowena refrained from pointing out that he'd become more liberal with his compliments since her appearance had improved. Certainly he was not so shallow as Mr. Galloway and his ilk, but she could not deny that his attitude toward her had changed subtly since seeing her in her new guise.

"Is your brother, Sir Nelson, to attend tonight?" he asked, when she made no reply.

She glanced at him in surprise. "Have you been making inquiries about my family, sir? Yes, Nelson is here. He was one of the first to arrive."

"Indeed? I should rather like to meet him. If you are any indication, he's likely to be an interesting man to talk to."

She felt flattered both by his compliment and this evidence of interest—wishing to meet her brother must indicate interest in her, mustn't it? Glancing up at him, however, she caught something in his expression that reminded her of the one he wore while playing chess.

"I'll introduce you at first opportunity," she told him, wondering if she had imagined it. What sort of strategizing could he be doing in a ballroom, after all?

"Thank you." He still looked somber, but before she could think how to ask about it, he smiled. "Care to attempt a twirl?"

Sudden panic drove all thoughts of Mr. Paxton's preoccupation from her mind. "A twirl? Do you think that's wise?" she whispered, as though he had suggested she petition Parliament to restructure the entire government.

"I believe you are up to the challenge," he responded with an encouraging wink that only flustered her further. "Take your hand from my shoulder, and turn to your right."

He removed his own hand from her back, lifting their joined hands higher, and she awkwardly followed his direction, turning about completely until she faced him again. She stumbled at the end of her twirl, but he quickly placed his hand at her back again, and she clutched at his shoulder for balance.

"Right," he said in apparent satisfaction, despite her clumsiness. "Now back to the steps: *one*, two, three, *one*, two, three." He counted until her steps were in time with his.

Relieved, she managed a shaky laugh. "At least I did not fall on my face. I think I would prefer not to attempt any more twirls at present, however." Indeed, her heart was hammering so quickly that it was all she could do to keep to the rhythm of the dance.

"Coward," he teased, just as Pearl had chided him yesterday. "I thought you more adventurous than that."

She raised her chin, spurred by his jibe to tell him she would attempt any maneuver he suggested, but fortunately the waltz came to an end just then. Casting about for something to say that would prove she was not afraid to try new things, she saw her brother approaching.

"Here comes Nelson," she said, abandoning her unladylike desire to have the last word. "Shall I introduce you?"

Mr. Paxton followed her gaze, successfully diverted. "Please," he replied, belatedly releasing his hold on her.

Rowena suppressed a small sigh as his hand left hers. For a short while, it had almost seemed—

"Ro, may I have a word with you?" her brother said the moment he reached them. He appeared vaguely troubled, she thought.

"Certainly. But first I'd like to introduce Mr. Paxton, a friend of Lord Hardwyck's. Mr. Paxton, my brother, Sir Nelson Riverstone."

The gentlemen shook hands. "Pleased to meet you,"

Nelson said distractedly. Rowena wondered what could have him so agitated.

"Likewise," Mr. Paxton responded. "I have heard your work at the Home Office spoken of highly."

Now Nelson's attention was caught. "Have you, then? That's nice to hear, I must say. We'll talk later, shall we? Need to have a quick word with my sister first."

"Certainly, certainly." Mr. Paxton bowed to them both and moved away.

Rowena frowned uncertainly at her brother. "I am engaged for the next dance with Lord Fernworth."

"Really? Making quite a splash tonight, I see. Good for you. But you can make it up to him later. I've just realized you're my best hope for dealing with a rather sticky situation." To her surprise, he actually flushed. "Ro, I have a problem, and I need your help."

Chapter 7

"**P**roblem?" Rowena asked her brother in surprise. "What sort of problem?"

Before he could answer, Lord Fernworth appeared to remind her of their dance. Judging by his slurred speech and silly grin, he had clearly had too much to drink already. Rowena was just as glad to have an excuse to put him off.

"Would you mind terribly if we had our dance another time?" she asked, trying not to let her distaste show. "My brother had a prior claim, which I had forgotten."

Lord Fernworth waved one hand grandly. "Of course, of course. Not much of a dancer anyway."

Shocked, Rowena wondered frantically if the whole room had noticed her inexperience. Surely, if the inebriated Lord Fernworth had been able to tell—

"Prefer to spend my time at the card tables, you see," he continued. "Takes practice to be a good dancer, and I've not had enough. Was hoping to convince you to sit it out, actually."

"I've had little practice myself, Lord Fernworth," she confessed in her relief. "I'll be happy to sit out a dance with you later."

"Certainly, certainly." His voice was too loud, his gestures too broad, but at least he was affable about it. With a final wave, he wandered away.

At once, Rowena turned back to Nelson. "Now, what is this problem you need me to help you with?"

"Let's get out of the crowd first," he suggested, indicating a pair of chairs in a corner, well away from both the dance floor and those milling about the edges.

Growing increasingly curious, Rowena accompanied him, waiting until they were seated to say, "Well?"

He ran a finger between his neck and cravat before answering. "It's, ah, rather embarrassing, actually. A problem of a, er, financial nature. Now that you've access to your inheritance, it occurs to me that you may be able to help. You see, I, ah . . ." He trailed off, clearly debating how much to tell her.

Striving to hide her astonishment that Nelson was actually asking for her help, Rowena touched his hand. "Come, you know you can trust me. Is it gaming debts?" Nelson had always had a weakness for cards.

He nodded, dropping his gaze from her direct one. "Aye, you've hit it. I'm in pretty deep—too deep, in fact."

Rowena felt her first real flicker of alarm. "What do you mean? Is the estate at risk?"

"No, of course not," Nelson said quickly, looking

up. "It's entailed. But I never should have . . ." Again he hesitated.

"Have what? What have you done, Nelson?"

"I've . . . I've pawned some of Mother's jewelry, for a start," he said.

She stared, anger beginning to stir. "Do you mean you brought it to Town with you?" That jewelry was among the few things they had to remember their mother by. "Which pieces?" she asked then. "Not the—"

He nodded miserably. "The diamond and emerald set—necklace, earrings and brooch."

Rowena jumped to her feet. "We must redeem them at once, then. Where is the pawnshop?"

Nelson pulled her back down beside him. "Shh! Don't make a scene, Ro. And it's no use—they'll have been sold by now."

"Sold? How long ago did you pawn them?"

"Back in June."

She stared at him in dismay. "And you've only become concerned now? Why? Because I'm in Town?"

He shrugged. "It's not the first time—that is . . ."

"You've done this before?" She'd suspected once or twice over the past year that Nelson was engaging in high play, but never had she suspected he had actually run into debt.

"Only things of my own, one or two smaller bits of jewelry Father left me, when I was badly dipped," he said, as though that excused his actions.

"But the diamonds weren't your own."

Nelson didn't meet her eyes. "Yes I know. They were yours. But I thought they would bring enough to finally satisfy him, and it didn't seem likely you would ever wear them."

She ignored the subtle insult. "But you still owe money, even after selling the diamonds?"

"He offered me another game, to wipe out my debts if I won. But I lost. And now . . . now he's threatening to bruit it about that I'm in dun territory if—"

"And who is 'he?'" she interrupted. "Who is this man who cheats men at cards, then extorts them?"

Nelson glanced about them in alarm, then shook his head. "Never said he cheated. I wouldn't dare, even if I believed it, which I don't. He'd likely kill me for it. A crack shot, everyone says. And very highly regarded among the intellectual set. Moves in higher circles than I do, anyway."

"Nelson!" exclaimed Rowena in exasperation. "Who *is* he?"

"Lester Richards."

"Lester Richards?" she repeated, stunned. "Mr. Lester Richards, the Spencean reformer?"

Her brother shrugged. "I don't follow such things, but yes, I'm sure it's the same man. He attends salons at Holland House, that sort of thing."

"But—I don't understand," she said lamely, seeing no point in telling Nelson that she positively idolized Mr. Richards. She had done so for nearly a year, ever since reading a persuasive essay he'd written promoting some of the very causes she herself espoused. How could he possibly be victimizing her brother?

"Nor do I, precisely," Nelson admitted. "He seems a likeable chap, if rather intense. Always asking questions about my work at Whitehall, that sort of thing."

Rowena was thinking hard. Mr. Richards, champion of the common man, must need the money for his cause—in which case she couldn't really blame him. "If you can't afford to pay, you must tell him so."

"Now why didn't I think of that?" asked Nelson sarcastically. "And then Mr. Richards can simply make certain no one will accept my vouchers again."

"Perhaps that would be for the best," Rowena told him bluntly. "In fact, I'm certain Mr. Richards would do so for your own good." That fit more with her idea of her hero.

Nelson seemed unmoved by such a charitable motive for his own ruin. "You don't know, Ro. You've no idea what it would be like: unwelcome at any of the clubs, merchants unwilling to extend credit—I'd be humiliated. I have a reputation to maintain, you know. Not to mention my position at the Home Office."

After a few more moments of thought, a bold solution presented itself. "Suppose I speak with Mr. Richards? I'm certain he will be perfectly reasonable, once he knows how you are placed." It would be the perfect excuse to finally meet her idol.

Though he looked skeptical, Nelson nodded. "I'm willing for you to try, anyway. Tell him I'll pay him the rest of what I owe him when I get the next quarter's rents."

"And we must look into getting Mother's jewelry back, as well. Find out what it will cost, if the pieces are still at the pawnshop, and I will give you the money." Rowena now regretted spending so much on clothing for herself.

Instantly brightening, he nodded. "I'll check, and let you know. You're the best of sisters, Ro. I should have known you'd come through." He leaned down to kiss her cheek. She accepted the caress guiltily, knowing she had another motive.

"And you *must* not gamble any more, Nelson," she added. "Promise me."

"Of course, of course." He flipped open a snuffbox and took a pinch. "I've learned my lesson."

She rose. "I should hope so. Now, I must find Lord Peter Northrup—I promised him the next dance." She couldn't help enjoying the surprise on her brother's face at this evidence of her popularity. "If you think of anything else I should know, you can send word to me here at Hardwyck Hall."

Nelson cheerfully waved her on her way. Too cheerfully, she feared, but she considered her promise to meet with Mr. Richards with growing enthusiasm. She'd dreamed of that meeting since first deciding to come to London. He was surely a man worth knowing—intelligent, committed to a worthy cause, and with the connections to enforce changes.

For a moment, the memory of Mr. Paxton's face distracted her. But handsome and intelligent though he might be, he did not seem to share her ideals for reform. Quite the opposite, in fact. How might he react to her future friendship with Mr. Richards?

Noel watched from the edge of the floor as Miss Riverstone made her apologies to Lord Fernworth, then accompanied her brother, who seemed agitated about something. But what?

Could Riverstone possibly suspect that Noel was on to him? No, most likely it was some personal matter completely unrelated to his mission. Still, he couldn't afford to let his best lead escape. He moved along the edge of the dance floor so that he could observe them from a distance.

As her brother spoke, Miss Riverstone herself became visibly upset, first seeming to accuse, and then to reassure him. So, big brother found himself in some sort of scrape, and little sister was promising to help him out of it? That was Noel's guess—and experience had proved his guesses accurate more often than not.

From the look on Sir Nelson's face as his sister left him, he clearly believed she could help him. She was intelligent, and her brother appeared to trust her. Might she possess the information Noel needed to solve his case? If Sir Nelson was the essayist, she would surely know it. Might she be aware of his treasonous activities as well? Surely she couldn't condone—

She was coming his way. Not wishing to be caught staring, he quickly turned to find himself facing Lord Peter Northrup and Harry Thatcher, who had been in conversation just behind him.

"—last night. Or so the servants claimed, according to the paper," Lord Peter was saying. "If they're right, it appears the Saint is still quite active among us."

Noel hid a smile. "So you're among the group that believes that the Saint of Seven Dials is a member of the *ton*?" he asked.

"He'd almost have to be, wouldn't he?" asked Harry, gesturing with a half-empty wineglass. "Not for a job like last night's—any street thief could have broken into an empty house, after all. But some of his more legendary heists have occurred in the middle of Society dos, where no one but high sticklers were present."

"Except servants," Noel pointed out. "He could simply be an enterprising footman."

Lord Peter nodded. "Just what I've said myself. No need for the Upper Ten Thousand to go about suspecting each other—though I'll admit it's possible he's one of us. Easier for a gentleman to ape a servant than—Ah, Miss Riverstone!" he exclaimed then, looking over Noel's shoulder.

Noel forced himself not to look around, though the temptation was strong. He could feel his body responding to her presence.

"Pray forgive me for not seeking you out sooner," Lord Peter continued. "This is our dance, is it not? Come, I'll tell you the latest news." He led her to the floor, chattering about the Saint's latest caper, while she listened with apparent eagerness.

Once her back was to him, Noel turned to watch her, his eyes enjoying her progress while his brain dissected the conversation just past. He hadn't expected the servants to find his card so quickly. Still, that might work to his advantage.

"Pretty thing, isn't she?" Harry said, breaking into his thoughts. "At least, if you like that bookish type. Can't say that's my usual style, but I'd not say no to a tumble with her."

Noel rounded on him, a swift, unreasonable anger nearly stealing his control. "I can't think Miss Riverstone is the sort to offer you one," he said coldly, fighting down an irrational urge to plant the fellow a facer.

"No, probably not, more's the pity," Harry responded, oblivious to Noel's sudden fury.

With an effort, Noel brought his emotions into check. He couldn't help thinking of some of the women Harry had seduced in Vienna. The very idea of Miss Riverstone being numbered among such ill-bred, willing wenches—Mentally, he shook himself. What was wrong with him? Harry always talked like this.

"So, what was this story you and Peter were discussing, about the Saint?" he asked, as much to change the subject as to learn what was being said about his adventure last night.

But as Harry related the details—accurate for the most part, but with some embellishments on the part of the servants—Noel found his attention drifting again to the dance floor, where Miss Riverstone was dancing the Boulanger.

She smiled up at Lord Peter as their hands touched. He spoke a few words and she laughed, then the movements of the dance parted them. But now she was facing Mr. Galloway again, and the fellow was leering at her even more offensively than he had during the minuet.

Clearly, Noel hadn't managed to discourage the fellow by drawing Miss Riverstone into talk of chess and politics. He would have to risk her ire by broaching those topics again, he supposed. Better that than she fall victim to a rogue like Galloway.

Because that would undermine his goal, of course. He needed to reach a level of intimacy with her where she would not hesitate to tell him everything she knew. Therefore, he must make certain she cared more about him than about any other man.

It made perfect sense.

*　*　*

By midnight, Rowena was ready to drop with weariness. She had now danced at least twice as long as the longest lesson she'd ever had. How on earth did Society ladies hold up, dancing for hours on end, night after night—in corsets? She wouldn't be plump for long, if she kept this up.

"Thank you, Lord Marcus," she said as an unnecessarily vigorous country dance ended. Clearly these Society types carried on until all hours on a regular basis—so she must learn to do likewise, if she was to fit in.

"The honor was mine, Miss Riverstone. Ah! That would be the supper dance," he said then, as the orchestra began a waltz. "If you will excuse me, I am promised to my wife for this one." He bowed over her hand and made a quick departure.

Rowena smiled after him, thinking how lucky his wife was to have such a devoted husband—as lucky as Pearl. Perhaps happiness in marriage for an intelligent woman was not so impossible as she had always—

"My dance, I believe?" came a familiar voice at her elbow.

Turning, Rowena fought down the blush that threatened at Mr. Paxton's appearance on the heels of her foolish fancy. He could have no notion of her thoughts, after all. She summoned a smile and a careless air.

"Thank you, sir. I am yet nervous of attempting a waltz with anyone else," she said, placing her hand in his outstretched one, determinedly ignoring the effect the contact had on totally unrelated parts of her body.

He placed his other hand at her back, intensifying

the effect. "You needn't be, from what I have observed tonight. You are extremely quick at covering any small errors you make while dancing."

Mortified that he had noticed such errors—and she knew there had been dozens—she averted her gaze as he moved her into the dance. "Thank you . . . I think."

He didn't respond for so long that she finally glanced up at him again, to find him looking sheepish. "That was a clumsy thing to say," he responded to her questioning look. "I'm not particularly gifted at compliments, am I? For that's what I meant that to be."

"And I should have taken it as such," she replied, her earlier embarrassment evaporating. "I've made no secret to you that I am unused to dancing. I only hope to keep some portion of the room relatively ignorant of that fact."

"I'm quite certain they have no suspicion," he assured her with a smile that set her nerves tingling again.

She wasn't sure whether she believed him, but was grateful for his reassurance nonetheless.

"I owe you another apology," he continued before she could respond.

"You . . . you do?" She'd have liked to blame her concentration on the steps of the dance for her conversational shortcomings, but she feared that was not the true culprit.

He nodded. "I had promised to introduce you to General Wellington. He left early, however, and heads back to Paris tomorrow."

Sudden disappointment stole a measure of Rowena's pleasure in dancing with Mr. Paxton. "I am sorry to hear that—but it is scarcely your fault, sir."

"No, I suppose not. And I did try to catch your attention earlier, while I was talking with him, but you were quite absorbed in the dance, and your partners, at the time."

Did she detect a faint trace of disapproval—even jealousy? Surely not, but it was pleasant to imagine. "I would far rather have spoken with the Duke, had I known," she said with perfect truth. He could be reassured or not.

"In recompense, suppose I repeat to you everything he said, over supper?" Mr. Paxton offered. "Mind you, I only spoke with him briefly."

"I—I should like that." She hoped he interpreted her response as pertaining to talk of the duke, not to the prospect of having supper together. That *was* what she meant, of course.

The dance ended, and he led her to one of the small tables set up near the buffet and held out a chair. "Do you suppose your brother would care to join us?" he asked, glancing about the room.

Again, Rowena couldn't help feeling a bit flattered that he wished to make her brother's acquaintance, but she had to shake her head regretfully. "I fear he has already gone. He . . . was not feeling well."

"Nothing serious, I hope." Did she imagine that glimmer of knowingness in his eyes? "Perhaps you can tell me a bit about him as we eat—after I tell you about Wellington, of course."

"Er, certainly," she replied, though of course she could not tell him about Nelson's dilemma.

"Would you like me to get a plate for you, or would you prefer to make your own selections?" he asked then.

"I will trust your judgment." She didn't relish the idea of choosing foods she could not see clearly. Tired as she was, she was sure to squint.

While Rowena waited for him to return, Pearl stopped at the table. "How are you holding up, Rowena? You've been every bit the success I predicted, you must admit."

Rowena returned her smile. "I won't deny I'm exhausted, but I have enjoyed myself for the most part. Thank you, Pearl."

"I'm sorry that I've been unable to introduce you to any of the intellectual set, as I'd hoped. Even the Duke of Wellington left before I could bring you to his notice. However, there is one gentleman—"

Mr. Paxton returned just then with two heaped plates, a footman with glasses hovering behind him. "Will you be joining us, Lady Hardwyck?" he asked pleasantly.

Pearl shook her head. "Luke is waiting for me over there, once I've had a chance to make certain everyone is well situated for supper. I hope you are finding everything to your liking."

He and Rowena both assured her that they were. She moved on to speak with Lord and Lady Mountheath and their daughters, leaving Rowena to wonder who she had been about to mention before Mr. Paxton had interrupted them.

"Wellington is pleased with the peacetime progress in Paris, but finds administrative duties terribly dull," Mr. Paxton said as he seated himself across from her.

"Indeed? What of the rumors that Napoleon may attempt another escape?" she asked, Pearl's unfinished sentence forgotten.

They talked of Wellington and the politics of war and peace as they ate, Rowena eagerly adding specifics to her more general knowledge of recent and current events. Mr. Paxton seemed remarkably well informed.

Every now and then something in his expression would recall her to the present. Was he amused by her interest in such things? But amusement did not seem to be the precise emotion behind the occasional unsettling intensity of his gaze. She tried to remind herself that such a thirst for knowledge was unconventional, even unladylike, but as long as he was willing to supply so much information, she was more than willing to absorb it.

"I'm now giving you more surmise than fact," he said at last. "As I said, I only spoke with Wellington for a few minutes. But you were going to tell me a bit about your brother, were you not?" Again, there was a certain acuteness to his gaze.

Suddenly self-conscious, Rowena glanced down and was surprised to see that she had eaten everything on her plate. So much dancing had given her quite an appetite.

"Yes, of course. What did you wish to know?"

"What sort of man he is, what sort of work he does. Are the two of you very close? Is he . . . protective of you?"

Rowena's breath caught. Was he asking whether he would need Nelson's permission to . . . to court her? No, of course he wasn't.

"I can't say we've been particularly close in recent years," she confessed. "Once he went off to Cambridge, I rarely saw him. From there, he went to the

Home Office, where Father obtained a position for him. Since Father's death, he has taken on more important duties there."

"What sort of duties?"

Rowena shrugged. "He's never discussed them with me, to be honest. I know more about his work from what I read in the papers than from anything he has said to me."

"The papers?"

"Well, nothing specifically about Nelson, of course, but occasional news items mention John Addington, under whom he works. They seem primarily concerned with implementing Parliament's charges for peacetime defense and the rebuilding of the economy."

She thought Mr. Paxton looked vaguely disappointed, but couldn't imagine why.

"Surely, now that you are in Town, you will be seeing more of him?" he asked. "He must have wished that, to send for you."

"Oh, he did not send for me," she exclaimed without thinking. "That is, he was pleased to see me, of course." That was stretching the truth a bit, but he would not know that. "But I decided to come on my own."

"Did you? Why?"

Rowena hesitated, trying to formulate an answer that would be both truthful and vague. But before she could manage it, she felt a touch on her shoulder. Glancing up, she saw Pearl and an unfamiliar gentlemen.

"Rowena, I promised to introduce to you the more interesting of my guests," Pearl said with a smile toward her companion. The wiry, dark-haired man returned it briefly, though his angular face, more interesting than handsome, remained somber.

"Mr. Richards, let me make known to you Miss Riverstone, my oldest, dearest friend. I can't help but think you will find her opinions both well-informed and interesting. Rowena, Mr. Paxton, may I present Mr. Lester Richards."

Rowena stared up at her idol, the chandelier behind him casting a halo of light about his head that blurred and exalted his features. Struck speechless, Rowena could only offer him her hand, scarcely noticing Pearl's departure. He bowed, never taking his piercing dark eyes—his most attractive feature—from hers.

"I am charmed to make your acquaintance, Miss Riverstone," the older man said in a deep, cultured voice. "Lady Hardwyck speaks highly of your . . . abilities."

Fighting down a blush, Rowena wondered whether he remembered the two rather gushing letters she'd written him. "Pearl is exceedingly kind. I am pleased to meet you, Mr. Richards. I would love to discuss Spencean philosophy with you sometime."

"I am at your disposal, of course." There was no denying the amusement in his eyes. No doubt he thought she was merely flattered to be meeting someone of his stature and speaking of things she didn't understand.

"Tell me, what think you of Mr. Spence's later treatises, where he elaborated on the natural law he first proposed in *The Real Rights of Man?*" she asked, both because she was interested and to show him she knew the subject well.

His brows rose, and she was gratified to see a dawning respect in his eyes. "I think—" he began, but was interrupted by a throat-clearing behind Rowena.

Guiltily, she turned. "Oh! Mr. Richards, Mr. Paxton is a friend of Lord Hardwyck's. He is in Town to catch the Saint of Seven Dials, among other things."

Mr. Richards inclined his head toward the younger man. "Honored, of course, Mr. Paxton. I have . . . heard of your work." His smooth voice dripped disapproval.

"And I have heard of yours, such as it is," Mr. Paxton replied, his tone no more cordial.

Frowning, Rowena glanced from one gentleman to the other. Clearly they had not met before, but their instant antagonism was unmistakable.

"I take it you do not approve of my efforts to correct an inequitable system of government." Mr. Richards' words echoed Rowena's thoughts.

But Mr. Paxton did not rise to the bait, as she had expected him to. "Your efforts to influence Parliament are of little consequence," he replied with a smile that did not reach his eyes. "It is your impact on impressionable young minds that I find cause for concern."

Unwilling to witness an argument between two men she would prefer to have as friends, Rowena spoke up. "Suppose you join us, Mr. Richards, so that we can all debate our varying views on the subject."

Rowena belatedly remembered that she had promised Nelson to plead his case with Mr. Richards—

though now she had met him, she found it even harder to believe he was pressuring her brother for money. This was clearly not the time, in any event.

"You are kindness itself, Miss Riverstone, as well as a born diplomat," he said. "Perhaps another time." With a bow, pointedly in her direction rather than Mr. Paxton's, he took his leave of them.

Chapter 8

Noel watched Mr. Richards' retreating back with a frown. He knew little of the man beyond the fact that he was a proponent of the so-called Spencean philanthropists. John Stafford, chief clerk at Bow Street, suspected that group of sedition, and Noel was inclined to agree.

Richards, if he recalled correctly, was actively recruiting more adherents to that cause. Surely, that was enough to explain his instant dislike of the man.

"Mr. Paxton?" Miss Riverstone recalled him.

Turning, he saw both concern and curiosity in her expressive gray eyes. Feeling compelled to reassure her, he managed a smile. "I'm sorry. You were about to tell me your reasons for coming to London, were you not?"

But she would not be so easily put off. "You clearly do not care for Mr. Richards. Why?"

"Some of his ideas are dangerous," he said carefully, not wanting to antagonize Miss Riverstone. He still had much to discover about her brother.

"Then so are my own, for I agree with most of what he stands for," she retorted. "I had thought you somewhat sympathetic to the plight of the common man when last we spoke on the topic."

"Sympathetic, yes." If only she knew. "But not to the point of overthrowing what has proved a stable and relatively just system of government. Anarchy is not the answer."

Miss Riverstone frowned. "I don't believe Mr. Richards advocates any such thing. Like me, he simply wishes for reform that will enable families who have farmed the same patch of land for generations to own that land."

"But if Parliament will not act, is the common man justified in taking up arms against his own government?" he asked, irked at her defense of the man. "Such ideas may sound good on paper, but in practice they are likely to lead to bloodshed and suffering."

"Of course I don't advocate armed rebellion," she exclaimed. "What makes you think Mr. Richards would?"

Noel started to reply, then realized he had no actual evidence—and would not be authorized to share it if he did. "I've seen his sort before," he said vaguely. "Professional agitators."

"So you don't actually *know*," she said in evident satisfaction. "I suspected as much. I won't have my good opinion of Mr. Richards swayed by mere speculation."

"Your good opinion—!" Noel was startled by a strong desire to shake her. Why should her opinion of Richards matter to him? But it did. It mattered quite a lot.

Abruptly, belatedly, it struck him that he was jealous—jealous!—of another man's influence over Miss Riverstone. And that, of course, was absurd. He needed to win her confidence and liking, but he could not allow *his* emotions to become involved.

"You're right, of course," he said with an effort. "While I won't deny I enjoy debating such matters with you, I have no real reason to slander Mr. Richards. My apologies."

Her expression softened, and Noel felt his pulse quicken. He felt the strongest urge to lean toward her, to . . .

"It is not I to whom you should apologize," she pointed out with a smile that forgave him.

Noel swallowed, thoroughly alarmed by her effect on him. It was just as well he was not required to stand at the moment, for that effect would be evident to the entire room. He had seen others brought low, even destroyed, by the allure of a woman. Then, he had not been able to understand such weakness. But now—

"If I should see Mr. Richards again, I will be more conciliatory," he said, hoping he would not be called upon to fulfill that promise. "Would you care for some sweetmeats?"

She shook her head—rather to his relief, since his body's response to her had not yet subsided. "I have eaten enough already to make me sleepy. When do you suppose I can escape without giving Pearl offense?"

"Some guests will undoubtedly leave after supper, though others will continue dancing for two or three more hours."

Her eyes widened with amazement. "More dancing? To think that I always regarded those in Society as lazy and useless."

"Useless some may be," he agreed with a grin, "but the social whirl can be gruelling for those determined to keep up with it."

"So I begin to perceive." Her voice held a hint of regret, and more than a hint of weariness.

Though aware of the danger, he could not help reassuring her. "You have used your energies far more productively, Miss Riverstone. Do not fault yourself for that."

She smiled gratefully at him. "Thank you. But now, I do believe I will attempt an escape, so that I may save a modicum of energy for tomorrow's activities."

Noel stood, finally able to do so without embarrassment. "Come. We'll stroll onto the terrace as we talk. We can make our way toward the garden door, and as soon as no one is looking, you may disappear inside that way. I can make your apologies to Lady Hardwyck once you are upstairs."

"You are very good to me, sir," she said, rising to place a hand on his outstretched arm.

He felt a ridiculous urge to confess to her his true motive in being kind, and squelched it at once. The mission was the thing, after all.

"Common courtesy is the mark of a gentleman, or so I have always heard," he said instead. "It is a designation I strive to merit."

"I too believe that a gentleman is evidenced by his behavior rather than the accident of his birth," she said as they moved toward the open French doors along the side of the ballroom. "As is a lady. I should wish to do as well in meriting that designation as you do that of gentleman, Mr. Paxton. But of that, I despair."

He glanced at her to find her gray eyes twinkling. "Why, Miss Riverstone, I do believe you are fishing for compliments. Far be it from me to refuse to rise to the bait."

They had reached the terrace now. A quick glance about showed no one observing them, so he led her down the broad stone steps into the gardens.

"Allow me to say that the world would be a better place were more ladies like yourself," he said as they moved along the graveled path toward the back door, between fragrant blooming rosebushes. "You have made the evening thoroughly enjoyable, and interesting as well."

Her eyes widened at his serious tone and he thought he could discern a blush by the light of the three-quarter moon. "Thank you. I . . . I must say the same for you."

They stopped near the door and Noel moved closer, probing her eyes with his own, trying to divine her secrets—for secrets he was certain she had. At the same time, her gray eyes searched his, threatening to unravel his own secrets. He felt another, stronger compulsion to tell her everything.

"Miss Riverstone—Rowena," he murmured.

She swayed toward him, almost imperceptibly, clearly eager to hear whatever he might say. Trapped between warring temptations, he gave in to the less dangerous of the two. Holding her gaze, he leaned down, resting one hand lightly on the nape of her neck. Her thick-lashed eyes drifted closed as he covered her mouth with his.

Noel thought to just brush her lips—a quick kiss to confuse her senses and keep her off balance. Instead, her sweet softness captivated him, demanding that he taste what she had to offer, to explore, to claim—

With a tiny sigh, she lifted her arms to his shoulders, clinging to him as though for support. Her answering kiss was innocent, inexperienced, but that made it all the sweeter. He found himself exulting that he was the first man to awaken this side of the serious Miss Riverstone.

Splaying one hand against her back, he drew her closer, intensifying the kiss, teasing at her lips with his tongue, coaxing them apart. Who could have guessed she would taste so good? He wanted—

Abruptly, she pulled away, staring up at him in near panic. "Oh! I—I— Good night, sir." Not quite meeting his eye, she turned and fled to the garden door, disappearing inside.

Noel stood watching after her, reflecting that it was just as well she had broken off that remarkable kiss. If she had not, he would almost certainly have accompanied her upstairs—and that was a commitment he was by no means ready to make.

Rowena ran up the back stairs and straight to her room, refusing to look back, refusing even to think, until she had barricaded herself inside. Was Mr. Paxton mad? Was she? What on earth had just happened?

"Miss? Is something wrong?" Matthilda emerged from the dressing room, her eyes wide with concern.

Managing a shaky laugh, Rowena shook her head.

"No, of course not. I am tired, that is all, and ran up here to escape before Lady Hardwyck could tease me into staying below. If you will unhook my gown, I can do everything else myself. I'm sure you want your bed as much as I do."

While the maid helped her to undress, Rowena tried to reel in her imagination. It was just a kiss, after all. Had she not read that men set little store by such things? It would not do to weave romantic fantasies about one single occurrence. No doubt she had said or done something to make Mr. Paxton think she was inviting such an attention, and he had felt it was only polite to comply.

That had not felt like a "polite" kiss, however.

"Thank you, Matthilda. Good night."

Slipping out of her shift and into her nightrail, Rowena shook her head. She would not know a polite kiss from a passionate one, never having experienced either. Perhaps he had meant it as a polite one and she had tried to turn it into something else. What must he think of her? Her cheeks burned with sudden embarrassment. Her inexperience must have been crystal clear to him. Was he even now chuckling at her expense?

She didn't know what to think, and her brain seemed too fuzzy to sort things out. She had not been exaggerating her weariness, but now her whole body tingled with newly awakened longings. Slowly, she climbed into bed, guiltily reliving every delicious sensation until she drifted off to sleep.

The day was well advanced when Rowena awoke, fully refreshed, if a trifle stiff from the unaccustomed exercise of the night before.

"Good morning, miss," Matthilda greeted her, bustling in as Rowena stretched the kinks from her joints. "Or good day, more like. It's nigh noon, but I dursen't wake you, late as you went to bed."

"And I thank you for that. I presume I've missed breakfast?"

The maid shrugged. "I wouldn't know, miss, but I can have a tray sent up if you'd like."

"No, I'll go down." She was eager to see Mr. Paxton again, though shy as well. Would he act differently toward her now? Should she act differently toward him?

Two new day dresses and another evening gown had been delivered while she slept, so Rowena donned a flattering yellow round dress with moss-green ruching about the neck and wrists. Not wishing to wait for Francesca, she had Matthilda pin her hair into a knot in back while allowing the rest to fall past her shoulders.

"You look a treat, miss," the maid assured her, and Rowena had to agree. Why had she eschewed bright colors all her life? As no guests were likely to be below so early in the day, she donned her spectacles and went in search of sustenance.

Pearl and Mr. Paxton were just leaving the dining room when she arrived.

"Good afternoon, sleepyhead," Pearl greeted her with a smile. "It seems Mr. Paxton was not bamming me when he said you were tired last night. In truth, I think you did splendidly for your first ball. I recall I slept until two the day following mine."

Rowena, acutely aware of Mr. Paxton's regard, returned Pearl's smile. "Then, as you were a mere sixteen while I am of a far more advanced age, I must credit myself with unusual stamina."

"You make it sound as though you are in your dotage," Pearl said with a laugh. "As we are of an age, I should take insult."

"No one could ever think either of you anything but young and vibrant," Mr. Paxton said gallantly. "Are you recovered from last night's exertions, Miss Riverstone?"

Something in his tone, and in his eyes, made Rowena blush, though it was a perfectly innocent question. "Yes, thank you. Or I will be, once I've had a bite to eat. Dare I hope—?"

"Yes, there's still plenty on the sideboard," Pearl assured her. "I expected you would be hungry when you finally emerged. But now you must excuse me. I need to speak with the housekeeper about arrangements for this evening's card party."

"And I must go out, I fear." Mr. Paxton sounded genuinely regretful, but Rowena tried not to read too much into that.

"How progresses your pursuit of the Saint?" she asked, more to remind herself of how divergent their ideals were than because she wanted to know.

He had started to turn away, but now faced her again, his gaze surprisingly sharp. "Slowly. Why? Have you heard anything?"

"I? Of course not," she said quickly, then immediately wondered if her vehemence might make it sound as though she were hiding something. Which she was, she realized, but it was of an emotional rather than a factual nature. She schooled her features to an expression of innocent interest.

He continued to regard her speculatively for a long moment, then gave a barely perceptible shrug. "I know you do not approve of my task, Miss River-stone, but I hope that if you hear of anything . . . irregular, you will tell me."

Rowena would not promise anything that might lead to the capture of the Saint, but she could not quite hold out against the plea in those intense hazel eyes.

"I truly have heard nothing, Mr. Paxton, and can't imagine that I will. But if anything happens that causes me concern, I will let you know."

"Thank you. That is what I had hoped."

Again, his expression gave his words added meaning, and she realized that her promise could pertain to much more than news of the Saint. Still, she found she did not wish to retract it. Something about Mr. Paxton compelled trust, whether she agreed with his principles or not.

"You two are free to make moon eyes all afternoon, but I really must leave you," Pearl said then.

Belatedly aware that she had been staring, Rowena dropped her gaze.

"A dozen or more people will be here at two for a trip to see the tigers at the Exchange," Pearl continued. "We will return in time to change for dinner and the card party. You will both come, will you not?"

Rowena nodded, but to her distinct disappointment, Mr. Paxton demurred.

"My business is likely to take longer than that, my lady, though I will be here this evening, of course. And if I finish sooner than expected, perhaps I may join you at the 'Change."

He took his leave then, and Pearl bustled off as well, leaving Rowena to a solitary breakfast and some much-needed thought. Any eagerness she had felt for the afternoon's excursion was dimmed by the news that Mr. Paxton would not be one of the party—and that was absurd.

To distract herself, she picked up the copy of the *Political Register*, which had been left in the dining room, as she had not been able to finish it the other morning. She was deep in an editorial on the injustices endured by factory workers in the north, when a noise behind her made her turn to find Mr. Paxton reentering the dining room.

"I felt the need for another cup of coffee," Noel explained, nodding to the footman to bring him one. "What have you there?" He had returned in the hope of speaking privately with her, and was delighted at his good fortune in finding her holding that particular paper.

She made a motion as if to hide it again, then lifted her chin and met his eyes squarely. "The *Political Register*. Are you familiar with it?"

"Indeed I am. I can't say I always agree with the views expressed therein, but it makes for interesting reading." He seated himself across from her. By unspoken agreement, neither referred with so much as a look to that remarkable kiss they had shared last night.

Some of the tension left her shoulders, as though his response reassured her. "I agree. Mr. Cobbett and his contributors have a way of cutting to the heart of the injustice and hypocrisy infecting England."

"And yet," he said, taking a sip from the cup just handed him by the footman, "some of those contributors hide behind false names or initials. Is that not a brand of hypocrisy in itself?"

Sudden alarm flared in her eyes. So, she *did* know something! "Can you really blame them, sir, when Cobbett himself was once charged with sedition, along with such luminaries as Leigh Hunt?"

"The Hunt brothers were merely unwise enough to openly criticize the Prince Regent. I tend to agree that imprisoning them was an overreaction on the Regent's part, and only served to make him look foolish. Cobbett and some of the others, however—"

"Exposing injustice is *not* sedition," she insisted passionately. "If anonymity allows the truth to reach the public, I cannot help but think it justified."

Surely, this was the fervor of a sister defending a brother? His pulse quickened as he sensed his quarry almost in his grasp.

"One would almost think you had a personal stake in protecting the identity of these anonymous writers," he said, watching her closely.

There was no mistaking her alarm this time. "Why do you say that?"

"You seem so passionate in their defense," he explained. Unbidden came a vision of how passionate she had been last night—how passionate she might prove in other endeavors as well. Hastily, he thrust it away.

"I, ah, share the opinions of some of those writers, so in that sense I suppose I feel a personal concern."

She still appeared more agitated than the discussion would seem to warrant, but he realized that she, too, might be remembering that kiss. He needed clearer proof.

"Have you no suspicion, then, as to who any of those writers might be? There is one in particular—" Reaching across the table, he twitched the paper from her grasp, his hand grazing hers in the process.

They were both ungloved, and he was startled at the impact of that brief contact. That she noticed it too was evident in her quick, indrawn breath and the widening of her eyes.

Steeling his emotions against such weakness, Noel quickly scanned through the pages. "No, he appears not to have an essay in this issue. If you are a regular reader, however, you are doubtless familiar with the author I mean. He signs his pieces 'Mr. R.' "

She swallowed convulsively, but then took a deep breath and met his eye. To his surprise, something like amusement flitted across her face. "I fear I pay little attention to the initials following the essays, Mr. Paxton. Do you recall the topics this particular writer addresses?"

"Oh, the usual rants about the evils of the landed class, the plight of the poor farmer, the conditions of the poorhouses. You know." He spoke disparagingly, hoping to goad her into defending the writer—and perhaps giving something away.

"Rants? Those essays are well researched, and quite logical in presentation—or so I have thought."

Noel couldn't suppress a triumphant grin. "Ah, then you *do* know which essayist I mean?"

Caught, she flushed scarlet. Still, he couldn't help but admire the way she lifted her chin and tried to brazen it through. "I find that true of virtually all of the essayists, with one or two exceptions."

"Of course." He let her see that he wasn't fooled in the least. "To be more specific, one such essay a month or two ago was emphatic in its defense of the Saint of Seven Dials as a champion of the common man. As you may imagine, that caught my attention."

In fact, that was the essay which had convinced Noel that the author and the Saint might be the same.

"He spoke of the necessity of the redistribution of wealth," he continued, "insisting that if Parliament would not see to it, the public should support the efforts of vigilante reformers like the Saint. He was rather persuasive, alas, which has not made my job any easier—nor more popular."

She shrugged slightly, taking a bite of shirred eggs that must be stone cold by now. "You already know my own views on the subject, Mr. Paxton. Is it any wonder I should be sympathetic to that essayist?"

He frowned, nettled that he'd given her a plausible counterargument. "I still find hiding behind initials cowardly," he said, and was rewarded by seeing her flinch. "If convictions are firmly held, should they not be stated openly?"

"Perhaps some writers have other reasons for disguising their identities," she suggested, her color still high. "A . . . man in the public sphere may hope to effect change through conventional channels even while he persuades the public through others." She motioned at the paper Noel held. "Were it known the two were one, it might make both avenues less effective."

"But when a man's public politics are at odds with his personal opinions—and writings—what then? Surely you cannot absolve such a man of hypocrisy." Sir Nelson was publicly allied with the conservative Tories, as his father had been. Else he would not hold a position of such importance in the Home Office.

She raised a skeptical brow above the rim of her spectacles. "Yes, I suppose that *would* smack of hypocrisy, but I cannot say that I know of any such man."

She was proving a tougher nut to crack than he'd anticipated, particularly after last night. Abandoning the matter of the mysterious essayist, he tried a different approach. "Tell me, Miss Riverstone, did your brother fight in the war?"

"Nelson?" She appeared genuinely surprised by the question, or perhaps she was merely startled by the abrupt change of subject. "Perhaps 'fight' is too strong a word, but he served briefly in the army, yes. Why?"

He ignored the question. "In what capacity? To what unit was he assigned?"

"To the Fifty-second Light Infantry, but he was injured in a minor skirmish shortly after his arrival in France. After spending several months in a field hospital, he was eventually sent home."

"And when might that have been?" he asked, abandoning subtlety in his eagerness.

"He returned in the spring of 1814, a few months before Father died."

So Sir Nelson *had* been in France when the Bishop had been passing information to Napoleon. He could not have been at Waterloo, but perhaps a confederate had planted evidence—

"Mr. Paxton?" He looked up to find her frowning anxiously.

And well she might feel anxious. He was more certain than ever that the Bishop and Sir Nelson were
one and the same. Still, he felt compelled to somehow
reassure her, to erase the worry from her eyes—if only
temporarily.

"I simply meant to make the point that a man who
went voluntarily into the army would be guilty of
hypocrisy if he were to criticize the war effort. Not
that I'm claiming your brother has done so, of
course."

She still looked dubious, and no wonder. His explanation sounded extremely feeble even to his own
ears. Quickly, he gulped down his cooling coffee and
stood.

"I really must go now, but I thank you for yet another stimulating conversation, Miss Riverstone."

"Um, yes, of course." She nodded to him almost
absently, apparently lost in her own thoughts now.

As he hurried out of the room, for a moment it occurred to him that he had perhaps been unwise to tip
his hand so soon. She was exceptionally intelligent,
and even if she had not yet pieced together his dis-
jointed questions, she would likely do so soon. He
would have to keep her off balance, keep her wondering about his motives.

Otherwise, his very life might be forfeit.

He didn't want to believe that Miss Riverstone
would intentionally put him at risk. But presuming
she did not know of her brother's treasonous activities, nor how dangerous the man could be, she
would have no compunction about warning him.
She would not know that Noel's life would be at
stake.

And if she did know . . . ?

Putting Miss Riverstone firmly from his mind, he left the house, hoping the inquiries he was about to make might solidify his case beyond doubt.

Rowena stared after Mr. Paxton, her mind in turmoil. What on earth had that been about? It was patently obvious that he was fishing for information of some sort, but what it might be, she had no idea.

For a few heart-stopping minutes she'd been convinced he'd identified her as MRR, but as he continued it seemed clear he believed her essays were written by a man. And he had called her arguments "persuasive," she recalled with a spurt of pride.

Then she frowned. What of that odd tangent about Nelson's army service? Mr. Paxton's "explanation" hadn't explained at all. Could he conceivably think that Nelson—or MRR—was the Saint of Seven Dials? Perhaps that all three were one? It was the only explanation she could fathom, but it made little sense.

She remembered the halfhearted promise he had extracted from her as he had left the dining room the first time. Yes, he must think she had information about the Saint, which must mean he at least suspected Nelson.

The very idea of Nelson writing her essays—or acting as the Saint—was so absurd she nearly laughed aloud.

Of course, he would find out soon enough that Nelson had been in the country while the Saint was active in London last winter. But she saw no need to disabuse Mr. Paxton of his amusing notion. While he pursued Nelson, he would not be pursuing the *real* Saint, whoever he was.

Still she could not ignore a small ache in the vicinity of her heart. Though she had tried not to, she had briefly allowed herself to believe that kiss last night had meant something to him. Now it seemed clear that he merely considered her a means to an end.

A spurt of anger abolished melancholy. Did he really think, if Nelson *were* the Saint, that she would betray her own brother? What kind of person would be capable of such a double betrayal, of both principles and blood—for a mere kiss?

No, she would think no more about the matter—or the man.

She had a mission in London, and any feelings she might have developed for Mr. Paxton would only interfere with that mission. Just as well she now saw him for what he was, and could nip such fledgling feelings in the bud.

She would use today and tonight strictly as the opportunities they were, to speak with men of political influence and to learn more about the undercurrents that bound or separated such men. Last night had been all but wasted in that sense.

But not completely wasted, she reminded herself. She *had* met Mr. Richards, and could look forward to future conversations with that most intelligent man. If he were not so much older than she—

No! She would certainly not entertain any romantic notions about Mr. Richards. Or Mr. Paxton, for that matter.

She signaled for a fresh pot of coffee, deliberately concentrating on what she would say to Mr. Richards about Nelson as soon as she had a chance for private conversation with him. The awkwardness of such a petition successfully distracted her for the remainder of her meal.

Chapter 9

To Rowena's surprise, nearly as many people arrived for the card party as had attended Pearl's ball the night before. Though the ball hadn't been quite the ordeal she had feared, she had hopes of feeling less out of her element tonight. At least with cards she need not fear treading on anyone's toes.

The trip to the Exeter 'Change had been rather disappointing, though she told herself that was because of the condition of the poor tigers. She had taken it upon herself to speak to the keeper, to the amazement of the other ladies present.

Mr. Paxton had not joined them, but after their conversation this morning she hadn't wanted him to. No, the real source of her disappointment was the absence of any men of influence she might cultivate. The party had consisted primarily of ladies, along with two or three young bucks who had only come along to spend time with said ladies. A pointless enterprise altogether.

"Well met, Miss Riverstone!" Mr. Galloway broke into her musings. Turning, she saw that he was again accompanied by Lord Fernworth and his cousin, Mr. Orrin.

"Good evening, sirs, my lord," she said with a smile, though these men would not serve her purpose either. "It is pleasant to see you again. I believe we will be breaking into various tables shortly."

"And Mr. Galloway promised you a chess match, if I recall," said Mr. Paxton, coming up just then to stand at her elbow. "I've already spoken with Lady Hardwyck to make certain a board is available."

Rowena fought to subdue the instinctive thrill that assailed her nerves at his nearness, sternly reminding herself of his true motive in befriending her.

"I had thought to play cards," she said, though in truth she would far prefer chess. She would do nothing to gratify Mr. Paxton, however.

"Come, there are four of us, not counting Stick-in-the-mud Paxton," Lord Fernworth exclaimed. "What say you all to a few hands of whist?"

He moved toward the nearest card table as he spoke, Mr. Galloway and Mr. Orrin following readily enough. Rowena glanced involuntarily at Mr. Paxton, who was frowning. That was enough to decide her. She joined the others.

"You'll partner me, will you not, Miss River-stone?" Mr. Galloway accompanied his request with a charming smile and a pleading look that was undeniably flattering.

Pointedly ignoring Mr. Paxton, she assented, taking the indicated seat at the table. The cards were dealt and the play commenced.

At first, Rowena found it hard to concentrate, so conscious was she of Mr. Paxton hovering just behind her. After a few minutes, however, he wandered off and she was better able to focus on the game.

Focus, in fact, was her main concern. She had to continually remind herself not to bring the cards ridiculously close to her face, that she might better see the pips. Nor would she squint. Therefore, it was a fairly easy matter to play less than her best, which no doubt pleased the gentlemen.

"Oh, dear, silly me," she said when she played a club instead of a spade for the second time. "I told you I was new to the game, did I not?"

Her poor play cost the first hand, but after that she paid closer attention—and held the cards just a tiny bit closer—and she and Mr. Galloway rallied to win the rubber, just as Mr. Paxton returned.

"Change partners for another rubber?" Mr. Orrin suggested.

But Mr. Galloway shook his head. "First, that chess match Miss Riverstone promised me. If you're still willing, that is?"

"Of course." Rowena thought he looked rather smug at the prospect, and was torn between wanting to put him in his place and wanting to frustrate Mr. Paxton's evident desire to see her do just that.

They passed Lord and Lady Hardwyck as they crossed the room to where the chessboard was set up, and Pearl pulled Rowena aside for a quick word.

"Remember, dear," she said softly. "Most men are not like Luke, or your Mr. Paxton—they like to win."

Rowena nodded, though she nearly lost the sense of what Pearl said. *Her* Mr. Paxton? She opened her mouth to protest the designation, but the others were watching now, so she turned and followed them.

Of course he was not *her* Mr. Paxton. How absurd. Surely Pearl couldn't know—?

"Here we are," Mr. Galloway exclaimed gleefully as they reached the chessboard. "I'll take black, of course."

Even without spectacles, Rowena's eyesight was sufficient for this game she knew so well—as long as she paid attention. Still, she was determined not to afford the hovering Mr. Paxton the satisfaction of seeing Mr. Galloway soundly trounced, much as that might gratify her own ego.

She made her first move, the perfectly conventional king's pawn opening. Unfortunately, within five minutes it was clear that Mr. Galloway was a far poorer player than even Pearl. Losing to him would be all but impossible.

The only thing that kept her from ending it sooner was the obvious disapproval radiating from Mr. Paxton. Rowena did her best to delay the inevitable, sitting back to make it harder to focus on the pieces, ignoring several obvious openings and even allowing Mr. Galloway to take her queen. She could almost feel Mr. Paxton stiffening with outrage, and had to hide a grin.

Finally, however, she had little choice but to checkmate the black king and win the game. To her amazement, Mr. Galloway seemed genuinely surprised to have lost.

"It seems Mr. Paxton was not exaggerating, Miss Riverstone," he exclaimed. "You are a formidable opponent indeed. My congratulations."

Rowena glanced about and realized with some dismay that a fair number of guests had gathered to watch the conclusion of the match—including Lester Richards. Mr. Paxton was frowning at her, which bothered her not at all, of course, but Mr. Richards' opinion was another matter.

It was all she could do to accept Mr. Galloway's congratulations graciously, as poorly as she had played. She prayed he would not suggest another match.

In fact, Mr. Galloway appeared more than satisfied to return to the card tables. "Now that I need not have *all* my wits about me, I'll try some of the claret," he said, plucking a glass from a tray carried by a passing footman. "Perhaps one of you gents would care to try your skill against our clever Miss Riverstone?"

But most of the other gentlemen and one or two ladies merely regarded her quizzically before beginning to disperse. She shot a defiant glance at Mr. Paxton, but then turned to find Mr. Richards watching her. She flushed, wondering how much of the game he had seen.

"I'd enjoy a match, if you would oblige me," he said, a smile making his face almost handsome. Well, not handsome, exactly, but . . . magnetic.

"Certainly, sir. I am pleased to see you again so soon," Rowena replied, fighting down sudden nervousness. Much as she would prefer not to, she really must mention Nelson to him tonight. She had promised.

"And I, you, Miss Riverstone. Shall we?" Deftly, he began resetting the board.

Though most of the spectators had drifted away, Mr. Paxton remained. Irritated, Rowena turned to him. "Surely you have better things to do than to watch me play again?"

Her words were rude and she regretted them at once, but he only smiled. "I find it quite an enjoyable pastime, actually. I'd like to play the winner if she—or he—doesn't mind."

"I've no objection, Paxton," Mr. Richards said. Rowena thought she caught a hint of eagerness in his dark eyes.

"Nor I," she echoed. Then, turning resolutely back to the board, she opened with the same move as before. How could she bring up Nelson's delicate problem with Mr. Paxton within earshot?

A few minutes' play proved Mr. Richards a vastly superior player to Mr. Galloway, though not of Mr. Paxton's caliber. Rowena concentrated, unsure whether she wanted to best her idol or not. She very much wanted to win his respect, but she feared alienating him. After all, there was the matter of Nelson's—

"Gadslife, Ro! Trust you to find a chessboard at a card party." Her brother's voice at just that moment made her start.

"Good evening, Nelson. You know Mr. Richards, I believe? And Mr. Paxton—you wished for a word with my brother, did you not?"

To her relief, Mr. Paxton took the cue.

"Indeed. Do you have a few moments, Sir Nelson?"

"Anything beats watching a chess match," Nelson agreed readily. "May as well watch paint dry, I say."

The two men moved away, and Rowena relaxed

marginally—though what she had feared, she was not sure. Seizing her opportunity before she could lose her courage, she said, "I understand my brother has been—unwise—in his gaming, Mr. Richards."

Her opponent was frowning at her last move, but at this he lifted his eyes to hers and smiled slightly. "I suppose one might say that. Sir Nelson's luck is such that he would do better to avoid games of chance."

"I agree. However—" But just then, two couples wandered over to watch the match, and Rowena was forced to drop the subject. "Perhaps we might talk of this later?"

"As you wish," said Mr. Richards mildly, his attention again on the board.

Noel wasn't sure whether to bless or curse his luck. He had wanted a conversation with Sir Nelson, but he very much preferred not to leave Miss Riverstone alone with Mr. Richards. There was something about the man—

"What did you have in mind to talk about, Paxton?" Sir Nelson asked, reminding him of his mission—the only thing that should matter now.

Besides, Miss Riverstone was scarcely alone. The table she shared with Mr. Richards was in full view of half the room.

"Your sister tells me you served in the army, Sir Nelson. I was wondering if we might have an acquaintance or two in common."

"Oh? Army man yourself, are you?" The stocky young man puffed out his chest a bit. "My time under Wellington was the most memorable of my life, I must say."

Noel was experienced in sifting men's words and expressions, but could detect no false note in Sir Nelson—not yet. "I'm a great admirer of Wellington myself," he said, "though I never held a commission under him. I did some courier work during the recent wars, however."

The Black Bishop would know what that really meant. But though he watched Sir Nelson's expression carefully, it showed not the slighted flicker of comprehension—merely mild curiosity.

"Courier? Delivering messages and such, you mean? Not a fighting man, then, eh? Though I suppose you must have ventured into danger now and again." He said it kindly, as though offering a sop to Noel's pride.

"Now and again, yes." Noel smiled, pretending gratitude while actually recalling the dozens of life-or-death situations he'd faced—more than many soldiers had faced, in fact. "I take it you saw your share of the fighting, then?"

Sir Nelson's fair skin pinkened slightly. "Not as much as I'd hoped, truth to tell. Took a bullet in the leg at Bayonne and though I wanted to get back into the fray, the surgeon wouldn't let me. Got to hear many a rare tale, though, let me tell you."

This echoed Miss Riverstone's account, though of course it would, if it were the cover story her brother had been using. Noel had serious doubts now, however. Unless the man was a superb actor, he was nowhere near clever enough to be the elusive Black Bishop.

"You spent some months in France, did you not? That must have been—interesting."

Sir Nelson shrugged. "Maybe if I'd been nearer

Paris, instead of trapped in a minuscule hamlet miles from anywhere. Since I speak only the sketchiest French, my only news came from fellow soldiers, wounded more recently than I. And, of course, from Captain Steen, who came to visit us when he could."

Noel's attention sharpened. "Captain Emory Steen?"

"Yes, of course. I was in his company, you know. Never progressed beyond ensign myself, thanks to that bullet."

"Of course." Noel was acquainted with Captain Steen. It would be an easy matter to verify Sir Nelson's story. If it checked out—which he unfortunately feared it would—that would rule him out as a suspect. Still, there were those essays, and his sister must have picked up her revolutionary ideas somewhere . . .

Noel glanced across the room, reassuring himself that Miss Riverstone was still engaged in her chess match—and nothing else. "Tell me, Sir Nelson, do you ever read the *Political Register?*" he asked in as offhand a manner as he could manage.

His companion frowned. "What, Cobbett's two-penny trash? My sister may believe the tripe he prints, but I've never wasted my time on it. Seditious drivel, if you ask me. Ro been spouting her theories to you or something?"

Again, though he tried, Noel could detect no trace of guile in the man. He seemed genuinely contemptuous. "Your sister and I have had some . . . interesting . . . discussions, yes."

"Told her she ought to keep her opinions to herself." Sir Nelson snorted. "Not that she'd listen to me, any more than she did to our father. Warned her she'd never catch a husband with that tongue of hers."

Noel had an intriguing vision of Miss Riverstone's sweet, pink tongue, darting between those perfectly shaped lips, touching, teasing—

"Er, yes, I see your point," he said before his distraction could be noticed. Then, feeling obliged to defend her, he added, "There are some who might appreciate her intelligence, however."

Sir Nelson grinned. "Like you, Paxton? Or maybe Lester Richards there—he's the intellectual sort."

Following his glance to the chess match still underway, Noel frowned. "A bit old for her, I'd say."

"Ro needs a firm hand," her brother said with a shrug. "A man closer to our father's age might be just the thing. Besides—" But then he broke off and shrugged again. "Think I'll find a baccarat table if you don't mind, Paxton. Care to join me?"

"Thank you, no." Positive now that Sir Nelson was not the man he sought, Noel was anxious to return to Miss Riverstone's side.

She knew the identity of that essayist, he was certain. If it was not her brother, it might be someone else she knew from Oakshire, which meant she was still his best lead—reason enough to stay close to her. If there was another reason, he chose to ignore it.

Rowena moved her knight back to the same square it had occupied three moves ago, trying to prolong the game until another chance for private talk presented itself. That effort had been aided by her eyesight.

Twice, she had mistaken a bishop for a pawn, to her detriment. Still, she had made steady inroads and now held a clear advantage on the board.

To her relief, Lord and Lady Norville finally moved away. She glanced up at Mr. Richards, ready to reopen the topic of Nelson's debts—only to see Mr. Paxton returning.

"Still at it, I see," he commented with a smile.

"The lady is quite skilled." Mr. Richards' voice held an edge Rowena had not noticed earlier. "Her primary fault seems to be indecisiveness."

Rowena managed a thin smile. His words stung, even though she had to admit that her attempts to delay winning made her seem to merit his criticism. Boldly, she pushed her black bishop from one corner of the board to the other.

"Caution is scarcely a fault," Mr. Paxton said. "She appears to have the upper hand, in any event." There was no mistaking the satisfaction in his voice—a satisfaction that nettled Rowena more than it flattered her.

"Appearances can be deceiving," Mr. Richards retorted, blocking the line between her bishop and the rook it threatened with a pawn.

She could now checkmate him in two moves, a fact Mr. Richards seemed unaware of. First the knight, then the bishop, and she would have him. But did she want to?

"So you have noticed that too, Mr. Richards? A perceptive man." Rowena suspected Mr. Paxton was referring to herself more than to the game. "For example, I'd have guessed, based solely on appearances, that you would not be a complacent loser."

So he was prepared to gloat the moment she won, was he? Unwilling to afford him the satisfaction, Rowena moved her queen instead of the knight. She didn't know what Mr. Paxton's game was, with kisses he refused to acknowledge and barbed comments to a man he scarcely knew, but she refused to play along with it.

"Nor am I a complacent loser," Mr. Richards admitted, moving his king out of danger and threatening her queen with his now-exposed rook. "It's as well that I rarely lose."

"Then I must count myself fortunate to witness such a rare event," responded Mr. Paxton. The smile he sent Rowena was both intimate and possessive, she thought.

Though her heart quickened its beat, she sent him a warning look. She would *not* be manipulated like some brainless miss, swooning after any man who flirted with her. Especially now that she knew his flirting disguised another purpose.

"How daunting to think your fortunes rely on my actions, Mr. Paxton," she said lightly, holding his eye for a long moment. Then, deliberately, she moved her black bishop back a single space, removing the last threat to Mr. Richards' king.

Instantly, her opponent took advantage of the opening. "Checkmate!" he cried triumphantly, taking her queen with his rook and pinning her king.

Rowena regarded the board in mock surprise. "Why, so it is. Mr. Paxton, did you not wish to play the winner?" She rose smoothly.

The look Mr. Paxton gave her said clearly that he knew exactly what she was about. "I did, though I confess I was hoping it would be you, Miss River-stone. I have quite enjoyed our previous games . . . all of them." He gazed pointedly at her lips.

Feeling the color surging to her cheeks, Rowena turned hastily away. Clearly, she was not so sophisticated as she had hoped. "Thank you, sir. And thank you for the game, Mr. Richards. I—I need to speak with Lady Hardwyck, but will return to watch your play."

Quickly, she walked away from the two men, not caring at the moment whether they laughed at her or engaged in fisticuffs. She wished only to be away from both of them and their smug maleness.

It occurred to her then to wonder what Mr. Paxton and Nelson had talked about. Nothing very involved, judging by how quickly Mr. Paxton had returned. She went in search of her brother, only to find him deep in a game of baccarat with several other men. For a moment, she tried to catch his eye to remind him of his promise not to gamble, but he refused to look her way. With a sigh, she left to find Pearl.

"What's this I hear about you playing nothing but chess at my card party?" her friend greeted her laughingly, beckoning for Rowena to join Lady Marcus and two other ladies with whom she stood chatting. "I thought you wanted to meet people."

"I started the evening with a few hands of whist," Rowena said defensively, not that Pearl seemed particularly upset. "The chess was primarily Mr. Paxton's idea."

Pearl's glance was rather too perceptive for Rowena's taste. "I see. His way of having you to himself at a crowded party?"

The two Melks sisters tittered. "I'd learn to play chess myself," said Miss Augusta Melks, "to spend time with that handsome Mr. Paxton."

"I haven't actually played with him tonight," Rowena said hastily, wanting to quash any speculation along those lines. It came too close to the truth for her liking. "Only with Mr. Galloway and Mr. Richards."

Again, Pearl seemed to be watching her closely. "Yes, I noticed. Did you—?"

"I managed to defeat Mr. Galloway after a hard-fought match, but I fear Mr. Richards bested me." Rowena answered the question her friend had been about to ask with a perfectly straight face, then turned to Lady Marcus. "Do you not play cards, Quinn?"

The diminutive brunette nodded. "I was doing so until a few moments ago, in fact. My husband made certain to teach me the more popular games. Still, it's pleasant to take a break from the competition and just chat for a bit."

Accordingly, the ladies did just that for a few minutes, though Rowena found her attention frequently wandering back to the ongoing match between Mr. Paxton and Mr. Richards. No, she would not look—not yet.

Her resolve lasted until Lord Marcus and Lord Hardwyck approached to claim their wives for new games just beginning. For a moment she wavered, knowing she would be wiser to accompany the others and distract herself with cards, but then curiosity won out. Excusing herself, she made her way back across the room, suddenly anxious to see how the chess match might be going.

Not until she was only a pace or two from the table could she see well enough to analyze the game, but it was instantly apparent that Mr. Paxton had played his best, unlike herself. In fact, she had scarcely reached the combatants when he made his final move.

"Checkmate," he declared. He accepted his opponent's grudging congratulations, then glanced up at Rowena with a smile that held more than a trace of mockery.

Though she knew the mockery was directed at her rather than Mr. Richards, she frowned. "Surely it is unsporting to gloat, Mr. Paxton?"

"Unsporting or not, he has earned it," responded Mr. Richards before he could answer. "I'd do the same in his position."

The two men stood, and Rowena glanced uncertainly from one to the other, struck again by how very handsome Mr. Paxton was. If only he shared the other man's sensibilities . . .

"Oh, surely not, sir," she protested. Mr. Richards wasn't the gloating sort—was he? She felt certain he would be above such pettiness.

He smiled at her. "Perhaps not. We'll have to play again sometime, Paxton. I find myself distracted in such a setting."

Did Rowena imagine it, or was Mr. Richards actually flirting with her? It seemed inconceivable—but heady. A great thinker and mover of events, attracted to her? She was suddenly more glad than ever that she had taken Pearl's advice and allowed him to beat her at chess. She returned his smile shyly.

"Would you care for some refreshment, Miss Riverstone?" Mr. Paxton asked then, his voice just a

shade too loud. "Of course, you are welcome to accompany us, Richards."

"Yes, I believe I will."

Rowena looked uncertainly from one to the other.
The animosity she had noted between them last night
was more pronounced than ever. Understandable,
perhaps, in Mr. Richards' case, as he had just lost at
chess. But surely Mr. Paxton—

With a spurt of pleasure, she suddenly realized that
she herself was the cause. He was at least a little bit
jealous. This, surely, must be how Pearl and other
popular ladies felt all the time. Fleeting as it surely
must be, Rowena could not help but savor the feeling
of pure feminine power.

Turning with a flirtatious smile on her lips, she suddenly froze. There, just behind the two men who so
improbably seemed to be vying for her attention
stood Lady Mountheath, with a disapproving frown.

It was not the frown that startled Rowena out of
her brief moment of triumph, however. It was the fact
that Lady Mountheath was wearing the emerald and
diamond necklace and earrings that had belonged to
Rowena's own mother.

Chapter 10

"**M**iss Riverstone," exclaimed Lady Mount-heath, coming forward with a smile as false as it was broad. "When I saw you last night, I assumed Lady Hardwyck had indulged you for the evening, but now it appears her kindness may have gone to your head."

Rowena blinked, tearing her gaze away from the woman's jewels to focus on her face. "I beg your pardon, my lady?"

"Just a kindly word of advice, my dear," the older woman said airily. "A companion who forgets her station may find herself disappointed when she discovers others are all too aware of her proper sphere, much as they may pretend otherwise for the course of an evening." She looked significantly at the two gentlemen flanking Rowena.

Taken aback as she was by the unexpected attack, Rowena realized what must be at the root of it. Lady Mountheath's two daughters had both been without partners for much of the ball last night. It must gall their mother to see Rowena—who she clearly regarded as their inferior—with two eligible gentlemen dancing attendance on her.

"I fear you are laboring under a misapprehension, my lady," she said as evenly as she could manage. "I am Lady Hardwyck's friend and neighbor, not her paid companion. Therefore, you need not fear for the social order on my account."

Now it was Lady Mountheath's turn to blink, as she absorbed this new, and clearly unwelcome, information. "My apologies," she finally murmured ungraciously. "I was merely attempting to save you from folly." Her expression implied that Rowena was still on the path to ruin. She started to turn away.

"And I thank you, my lady," Rowena said, quickly adding, "Those . . . are lovely jewels you are wearing tonight. You have exquisite taste."

Her words had the desired effect, for Lady Mountheath turned again to face her, her smile now appearing quite genuine. "Why thank you, my dear. They were a gift from my husband only last week. So extravagant of him, but he knows how well emeralds become me." She patted her lilac turban complacently and Rowena noticed the wispy strands of faded red peeking from beneath it.

"Yes, very flattering," Rowena forced herself to say, hoping for more detail.

"I wouldn't be surprised to learn he had them commissioned specially," Lady Mountheath continued. "He wouldn't tell me from which jeweler he purchased them, doubtless because he knew I'd be cross if I discovered how much he spent on me." She then fixed Rowena with a stern eye. "A just reward for conventional behavior, Miss Riverstone. See that you remember that lesson."

With a sententious nod of her turban, she sashayed off, clearly satisfied that she had prevailed in the encounter.

"Hmph. I'm not surprised her husband wouldn't say where he bought those jewels, considering that it was a pawn shop," Rowena muttered to her retreating back. "Extravagant, indeed."

"A pawn shop?" Mr. Paxton asked in obvious amusement. "What makes you think so?"

Rowena flushed, embarrassed that her companions had heard her words. There was nothing for it now but to explain—or be thought intolerably petty. "Those jewels were my mother's. I discovered only last night that my brother sold them to . . . to meet an obligation." She glanced significantly at Mr. Richards, who had the grace to frown.

Mr. Paxton chuckled. "And that dragon flaunts them as proof of her husband's devotion. If she only knew!"

"Please, you won't say anything?" Rowena turned pleading eyes first on Mr. Paxton, then Mr. Richards.

Both gentlemen shook their heads. "You may depend upon my silence," Mr. Richards said gallantly. "I would not wish your brother—or you—embarrassed in any way."

Was he trying to tell her that he would forgive the remainder of Nelson's gaming debts? But of course she could not ask him in front of Mr. Paxton. She didn't wish to lower his opinion of Mr. Richards any further than it was already.

"Nor I," Mr. Paxton echoed after a pause. "Now, shall we continue to the buffet tables?"

Much of Noel's pleasure at beating the arrogant Mr. Richards at chess had been lost when Miss Riverstone had smiled so sweetly at the fellow, and now she was doing it again. Couldn't she see that he was nowhere near as clever as she'd believed? Hadn't her own match against the man taught her that?

In addition, there was something less than candid about the fellow, though he couldn't quite put his finger on it. Something about the way his eyes failed to reflect his expressions, perhaps. He'd learned over the years to trust his instinctive response to people, and his instincts told him not to trust Mr. Richards.

Or perhaps it was merely jealousy telling him that.

"The company is beginning to thin," he commented. "Between chess and conversation, the evening has passed remarkably quickly." Perhaps Richards would take the hint.

Miss Riverstone set down her empty ratafia glass and glanced about the ballroom. "It certainly has. I hope Pearl won't scold me for playing but one card game, after all of her coaching—and yours, sir."

"Surely you don't allow yourself to be *scolded*, Miss Riverstone?" Mr. Richards said, raising one brow. "You acquitted yourself quite well against that harridan, Lady Mountheath, earlier."

She dimpled up at him in a way that made Noel grit his teeth. "Thank you, Mr. Richards. Perhaps we should have quizzed her on the treatment of her servants, for Pearl hinted to me that it is abominable. As for scolding, Pearl is a good friend and means it in the nicest possible way."

"I am reassured. A woman of your intelligence need apologize to no one, you know."

Miss Riverstone pinkened slightly at Richards' intimate tone, and Noel cleared his throat loudly to remind them both of his presence. "I'm glad to see, Miss Riverstone, that you are not so tired this evening as you were last night."

She turned to him and he held her gaze, smiling down into her eyes until she could see what kindled in his own. Her eyes widened and she pinkened further—clearly remembering as vividly as he how last night had ended.

"That's scarcely surprising." Mr. Richards' scornful voice broke into the private moment. "Chess and cards are hardly as strenuous as dancing—frivolous pursuit that it is."

"Very true," Noel agreed, still not taking his eyes from Miss Riverstone's. Her lashes were remarkably dark and thick, he noticed. Beautifully so. "Dancing was not quite the ordeal you expected, however, was it?"

She parted her lips to answer, and Noel found himself mesmerized by the shape of those lips, the memory of—

"There you are, Rowena." Lady Hardwyck's voice came from behind him, before a word escaped the exquisite lips he was watching. "I'd like to introduce Mr. Robert Southey."

Miss Riverstone blinked and turned, the spell broken. She greeted Mr. Southey eagerly, but Noel tried not to take offense. Southey was a celebrated essayist, poet and biographer—someone bound to appeal to anyone of Miss Riverstone's intellect and sensibility.

"Charmed, Miss Riverstone," the newcomer said, bowing over her hand. Lady Hardwyck then introduced Noel and Mr. Richards, though it was clear at once that the latter was already acquainted with Mr. Southey—and that the two were not on the best of terms.

"I'll speak with you later, Miss Riverstone," Richards said after the most formal of greetings and an awkward pause.

She nodded, but scarcely seemed to notice his defection, so interested was she in hearing Mr. Southey's critique of a new play he had seen the week before. Noel could not regard Mr. Southey as a threat, given the man's age and marital status, so allowed himself to relax—only then realizing how tense he had been.

"Might I prevail upon you to make a fourth at whist?" Lady Hardwyck asked Noel then, and he hesitated only the barest moment before assenting. He could not afford to have his interest in Miss Riverstone marked again by his hostess. Miss Riverstone's continued conversation with Mr. Southey meant that she was safe for the moment from Mr. Richards' return.

Noel couldn't claim to play his best, distracted as he was by discreetly watching Miss Riverstone. She and Mr. Southey moved to another table to play at piquet, where they were soon surrounded by several others of the literary set.

Determinedly, Noel turned his attention back to his own game. What did he hope to gain from his observation of Miss Riverstone, anyway? Now that he'd ruled out her brother as a likely suspect, she had little bearing on his case.

Or did she?

"Mr. Paxton?" Miss Cheevers, his partner, recalled him to the game.

"Sorry." He played a card almost at random.

There was still the matter of those essays which, according to the clerk he'd questioned at the *Political Register*, had been posted from Oakshire. He glanced in her direction again—to see her rising from the piquet table.

"Your game again," Miss Cheevers said to Lord and Lady Hardwyck, with understandable irritation. "Mr. Paxton, will you deal?"

But Noel rose. "I beg you will excuse me. I seem to be too tired to concentrate properly." He beckoned to Harry Thatcher, just passing with a group of other men. "Take my place, won't you, Harry?"

With a shrug, Mr. Thatcher assented, freeing Noel to follow Miss Riverstone, who had just disappeared in the direction of the back staircase. Quickening his pace, acknowledging greetings from the two Mountheath sisters with only a nod, he reached the landing just as Miss Riverstone began to mount the stairs.

"Escaping again?"

She turned with a gasp. "You startled me, sir. But yes, I had thought to retire. It is well past midnight, after all."

"I've also had enough of games and chatter for one evening," Noel confessed. "May I escort you upstairs?"

She frowned, her cheeks brightening. "Surely that wouldn't be proper?"

"Who is to know?" he asked reasonably, though she was perfectly correct. "Besides, is not propriety one of those social constructs you despise?"

One corner of her mouth quirked up, fascinating him. "So I have always claimed. Come, then. We will escort each other."

Now that was a fascinating concept.

"It appears your brother does not share your political views," Noel commented casually as they mounted the stairs together.

"Nelson?" She chuckled—a low, erotic sound. *Erotic?* "Rather the opposite, I should say. It's why he—and my father—never wished me to come to Town. I fear I've been rather an embarrassment to them."

Noel didn't see how this intelligent woman could be an embarrassment to anyone. "Someone must have shaped your views," he persisted. "An uncle? A neighbor?" Perhaps whoever was writing those essays?

"My mother was rather a free thinker for a woman but she died when I was fourteen. I have shaped my own views, after reading widely. I need no man's sanction to form opinions." She spoke archly, daring him to doubt her.

And indeed, he could not. In fact, he could scarcely think, with her gazing up at him like that.

They had reached the upper hallway, where the bedrooms were situated. He wondered which was hers.

"You are unique, Miss Riverstone," he said warmly. "Or—may I call you Rowena? I feel I know you quite well, for all we've only been acquainted a few days."

"I . . . I was thinking the same," she said in a voice that was almost a sigh. "Still, Mr. Paxton—"

"Noel," he corrected her gently.

She smiled, a small, shy smile. "Noel, then. But I was going to say, as well as we understand each other, we seem to disagree about a great many issues."

He moved closer to her. "But that is what makes things so interesting."

"Yes," she agreed, her wide gray gaze probing his own.

As before, he could not seem to stop himself. As he lowered his head, she parted her lips slightly, her tongue flicking out to moisten them. That tiny motion undid him. With a guttural moan, he pulled her against him, claiming her mouth with a fierce kiss.

At once, her arms went about him, urging him closer, even as her lips responded eagerly to his claim. Somehow he had known, had known from the first, that she was capable of such passion, that a fire was concealed beneath her prim exterior—not so prim anymore.

His hands roved up and down her back, exulting in her lush curves, the way her small waist flared to generous hips. She twined her fingers through the hair at the sensitive nape of his neck, slid one hand across the breadth of his shoulders, his back.

Noel felt his breath coming in quick, shallow gasps. Never could he remember wanting a woman so desperately as he wanted Rowena. He tried to remind himself that she was a means to an end, but the feather-light explorations of her fingers, now stroking his ears, drove him past rational thought. Teasing her lips apart with his tongue, he tasted all her kiss had to offer, demanding that she do the same.

Nor did she hesitate. She twined her tongue with his, a joining that went beyond the mere physical. It was as though their very souls touched.

It was that sense of connection, of vulnerability, that recalled him to his senses—the knowledge that he danced on the edge of a precipice that he longed to plunge over until he lost himself in her entirely.

"I—we—" he murmured into her hair.

"Yes?" she breathed, then, "Oh!" much more distinctly. Taking a quick step backward, she stared at him, clearly aghast. "Oh, my."

"Indeed. I had no—That is, I suppose I should apologize, but—"

"No, don't. Unless . . . you are sorry?"

Slowly, he shook his head. "Not in the least, unless I've distressed you."

Again, that half-smile that made him want to kiss her again. "Confused, perhaps. But distressed? No."

"I'm glad. I never want to be a source of pain to you, Rowena." He realized he meant it—which presented him with a problem.

"Thank you. That is—this morning I thought—"

"Yes, I know," he said before she could say too much, tempt him to promise things he was not ready to promise. "I handled that clumsily, and for that I *do* apologize."

She smiled her acceptance of his apology and suddenly she was in his arms again, though he couldn't have said who moved first. Only that it seemed the most natural thing in the world.

Again he felt as though he were falling as desire swept away reason. Her tentative touch revealed her innocence, unleashing a fierce need in him to show her new delights, to be the one who led her through the maze of adult pleasures.

Dimly, in some far-off corner of his mind that still clung to the capacity for reason, he registered the fact that they were exposed here in the hallway. A servant might appear at any moment.

"Which is your room?" he murmured against her lips.

He felt rather than saw her swallow. "Here." She half turned, taking a step toward the next door on the left. "But my maid—"

Abruptly, reason returned. What on earth had he been contemplating? Had she been ready to allow—?

"Your maid. Yes, of course. I do apologize. I've overstepped—that is—Good night, Miss Riverstone."

Though his body protested, he turned from her and strode down the hall to his own room only two doors away. Not trusting himself to so much as glance back, he shut himself inside and leaned against the door, gulping great draughts of air in an effort to calm himself.

"Sir?"

Damn. "I'm fine, Kemp. I just need to think."

His manservant took the hint at once and withdrew without another word.

Was he mad? More than one French beauty had attempted to cloud his mind during the war. Always, he had been able to take his pleasure while keeping his mind, his mission, perfectly clear. Why should this be any different?

Perhaps he was simply out of practice. Still, did he dare risk his investigation—and perhaps men's lives—on the assumption that he would be able to rein in his emotions where Rowena Riverstone was concerned?

"Kemp?"

"Sir?" The man emerged from the dressing room.

"Pack my things. We're returning to our lodgings tonight."

He needed to put some distance between himself and Rowena Riverstone, so temptingly situated only two rooms away. Then, perhaps, he'd be able to recall just how vital his mission was.

Rowena stared, openmouthed, as Mr. Paxton—Noel—disappeared into his room without a backward glance. How could he have altered so abruptly? A moment ago, he had clearly wanted her, wanted—

She put her hands to her flaming cheeks. He'd wanted what she had wanted—what she'd actually been prepared to allow. Was she mad? If her bedchamber had been empty, with no maid to concern them, she had little doubt she and Noel would be in there now, and her virtue on its way to becoming a mere memory.

Thank heaven he had come to his senses, she thought with a discontented sigh. Turning the handle, she entered her room—only to find it empty after all.

"Matthilda?" Though the small fire had been recently tended, there was no answer.

In sudden frustration, Rowena snatched up her hairbrush from the dressing table and flung it across the room. They could have been alone after all! Why, oh why, had she mentioned her maid? She half turned back toward the door, thinking to somehow recall Noel, to let him know, but caught herself before she'd taken a step.

Really, she *must* be mad. Matthilda had likely gone down to the kitchens, and would be back at any moment. And even if she weren't, did she, Rowena, really hold her virtue so cheaply? Could she seriously contemplate destroying her reputation for a fleeting moment of passion?

Yes, she realized, she quite definitely could. She could imagine doing so all too vividly. Not that it meant she *would*, of course . . .

With another sigh, she crossed the room to retrieve her hairbrush, then seated herself at the dressing table to unpin her hair and brush it out with vigorous strokes. The rhythmic action calmed her, and gradually the jangling of her nerves, sensitized to a screaming pitch by Noel Paxton's kisses, quieted. When Matthilda entered a few minutes later, she was able to greet the maid with reasonable equanimity.

"Miss! I did not expect you so early. I'd have come up sooner, if—"

"It's no matter, Matthilda. I've only been here a moment. Run back downstairs and see if a bath might be possible, then come back to help me out of my gown."

A few minutes later, a tub and steaming kettles were brought. While the tub was filled, Matthilda undid the row of hooks down Rowena's back, then lifted the blue gown over her head. Not until she was alone again, lowering herself into the bath, did Rowena allow her thoughts to return to Noel Paxton.

What might he be doing, two rooms away? Was he,

perhaps, thinking of her? Would he have heard the servants bringing her bath water, know that she was now in here completely unclothed?

"Oh, stop it," she said aloud to the empty room.

She had read widely enough to know that men rarely set as much store by kisses, or even lovemaking, as women did. History was littered with stories of women who had foolishly given themselves to undeserving men, only to find themselves ruined and alone.

Of course, there were other stories that ended quite differently, and it had certainly *seemed* as though—

No. She could not count on that. He might have been merely dallying with her. Still, why could she not dally as well? Rowena had never entertained romantic expectations of marriage and family. Her dreams had run rather to ambition and influence, as a man's might. So why could she not take her pleasure as men did?

The novel notion intrigued her.

She would not discourage Noel, she decided. If he wished to pursue a dalliance, she would indulge him and take what enjoyment she might from it, without expecting anything more. That would leave her heart and her mind free for more important things.

If men could separate their emotions from their physical pleasures, then so could she.

But as she drifted off to sleep an hour later, her dreams inexplicably involved Noel Paxton not only kissing her, but declaring his undying love—a love she professed to return.

Chapter 11

"**G**one?"

Rowena had dressed with extra care for breakfast, even leaving her spectacles upstairs, only to have Pearl inform her that Mr. Paxton had packed his things and left late last night.

"He said he had things to attend to at his lodgings—that he would be working more closely with Bow Street for a few days, which made staying nearby more convenient," Pearl explained. "I daresay we shall still see something of him, however, as the investigation cannot take up all of his time."

"I daresay," Rowena echoed hollowly. He had said nothing last night about his investigation, nor about leaving. She suspected his decision had been made after the passionate moment they had shared in the upstairs hallway.

But what did it mean?

"You sound tired, dear." Pearl peered at her in evident concern. "It's as well that it is Sunday, and that we have no particular plans for the day. I recommend you take the opportunity to rest."

Rowena nodded, then turned away to fill a plate from the sideboard before Pearl could read her expression. "Yes, I'm sure that would be best. Then I will be fresh for whatever you have planned for tomorrow."

"A picnic in Green Park, to be sure. If the fine weather holds, it will be perfect for a day out of doors. You'll want to choose a dress with a matching parasol, of course, to keep your freckles to a minimum."

While Pearl elaborated on her plans, Rowena's thoughts returned to Noel, though she tried to appear interested in both her breakfast and Pearl's words. *Had* he run away from her? Why? Was she really so threatening—or so distasteful?

But he had not seemed to find her distasteful last night.

Though she tried to distract herself with both reading and writing, by the end of the day Rowena had examined every conceivable explanation for Mr. Paxton's removal, finding none of them satisfactory. The one she wished most to believe—that he had felt honor bound to remove himself from the temptation to sully her virtue—seemed the least likely of all.

Nor was she satisfied with a second draft of the essay she had written for the *Political Register*. Reading it over, she saw that the opinions of both Mr. Richards and Mr. Southey had crept in, along with the mitigating influence of Noel Paxton's views. Had she always parroted the opinions of others like this, with no original thoughts of her own?

Pulling out copies of her previous essays, she realized that, to some extent, she had. In fact, her first two essays had been drawn almost entirely from Mr. Richards' letters. She had even used his handwriting as a model, to disguise her own as a masculine hand.

Surely she was capable of more independent thought—and expression—than she had shown so far. Picking up her pen, she began the essay afresh. Finally, after much work, she was satisfied that the opinions in the essay she would post in the morning were her own and no one else's.

Still, she went to bed that night in a far less complacent frame of mind than she had done the night before. Her life seemed to be teetering on the verge of some change—but whether for better or worse, she could not at all determine.

Noel also spent much of Sunday reading through all of Mr. R's essays, but with a far different purpose. A previous visit to the office of the *Political Register* had yielded the original of one of those essays. Now he carefully reexamined both the hand and the content, again comparing both to letters given him by the Foreign Office—letters known to have been sent by the Black Bishop.

While the writing had clearly been disguised in both cases, there were enough similarities to make it likely that the same hand had penned both, allowing for differences in pens and circumstances. And the similarity of expression struck him even more forcefully than before.

That one phrase, "the sacrifice of men as beasts," while perhaps not unique, was unusual enough to stand out when it appeared in both Mr. R's work and a letter from the Bishop.

He paused then, struck. Had not Lester Richards said something similar last night, while talking with Rowena? At the time, Noel had been watching the lady's face, trying to convince himself that she felt no more than intellectual interest in the other man. Now he recalled some of the actual words that had been spoken.

Mr. Richards? Surely it could not be so easy as that? Nor could he quite trust himself to be objective, given how much he resented the fellow's influence over Rowena. Still, he was duty bound to follow any lead—and he now had an idea of how to do so.

Early Monday morning, Noel again presented himself at the *Political Register*, pleased to discover the clerk who had helped him before, a Mr. Bell, was there. Noel waited until the other clerk was busy on the other side of the small, paper-filled room to put forth his plan.

"Those letters you mentioned before, the ones that have accumulated for the anonymous essayist Mr. R over the past few months," he said softly. "I've an idea how they might be delivered."

The bespectacled young man looked both pleased and surprised. "Do you, sir? Mr. Cobbett would be pleased to do so, I know. He's been so concerned some might be important, or of a timely nature, that he talked about opening them, but felt it would be a breach of privacy to do so."

"He never tried to trace those essays back to their source in Oakshire for that purpose?"

The clerk shrugged. "He would have, I'm sure, had any of them been delivered other than by post. There's another anonymous writer, an LB, who has his pieces delivered by a footman. That made it easy enough to figure out who he was—and to send on any letters he receives, the same way. He doesn't get nearly so many as this Mr. R, though."

"A popular and controversial writer, I perceive." Noel was not surprised, as the essays were both thoughtful and articulate, forcing one to reexamine long-held beliefs. That would draw both support and condemnation, both no doubt equally vehement.

"Oh, aye, he is that. Do you have an address we can send the letters, then?"

Noel shook his head, to Mr. Bell's obvious disappointment. "Not an address. A plan. How if you were to print a notice in this week's *Register*, saying that Mr. R could retrieve his letters himself?"

"I can't imagine he'd come here and risk anyone knowing who he is," said the young man skeptically.

"No, of course not. That's why the notice will specify a different location—one that he will choose himself. He can post a note to you, saying where the letters are to be left, and he can then retrieve them at his convenience. That should preserve his anonymity."

The clerk's brows rose with respect. "It's a good plan, sir. I'm sure Mr. Cobbett will approve. Am I right, however, in thinking that you will wish to know the location, once we receive his reply?"

There was no denying the young man was intelligent. But then, Cobbett would never have fools working for him.

"Yes, but no one else. I won't publicize his identity, I promise you."

"You said before that you're concerned with a matter of national security. I assume you don't want me to tell Mr. Cobbett about that part?"

Noel handed the clerk a few gold coins. "Not just yet. But if I am right, you will have done a very patriotic thing, Mr. Bell, believe me."

"I admit I'm a bit more conservative than some of our contributors," the young man confessed. "Certainly, I wouldn't want to see England go the way of France."

"That's precisely what we may be preventing."

Seating himself at the desk, Noel jotted down the wording for the notice, subject to Mr. Cobbett's approval. While he wrote, the morning's post came, diverting the clerk's attention until Noel handed him the notice.

He glanced up to take it, then back at the letters in his hand. "Sir!" he exclaimed, just as Noel was turning to go. "You may wish to see this." He held out a sealed envelope.

Curious, Noel took it. Even had it not been addressed in the distinctive disguised hand he had spent yesterday examining, the scrawled "Mr. R" on the corner of the envelope declared its source. And it had been posted this very morning, right here in London.

"Interesting," he said, handing it back to the clerk. "This makes me even more hopeful that this fellow will have his letters by the end of the week."

He would make certain inquiries into Richards' activities and try to discover his whereabouts during the war. If that did not rule him out as a suspect, this trap with the letters should prove that he was indeed the mysterious essayist—and the traitor Noel sought.

Lady Hardwyck had planned an excursion to

Green Park this afternoon, he recalled. Though he had intended to keep his distance from Rowena for a few days, he could not afford to ignore an opportunity to observe Mr. Richards more closely, nor an obligation to protect others from a possible traitor.

If he should be thrown into Rowena's company in the course of his investigation, it was simply the price of duty—a price he was more than willing to pay.

The lovely weather, particularly after the unusually dull summer that had cast a pall over England, drew a considerable crowd to assemble in Green Park for the day.

Rowena felt she looked her best in her green-sprigged white muslin with matching parasol—fresh, summery, and ready to captivate any man who looked her way. If Noel Paxton was frightened away by the idea of a dalliance, she would simply find her diversions elsewhere.

The rainy summer had rendered the triangular park as green as its name. Situated directly across Picadilly from Hardwyck Hall, it had been easy for Pearl to arrange to have vast quantities of refreshments carted over in baskets and barrows. Chairs were set up and cloths spread on the grass for the comfort of the guests.

Rowena settled herself on a white, lacy coverlet that complemented her gown and gazed about. Though people at any distance faded into a colorful blur, she did not *think* Noel was in attendance. Mr. Galloway was near enough to identify, however, as were Lord Peter and Mr. Thatcher, all potential "diversions."

Unfortunately, the first man to come her way happened to be her brother.

"Should you not be at the Home Office?" she greeted Nelson as he approached. It did not suit her purposes at all for him to attach himself to her for the day.

He shrugged. "A man must eat. Here, at least, I needn't pay for my food. I'll return to the Office in an hour or so." Dropping down on the cloth beside her, he added, "I needed to speak with you, as there was no opportunity last night. Have you talked with Richards?"

Though she did not feel at all like discussing Nelson's problems on such a lovely day, she nodded. "Briefly, but we were interrupted before I could ask him to forgive your debt. I did think he seemed sympathetic, however, and—oh! I know where Mother's jewels are."

"Do you?" he said eagerly, then frowned. "You haven't been visiting pawn shops unaccompanied, have you, Ro?"

"Of course not. As you said, the jewels would have been sold by now—and so they were. To Lord Mountheath, who gave them to his wife. She was wearing them last night."

Nelson puckered his brow. "They're well and truly gone, then, for there is no way to buy them back without an explanation—and we can trust Lady Mountheath to spread the story far and wide, should she get wind of it."

"Yes, I know," Rowena said with a sigh. "Still, I feel better knowing where the pieces are. And it's rather amusing to think of Lady Mountheath flaunting our mother's baubles with no notion that her husband redeemed them from a pawn shop."

"I suppose that's true," Nelson agreed with a chuckle. "But that don't help with the larger problem of the five hundred pounds I still owe Richards."

Rowena gasped. "Five hundred pounds? I had no idea it was so much. How could you possibly—" She broke off. "That is quite a sum to ask Mr. Richards to forgive. No doubt he has plans for it already."

Nelson nodded glumly. "No doubt. Though he's hinted he'd be willing to accept information in exchange for a portion of it."

"Information? What sort of information?"

"From the Home Office. Details about old spy cases, mostly."

Rowena frowned. "But the war is over. What would anyone want with such information?"

"I have no idea. Far as I can tell, what he wants isn't even secret, though it's not something anyone outside the Home Office would be likely to know about."

"He actually asked you for such information? And you're considering giving it to him?" She was struggling to understand both her brother's reasoning and Mr. Richards' motives.

Nelson shrugged. "As I said, it isn't sensitive or secret. Mostly cases that were closed by the Foreign Office and turned over to us. Can't imagine why he might want such stuff, to be honest."

Rowena was thinking hard. If Mr. Richards needed information or even money for his cause, could she really fault him? "Perhaps he intends to write a treatise, or even a book, on such things," she suggested.

"Perhaps. Anyway, what can I do? It's either tell him what he wants to know or pay him money I don't have."

"No," Rowena said firmly. "Let me speak with him again. Today should provide an opportunity. It would be far worse for your superiors to discover you passing along information—even information that seems perfectly innocent—than for Mr. Richards to publicize your debts."

Nelson was clearly skeptical. "I'd prefer neither occur, but perhaps you are right. I'll give you your chance before I tell him anything. Let me know how it falls out."

"Yes, I'll send word, or tell you the next time I see you."

He clambered to his feet. "You *are* a good sister, Ro! Now, I'm going to go see what it is they're putting out on those tables, before I have to return to Whitehall."

Rowena watched him go with mingled affection and exasperation, wondering if she were really doing him a favor by allowing him to avoid the consequences of his poor judgment. He was her brother, however, so she would do what she could for him.

Half rising, she looked to see whether Mr. Richards had arrived, only to discover him approaching her, along with Lucinda and Augusta Melks and Mr. Galloway.

"Miss Riverstone," he greeted her. "I thought you might like some refreshment, as your brother did not think to provide you with a plate." He handed her an assortment of small sandwiches and a glass of lemonade before taking his place beside her.

The others arranged themselves about the white cloth with their own plates and glasses in hand. Rowena glanced at Mr. Richards, then away, wishing he were as young and handsome as Noel Paxton—then immediately despising herself for such a wish.

"Mr. Richards tells me he succeeded where I failed last night," Mr. Galloway commented.

The ladies, Rowena included, regarded him questioningly.

"At the chessboard," he clarified. "Miss Riverstone is quite the whiz at chess, you must know."

"Indeed?" Miss Augusta regarded Rowena quizzically. "You must be very clever, then—but I suppose that is to be expected in Lady Hardwyck's good friend, as she is so clever herself."

Rowena was uncertain that the comment was meant as a compliment, but smiled her thanks. "Mr. Richards defeated me, however," she said to deflect attention.

"Miss Riverstone plays very well," he said in a manner some might have called condescending. "She needs to learn more focus, and to restrain her emotions from interfering with her reason. I have hopes of schooling her into a truly superior player one day."

Her pride severely stung, Rowena had to make an effort to keep her expression pleasant. "I am unused to playing amidst a crowd. I assure you that in quieter surroundings, I am able to focus quite well." *And would have beaten you last night, crowd or no, had I chosen to do so,* she added silently.

"No doubt, no doubt," he replied placatingly—which only served to irritate her further.

"I should like a chance to prove it to you sometime, sir."

He actually looked surprised—though still complacent. "Of course, my dear. Of course."

"It is a lovely day, is it not?" Miss Melks asked then, in an obvious attempt to change the subject. Her sister quickly agreed.

The others took the hint and conversed on more general topics while enjoying their sandwiches and other dainties. After half an hour, Miss Melks held out her hand to Mr. Galloway. "Sir, you promised to show Augusta and me the swans, did you not?"

"I did indeed." Leaping to his feet, he helped first Lucinda, then Augusta to rise. "Would you care to join us, Miss Riverstone?"

"Perhaps in a few moments," she replied. This might be her best chance to have a private word with Mr. Richards, though in truth she had little desire just now to ask favors of him.

Surprisingly, he broached the subject before she could. "You seemed in rather deep conversation with your brother earlier," he commented as soon as the others were out of earshot.

"Yes, Nelson is concerned about his debt to you," she admitted candidly. "He was asking my advice on the matter."

Mr. Richards frowned. "I am sorry to hear that he has troubled you. I would not have expected a gentleman to run to a lady with his problems, even an exceptional lady like yourself." He did not, Rowena noted, offer to solve the problem himself.

After a slight pause, she said, "Nelson has faith in my intelligence, Mr. Richards—more faith than you seem to show. You have put forth persuasive arguments for the equality of men. Do you not feel women should be accorded the same rights and respect?"

Though he appeared startled, he answered readily enough. "Men have a duty to protect the women under their care. While some, like yourself, possess abilities beyond the norm, you must admit that there are many things women are ill suited for."

"Like chess?" she asked, the stirrings of a plan beginning to form. Perhaps she would not have to beg after all.

He smiled. "Like chess—though you do show great potential."

"I am happy to hear it. I was quite serious when I said I should like another chance to demonstrate it. I might surprise you."

"I am at your disposal, of course. You have merely to name the day." The complacency on his face made it perfectly clear he expected no different outcome.

Time to put her plan to the test. "How if we play for stakes next time?" she asked. "That might help me to—focus."

He raised a thin brow. "What stakes did you have in mind?"

"My brother's debt," she responded. "If I win, you will agree to forgive the remainder. If you win, I will see that you are paid twice what he still owes you."

"I see that recklessness runs in your family, Miss Riverstone. How can I, in conscience, accept such stakes, knowing that I am the superior player? I was distressed enough to discover jewelry of undoubted sentimental value to you had been sacrificed to this debt already."

His concern softened her pride enough to allow a genuine smile. "As it was my suggestion, your conscience is clear. I told you I was not at my best last night. I wish an opportunity to show you I can do better."

He sighed, though she imagined that she caught a glint of eagerness in his eyes. "Very well, if you insist—and if your brother agrees. I would prefer not to have a lady indebted to me."

"I will speak to him, of course." Rowena fought to hide the triumph she felt. "Any debt will be in his name, not mine."

Mr. Richards rose. "I have a previous engagement tonight. A . . . personal matter. Perhaps tomorrow evening? What does Lady Hardwyck have planned?"

"A musicale, I believe. But it may be possible to find a quiet corner for a game, away from the crowd."

"I will look forward to it, Miss Riverstone. Now, if you will excuse me, I need to make certain preparations before this evening." He bowed and left her.

Rowena wondered what he might have planned— for he had seemed almost deliberately mysterious. Something to do with his efforts at reform, perhaps? The Spencean societies were under close surveillance by the authorities, she knew. If he were involved with them, it would make sense that he would not broadcast it.

For a moment, she almost regretted what she would do tomorrow night, but then she remembered his patronizing attitude and smiled. It seemed that even a forward thinker like Mr. Richards had a thing or two to learn.

Noel stood at the edge of Green Park, watching as Mr. Richards took his leave of Rowena. They had spent nearly fifteen minutes *tête-à-tête*, though of course they were in plain view of the rest of Lady Hardwyck's guests. Still, he could not quite suppress an instinctive urge to protect her.

Though he had promised himself he would keep his distance, as soon as Rowena was alone he found himself moving forward. He had a few moments to observe her closely before she saw him—to notice how lovely she looked in her fresh white dress, her coppery curls pulled back with a fetching green ribbon.

"Good afternoon, Rowena." He kept his voice low, not certain whether she would want anyone else to know she had given him permission to use her name.

She turned quickly, a smile lighting her face for an instant before her expression turned guarded. "Mr. Paxton. I had understood you would not be able to come today."

He shrugged. "I was able to conclude my business early." Though she did not invite him to sit, he lowered himself onto the cloth beside her.

"And what business might that have been?" Her gray gaze was as direct as her question, seeming to see right through him. He found himself oddly distracted by the attractive pattern of freckles dusting her nose.

"My investigation into the Saint of Seven Dials, of course."

He was not surprised when she looked doubtful.

"And that necessitated you leaving Hardwyck Hall like a thief in the night?"

Her phrase startled him. Surely, she couldn't suspect—?

"I did feel I could more effectively follow some new leads from my own lodgings near Bow Street, but—no. I admit my precipitousness was prompted by other concerns." Even now, when he should be planning his next move after this morning's inquiries, he found her nearness thoroughly—and pleasantly—distracting.

She lowered her voice. "Last night, I told you not to apologize unless you were truly sorry—and yet you did apologize. I am sorry if I have been a cause for regrets, Mr. Paxton."

"Noel," he reminded her, even though a more formal footing would be wiser. "And my only regret is that I may have distressed you by my actions."

"Yes, I was distressed." Still, she regarded him with that clear, gray gaze. "To learn that you had fled in the night was quite distressing—for a moment or two. I realized, however, that it would be foolish to allow your actions to affect me so."

"I did not *flee*, precisely," he felt obliged to protest. Then, leaning forward to add weight to his words, he added, "I must confess that your actions affect me, whether the reverse is true or not."

Though her color rose, she did not drop her gaze. "My effect upon you seems inconsistent at best, sir. How am I to interpret that?"

He had no idea how to answer her, so instead he rose and extended his hand. "Would you care to walk with me for a bit?"

"Very well." She allowed him to help her to her feet, her small hand warm beneath the thin lace glove she wore. "You did not answer my question," she reminded him as they turned toward the small pond in the center of the park.

"Because I'm not certain of the answer myself," he confessed truthfully. "I can't deny that I am drawn to you. I've never met another woman of your intelligence and candor—and loveliness. But my investigation is at a critical juncture, and I fear I cannot afford the level of distraction you afford."

This was also true, though his investigation was not the one she believed it to be.

"I, ah, never intended to *distract* you, of course," Rowena said after a pause. "Or, at least, perhaps I did—but I never expected it to work."

He glanced down at her in surprise, but she was gazing off into the distance, her cheeks still pink despite the parasol that shaded them from the August sunshine.

"I am flattered that you wished it—and I can assure you that it did indeed . . . work." He did not bother to hide his smile, as she was not watching him.

"So what shall we do about it?" she asked then, finally turning to meet his eyes.

Again startled—and charmed—by her directness, he quickly schooled his expression to one of proper seriousness. "I am open to suggestions. What should you prefer?"

She frowned, apparently not seeing the humor in this unconventional conversation. "I suppose it would make the most sense for us to avoid each other. While I would prefer to, ah, distract you from your investigation of the Saint of Seven Dials, it seems unsporting of me."

"That's unusually gallant of you, Rowena, presuming that avoiding me entails any sacrifice on your part. I would have thought your championship of the Saint would take precedence over the demands of sportsmanship."

She regarded him uncertainly. "Are you poking fun at me? However, I do see your point. Perhaps my priorities are askew."

"I would be surprised to find your priorities anything other than well thought out."

Finally, she smiled, an arch smile that only made her more fetching. "I'm pleased that my lack of social experience is a source of amusement to you, sir. On further thought, however, I see little point in our continued association."

"Oh?" Every statement she made seemed more surprising than the last. Noel was enjoying this conversation immensely.

"We have so little in common," she explained. "You are a proponent of the status quo, putting man-made laws above essential justice, while I am an unrepentant idealist."

He nodded. "I see. But what of chess? We have that in common, as well as a mutual enjoyment in arguing our differing views."

Her glance slid away from his again. "That . . . that is true. But scarcely enough to base a lasting—friendship—upon."

Noel abruptly realized that he wanted Rowena Riverstone for much more than a passing dalliance. He wanted to explore every facet of her mind as well as her body, to take his time getting to know her better than she even knew herself. He wanted her for life.

That shattering discovery sobered him as nothing else could have done. How could he have allowed this to happen, particularly now? But the fact was undeniable.

"Perhaps," he finally admitted, bringing his attention back to her words with an effort. "But friendships have flourished on far less, from my observation. Nor am I convinced that our ideals are so divergent as you seem to believe."

"Then—do you not wish to avoid me after all, despite the danger you claim I present to your pursuit of the Saint?" The look she sent him from under her lowered lashes was positively flirtatious, both out of character and exceedingly alluring.

Though still shaken by his discovery, Noel couldn't help grinning. "So you have decided to do your part to save the rogue, have you? But no—I cannot honestly claim that I wish to avoid you. Quite the opposite, in fact."

"Does that mean you will be returning to Hardwyck Hall?"

Noel considered. He still had numerous inquiries to make, and likely numerous forays as the Saint, to discover what he needed to know about Mr. Richards. In addition, there was his plan to positively identify the mysterious Mr. R once and for all.

"In a day or two, perhaps," he replied. "I do have certain responsibilities that I cannot ignore, much as I might like to. Once I have discharged them, I hope to have opportunity to turn my attention to more pleasant pursuits."

"Once you have captured the Saint, do you mean? Do you believe you are only days from doing so?" There was no mistaking her alarm. Noel rather enjoyed her concern for the Saint, construing it as concern for himself even though she could not know that.

He shrugged. "I dare not be so specific, but my investigation is progressing. I begin to understand the Saint quite well, in fact."

"Yet you still wish to put a stop to his work? You disappoint me, sir." Her eyes reproached him even more strongly than her words.

Noel wished, more than ever, that he could tell her the whole, not only about being the Saint, but about his suspicion that Mr. Richards was the traitorous spy he sought.

It was too soon, however. Too many pieces of the puzzle were yet missing. If he believed she was in any danger that would change things, but that seemed unlikely. She posed no threat to the Black Bishop, after all.

"Perhaps when you come to know me better, you will feel differently." It was all he dared to say, and it was not enough to erase the censure from her eyes.

He felt a strong desire to please her, to give her some tangible evidence of the feelings he finally admitted to himself. The perfect compliment, the perfect gift—

Her mother's jewels? He recalled how upset she had been Saturday night to see them upon Lady Mountheath's arrogant neck. Surely it would please her to have them back.

While he, Noel Paxton, could not approach Lady Mountheath about them without giving rise to dangerous speculation, the Saint was under no such constraint. The Saint worked anonymously.

And tonight, in keeping with his legendary *modus operandi*, the Saint would restore those jewels to their rightful owner.

Chapter 12

Rowena released Noel's arm as they reached the pond. He had that look again, the one he wore during chess matches—and this time she feared it boded ill for the Saint of Seven Dials. She had let his flattery distract her, even as he claimed she distracted him, but she saw now that they were as much at odds as ever on this one point.

"Do you know—or think you know—who the Saint really is?" she couldn't help asking, though she doubted he would tell her.

Nor did he. "See, here is the risk I spoke of. I find myself sorely tempted to tell you all I know, but that would be most unwise. Let us say that I suspect the Saint may reveal himself soon—perhaps to you as well."

Now *that* was an intriguing notion. But she saw from his expression that he would say no more on the subject. Had he meant it when he said she was lovely? No, she could not ask him that, either, without sounding both foolish and insecure.

"Will you be at the literary gathering Lady Hardwyck has planned for tonight?" she asked instead.

To her disappointment, he shook his head. "I am
otherwise engaged. It sounds like something you will
thoroughly enjoy, however. I daresay you will scarcely
miss me."

In truth, she was looking forward to this gathering
more than any other event Pearl had scheduled.

"Of course I will miss you," she replied automatically, then wondered if she should have been so honest. He said he admired her candor, but all too often it
was simple lack of forethought. Why could she not
treat conversation more like chess?

He smiled. "I must comfort myself with that, while
I conduct my dull, official business tonight." Pulling
out his pocket watch, he frowned. "I must go. I have
been here longer than I had planned."

Though he sounded genuinely regretful, Rowena
gathered what was left of her dignity. She did not wish
him—or anyone—to think she could not enjoy herself
without him. "Of course. It was pleasant to see you
again."

The glimmer in his hazel eyes told her he knew that
she had deliberately refrained from calling him by
name, thereby not committing herself to intimate—or
formal—appellation. "The pleasure was all mine,
Rowena."

To her surprise, he raised her hand to his lips, his
thumb stroking her wrist as he held it for a long moment. Unbidden, all of the feelings he had aroused in
her two nights before came flooding back—as he no
doubt intended.

"Until we meet again," he said softly, his eyes

probing hers, reading her emotions. Then he released her and turned away. As he had done Saturday night, he left her without a backward glance.

Rowena stifled a sigh, but not an unhappy one. This time, he had left her with an unmistakable promise to meet again—and to pursue their friendship, or whatever it was that was growing between them.

"Sir Nelson Riverstone? Are you sure?"

Noel had spent the afternoon and evening tracing Mr. Richards' movements over the past few weeks. That the man was fond of gaming and generally won did not surprise him. Discovering that Rowena's brother had lost heavily to him did, however.

"Aye, fair dipped he must be by now," said Willie, the proprietor of a popular gaming hell on Jermyn Street. He had acted as Noel's eyes and ears before— for a fee. "Last time they played, it was for double or nothing."

"And I take it Sir Nelson lost again."

The other man nodded. "Always loses, far as I can tell. Dunno why gents like that keep playing, though it keeps me in business. Must be a sickness, I'm thinking."

If Sir Nelson's luck was that bad, it seemed unlikely Richards was cheating him, as Noel had first hoped. Still—"Who else is deeply in debt to Mr. Richards?"

But Willie shrugged. "There was another government chap—Grant? Something like that. He lost a good bit of blunt, but was able to pay. Haven't seen him in here lately, though."

"Geraint?"

"Aye, that was it. Know him, do you?"

"I did." Roger Geraint was the agent who had been in London investigating the Black Bishop until his untimely death a few weeks since. It had appeared he had been murdered by footpads, but those at the Foreign Office suspected otherwise—and so did Noel.

"Richards suckers them in the usual way," Willie volunteered. "Loses a game or two, till they get cocky, then cleans 'em out."

Noel nodded. It was a familiar tactic. "You've been helpful, as always, Willie." He slipped the man a five-pound note.

"Always willing to do my part to keep London safe," he said, tucking the note into his breast pocket with a grin. "Just you let the chaps at Bow Street know how cooperative I've been—and that I run an honest house."

Noel clasped the man's grubby hand in his own. "Of course. May you have a profitable evening."

Walking back to his lodgings, he considered what he had learned today. It was little enough, really. Richards had lived in London for the past year or so, but where he had been before that, no one seemed to know. France was a possibility, of course, but he had no proof of that. That he could have been at Waterloo seemed unlikely, in any event.

Though he mingled with the intellectual set, he seemed to have formed no real friendships. His entrée to that circle was primarily by way of two treatises he had written last autumn on the Spencean ideal of the rights of the common man—the same treatises that had recommended him to Rowena Riverstone.

He appeared to have no family in Town, though Lord Peter Northrup had said something about his father having worked at Whitehall some years ago. Noel would have to follow up on that. Nor did he seem to have any noticeable means of support, beyond his skill at the card table.

Having supported himself in the same way for a time, Noel could not condemn the man for that. But he wondered now whether Richards' gaming concealed a darker purpose. Blackmail, perhaps? Geraint had been privy to all of the information the Foreign Office had accumulated about the Black Bishop, and Sir Nelson had access to data that might be useful to a traitor as well.

Geraint would have refused to tell him anything, which might explain Geraint's murder. But what of Sir Nelson? Rowena said her brother had sold those jewels, presumably to pay a gaming debt—to Richards? He remembered now the look Rowena had directed at Richards after divulging her secret.

He remembered also how agitated Sir Nelson had been that first night, at the ball. What was Richards demanding from him? He meant to find out.

Now, however, he had other business to attend to. A change of clothes, a bite to eat, and then a clandestine visit to the Mountheath house. The Saint of Seven Dials had an interesting evening ahead of him.

Rowena was enjoying herself even more than she had expected. Never before in her sheltered existence had she had such a wonderful opportunity to exchange views with so varied a group of well-read, intelligent people. It was an exhilarating experience.

At the moment, she found herself in animated conversation with Leigh Hunt, Robert Southey and Lord and Lady Holland, of the vaunted Holland House circle. Talk of poetry had given over to politics, Rowena's particular interest.

"Then you feel the Luddites were justified?" she asked Lady Holland. "I read Lord Byron's opinion on the subject some years ago, and thought them well reasoned, though I felt the weavers should have done more to prevent violence against persons."

"Violence will undermine any cause," said Southey, "though I know not all agree with me."

This sparked another lively discussion, to which Rowena listened avidly, occasionally offering an opinion of her own. Indeed, this was the very sort of thing she had hoped to find in London.

At one point, Lester Richards was mentioned, with Mr. Hunt expressing some surprise at his absence, "—for he generally shines in a milieu such as this," he said.

"He mentioned a personal engagement of some sort," Rowena offered. "And indeed, he did express his regrets."

Mr. Southey snorted. "One of his damned Spencean meetings, I'll warrant. Stirring up the very kind of violence we discussed earlier. Of course, like Byron, Richards believes I traded my principles for position when I became poet laureate. But with age comes perspective, leading, I believe, to reason."

"So you feel Mr. Richards has not yet attained that degree of perspective, or reason?" Rowena had noticed the constraint between the two men Saturday evening. This helped to explain it.

"He seems the sort who would go to any lengths to further his ends—legal or illegal, peaceful or violent,"

Mr. Southey said with a shrug. "I have come to believe that the end does not in all cases justify certain means."

Rowena nodded noncommittally, but she was then struck by a sudden thought. Might Mr. Richards' principles lead him even to theft for a good cause—as the Saint of Seven Dials? The more she considered it, the likelier it seemed.

Stealing Rowena's jewels was going to be harder than Noel had anticipated. The Mountheaths were dining at home tonight, with another couple he had identified as Lord and Lady Plumfield. Shouldn't all of these people have retired to their country estates by now? he wondered irritably as he watched the dining room from atop the garden wall, using a small spyglass.

Lady Mountheath was wearing the jewels in question: diamond earrings, necklace and brooch with emeralds interspersed. Which meant he wouldn't be able to act until the Plumfields left. He would watch to see where Lady Mountheath placed the jewels before going to bed—and pray it would not be in her own bedchamber. He settled himself more comfortably on the wall to wait.

Presently, the ladies went into the parlor while Lord Mountheath, Lord Plumfield and a young man Noel presumed was Plumfield's son remained in the dining room over brandy and cigars. He couldn't see the parlor from this vantage point, but that scarcely mattered.

Noel was considering leaving and coming back later when the gentlemen rose and left the dining room. He jumped from the wall, making little noise in his thin-soled shoes, though his toes stung at the impact. Cautiously, he circled around to the other side of the garden, where he might have a clear view of the parlor.

Applying his spyglass again, he watched the two Mountheath girls flirt shamelessly with young Plumfield while their parents discoursed on undoubtedly boring topics. Fairly adept at lip-reading, a skill he had developed during his Puss in Boots days, he identified such words as "drainage," "imports," and "sleeves."

Eventually, they ran out of conversation—or perhaps were as overcome by boredom as Noel was—and the Plumfields took their leave. Lord and Lady Mountheath appeared to have little to say to each other once they were gone, though Fanny and Lucy giggled together as they left the room—no doubt comparing notes on the young man.

Again Noel crept through the garden, trying to keep Lady Mountheath in his sights. The angle was wrong for viewing the upper floor, where the bedchambers would be—all he could see were ceilings. No one lingered below, however, which meant the jewels had likely not been put into a safe or strong box there.

He sighed, settling in for another tedious wait until at last all lights in the house were extinguished. Now, finally, he could make his move. All doors and windows were locked, of course, but that was small deterrent. Plying his lock picks, he soon had the back door open and was creeping up the stairs in search of his goal.

Reaching the upper hallway, he was able to identify Lord Mountheath's chamber by the loud snores resonating behind the door. The next one along was likely to be his wife's. Slowly, he turned the door handle, only to find it locked as well. What the devil did the woman fear in her own house?

With an inaudible sigh, he again pulled out his picks, and in a moment was able to push the door open. One hinge protested, and he froze, listening for any movement from the direction of the bed. None came, so he moved forward—only to see the bristling whiskers of Lord Mountheath, the lone figure in the bed.

Noel backed out of the room as softly as he had entered, closing the door behind him after oiling the offending hinge. Was Lady Mountheath the snorer, then?

He went back to the first door, unlocking it as he had the other. The resonant snoring and wheezing doubled in volume, nearly rattling his teeth from his head. The faint light from the window revealed a frilly nightcap on the occupant of the bed, however. He was in the right room.

Turning his attention to the dressing table, he silently examined the assorted boxes and jars cluttering its surface. Opening first one, then another, he reflected that he was unlikely to be heard over the fearful din of Lady Mountheath's snoring. No wonder her husband slept in a separate room.

He had gone through almost every receptacle and drawer and was regretfully coming to the conclusion that the jewels must be elsewhere, when his fingers contacted something cold and hard at the bottom of a box of ribbons. One by one he extracted a brooch, necklace and earrings. Success!

After verifying that these were indeed Rowena's jewels, Noel pocketed them, then hesitated. Should he—? He glanced over his shoulder at the raucous sleeper, then grinned. Quickly, he pulled a card from the pocket where he'd stowed the jewels, placed it beneath the ribbons, closed the box, and left.

Rowena stifled a yawn. Fascinating as the conversation had been all evening, she couldn't deny that she was beyond tired. As the last of the guests took their leave, a glance at the clock on the drawing room mantelpiece showed it to be past two.

"Goodness, do they always stay so late?" she asked Pearl once the door had closed on Lord and Lady Holland, the last to leave.

"Not always, but frequently. I thought you were beginning to get used to Town hours?" her friend chided her.

Rowena smiled, despite her weariness. "Beginning, yes, but I fear it will take time. Thank you for a most fascinating evening."

"I knew you would enjoy it. Now, don't you wish you had come to London long before? I told you how many interesting people you would meet here."

"Yes, of course you were right—aren't you always?" Rowena did not point out that she could scarcely have come on her own over her father's or brother's protests before coming into her inheritance. "Now, can't we please go up to bed?"

By the time Rowena reached her chamber, she was

half prepared to go to bed fully clothed, she was so tired. However, one look at Matthilda's frightened face roused her to alertness.

"What is it?" she asked, instantly concerned.

The maid held out a small, wrapped package with trembling hands. "Oh, miss! I only stepped out for a few moments—down to the kitchens to fetch hot water for your washing up—and when I came back, this was on your pillow."

Rowena took the package with a frown. "Did you ask Molly if she knew anything about it?" The chambermaid occasionally entered the room to change linens and dust.

"Yes, miss, it was the first thing I thought to do. She has no more idea than I how it came there. Do you think it was housebreakers?" Matthilda twisted her hands together.

"A housebreaker who leaves gifts instead of stealing? Unlikely, I should think. Well, let's see what it is, shall we?" Rowena proceeded to untie the jaunty bow and unwrap the parcel.

When her fingers touched something hard within, she felt a sudden prickling of foreboding. Quickly, she tore away the rest of the paper, only to gasp at what lay revealed. Her mother's jewels, all of them.

"How—? You are certain you saw no one, Matthilda?"

"No, miss, on my oath." She leaned forward to look at what Rowena held. "Oh! Were those not Lady Riverstone's?"

Rowena nodded, still staring at the diamond and emerald set in puzzlement.

"Likely you left them somewhere, and they was returned." Matthilda was clearly relieved, the mystery
solved in her mind.

But not in Rowena's. "Yes, I'm sure that was it.
Doubtless tomorrow we'll find out who left them."

She thought that unlikely, however. Whoever had
returned the jewels had either redeemed them or,
more likely, stolen them from Lady Mountheath.
Just now, though, she was too tired to puzzle out the
possibilities.

"We're clearly in no danger, in any event. Help me
get ready for bed, Matthilda."

It was as well Pearl had planned nothing before the
evening's musicale, for Rowena did not rise until well
past noon the next day. Almost the first thing she saw
upon waking were her mother's jewels, lying where
she had left them on her dressing table.

This was a mystery she was determined to solve—
but if the jewels *had* been stolen, she'd best keep them
hidden for now. She wrapped the jewels in a handker-
chief, tucked them in the back of the drawer of the
writing desk, then rang for her maid.

"You have just missed our first callers," Pearl
greeted her when she came downstairs half an hour
later. "Mr. Richards particularly asked for you, and
left these." She indicated a small but lovely arrangement of carnations and sweetpeas.

Rowena felt absurdly flattered. No gentleman had
ever sent her flowers before. "That was most kind of
him."

"He apologized for his absence last night, but said
that you would understand that some business is

more important than socializing." Pearl's expression was frankly curious, but Rowena could not answer her unspoken question.

"He did not tell me where he would be—" she began, then stopped, struck by a wild suspicion. The jewels—could that be what Mr. Richards had been doing last night? He had expressed regret for involving her in Nelson's debt to him. Was this his way of repaying her?

"Rowena?"

Shaking her head, she managed a smile. "I was trying to remember just what he said yesterday, but it was nothing to the point. I have no idea what business he meant. Perhaps he will explain later."

Pearl looked as though she meant to ask more questions, but just then another caller was announced—Noel Paxton.

"Good day, ladies," he said with a bow. Rowena could not help noticing how exceedingly handsome he looked in his well-cut riding coat and top boots. "I trust I find you both well."

"Quite well, thank you, Mr. Paxton," Pearl replied. "We missed you last night."

"Duty does not always allow me to follow the dictates of my . . . wishes," he replied with a glance at Rowena that made her pulse quicken. Had he almost said "heart"?

Pearl was clearly not oblivious to the unspoken exchange. Rising, she said, "I must go speak with the housekeeper for a moment. Pray excuse me, Mr. Paxton. I won't be long." With a sunny smile, she left the parlor, though of course she did not close the door behind her.

"How went your 'dull, official business?'"
Rowena asked, more for the sake of saying something
than because she wished to hear the details. He was
unlikely to give them to her anyway.

Nor did he. "Parts of it were dull indeed, but rewarding nonetheless. I hope your evening was more
interesting, and equally rewarding?" He moved to sit
across the tea table from her.

"Oh, quite." She proceeded to relate some of the
more fascinating discussions, watching his expression
as she mentioned one or two controversial points.
"Mr. Southey is more conservative than I had expected, but Mr. Hunt was all fire and enthusiasm."

"I can see I would have been entirely out of my element, then," he said with a smile. Then, with a stud-
ied casualness that Rowena found rather amusing, "I
presume Lester Richards made one of the company?"

"No, he was unable to attend." At the flash of satisfaction in his eyes, she could not help adding, "But
he sent those flowers by way of apology."

Noel frowned at the arrangement she indicated.
"Did he indeed?" He seemed to struggle with some
decision, then moved his chair closer to hers.
"Rowena, I hope you will not put too much trust in
Richards. I have reason to believe he may not be as he
appears."

So he *did* suspect Mr. Richards was the Saint.
Rowena felt some satisfaction that she had come to
the same conclusion on her own. "I imagine most
men are not quite what they seem," she replied.
Somehow, she must deflect Noel's suspicions.

He leaned forward, placing one hand over hers.
"Perhaps you are right. I wish—" He broke off

whatever he had been about to say, his gaze locked with hers. Slowly, he closed the short distance between them.

Rowena felt her heart thundering as his lips touched hers. Vainly, she tried to remind herself that she could not put her trust in this man, either—that he represented all she felt obliged to oppose. But her brain was rapidly giving way to her body and emotions, which pled Noel's case most forcefully.

For a blissful moment, she allowed sensation to take over, parting her lips to allow him to deepen the kiss. Their hands clasped between them, and again he stroked her wrist above her glove, sending spirals of delight up her arm and into her vitals. His kiss was tender rather than demanding, but still she felt an irresistible urge to give herself up to him, body, soul and mind.

"Rowena," he whispered against her lips, the vibration cascading through her body, making her very nipples taut. "I—"

Footsteps sounded in the hallway, and they abruptly broke apart. For a moment they stared at each other, Rowena noting with both satisfaction and alarm that his color was as heightened as hers must be. Then they both swung around to face the door with polite, social smiles.

"That is settled," Pearl declared as she entered. "I feared we would not be able to get enough fish for tonight's dinner, but Mrs. Potts assures me—" She broke off, her brows rising as she looked from Rowena to Noel and back. "You two haven't been arguing again, have you?"

Rowena felt her lips twitch and beside her, Noel's

cough sounded suspiciously like it had been converted from a laugh.

"Not about anything of importance," Rowena managed to say with a straight face. "Don't worry, Pearl. Both of us quite enjoy—arguing. Do we not, Mr. Paxton?"

"We do indeed," he asserted. "Now, what were you saying about the fish?"

Chapter 13

"Have you no leads at all?" Sir Nathaniel Conant, chief magistrate of the Bow Street Runners, ran a hand through his hair in evident frustration.

Noel looked the older man in the eye and shook his head. He hated to deceive Sir Nathaniel, but his true superiors were at the Foreign Office, and they had approved this course. No Saint of Seven Dials had ever killed or even harmed anyone, after all, while the Black Bishop was a genuine danger.

"As you know, I felt I had good evidence against Lord Hardwyck, but further investigation proved me wrong."

"Thank heaven for that, at least!" Sir Nathaniel exclaimed. "I don't like to think of the repercussions were we to attempt to arrest a peer of the realm on less than complete proof of guilt. But I'm under quite a lot of pressure now, what with this latest robbery at the Mountheath house."

Keeping his expression carefully neutral, Noel said, "It does seem strange that the Saint would target a household he had stolen from already. Has he ever hit the same place twice before?"

"No. And why it had to be Mountheath—! You can't imagine what it was like last spring, after the first theft from that house. Lady Mountheath sent a footman round every day—twice, some days—to ask about our progress. Had her husband stir up sentiment to launch a parliamentary investigation into our workings. I'm still dealing with the consequences of that."

Noel hadn't known the Mountheaths were behind that, but doubted he'd have acted differently if he had. Rowena deserved to have those jewels back, and Lady Mountheath deserved whatever came her way, as many young reputations as she had shredded over the years. Even his own sister Holly had not escaped the harridan's barbed tongue in the early days of her marriage.

"Perhaps that is why the Saint seems bent on harrassing the Mountheath household?" Noel suggested. "If he follows such things, he may fear that their interference will make his task harder."

"Damned foolish of him, if so," Sir Nathaniel declared. "This is only bound to redouble their efforts. Ah, well." He heaved a heavy sigh. "What comes, comes. Perhaps he's becoming careless and we can use that to finally rid London of the scoundrel."

Noel nodded. "Perhaps. I'll redouble my own efforts, sir, and report any progress."

"You do that, Paxton. And see you *do* have progress to report by the next time we meet."

Noel was still reflecting on his interview with Sir Nathaniel when he arrived at Hardwyck Hall that evening for the musicale. He'd been in some interesting situations over the course of his undercover career, but never had he been cast as his own quarry. While he couldn't deny the humor of his predicament, the moral implications were a bit bothersome.

If he could finally bring the Black Bishop to justice, however, it would all even out. More than one battle had been lost due to his duplicity, not to mention the men he'd had murdered or executed. As soon as he'd paid his respects to his hosts, Noel went in search of the one person he believed might help him to balance the scales.

"Ah, Miss Riverstone. You are lovely this evening, as always." And she was, arrayed in turquoise satin and pristine white lace. Surrounded as she was by other guests, he was forced to greet Rowena more formally than he'd have preferred.

Even so, her cheeks pinkened at his words. "Good evening, Mr. Paxton. I am pleased to see that your duties allowed you to attend."

"I made a particular effort to conclude my business early today."

"Music lover, are you, Paxton?" Harry Thatcher asked, coming up just then. "I seem to remember you saying so in Vienna. Charmed to see you again, Miss Riverstone."

She bobbed a quick curtsey. "The pleasure is mine, Mr. Thatcher. So you were at the Congress of Vienna as well? Perhaps you can tell me more about what it was like there than Mr. Paxton has been willing to do."

He bowed over her hand with the slow smile Noel

had seen him use all too effectively on other ladies. "It would be my extreme pleasure, Miss Riverstone. Would you care to retire to a private corner somewhere so that I may regale you with my stories?"

"I'm sure Miss Riverstone is too well versed in the proprieties to consent to being alone with you, Harry." Noel tried to keep the edge from his voice. "There's no reason you can't tell about what little you did there that is fit for a lady's ears in a more public forum."

The laughter in Harry's eyes showed that his flirtation had been designed to get just such a reaction from Noel. "I suppose you're right, Paxton—more's the pity. Do seek me out later, Miss Riverstone, won't you?" With a jaunty wink at Noel, he sauntered off.

"You do not approve of Mr. Thatcher?" Rowena asked, watching Harry disappear into the passage leading to the smoking room.

"Oh, he's an amiable enough rogue," Noel admitted, "but more used to dealing with high flyers and serving wenches than ladies of quality like yourself."

Rowena regarded him quizzically. "It's very touching that you feel obliged to protect me from various gentlemen, but I can't think it's necessary."

"I'm not—," he began, then realized that was precisely what he'd been doing, both yesterday afternoon with Mr. Richards and now with Harry. "I don't wish to see you hurt," he concluded, holding her gaze to prove his sincerity.

Her eyes widened at what she saw in his. "Oh." The word was almost a sigh.

Again, he was seized by a desire to take her in his arms, to prove with his lips, his body, just how strongly he felt. But of course that was impossible in this setting. In fact, Lady Marcus was approaching them just now.

"Rowena! Just the person I was looking for. You'll appreciate the humor in my latest blunder without making fun of me." She paused, glancing at Noel uncertainly.

He took the hint at once. "I believe I will visit the buffet tables before the entertainment begins. May I bring you ladies anything?"

They declined, and he moved away, scanning the room as he went. There was Richards, just entering. Noel was determined to keep a close eye on him, watch who he spoke to, how he conducted himself. Particularly around Rowena.

In fact, Richards was already heading her way, a certain intensity in his eyes that Noel found disturbing. Snatching up a canape to preserve his pretense of wanting food, he turned to follow his quarry at a discreet distance.

Deep in animated conversation with Lady Marcus, Rowena did not notice Richards until he spoke to her—perhaps because she was again without her spectacles. Though she smiled most pleasantly, Noel was pleased to note that her color did not change, as it had when she greeted himself.

Moving closer, Noel was able to hear snatches of their conversation.

"—my friend, Lady Marcus," Rowena was saying.

Richards bowed. "Charmed, my lady. Any friend of Miss Riverstone's must be worth cultivating, from my limited experience."

What might be the man's motive for ingratiating

himself with Rowena? If he were extorting her brother for information, as Noel suspected, perhaps he merely hoped to allay suspicion by also befriending the sister. Or did he perceive in her a kindred spirit who might be induced to help him in whatever seditious plans he was now formulating?

Either way, Noel felt duty bound to interfere.

"I believe the first performance will begin shortly," he said, rejoining the group. "We may wish to move into the gallery and take our seats."

Richards shot him a look of barely concealed dislike, quickly schooled to one of cool politeness before the ladies could note it. Lady Marcus excused herself to go in search of her husband, and the remaining three turned toward the archway leading to the gallery, where the first performance was to be held according to the programs Lady Hardwyck had provided.

They had taken only a step or two, however, before they were accosted by Miss Fanny Mountheath. "Miss Riverstone, how nice to see you again," she said with a falsely bright smile. "And you, too, Mr. Paxton. I trust you have all heard the news? My poor mother."

"Yes, I read of it in the afternoon papers," Rowena replied. "Is it certain that the Saint of Seven Dials was the culprit?"

"Oh, yes—he left one of his calling cards in my mother's very bedchamber! I declare, I shall be afraid to sleep for weeks now. It is most oversetting, as you can imagine. Mr. Paxton, perhaps you should call on us to allay my mother's—and my—fears." She batted her eyelashes at Noel.

Trapped, he forced a smile. "Certainly, if you feel it

would help. Remember, however, that the Saint has never yet harmed anyone, according to all I have been able to learn of his activities. You are doubtless quite safe from physical danger."

Clearly, this was not the level of sympathy she had hoped for. "You are the expert, of course," she said with an unattractive pout. "I do hope you will catch him soon, however. Oh, mother is beckoning to me. Good evening."

She hurried off and the trio resumed their progress toward the gallery. Rowena, to Noel's irritation, took Mr. Richards' arm rather than his own.

"I have reason to thank you, I believe," she said to Richards as they walked, in an undertone that Noel had to strain to hear. He managed to appear oblivious and disinterested, hiding his shock at what must surely be her meaning.

There was a pause, then Richards replied, "My goal was to please you, Miss Riverstone."

"You most definitely succeeded. And you may trust—" With the corner of his eye, Noel saw her looking over at him. "Thank you," she finished in a whisper, clearly not wishing to say more in Noel's hearing.

The long gallery, hung with dozens of portraits of Hardwyck ancestors, had been converted for the evening into a performance hall, with a small dais erected at one end and chairs placed for the convenience of listeners. Rowena selected a seat near the dais, and Richards and Noel sat on either side of her.

Noel was quite aware that Rowena wished to have a private word with Richards after their brief exchange, but he was determined to prevent it. Clearly, she had been referring to the return of her mother's jewels—the jewels he himself had procured for her, at great risk.

After their conversation this morning, it had occurred to him that she might interpret his warning against Richards as evidence that Noel suspected him as the Saint of Seven Dials—a result he had not considered at the time. It seemed he was right.

The music began, a haunting air by one of Europe's most accomplished flutists, but Noel scarcely heard it. He was overcome instead by the irony of his situation. Not only could he not claim credit for the favor he had done her, he must sit idly by while she showered his enemy with gratitude—a gratitude Richards was all too likely to exploit.

It was more imperative than ever that he not allow Rowena and Richards a moment alone, he realized. If he did, she would doubtless use that opportunity to warn Richards against him.

At best, Richards might inform her that he was not, in fact, the Saint. While Noel did not like giving Rowena one more reason to admire the man, her assumption did offer Noel himself extra protection from her perceptiveness. At worst, Richards might guess Noel's true intent, which could have disastrous consequences.

He would simply have to stick as close to Rowena Riverstone as her own corset.

And *that* intriguing image served to divert his mind for the remainder of the performance.

"What are you about tonight?" Rowena hissed as Noel accompanied her to the buffet tables between performances. "I am quite capable of filling a plate on my own, you know."

She realized she was being rude to him—again—but she was becoming concerned that she would never get a chance to arrange that most necessary chess match with Mr. Richards with Noel hovering this way.

"Of course," he replied, appearing not the least put off by her rudeness. "I simply enjoy your company, and the opportunity to be of use to you. The meat pies and the fruit tarts look remarkably similar, and I would not wish you to choose the wrong one by mistake."

He was referring, she knew, to her poor eyesight, but at least he did so subtly. Nor was the potential blunder he mentioned particularly unlikely.

"Very well, sir, if you insist," she said with a reluctant grin. "You may select a light repast for me—more fruit than meat, I think."

Mr. Richards had moved further down the table, making it impossible for her to broach the subject of the chess match just then. She wondered if he had reconsidered. After all, why should he risk losing what Nelson owed him for the chance at doubling an amount Nelson already could not pay? He might consider her assurances of payment worthless.

She moved in his direction, Noel close behind her as he filled two plates with select dainties. With sudden inspiration, she turned. "I believe I should like one of those . . . things . . . at the far end of the table," she said, pointing at an item she could not identify at that distance.

He looked. "A jug of cream?"

"No, next to that." She ignored his obvious amusement.

"Ah. The bowl of sugar lumps."

She glared at him. "Yes. The sugar lumps. I should like one."

Though his lips twitched, he went to do her bidding. Quickly, she moved forward to take advantage of the brief respite. "Mr. Richards," she said softly. "Are you still willing to allow me the rematch we discussed yesterday?"

He turned in evident surprise. "Of course, Miss Riverstone." Then, glancing behind her, "If you think you can shed your shadow for an hour."

Rowena was about to warn him about Noel's suspicions—fear that she might do so must explain his refusal to leave her alone with Mr. Richards—but it was already too late.

"Your plate, Miss Riverstone, complete with the sugar lump you requested," Noel said, rejoining her.

Earlier, when he had looked into her eyes while assuring her that he wished to keep her from harm, she had felt as strongly drawn to him as she had this afternoon in Pearl's drawing room. Now, as frustration warred with attraction, she thought how perverse it was that this particular man should have such an unsettling effect on her.

"Thank you, Mr. Paxton," she said, willing her color to remain neutral. "Mr. Richards and I were just discussing the possibility of another chess match later, when the guests disperse to hear some of the lesser performances."

There. If he would not leave her side, she would simply have to carry out her plans for the evening with him in attendance. He need not know about the stakes.

"Splendid. Much as I enjoy music, I enjoy watching skilled chess players matching wits more. And I imagine we shall still be able to hear some of the performances from whatever location we find for a table and board."

"Perhaps you would be so kind as to find Lady Hardwyck and ask her when and where we might play?" That would give her the chance she needed to warn Mr. Richards.

"No need. Here comes Lady Hardwyck now." If he knew what Rowena intended, he hid it admirably under a serene smile. "My lady, a word with you?"

At his behest, Pearl joined them. "There is no problem with the food, I hope? After the dust-up about the fish this morning—"

"No, no, everything is perfection," he assured her. "A credit to your organization and generosity. We were merely hoping you might do us a favor."

Unwilling to let Noel arrange everything, Rowena spoke up. "Mr. Richards and I were hoping to play a game of chess during the course of the evening, once the lead performers had concluded. Would it be terribly unsocial of us to do so?"

As she had feared, Pearl frowned. "Mr. Richards, you must know that this is Rowena's first visit to Town. You mustn't encourage her to act the hermit here, as she has done all her life in the country. I wish her to enjoy what Society has to offer."

"Oh, but—" Rowena began to protest, but Mr. Richards cut her off with a bow.

"Surely, Lady Hardwyck, it is possible for her to

enjoy both Society and her favorite pursuits? I had no mind to closet her away in a private room, I assure you. Merely some out-of-the-way corner, where we can still hear and see what is going forth."

Though she still shook her head at Rowena, Pearl smiled. "Of course I will not *forbid* it. I'll speak to one of the footmen and see that a board is set up. Would that alcove be acceptable?" She pointed to a recessed archway along the side of the ballroom.

"Thank you, Pearl. That would be perfect," Rowena said gratefully. Perhaps too gratefully, for Pearl shot her another keen glance.

"You are not finding so much activity upsetting after the quiet life you have led, are you, Rowena? My intent was to stimulate, not to overwhelm."

Suddenly self-conscious in front of these two gentlemen she wanted to impress, Rowena shook her head. "Not at all. I merely wished a chance to revenge myself for Mr. Richards' win the other night, and this seemed a good opportunity."

Pearl gave her a long look, which Rowena knew was an unspoken reminder that gentlemen preferred to win. This time, however, she could not oblige. Nelson's future was at stake. She met Pearl's gaze steadily and her friend gave it up with a slight shrug.

"Very well. But mind your competitive nature does not get you into trouble one day, dear."

Pearl left them to signal to a passing footman, and Rowena turned her attention to her well-filled plate, preferring not to comment upon Pearl's last remark.

Noel, however, seemed unwilling to let her ignore it. "I have never considered a competitive nature to be a flaw. Have you, Mr. Richards?"

"Certainly not in a man," Mr. Richards agreed. "However, it is far more—unusual—in a woman, and perhaps less useful for the role she typically fills in our society."

"Do you think so, sir?" asked Rowena. "In my few days in Society, I have noted many instances of competitiveness among women, though what they frequently compete for is attention and status, rather than victory in games or war."

"They compete for husbands, you mean—husbands that will provide them status, safety and respectability. Once married, however, they have little to strive for—which is no doubt as it should be."

"I must disagree," Noel said before Rowena could respond to this attack upon her sex. "Lady Hardwyck still works to better the lot of the poor and oppressed, nor is she the only married lady I can point to who continues to put her abilities to good use. My own sister—"

"Hardly typical examples," Mr. Richards pointed out. "Lady Hardwyck is wife to one of the richest men in England, while your sister, Lady Vandover, is in training to become Duchess of Wickburn one day. More is expected of women in such positions."

Rowena had been about to mention the accomplishments of women of lesser status, even commoners, who had set up orphanages and hospitals, but Mr. Richards' words sent such arguments out of her head. Noel Paxton's sister was to become a duchess? Why had he never mentioned such a thing to her?

She stared at him accusingly and he turned, as though feeling her eyes upon him. He gave her a rueful smile and a slight shrug before turning back to Mr.

Richards with examples of his own that showed women quite capable of accomplishing worthy goals, regardless of their positions in Society.

Gathering her wits, Rowena reentered the discussion, but she was torn. Lester Richards in person was proving rather different from what she had expected of the man she had idolized. He clearly held women in generally low regard, and then there was the matter of his gaming for high stakes and pressing Nelson for information from the Home Office, which seemed underhanded if not treasonous.

Was it possible she was wrong about him being the Saint of Seven Dials? But no, he had all but admitted it when she had thanked him for retrieving her jewels.

And then there was Noel Paxton, who derided views she held dear—including those she herself had expressed as MRR—and whose stated goal was to put an end to the noble Saint's career. Yet here he was championing the contributions of women, just as he had more than once shown admiration for her own abilities. Not to mention the sheer physical attractiveness of the man . . .

Was she really so shallow as to allow *that* to color her perceptions of the two? True, Noel Paxton fit the physical image of a hero better than Mr. Richards did, but one could never judge by appearances.

Could one?

"The next performance is beginning," she said to the two men, as much to distract herself from her disturbing ruminations as to quiet their argument, an argument that put her preconceptions about both at risk.

The singer and her accompanying pianist were both exquisitely skilled, and for a brief time Rowena was able to concentrate on the music rather than her jumbled emotions. At the conclusion of the performance, she excused herself to go to the ladies' withdrawing room, feeling strongly that she needed a respite from both gentlemen.

Once there, however, she discovered that the conversation of the ladies who had retreated to adjust the pins in their dresses or to avail themselves of the necessary was all about the Saint of Seven Dials and his latest daring exploit.

"—from her very bedchamber while she slept, can you imagine?" Miss Augusta Melks was saying.

"Had it been my bedchamber, I might have invited him to stay," responded Miss Stuckton with a giggle. "Oh, to discover who the Saint really is!"

Rowena left the room more disturbed than before. It occurred to her that she would never be able to wear her mother's jewels again—at least, not in public. To do so would be to advertise her connection to the Saint. Oh, this was becoming far too complicated!

Returning to her pair of self-appointed escorts, she noticed that the chess board she had requested had been placed in the alcove. Mr. Richards had noticed it as well, for he pointed it out the moment she rejoined them.

"Yes, let us play," she said at once.

Much as she had looked forward to this game, she was now only anxious to have it over. At least then she would have one less thing to worry about, and could perhaps devote her mind to untangling her conflicting emotions.

Chapter 14

Lester Richards carefully concealed his eagerness as he followed Miss Riverstone to the alcove where the chessboard had been set up for their match. A few inquiries had revealed that she did indeed have the means to make good on twice her brother's debt. One thousand pounds would be almost as useful to him as the information he had hoped to extract from Sir Nelson.

With that kind of money, he'd be able to buy the allegiance of a Home Office clerk lower in status but more willing to snoop. He'd also be able to ensure the privacy of his next meeting, as well as the critical one planned for next week—the one that should finally start the wheels turning for the downfall of England's damned aristocratic class.

For Lester Richards was a republican in the truest sense of the word. He had been fired with enthusiasm for the French Revolution as a lad of fourteen, when first hearing about it from his French mother, exiled by his autocratic father to chilly Cumberland. No excesses could be too great if they brought about the ideals of liberty and equality for all men.

Later, he had done his part to keep King Louis XVIII from the throne. Though he had failed at that, he was determined to bring about a new order here in his native England. At present, the radical Spenceans seemed his best means to achieving that end.

Therefore, he had insinuated himself into their midst until he became a leader of sorts, at the same time ferreting out and destroying all evidence—and men—that could link him to his former identity as the Black Bishop, one of Napoleon's staunchest, most useful supporters. For both enterprises, however, he needed information—and money.

"Shall I take white again?" Miss Riverstone asked when they reached the table.

"Of course," he said, moving to the side where the black pieces were arrayed.

Why the silly chit wanted a rematch, and for such enormous stakes, he had no idea. She seemed reasonably intelligent for a woman, so she must know she was incapable of besting him. Perhaps this was a way for her to contribute to his cause—a cause she seemed to approve—without publicly declaring her sympathy?

Whatever her reasons, he was more than willing to take her money.

Miss Riverstone took her chair, which that irritating legalist Paxton held out for her. The man had stuck to them both like glue all evening, and Richards did not believe admiration for Miss Riverstone was his sole reason.

One of his confederates had informed him earlier today that Paxton had been snooping about the gaming hells, asking questions about him. He had apparently been an acquaintance of Geraint's, the fellow Richards had had to dispatch when he grew too inquisitive. It appeared Paxton might have to follow his friend—a prospect Richards found not the least bit distasteful.

"I trust these surroundings are less distracting than those of the card party?" he asked as Miss Riverstone opened the game with her king's pawn.

"Yes, I believe I will be able to concentrate properly this time."

There was something almost smug in her expression, and he realized in sudden alarm that no one had witnessed their wager yesterday. Suppose, after losing, she planned to deny it had taken place? It was the only thing he could think of to account for her complacency, given his superiority as a player.

"Perhaps we should restate our terms, for the record," he said before making his first move. Paxton might be an enemy, but he was one of those honorable sorts and well regarded, which made him an adequate witness.

Miss Riverstone was clearly startled—and displeased. "Our terms?"

"Double or nothing for your brother's debt," he stated clearly, enjoying her anxious glance at Mr. Paxton. "He owes me nothing if you win, but one thousand pounds if you lose."

She glared at him, which must mean he had been right about her intention. "Yes, of course," she said stiffly. "It is your move, sir."

Paxton, he noted, looked interested but not particularly surprised at the stakes. If anything, he appeared amused. No doubt he would enjoy seeing the chit get her comeuppance after the merry chase she had led him all evening.

Richards moved his own king's pawn ahead two spaces and the game was underway.

Perhaps Miss Riverstone really had been distracted Saturday night, he thought several moves later. Certainly, she seemed far more competent this evening—or, perhaps, the stakes really did give her more focus. Not that it would matter, of course. He took one of her pawns with his white bishop.

She frowned, then murmured, "One moment." Opening her reticule, she pulled out a pair of spectacles and perched them on her nose. "Now, then."

Ah, so the lady was nearsighted, was she? No wonder she had played so inconsistently before. Still, he was not worried. The spectacles might give her confidence, but they could scarcely improve her strategy.

Miss Riverstone moved a knight, simultaneously threatening his queen and his white bishop, and it was his turn to frown.

Ten minutes later, Richards stared at the board in stunned silence. She had beaten him. The bespectacled bitch had beaten him—and in fewer than twenty moves!

"Checkmate," she said unnecessarily. "Mr. Paxton, you witnessed the terms of our wager. My brother's debt is now discharged. I thank you, Mr. Richards."

Disbelievingly, Richards raised his eyes to hers, to find her smiling—a smile he felt a violent urge to wipe from her face. He wanted to deny the terms, but it was too late. He himself had stupidly insisted on a witness, and now he was stuck for it.

"Yes, of course," he grated, pulling Sir Nelson's vouchers from his pocket. With an effort, he managed to refrain from flinging them in her face, instead depositing them in the center of the chessboard. "Here. You may inform him yourself. If you will excuse me?"

He stood, bowed, and strode quickly away, before his temper could betray him. How in hell could the chit have beaten him? She had played him for a fool, for it was clear she must have lost intentionally before. Never would he have believed a female brain capable of that level of play.

Obviously Miss Riverstone was a freak of nature, possessing a man's brain in a woman's body. Because of her, he had lost not only the money, but his only hold on her brother.

With a curt nod to his hosts, he retrieved his hat and coat and left Hardwyck Hall. Clearly, something would have to be done about Miss Riverstone. She was too clever by half, and no doubt deep in her brother's confidence, and perhaps Paxton's, as well.

It appeared Paxton was not the only person who would need to be eliminated to safeguard his plans.

"Well done," Noel declared the moment Richards was out of earshot. "Now don't tell me you didn't enjoy giving the fellow his comeuppance, apart from the money."

Rowena's smile was slightly sheepish. "I confess that his arrogance made it far easier to beat him with a clear conscience. But—I hadn't intended anyone else to know about my brother's poor judgment."

So that was why she had appeared so distressed when Richards called Noel to witness the wager. He had to laugh. "I suspect had Richards known how the match would fall out, he would have been perfectly happy to keep Sir Nelson's secret."

She stared at him. "Surely you do not believe he would have reneged on the wager?"

Noel shrugged. "I believe he was concerned that you might do so. It's the only conceivable reason for him to have made the terms public as he did."

Rowena's eyes narrowed in outrage. "How despicable! But you are only surmising, of course. We don't *know* that was his design."

"No, no, of course not." Noel reminded himself that Rowena had long been an admirer of Richards, however mistakenly. Her opinion would not be overthrown in an instant. "Do you feel up to another game?"

"Oh!" She glanced down at the board in surprise. "I hadn't really considered it, but I'm willing if you are."

"More than willing," he assured her with a warmth that made her color rise. Deftly, he reset the board, black toward himself. "This will make it easier for you to compare my play to Richards'," he explained with a grin.

She smiled back, having apparently regained her composure. "There *is* no comparison—you know that. Much as I might admire his opinions on social issues, yours is the superior mind." She colored slightly again, and Noel wondered what other comparisons she might be making.

Concealing a smile, he said, "I'm glad to hear you say so."

For a long moment she regarded him uncertainly, then moved a pawn to open the game. "It's been clear from the first that you do not care for Mr. Richards, and now I believe I understand the reason."

"Do you indeed?" He moved a pawn of his own. "Perhaps you will enlighten me, for I am having some difficulty narrowing my reasons down to only one."

She raised her chin to regard him squarely. "Now that you have undoubtedly realized my brother cannot possibly be the Saint of Seven Dials, you have turned your suspicions upon Mr. Richards. I assure you, however, that you are mistaken."

"Am I?" Noel asked, not bothering to hide his amusement. "How can you be so sure?"

"He, ah, told me where he was last night, and it had nothing to do with Lady Mountheath."

She was clearly lying, for Noel had made certain she had no opportunity for private conversation with Richards all evening. Was it really Richards himself she was trying to protect, or the Saint of Seven Dials?

"It is your move," he pointed out.

With an impatient frown, she looked at the board and moved another pawn, seemingly at random. "Well?" she challenged him.

"I don't find myself at an impasse just yet." He shot her a grin and brought a knight out onto the board, leaving her to wonder whether his words referred to the game or the Saint.

For half a dozen moves, they played in silence. Then, casually, Noel remarked, "My inquiries indicate that the jewelry stolen last night from Lady

Mountheath just happened to be that which you identified as your late mother's—and that nothing else was taken. Don't you find that intriguing?"

"Really? How . . . how curious." Though she tried for an air of surprised curiosity, her color betrayed her.

Noel managed not to smile. "I thought so. You'll let me know, of course, if those jewels should mysteriously turn up."

She swallowed. "Of—of course." Barely glancing at the board, she reached for her black bishop. Before she could touch it, however, Noel covered her hand with his own. Her eyes flew to his face in sudden alarm.

"It's my move," he said gently.

She snatched back her hand as though he had burned her. "My apologies. I am not usually so inattentive."

"Yes, I know. Not unless you are letting other gentlemen win, at any rate."

A reluctant smile tugged at her lips. "You are not going to let me live that down, are you?"

He shrugged. "I was never one for holding grudges." That was not quite true, he realized. He'd held one against the Black Bishop for years—but that was different.

"I'm happy to hear that," she said softly, almost wistfully.

Though her hand now rested on the table beside the board, he again covered it with his own. "We are not really on opposite sides, Rowena. I wish you would trust me."

This time she did not pull her hand away. "As you trust me?" she asked with a raised brow. "When did you mean to tell me that your sister was married to the heir to a dukedom?"

"I didn't think—that is, it never seemed something I could introduce into a conversation without sounding pompous. Why should it matter, anyway?" They both knew, though, that it did.

Instead of answering, she asked another question—a more difficult one. "Tell me, what evidence do you have against Mr. Richards?"

"I cannot do that," he replied, though in truth he wished he could. Surely, if she knew what atrocities the man had committed, she would never want to see Richards again.

"Because you do not trust me not to warn him?"

"Would you?" he asked, trying to read her expression. To his disappointment, she would not meet his eyes.

"Perhaps you are wise after all not to trust me," she confessed after a long pause. "It is still your move."

Frustrated that she had shut him out, and equally frustrated that he could not tell her the truth—all of the truth—Noel removed his hand from hers and turned his attention back to the game. Or, at least, he tried to.

Separated only by the small table, he found Rowena's nearness thoroughly intoxicating—the curve of her face, the shimmer of her hair, the smoothness of her skin, her faint, feminine scent. He thought back to the first night he had met her and found it incomprehensible that he had not known at once that she was unique, the missing piece of his own soul.

Wanting to hear her voice again, he finally broke

the silence with a topic sure to interest her. "The new *Political Register* is out today. Have you seen it?"

"I, ah, was able to glance at it this afternoon, though I have not read it thoroughly yet," she replied. "Mr. Cobbett's essay on the weavers was most interesting, I thought."

"Yes, most interesting," he agreed. But not disturbing, particularly—and Rowena suddenly seemed quite disturbed. "I was more taken by the anonymous Mr. R's latest offering, however," he said, watching her.

Her eyes were on the board, so he was still unable to divine her emotions. "Were you?" she asked with careful indifference, as she took his remaining bishop with a knight. "In what way?"

"I thought he pilloried the aristocratic class quite effectively, using both humor and truth to point up the hypocrisy one often sees at gatherings such as these. I believe it may be his best essay yet. Not, of course, that I agree with his premise that the lower classes are more honest."

"Do you not think so? I have never heard my maid, for example, speak in such a two-faced manner as some of the high-born ladies I have met since coming to Town."

He surveyed the board, carefully positioning a rook to defend his queen before replying. "Your maid no doubt has learned her values primarily from you, so that does not surprise me."

She blushed charmingly at the implied compliment. "You do not think her typical, then?"

"I imagine that I have had more opportunity than you have to observe the lower classes in their more depraved moments," he said. "Believe me, there is dishonesty enough to go around for all classes. If anything, the aristocracy is frequently constrained by Society's expectations from descending to true viciousness."

"That all depends on how one defines viciousness," she argued. "Not many dukes resort to highway robbery, I'll grant you, but is that not because they have no need to do so? Is it any less vicious to tax a man to the point of destitution than to take valuables from a wealthy man to supplement an inadequate income?"

Though she attracted him more than ever in her passionate defense of the downtrodden, her championing of this particular essay nettled him—particularly since he suspected she knew that Richards had written it.

"The former, at least, is less likely to result in loss of life or limb for either party." His voice was perhaps sharper than he had intended.

"So you do support theft by the government? That strikes me as the very height of hypocrisy." She made a sweeping movement with her hand to underscore her point, accidentally knocking a few pieces from the board to the floor. "Oh! I did not mean—"

Noel retrieved the pieces, but did not set them back in their places. "Neither of us seem to be playing at our best just now anyway. What say we postpone this match until another time?"

"Very well," she agreed with a rueful nod. But then she glanced up at him mischievously. "Do you also concede the point I was making?"

"You vixen," he said with a chuckle. "I concede neither the game nor the argument. I perceive, however, that most of the guests appear to have left. Perhaps we might continue the latter in more private surroundings?"

She regarded him uncertainly. "Private?"

"Nothing scandalous," he assured her, though his thoughts were definitely tending that way. "I had in mind the parlor." The parlor where he had stolen an extremely sweet kiss that afternoon.

That she also was remembering was evidenced by her agitation. "I—that is—do you not wish to return to your lodgings soon?"

He shook his head. "I am staying here again. I realized that where I am lodged makes little difference in how I carry out my investigation, so it seemed churlish to spurn the Hardwycks' hospitality."

In fact, Luke's expression had been far too knowing when Noel had requested his room back, using the same excuse. His true motive was to keep a closer eye on Rowena, to prevent Richards from somehow using her, and to prevent her from telling Richards too much. At least, he was fairly sure that was his true motive.

"Oh," she said faintly. "I see. Yes, I suppose we can repair to the parlor—but only briefly, as it is growing quite late." She nodded in the direction of a tall clock in the corner of the ballroom.

"I know I teased you earlier for leaving off your spectacles," Noel said, "but now I rather regret you wearing them, for now I cannot pretend it is earlier than it is."

"Why?" Rowena asked as they rose. "I mean, why do you tease me when I don't wear my spectacles?"

He took her hand and placed it on his arm so that

he could escort her to the parlor and was pleased when she did not resist. "Because I prefer you to wear them in public."

"Why?" she asked again. "Why should it matter to you?"

They moved out of the ballroom and down the passage to the parlor, which was still lit by numerous candles, though it was empty. Just inside the doorway, he stopped to look down at her, his expression serious.

"Because I don't want other men realizing how lovely you are, Rowena. I had hoped to keep that knowledge to myself."

Rowena stared up at him, her heart pounding in slow, heavy strokes. "Do you really think I'm pretty?" she asked, then immediately wished she could snatch the question back, lest he think she was fishing for compliments when it wasn't that at all.

"Don't sound so disbelieving," he chided her gently. "Your own glass must tell you that—assuming you can see it clearly enough." A wink took any insult from his words.

"But I recognized your beauty even before you turned yourself into a Society miss," he continued, to her amazement. "I rather enjoyed thinking I was the only one to perceive it, beneath your severe gowns and hairstyle—and your spectacles. But now it is revealed for all the world to see."

Rowena felt as though she would melt on the spot, but made an effort to rally herself. "You fear the competition, do you?" She forced herself to speak lightly, though she very much wanted to hear his answer.

"Craven as it sounds, I believe I do," he replied.

"The thought of you becoming as—friendly—with another man as you've been with me is almost unsupportable."

"It is?" The words escaped her like a sigh.

He nodded, gazing deep into her eyes, and then she was in his arms, as easily and naturally as though she belonged there. When his lips touched hers, she knew she had been waiting for this moment all evening— ever since their last kiss, in this very room. Rather than satisfy, his kisses seemed to create in her a hunger for more—and more.

His hands roamed up and down her back as he explored her mouth, her throat, her ears, with his lips. Incapable of thought, Rowena gave herself up to his caresses, reveling in the sensations he produced in her. Tentatively, she ran her fingers along his jaw, rough now with a day's growth of beard. Why that should excite her, she had no idea.

Finally, he lifted his head to gaze down at her again. "This wasn't supposed to happen, you know."

"Kissing me again?" She hadn't intended it either.

"Falling"—he cleared his throat—"under your spell. I've come to care very deeply for you, Rowena."

Her breath caught, and she stared up at him, unable to speak. Surely he hadn't been about to say—? But his eyes told her that he had. She felt something inside her unfolding, expanding, like a rose bursting into bloom from the sunshine of his regard.

Was this love? She rather suspected it was, though until this moment she had never quite believed in the romantic emotion. Should she tell him? If she said the words, would he? She found her courage not quite equal to that test.

Watching her face, his eyes suddenly grew guarded. "I'm sorry. I should not have—"

She interrupted him with a kiss, afraid to hear a retraction of what he had so nearly said, but almost equally afraid that he would speak more plainly. She felt as though they both teetered on the edge of a precipice, from which there would be no returning once the words were clearly spoken.

Though his lips made it all but impossible to think, she tried, while there was yet time, to remind herself of the differences that divided them. Noel still pursued the Saint of Seven Dials, something she could not possibly condone. Could she?

No, no, she mustn't do that, no matter how desperately she wanted to confess her own feelings, and to hear his in return. Before she could give her whole heart to him, she must somehow try to persuade him to her own views, convince him to give up the hunt. She could think of only one way to do so.

"Let's go upstairs," she whispered against his lips.

Chapter 15

A t first Noel felt sure he was hearing what he wanted to hear instead of what Rowena had really said, there was so much unspoken between them already. Surely, she couldn't mean—? But already she was urging him toward the door of the parlor.

As though in a dream, he went with her, his senses overwhelmed by her taste, her scent, the silky softness of her hair and skin. Taking him by the hand, she headed for the stairs and he followed, unable—or unwilling—to resist.

A murmur of voices warned them a moment before Lord and Lady Hardwyck appeared on the landing before them, having just bidden the last guests farewell. Rowena released Noel's hand and he followed her lead by focusing on his hosts rather than this girl who had quite definitely cast a spell over him, even if he had chosen those words to mask what he had nearly said instead.

"Another success, my lord, my lady," Noel said, his voice sounding odd and stilted to his own ears.

"I thought so," Lady Hardwyck agreed with a smile that showed no trace of suspicion.

Luke's glance, however, was more perceptive. "Ready to retire, are you? It is growing rather late. Your man should have your previous chamber ready for you, I should think."

"I'm more than ready for my own bed," Lady Hardwyck declared. "Come, let's all go upstairs. We can discuss the relative merits of the evening's performers tomorrow."

A glance at Rowena showed her clinging to a polite smile with evident effort, making Noel wonder if she was as frustrated by the interruption as he was. Surely, though, it was just as well?

Though he had all but declared his love, he had made her no offer—nor had she indicated that she expected one. In fact, he recalled, now that the capacity for thought was returning, she had not mentioned her own feelings at all—not in words, anyway. He had no doubt read far too much into her seeming invitation. It would be madness to assume otherwise.

Madness seemed to be the order of the evening, however. As they reached the upper hallway and bid each other good night, Rowena held his glance while he bent over her extended hand, and mouthed the words, "Later. Join me."

Noel nodded slightly, then turned to bid his hosts good night, assuring himself that they had not witnessed the silent exchange. Rowena entered her chamber, then Noel entered his, while Lord and Lady

Hardwyck proceeded to their corner suite at the end.

Kemp awaited him, of course. "Would you care for a brandy before bed, sir?" he asked as he helped Noel out of his tailored coat.

Noel's only desire was to have the chamber to himself, so that he could think things through. Rowena knew who Mr. R was, of that he was certain. If he went to her now, could he persuade her to share that knowledge with him? Or was that a despicable motive for something he very much wanted to do anyway?

"No, thank you, Kemp. I'll sleep well enough without any brandy tonight, I believe."

The manservant bowed and left Noel to snort at his own words. Whatever he decided to do now, he would not be sleeping anytime soon, of that he was certain.

"That will do, Matthilda. Thank you." Rowena had never been so nervous in her life. But whether she was more terrified that Noel would come to her chamber before she could rid herself of her maid, or that he would not come at all, she could not say.

His nod had implied that he would come—hadn't it? Would he reconsider, now that he was away from her "distracting" influence? She found it hard to believe she could have such an effect on a man of Noel Paxton's intellect and resolve, but his actions and words seemed to prove that she did.

Matthilda was still puttering about the room, hanging Rowena's gown in the clothespress, tidying the dressing table and turning down the oil lamp on the bedside table. Rowena's agitation increased to unbearable levels.

"I said that would do," she said, more sharply than she intended. "Good night, Matthilda."

The maid sent her a startled glance but asked no questions, merely bobbing a curtsey. "Good night, miss. Sleep well."

Rowena knew there was little chance of that.

She listened as Matthilda's light footsteps receded down the hall toward the servants' stairs. And kept listening, for any other sound in the hallway. Would he come? Could she really go through with her outrageous plan if he did?

As the silence lengthened, she began to relax. Of course he would not come. Noel Paxton was a gentleman, with a high regard for the law and the proprieties. And she was a lady, who had no business attempting a seduction, not even for the noble purpose of keeping the Saint of Seven Dials safe from the law.

That *was* her purpose, wasn't it?

Not that it mattered now, anyway. She had no doubt read too much into what Noel had almost said—or what she *thought* he had almost said. With a sigh of mingled disappointment and relief, she turned toward her bed, then froze. Was that a step in the hall? No, she was imagining things. But then came another sound, a soft scratching at her chamber door.

Her heart pounding frantically, Rowena moved to open it. Noel stood there, more handsome than she'd ever seen him, wearing only shirt and breeches, his collar open to reveal a disturbing triangle of throat and chest. His curly hair was disordered and damp, as though he had already washed for bed. For a moment she thought she might swoon, then chided herself for such foolishness.

"I—I hoped you would come," she whispered, standing aside to let him enter. She needed to maintain complete control of her emotions if she was to put this opportunity to proper use.

He stepped past her, softly closing the door behind him without taking his eyes from her face. "I nearly convinced myself I had imagined—or at least misunderstood—your invitation." His voice held a question.

"No, you did not misunderstand," she said, hoping he would not notice the trembling that had begun in her midsection and now spread to her extremities. She wanted to ask a similar question of her own, but feared her voice might fail her—and feared his answer, as well. Instead, she smiled what she hoped was a seductive smile.

His gaze dropped to her lips, then returned to her eyes. He took a step nearer and she could feel the warmth emanating from his body, though he did not touch her.

"Are you certain that *you* understand what you are asking?"

She wasn't certain of that at all, but she nodded firmly. "Of course. I am . . . very well read, you know."

One corner of his mouth quirked up in a half-smile that sent odd sensations through her chest. "I'm aware of that. But there are some things one really cannot learn from books."

He was giving her a chance to reconsider and, cravenly, she was tempted to take it. For all of her studies of political intrigue, she actually knew very little of what went on between a man and a woman. For the first time, she regretted that she had not included romantic novels in her extensive reading.

"Then it is time I supplemented theory with practical application, is it not?" she forced herself to say, lifting her chin to look him full in the eyes—eyes that had darkened from hazel to dusky brown.

"Ever the academic," he murmured, moving even closer, until the fabric of his fine lawn shirt brushed against the thin cotton of her summer nightrail.

She tilted her face up for his kiss and he obliged her, his warm, firm lips taking possession of her own. His arms went around her, and her trembling subsided, to be replaced by a swirling need for something she could not define. Her noble plan forgotten, she clutched at him, pulling him closer, wanting more contact, more of . . . everything.

Noel's low, throaty growl inflamed her further with the evidence that he desired her as much as she desired him. He deepened the kiss, stroking her tongue with a rhythm that pushed her need to new levels. She heard another growl, and realized with a start that it had come from her own throat.

Pressing the length of her body against his, she reveled in the hardness of his chest, the strength of his arms around her—and in his insistent maleness, straining against his breeches, against her belly, proving just how much he wanted her.

Her body clamored for more, but she had no idea how to satisfy that longing. What should she do next?

He did it for her. Still kissing her deeply, he slid one hand to her shoulder, then her throat, deftly untying the ribbon that closed the neck of her nightgown. His lips followed his fingers, trailing kisses from her mouth to her shoulder, then to the hollow at the base of her throat, even as he undid the next fastening of her gown.

Swallowing convulsively, Rowena tilted her head back, giving him free rein to do what he would. Never had she imagined the sensations that swirled through her at his touch, and now she could imagine nothing worse than a cessation of his exquisite attentions.

Dimly, in the back of that tiny part of her brain that still clung to the capacity for thought, she remembered that she was supposed to be doing the seducing. Her hands clutched at his shoulders to keep her upright, but now she let go with one hand to fumble with the fastenings of his shirt. The angle was quite different from undoing her own buttons. That and the sweet distraction of his fingers against her flesh made her clumsy.

"I rather like this shirt," he said against her ear, a hint of a chuckle in his voice. "Let me help you, before my buttons are scattered about the room."

She knew she should be embarrassed, but somehow she was not. She was only anxious to proceed, to feel more of him against more of her. Judging by the speed at which he undid his buttons, he shared her eagerness. They embraced again, this time with much of her upper body exposed to his now bare chest, his shirt hanging completely open.

Though her breasts were still covered by thin cotton, the space above and between them was not, and the soft roughness of the hair on his chest stimulated her sensitive flesh to new heights of desire.

She could not bare more of herself to him without breaking contact, however. Her nightrail opened only to breast level. To remove it, she would have to take it over her head—an irrevocable step. Did she dare? Could she not?

Noel's hands were at her back now, massaging her spine between her shoulder blades, at her waist, lower. Sliding her own hands up to his shoulders again, she pushed his open shirt back, revealing more of his chest. He took his hands from her for an instant, but even that brief loss of contact made her whimper.

"Sshh," he whispered against her lips. Quickly, he shrugged out of his shirt, letting it fall to a heap on the floor, then his arms were around her again.

Now her hands had free access to the whole of his upper torso, and she made good use of that freedom, exploring his sides, his chest, the firm planes of his back, where she felt faint ridges that might be scars. His body was so different from her own, so beautifully *male*. She wanted to know it better.

Meanwhile, his hands were doing their own exploring, through the fabric of her nightrail. They spanned her narrow waist, then slid lower to cup her bottom and pull her tighter against him. He bunched up the thin cotton, and she could feel the hem moving up her calves, then her thighs.

In a moment he had it about her waist, and she was acutely aware that she had nothing beneath it, that nothing now stood between her lower body and his hands, his eyes. Her own eyes were tightly closed, but when he gently broke their kiss, she opened them to find him gazing earnestly at her.

"May I?" he asked softly.

She knew he was asking her permission to divest

her completely of her nightrail—to remove her last shred of defense against his touch. She nodded silently, not trusting her voice.

With a swift, fluid movement, he lifted the sheer fabric up and over her head, tossing it behind her. Then, gently clasping her shoulders, he smiled. "You are even more beautiful than I imagined."

Beautiful. No one, not even her mother, had ever called her beautiful before. But he seemed to mean it, his eyes admiring, even reverent. Still, Rowena had to fight an urge to cover herself, to shield her body from his eyes. Though she hadn't summoned it, sanity began to return. What was she doing?

Oh, yes. She was going to convince him to leave the Saint alone. Then she could be done with intrigue, admit her feelings for him, be his in every possible way. Was this the right time to ask? If she allowed him to take her, to compromise her, would it be too late? But what if she spoke too soon? Her desire to do nothing to stop him warred with her weakening resolve to appease her conscience.

He leaned forward to kiss her again, one hand coming up to cup her breast, and thought left her again, replaced by pure sensation. Again, she clutched at his shoulders, his back, pulling him against her so that her breasts rubbed against the firm roughness of his chest. It was an exquisite feeling.

Taking a step backward without releasing her hold on him, she guided him toward the bed. She had no idea what she would do once they reached it, but trusted that he would. A tendril of fear snaked through her—fear of the unknown—but she ignored it. She craved, and she must be satisfied.

He resisted her, however. "Rowena, you must be very sure," he murmured. "In a moment, I fear I won't be able to stop myself."

"I'm sure," she said, but then glanced up, into his burning eyes. Surely, his desire for her was at fever pitch now, as hers was for him. She *must* take this chance. "First, though," she forced herself to say, "won't you please promise me that you'll give up your investigation of the Saint of Seven Dials?"

Noel felt as though she had dashed cold water on him, chilling the blaze that had been consuming him an instant before.

"Is that what this is about?" he demanded, sick disappointment coiling in his stomach. "You are willing to—to trade yourself for my promise?" He wasn't sure whether he was angrier at her or himself. Certainly, he had known better than to come here.

Her gray eyes flew open, revealing dismay, fear, and desire. It was the desire that almost undid him again, but he made himself hold her at arm's length, trying to ignore the way her nude body enticed his own.

"No! That is, I hoped that . . . that if you cared for me, you might be willing to change your mind. To . . . to please me." She made a motion as though to cover her nakedness, and he released her.

Her words only confirmed his accusation. "Perhaps you would consider another sort of trade," he said, his ego still smarting. "Tell me who Mr. R is, and I'll consider leaving off my pursuit of the Saint."

She stared at him for a long moment, then knelt quickly to retrieve her nightrail and clutch it to her chest, concealing her charms. Though that should have made it easier to bring his desire for her under control, it did not.

"You—you say that very glibly," she finally said. "Was that *your* design in coming here, to get that information from me? Not that I know the answer, of course."

He hesitated, for that *had* been the reason he'd used to justify his presence here—though he knew it was not the real one. At his hesitation, as good as a confession, hurt flared in her eyes. Hurt, followed almost immediately by anger.

"So, you meant to use me—to seduce me for information? Is that why you said . . . what you did, downstairs?" The glitter in her eyes was more than anger. She was dangerously close to tears, and Noel was not sure what he would do if she cried.

"No! I meant—that is—" Why was he on the defensive? He should be doubly glad now that he had stopped short of a declaration. "You are a fine one to talk. It appears that neither of us had completely pure motives for this . . . rendezvous."

"Pure—!" She whirled from him, affording him an excellent view of her shapely bottom before she moved behind a chair. Hastily, clumsily, she pulled her nightrail back on, then folded her arms across her breasts as she faced him again.

For a long moment she stared at him across the dim room, as though trying to decipher his thoughts from his expression. He doubted she would have much success, as he could not decipher them himself. Regret, anger, guilt—and a substantial amount of lingering desire—warred within him.

"I . . . I thought—" she began, one hand fluttering free to reach tentatively in his direction.

"Yes, so did I," he responded. "Perhaps we were both mistaken. In any event, I must apologize, for I had no business coming here in the first place, whatever my motives. You are an innocent, but I am wise in the ways of the world. Just as well we stopped when we did."

Rowena swallowed visibly, her eyes so bereft that he longed to comfort her. But he dared not move closer, knowing how strongly she affected him, how easily he could lose his hard-won control.

"Do you really think so?" she whispered.

She really was an innocent. "Had we not, you would have found yourself bound to me for life, willing or no," he explained. "Is that what you would have wanted?"

She looked away, and even in the dim light of the oil lamp he could see her cheeks darken. "I would not have expected you to marry me, of course. I can't imagine that we would suit, as different as our views are."

"Had we finished what we began, I would have married you, nonetheless," he told her, knowing it was true—and now regretting that they had stopped for a whole new reason. "I would not have been able to live with myself otherwise. In fact, I should offer for you even now, considering how far things have gone."

"You needn't worry for my reputation," she said, still not meeting his eye. "No one knows you are here, so it is in no danger. And even if it were, I could simply return to River Chase. You are under no . . . obligation to me, sir."

The "sir" chilled him, but he could in honor do

nothing now but leave. She had made her feelings clear. "Very well, Rowena, I will not press you. But we must be very discreet, to be certain no hint of this becomes known."

"I think that will not be difficult."

Perhaps it would not be difficult for her—though he would swear she had desired him nearly as much as he had desired her just a few minutes earlier. Clearly, though, however passionate she might be, her heart was not touched.

"No. No, I suppose not. Good night, Rowena." He waited for a moment, hoping she would look at him, that he might divine something of what she felt. When she did not, he scooped up his shirt and left the chamber.

Rowena remained where she was, one hand tightly gripping the chair back for support, until his steps receded down the hall. Then she collapsed into the chair, buried her face in her hands and sobbed.

Waking late the next morning after only a few hours' fitful sleep, Rowena took breakfast in her room. She could not bear to see Noel across the dining room table downstairs. In fact, she was not sure she could ever bear to face him again. What a horrible mess she had made of everything last night!

She should never have invited Noel to her room, she realized that now. Her plan to convince him to leave the Saint alone had been merely an excuse, a salve to her conscience. The truth was, she had wanted his kisses, his touch, and more—something she would never have now. If she had only remained quiet . . .

But no. Then she would be ruined, and by Noel's own admission would have essentially trapped him into a marriage he had never actually said he wanted. Nor did she want it herself—did she?

Of course she didn't. Neither of them would be happy. She was too independent and he was too rigid. It would never work.

Tonight was to be another ball, but she intended to stay in her room, perhaps pleading illness. Certainly, she was mortally tired. She was just considering returning to bed when a tap on the door heralded the appearance of Pearl herself, who appeared depressingly cheerful and fresh to Rowena's scratchy eyes.

"Here you are, sleepyhead," she cried. "There are callers below already, and more than one has asked specifically for you—and you not even dressed to go down yet."

"I . . . did not sleep well," Rowena responded with perfect truth. "Perhaps you can make my apologies?"

Pearl regarded her closely—so closely that she was sure her friend would somehow divine what she had done—no, nearly done—last night. But Pearl only said, "You do look rather pulled. However, I have just the thing to cheer you. Wait here."

She hurried out, and returned a moment later with a small parcel. "It arrived less than an hour ago. I was worried it would not be here in time for tonight's ball, as it was to have been delivered yesterday." As she spoke, she pulled away the paper, then held up the most exquisite reticule Rowena had ever seen.

"Why, it is in the shape of a book," she exclaimed.

"Yes. I thought of you at once when I saw it at Mellon's on Friday. I'd hoped to give it to you for that ball, but the last one had been sold. But see? The colors match the dress you plan to wear tonight, so this is even better."

Indeed, the diminutive book-shaped purse was the same blue as Rowena's new ballgown. Charmed, she opened and closed it, smiling her thanks at Pearl. "It's perfect," she said, realizing that there could be no question of crying off attending tonight's affair now.

"There, did I not say it would cheer you up? Get dressed, do, and come downstairs. I must hurry back myself, as more callers will doubtless have arrived by now."

Pearl rushed off, leaving Rowena to toy with her gift. Interesting that Pearl should want her to carry this, when she had earlier tried to disguise Rowena's bookishness. Not that it had done much good, of course. She knew full well that by now she had been branded a bluestocking by nearly everyone who had met her.

And so what if she was? If Noel had done nothing else for her, he had shown her how much happier she could be when she was herself—playing chess, arguing politics . . . kissing him.

No! That part was not her. It couldn't be. Studious Rowena Riverstone, a wanton? Absurd. It was simply an error in judgment, nothing more.

But he *had* praised her latest essay—even if he had no idea she had written it. She picked up the *Political Register*, which she'd had Matthilda bring up with her breakfast tray, though the meal was still untouched.

Noel had said this was MRR's best essay yet, she remembered with a reluctant smile. Reading over it, she had to agree. She must work harder in future to convey her own opinions, as they could clearly hold their own against those of the other contributors, learned men all.

Turning the page, her eye fell on a small, boxed notice at the bottom that she had not noticed in yesterday's quick perusal.

To MRR: The PR has 16 letters to forward. Please advise where we may send or deposit them for your convenient retrieval.—WC

Rowena frowned. Sixteen letters, for her? It had never occurred to her that people might write to MRR—though it should have, since she had written to Mr. Richards after reading his treatise. Sixteen letters! What might they say? And how could she obtain them without disclosing her identity?

She read the notice again. *Send or deposit.* Presumably she could choose a location, they could leave the letters there, and she could retrieve them later, with no one the wiser. But what location?

Green Park was just across Picadilly from Hardwyck Hall. She recalled a large, lichen-covered rock near the entrance, with a small stand of trees nearby. Perhaps the letters could be left behind that rock? They would be at the mercy of the elements, but the weather was fine just now. If she retrieved them soon after they were left, they should not be damaged.

Her decision made, she went to the writing desk for paper and pen and wrote a quick letter requesting that the letters be deposited by that rock by noon tomorrow. She folded it, addressed it as she did her essays, then rang for Matthilda.

"Help me into the yellow round dress, please," she said when the maid appeared. "It's time I went downstairs."

Once she was dressed, she picked up the letter she'd just written and handed it to Matthilda. "Post this for me as soon as possible. Do as you did Monday—tell no one what you are doing, and return as quickly as possible."

"Yes, miss." Though Matthilda looked curious, just as she had on Monday, she asked no questions. She took the letter and left.

That brief flurry of excitement over, Rowena returned to her earlier brooding, but found she did not feel so hopeless as she had before. The thought of those letters and what might be in them lifted her spirits somewhat. Perhaps it was even possible that she and Noel could come to some sort of understanding.

Still, the idea of facing him after last night made her flush with anticipated embarrassment. What could she possibly say to him? What might he say to her? Aside from the way they had parted, he had seen her *naked*.

Before leaving the room, she donned her spectacles. Pearl should not mind, since her gift underscored her bookishness. Besides, being unable to see clearly made her feel vulnerable, and she already felt quite vulnerable enough.

Chapter 16

Lester Richards summoned a smile for Miss River-stone when she entered the parlor. Last night he had let his temper get the better of his judgment, but once it cooled he realized that he could still make use of the girl, oddity that she was.

She was already sympathetic to the Spencean cause. With some flattery, she might be induced to get the information he needed from her brother. Or, he might convince her to give him specifics on Paxton's movements and motives, should she discover them.

For either purpose, he needed her trust.

"Miss Riverstone," he exclaimed, rising as she entered. "You look particularly lovely today." She did not, of course, wearing those damned spectacles again, not to mention the freckles marring her face. "I hope you will forgive my churlishness last night."

As he'd hoped, she moved at once to sit by him, ignoring Paxton, who had also risen at her entrance.

"Thank you, Mr. Richards. But I thought you remarkably polite, given the circumstances."

He must have hid his anger better than he'd realized. Habit was a useful thing, he reflected.

"I am relieved to hear it," he said with perfect truth. "Dare I hope you will allow me a dance this evening, in that case?" A plain, bookish sort like Miss Riverstone should be absurdly easy to charm.

"Certainly," she responded with a smile.

Lady Hardwyck then called her attention to the other callers, including that insufferable pup Galloway who persisted in pursuing her. When she finally met Paxton's eye, Richards noticed that her color rose and that she quickly glanced away. Paxton seemed similarly affected, though he concealed it better.

So the wind lay that way, did it? So much the better. It would make the chit excellent bait to lure Paxton to his doom, once Richards had what he needed from her. Then, he could rid himself of two problems with one stroke.

Noel kept his expression rigidly neutral. He would have avoided this encounter entirely if he did not feel an obligation to keep both Richards and Rowena under observation. Facing enemy fire would have been preferable, however.

He had watched as Rowena accepted compliments from Richards, fighting down a ridiculous urge to call the man out on the spot. Not only had he said nothing to reasonably provoke such a response, but any openly hostile action toward Richards on his part would certainly endanger his mission.

He could not see Rowena again without remembering—all too vividly!—how she had felt in his arms last night, how lovely she looked unclothed. It was all he could do to disguise his physical reaction to that memory.

When she spoke with Galloway and his cousin, it did not cause Noel the same pang of jealousy—probably because she had not been protecting either of them when she pretended to want him last night. If she had been pretending. Surely such an innocent could not counterfeit her body's responses so convincingly?

When she finally turned toward Noel, her reluctance was obvious. "Mr. Paxton." She coolly inclined her head, though her heightened color revealed her disquiet.

"Miss Riverstone," he responded just as coolly. When he tried to hold her gaze she flinched away, turning back to Richards at her side.

Damn him.

He did not, of course, believe that Rowena had any *romantic* inclinations toward Richards. She simply admired his mind—and, if he was who Noel thought he was, he was certainly crafty enough. Soon, he hoped to have the necessary proof . . .

Smiling fixedly at Lady Hardwyck as she chatted with the others, Noel felt sudden doubt. Was it possible that he was blinding himself to evidence that might point to other suspects simply because he so badly wanted Richards to be a villain? Surely not. Surely he was more objective, more professional, than that.

Now, however, he wondered. Rowena Riverstone clouded his thinking. She had done so almost from the first evening he met her. What if he were now pursing phantasms because of it?

All he had on Richards so far was an unusual turn of phrase and the circumstantial evidence of his gaming with certain men. Suppose his trap for the essayist did not work? He would be no further ahead than he was now. He needed more.

It was sheer torture pretending interest in the chatter around him as he waited for Richards to take his leave. When he finally did, Noel waited only a moment or two before rising himself.

"Pray excuse me, Lady Hardwyck," he said, resolutely refusing to glance Rowena's way. "I have business to attend."

"Of course," his hostess responded. She cast a curious look at Rowena, but Noel would not follow her gaze. "We will see you tonight, then."

He bowed his assent and headed up to his chamber to retrieve his hat and inform Kemp of his plans. There was one person who must have information on Richards' whereabouts during the war, solidifying his case against the man—or destroying it. He would discover where Richards' father might be and arrange an interview.

Rowena was finding this ball to be a vastly different experience from her first, the week before. This time she knew well over half of the attendees—and could recognize them, as she was wearing her spectacles.

Pearl had frowned when she'd come down for dinner with her eyeglasses on, but then had shrugged. "I suppose you've made most of the first impressions

you're likely to by now, and I couldn't very well expect you to go about half-blind indefinitely. You've
been a good sport, Rowena."

"Could I do less, after all you've done for me?" she
had responded.

At the moment, however, Rowena wondered
whether introducing her to Noel Paxton counterbal-
anced all the good Pearl had done. Judging by the
wretched feeling in the pit of her stomach when he entered the ballroom, she thought perhaps it did.

Meeting his eyes across the room for only the
briefest instant brought all the wanton feelings from
last night flooding back, just as seeing him in the parlor this afternoon had done. Now, though she refused
to look his way again, her whole being was focused on
Noel, half a room away. She felt his eyes upon her like
a physical caress—or was she only imagining that?

Her dance card was nearly full, but she had left the
waltzes open, using the excuse that she was yet too
unskilled at that dance. She knew, however, that she
was secretly hoping Noel might claim those dances as
he had before.

"Good evening, Rowena," Lady Marcus greeted
her just then, giving her a welcome excuse to turn her
back to Noel, who was moving slowly in her direction. "Are those spectacles new? They're really quite
becoming."

Rowena had to laugh at Quinn's diplomacy.
"Thank you, but no. I've worn them most of my life,
and only left them off earlier at Pearl's insistence. It's
much nicer to be able to see, however."

"My, that was courageous of you, I must say. I
imagine it was rather distressing not to be able to see

things clearly, especially with so many strangers about."

"Yes, it was, rather. But a novel experience nonetheless. If nothing else, it forced me to give my full attention to whoever I happened to be speaking with, as I could not recognize anyone more than a few paces away."

Now, however, she could see people all too clearly—including Noel, who had just moved past them to exchange greetings with her brother. Rowena's heart did an odd little flip at the sight of his handsome profile.

Quinn was chuckling. "That explains why the gentlemen were all so taken with you. They love nothing more than a woman who will give them her undivided attention, I have noticed."

"A lesson I will try to remember," Rowena said lightly. "I see my brother over there. If you will excuse me, I need to speak with him before the dancing begins."

By the time she reached Nelson, Noel had moved on, to her relief—and disappointment. "There you are, Ro. Any progress?" Nelson greeted her eagerly.

Hastily, she pulled her attention back to her brother. Noel's movements were nothing to her, after all.

"Yes indeed. Substantial progress," she replied. "You are no longer in debt to Mr. Richards." She pulled his vouchers from her book-shaped reticule and handed them to him.

He took them, his mouth dropping open in surprise. "How the devil did you persuade him?" His eyes widened in alarm. "You didn't do anything—improper, did you, Ro? I told you Richards is a crack shot. I'd as soon not be obliged to call him out to defend your honor."

Rowena choked on a laugh that was almost a sob, remembering just how improper she'd been—though not with Lester Richards. "Of course not, Nelson. How can you ask?" She would *not* blush. "I wiped out your debt with a wager of my own, if you must know."

His eyes widened even further. "You played Richards at cards—and won?"

"Not cards. Chess." *That* memory still had the power to make her smile.

Nelson stared at her a moment longer, then began to laugh. "And I always said you were wasting your time at that game. Damned if you didn't find a way to make it pay off!" He clapped her on the shoulder as he might a man. "You're too clever by half, Ro, but for once I'm dashed grateful for it."

"Clever. Yes." She had apparently exhausted her cleverness on that chess match with Richards, judging by her behavior for the remainder of last evening. "At any rate, you need not worry now about passing along any information to Richards and endangering your position at the Home Office." Curiosity about that still nagged at her.

Her brother gave her an awkward hug, then quickly released her, glancing about in some embarrassment. "You're the best sister a fellow could want, Ro. I'm glad you're here in London—and glad you've become such a success. I expect I'll have some buck calling on me one day soon, asking for your hand. Who'd have thought it?"

"I don't think you need worry about that just yet," she said, coloring despite her best efforts.

"Won't be long, mark my words. And don't sell yourself short, Ro. You deserve all the happiness a woman can have."

He left her then, to go in search of a card game at one of the tables set up in the alcoves. Rowena stared after him sadly. Whether she deserved happiness or not, she had ruined her best chance at it with her actions last night.

Again, she involuntarily picked Noel Paxton out of the crowd. She might have been truly happy with him, she realized, despite their differences. Ironic that she had not seen it until now, when she had given him a thorough disgust for her.

"The dancing is about to begin." Mr. Richards' voice snapped her out of her mournful reverie. "I believe the first is mine?"

She turned, forcing a smile to her lips. "I am flattered you remembered," she said. Then, realizing this might be her best opportunity for a private word with him, she lowered her voice. "Before we are separated by the dance, there is something I must tell you, Mr. Richards."

All day she had wavered between her duty to the common man and what Noel might see as a betrayal. But had he not betrayed her already? He had claimed to care for her, but today he had demonstrated his indifference. Painful as it was to contemplate, it appeared that he really had only hoped to learn the identity of the essayist from her.

Suddenly she remembered those sixteen letters she

hoped to retrieve tomorrow. What might be in them? Was it possible one would be from Noel? If so, would she dare to somehow reply?

Mr. Richards was watching her expectantly, so she put that matter from her mind for the moment. Taking a deep breath, she continued.

"I know who you really are—but I fear Mr. Paxton suspects you as well. You must be on your guard against him."

"Who I really am?" His dark brown eyes bored into hers with an intensity that made her shiver. Almost, she would have called it sinister—but that was absurd, of course. "And how came you by this knowledge, Miss Riverstone?"

"It was a matter of deduction," she explained. "Your convictions, with which I am well acquainted through your writings, as well as something Mr. Paxton said. And, of course, there was the matter of the jewels."

He blinked, breaking the intensity of his gaze. "Of course," he said slowly. "Your mother's jewels . . . stolen from Lady Mountheath. You will want them back, of course."

Rowena frowned uncertainly. "Yes, as I said last night, I appreciated—"

"The music is beginning. Later we shall discuss their return, shall we? It occurs to me that you may have something I want as well." With that cryptic comment, he led her into the opening dance.

Mechanically going through the movements of the minuet, Rowena's mind worked furiously. Mr. Richards spoke as though the jewels were still in his possession, when they had been returned to her the very night they were taken from the Mountheath house. Could she have been mistaken? But he had admitted just now that he was the Saint, hadn't he?

Glancing down the line of dancers, she saw Noel partnering Augusta Melks. He turned his head just then and their eyes met before she could look away. She felt an instant connection, a communion, mind to mind—and then it was gone as another dancer blocked her line of sight. When she could see him again, he was not looking her way.

Shaken, she had to concentrate to avoid losing her place in the dance. Surely she had imagined that link between them? A few kisses and one evening of wanton caressing could not forge such a thing—could it?

But no, it was more than that. She remembered their chess games, their conversations, both of them taking enjoyment in disputing each other's views. They had far more in common than she had been willing to admit, despite their differing opinions on certain issues.

She turned to face Mr. Richards again, and his gaze was overtly admiring. Rowena knew she should be flattered—the man was her longtime idol, after all—but instead she felt uncomfortable, even vaguely repelled. He was almost old enough to be her father, and she couldn't help remembering his patronizing comments at yesterday's picnic.

No, she did not feel the rapport with Mr. Richards that she felt with Noel Paxton, despite her endorsement of his opinions. Most of his opinions. Not the ones pertaining to women, of course.

"Shall we go to the refreshment table?" he suggested at the close of the dance. "That will give us an opportunity for conversation."

"I fear I am already engaged for the next dance with Mr. Thatcher," she said with feigned regret. In fact, she felt more relief than regret—and chided herself for it. Surely she did not think Noel was right, that Mr. Richards was somehow dangerous?

Mr. Thatcher appeared at her elbow then, and Mr. Richards bowed. "Of course. Later, then."

"Odd fellow, Richards," Mr. Thatcher said as he led her back to the floor. "Radical sort. Did he say anything to upset you, Miss Riverstone?"

She realized she must have let some part of her sudden distaste for her erstwhile idol show in her expression and quickly summoned a smile. "No, of course not. He merely wished me to sit out a dance with him."

"His loss, my gain," her partner said with a roguish smile. "Never thought I'd seek out a lady in spectacles— intimidating, don't you know—but I'm willing to risk having my egotism deflated for a dance with you, Miss Riverstone."

Rowena had to laugh at his outrageous flattery. "Intimidating? I find that hard to believe, Mr. Thatcher." Harry Thatcher was a longtime acquaintance of Noel's, she recalled. Did she dare question him about his friend?

The country dance began, and Rowena was again impressed at how well Mr. Thatcher compensated for his missing left arm. One scarcely even noticed it, as he seemed not to.

"How well do you know Mr. Paxton?" she asked

with all the nonchalance she could muster, when the movements of the dance brought them back together for a time.

"Noel?" He glanced across the room, where the gentleman in question was one of another set of dancers. "Haven't seen too much of him since his return to London, but we had some good times in Vienna. Bang-up sort. He can carouse—and fight—with the best of 'em, and match me bottle for bottle at the table."

This was a picture of Noel she would never have suspected. She had assumed his duties in Vienna had entailed delivering messages and attending meetings, interesting in its way, but involving little risk or adventure. Before she could request more details, however, the dance separated them again.

"I've noticed Noel watching you," Mr. Thatcher commented when they were able to speak again. "You could do worse, Miss Riverstone, if you'll excuse my impudence in saying so. Of course, you could also do better." He winked suggestively.

Again she had to laugh, despite the jumble of emotions that assailed her at his endorsement of Noel. "You do not seem the sort to be hanging out for a wife." But then, neither did Noel.

"Gad, no!" he exclaimed, and his horror seemed only partially feigned. "Just innocent flirtation, don't you know. Not looking for a straitjacket, not at this stage of my life."

Rowena suspected that a good woman might do wonders for Mr. Thatcher, but he was not the one she was interested in at the moment. "Pray do not panic, sir. You have raised no expectations. But what makes you think Mr. Paxton feels any differently?"

She had to wait for his answer, as they were temporarily separated again, which gave her time to regret her bold question. What if he repeated it to Noel? She would die of embarrassment.

When he took her hand again, he appeared more thoughtful, less the devil-may-care rake that he usually projected. "Don't tell Noel I said so, but he has the look of a man ready to settle down. 'Course, I could be wrong. I'd never want to be instrumental in leg-shackling a friend."

At least it appeared he was unlikely to share their conversation with Noel, she thought with relief. "I suspect you may be mistaken, Mr. Thatcher. Mr. Paxton seems quite single-minded in his pursuit of the Saint of Seven Dials. I'm sure no other thoughts have room in his head at the moment."

"Yes, Noel's become rather a stick-in-the-mud of late," Mr. Thatcher agreed. "Seems he's forgotten how to have fun. I'll have to see what I can do about that. I owe him a favor, after all—maybe even my life."

The dance ended then, and he bowed and left her before she could ask him to explain that remarkable comment. Frowning, she turned—to find herself face to face with Noel himself.

"Dare I hope you have a waltz yet open?" he asked, his voice raising all of the tiny hairs on Rowena's body as the orchestra played the opening strains of just that dance.

She opened her mouth, but no sound came out. Clearing her throat, she tried again. "As it happens, I have." Her voice sounded high and breathy, totally unlike her.

"Good." Smiling down into her eyes, holding her gaze with the question in his own, he took her hand and led her into the dance.

For several long moments, Rowena could not bring herself to speak, so distracted was she by the sensation of his hand against her back and the memories—and desire—that sensation aroused. The silence between them lengthened to awkwardness, and finally she forced herself to say what she knew must be said.

"I . . . I must apologize for my behavior last night. It was forward, and unladylike, and completely improper."

She waited for the disgust he must feel to show in his expression at the reminder, but instead his grip on her hand tightened and his eyes seemed to grow warmer. She felt her breath quickening, despite their surroundings.

"I cannot deny that however improper it might have been, I found your behavior more than enjoyable," he said softly, ensuring that no one around them could possibly overhear. "I am more concerned about the motives for it than the behavior itself."

Impossible to tell him what she now knew was the truth—that she had simply wanted him. That she wanted him even now. It would only confirm her as a wanton, not to mention opening her to humiliation, should he feel differently. At the same time, she did not want to anger him as she had last night.

Instead, she tried to skirt a line between the noble reasoning she had used to convince herself last night, and today's realization. "I seem not to have been thinking entirely clearly last night." That was true enough! "I thought I could both follow my inclinations and justify my indiscretion by attempting to dissuade you from a course you already knew me to oppose."

"I see." Though his grip did not loosen, there was an indefinable withdrawal in his eyes. "Tell me, what were you speaking about with Richards, earlier?"

Completely unprepared for the question, Rowena missed her step and came down hard on his foot. "Oh! I beg your pardon."

Deftly, he guided her back into the motion of the waltz. "I'm not so easily distracted, you know. Will you answer my question?"

"I did not tread on your foot intentionally," she protested, as much to give herself time as because it was true.

Noel would surely be angry if she told him she had warned Richards against him. He would see it as a betrayal—which, she admitted, it was, but one she felt justified in, given the good the Saint was doing for the poor of London.

He did not argue her defense but merely waited, watching her with that intensity that both excited and disturbed her. With an effort, she pulled her glance away to look over his shoulder.

"I, ah, attempted to verify a theory about Mr. Richards," she finally said evasively.

"That he is the Saint of Seven Dials." It was not a question.

Her gaze snapped back to him, to find him regarding her with that analytical expression he sometimes wore. "I knew you suspected him," she admitted, though clearly he was already aware of that.

"And now Richards knows it too?" There was no expression in his voice, but still he accused her.

Unfortunately, she could not deny it, much as she wanted to. She simply could not lie to this man. It appeared she would not make a good politician after all. "Yes," she whispered, not meeting his eye.

"You seem to have chosen your loyalties, though I fear you may find them misplaced. You are meddling in things you do not understand, Rowena."

Her pride stung, she lifted her chin. "How do you know what I understand? I have read"—she almost added "and written," but caught herself in time— "extensively about the Saint. I daresay I understand him as well as you do."

"I rather doubt that." Surely, that was not amusement she heard in his voice? "In any event—"

"It appears you have as low an opinion of a woman's intelligence as Mr. Richards does," she snapped, angry herself now. "I do seem to have faltered in my judgment—of you."

He smiled, but it was a mirthless smile. "Anyone can make an error in judgment when lacking relevant information. I have certainly done so myself, on more than one occasion."

What was he saying? That there was more to himself than met the eye, or was he referring to Mr. Richards—or to her? Not that it mattered. "One must make decisions based on the information available, mustn't one?" she challenged him.

"But one must also be careful not to ignore the facts, seeing only what one wishes to see."

The dance ended, and he released her at once,

though still he held her eyes with his own, daring her to look away. Clearly, he thought she was granting Mr. Richards additional virtues because of her prior admiration of the man—but that was absurd. Both men had strongly implied that Richards was the Saint. It was not some foolish fantasy she had invented.

"I pride myself on my objectivity," she told him. "I always consider all options before making a move, as you have seen at the chessboard."

"Always?" He raised a skeptical brow.

Last night she had not followed that maxim—quite the opposite, in fact. She knew he was reminding her of that, and she felt her color rising against her will. "Almost always," she amended, refusing to look away this time.

The first real smile she had seen on him today briefly lightened his features. "I've said before that I admire your honesty. Perhaps we can continue this discussion over supper, if you still have that dance free?"

Before she could answer, a soft throat-clearing sounded at her elbow. "Miss Riverstone?" It was young Lord Roland, to whom she had promised the next dance.

She smiled at the newcomer, then turned back to Noel. "Supper, then," she said, though she suspected she might be making yet another error in judgment by agreeing. He bowed, and she took Lord Roland's arm so that he could lead her to the quadrille just forming.

Noel watched Rowena take her place in the set, then turned away with a frown. He'd expected that she would warn Richards given an opportunity, but he wondered very much what she had actually said—

and how he had responded. Would he interpret her warning as pertaining only to the Saint, or would he guess that Noel suspected him of something far more sinister?

If the former, Rowena's assumption no doubt amused him mightily. If the latter, he might become desperate. Either way, Rowena herself might now be in danger. But how could Noel possibly convince her of that without telling her the truth, not only about Richards, but about the Saint?

He reminded himself that he still had no clear proof that Richards was the man he sought, though he hoped to within days. For the first time since suspecting him, Noel hoped he was wrong—but his instincts claimed otherwise. Until he knew for certain, he had to somehow protect Rowena, with or without her consent.

With that goal in mind, he kept a discreet watch on her for the next two hours, even as he danced with other ladies. Twice Richards approached her, but both times she smilingly rebuffed him to dance with her next promised partner. It was difficult from a distance to read the nuances of her expression, but Noel felt almost certain that she wished to avoid Richards.

Perhaps his words had not been entirely without effect, then. He could only hope so, for her sake.

And his own.

Chapter 17

Rowena was more than ready for this interminable evening to end. She felt as though her emotions had been put through a wash wringer, twisted and distorted until she no longer knew how she felt or what she believed. All she had felt sure of had been called into question, and she didn't much care for the sensation.

"I thank you for the honor, Miss Riverstone," said Mr. Orrin with a bow as their cotillion ended.

She smiled in response, her nerves stretched to a screaming point in painful anticipation. The supper dance was next, but she did not see Noel. Would he appear to claim her as promised? Did she want him to? What could she possibly say to him after their last exchange?

"Miss Riverstone," came a voice from behind her—a voice she was almost beginning to dread this evening, contrary as that seemed. "You mentioned earlier that you don't waltz. Might that mean we can finally talk during this dance?"

Summoning a bright smile, she turned to face Mr. Richards, nearly ready to agree. Perhaps it would allow her to figure out *one* of the conundrums besetting her. "I take it you do not waltz either, sir?" she asked, stalling for time until she could decide what to do.

"Dancing is a foolish pastime, in my opinion, intended to make the mating ritual easier for those who lack the address to go about it in a more direct and rational way."

His dark eyes held hers as he spoke and a shiver went up her back at his apparent meaning. Not a particularly pleasant shiver, unfortunately.

"Of course," she said in automatic agreement, but then realized that she was again parroting his opinion rather than proclaiming her own. "But I believe there is more to dancing than that. I find it a metaphor for the strictures of Society—some foolish, certainly, but some quite sensible."

"Do you indeed?" he asked in apparent surprise, but then smiled suggestively again. "But surely you don't believe those strictures apply—"

"My apologies, Miss Riverstone," Noel interrupted him, appearing without warning from behind a pillar. "Our dance, I believe?"

Rowena turned with a relief she feared she did not completely conceal. "Mr. Paxton! I assumed you were otherwise engaged."

"Never." Though his smile was as suggestive as Mr. Richards' had been, it warmed Rowena rather than chilling her. "Shall we?"

"The lady does not waltz," said Mr. Richards, an edge to his voice. "She prefers to sit this dance out, Paxton—with me."

Noel turned to the man, his brows raised. "The lady waltzes beautifully, with the right partner. You do not give her enough credit—still."

Mr. Richards' complexion darkened at this oblique reference to last night's chess match. "And you seem to have a habit of putting your nose where it doesn't belong," he snapped. "The lady and I were conversing."

"I find that I can learn quite a lot by putting my nose where others would prefer I did not," Noel responded with an enigmatic half-smile. "In any event, Miss Riverstone promised this dance to me earlier, did you not?" He turned to her for verification.

Embarrassed in the extreme, Rowena nodded. "He is right, Mr. Richards, I did. I . . . I am improving slightly at the waltz, with practice, though I am by no means proficient."

"Practice improves all skills," Noel said, his eyes giving his words an added meaning that embarrassed her further. "Shall we?" he said again.

This time, she put her hand in his. "My apologies, Mr. Richards. I did promise."

"Then you surely realize now that one should not make promises lightly, or without proper fore-thought," Mr. Richards said with a darkling glance at Noel. Then, he seemed to recover himself. "No matter. We will continue our conversation later."

As Noel led her to the dance already in progress, Rowena decided that "later" would not be tonight. She would retire immediately after supper, as she had before. She'd had enough emotional turmoil for one evening.

"Now then," said Noel, placing his hand at her

back to guide her into the movements of the dance. "Am I mistaken, or were you just as glad of an excuse to break off that talk with Richards?"

She looked up at him in surprise, trying vainly to ignore the sensations—and emotions—that rippled through her at his touch. "How could you—That is, he has seemed unusually determined to speak with me alone this evening, since our earlier conversation."

"And that makes you uncomfortable."

She nodded. Now, why had she admitted that to a man who was certainly Mr. Richards' enemy? "I don't really know him that well, after all," she temporized.

"Precisely the point I tried to make earlier," he said. "I know you think his motives are entirely noble, but I have reason to believe otherwise. I wish you would trust me, Rowena." The warmth in his eyes nearly made her melt, right there on the dance floor.

Valiantly, she tried to rally her reason. "How can I, when we are so ideologically opposed?" she made herself say. "Would you have me sacrifice my principles on the altar of that trust?"

To her surprise, he smiled. "I think we are not so opposed as you believe, Rowena. As I said, you have based some of your opinions on insufficient information."

"And will you supply the information I lack?" It was both a challenge and a plea, but he shook his head with apparent regret.

"I can't—not yet. That is why I want you to trust me, until I am able to do just that."

He seemed to be speaking in riddles, and it frustrated her that she could not decipher them. Normally, she was quite good at riddles. She made one more attempt. "Are you trying to tell me that Mr. Richards is *not* the Saint of Seven Dials?"

"Please, Rowena, do not press me for information I cannot safely give you just now. If all goes as I hope, my mission will be accomplished within days. Then, I will tell you everything."

Within days? He expected to have the Saint arrested within days? Or did he mean something else entirely? Though she asked no more questions, Rowena by no means intended to give up trying to figure out what was going on. To do so would be to betray who she was and all she believed in.

She thought back over the recent exchange between Noel and Mr. Richards. The older man seemed to be subtly threatening Noel, a threat that Noel had turned back upon him. They had all but openly acknowledged themselves as opponents—and not, she thought, simply for her affections.

Clearly, she would have to choose her loyalties, and choose soon, if she was to have any hope of affecting their contest.

The dance ended, and Noel led her in to supper. As before, he attempted to find a table where they might be private, but unfortunately they were joined almost at once by Lord and Lady Marcus.

"I see that your spectacles have in no way diminished your popularity," Lady Marcus remarked, seating herself next to Rowena.

Noel glanced at Rowena in surprise, drawing a confused look from her in return.

"Why do you look at me like that?" she asked him.

He smiled sheepishly. "I, ah, hadn't noticed that you

were wearing your spectacles tonight," he confessed.

"Knowing how observant you generally are, sir, I believe I will take that as a compliment," she said.

The other couple chuckled, and Noel joined in, still feeling foolish. It was true, however. Her eyeglasses were so much a part of her that he *hadn't* noticed. Certainly, they did not diminish her attractiveness. He wanted her more than ever.

He and Lord Marcus excused themselves to fetch plates of food for themselves and the ladies. Footmen were circulating with trays of drinks ranging from champagne to lemonade.

"Glad of this chance for a word," Lord Marcus said as soon as they were out of earshot. "I'm hoping you can meet with Luke and me later this evening. We're wanting to finally do something about Twitchell, who's become even more abusive of late."

"Certainly," Noel agreed. The vicious thief-master was a problem he'd been hoping to solve himself.

Other gentlemen joined them then, so the subject was dropped. When they returned to the table, the ladies were deep in conversation, but turned to greet them with smiles. The four of them talked primarily about the deplorable conditions of London's work-houses during supper.

Rowena was animated on the topic, and Noel enjoyed watching and listening to her, though he took a smaller part in the conversation than the others. He also noticed the overt affection between Lord Marcus and his wife, a rarity among their class that they shared with Lord and Lady Hardwyck.

It was what he wanted for himself, Noel realized, his gaze again going to Rowena. She glanced his way just then, and for a long moment their eyes locked. Hers still held a certain reserve, as well as a question— a question he dared not answer yet.

"Goodness, was the supper break so short at the last ball, or is it merely the company that has made the time pass so quickly?" Lady Marcus exclaimed as the orchestra began the next dance number.

"The latter, I'm sure," Rowena replied. "I have enjoyed our conversation immensely. Now, though, I pray you will all excuse me. I made a point of committing to no dances after supper, knowing how tired I was likely to be—and so I am."

Noel and Lord Marcus rose to help the ladies to their feet. "You plan to escape yet again, then?" Noel said to Rowena in an undertone. "Would you care for an escort?"

"Marcus wishes to talk to Lord Hardwyck later, so we will enjoy another dance or two," Lady Marcus said. "Sleep well, Rowena. Perhaps we can go shopping together later this week."

Rowena agreed that she would like that, then turned back to Noel. "I am quite capable of finding my room unassisted," she told him archly. Then, glancing over his shoulder, her expression changed. "However, if you would care to accompany me as far as the stairway . . ."

He extended his arm and she took it. As they walked, he cast a quick look behind him to see Richards watching them with a frown. So, she was still eager to avoid the man. Good.

"You do not seem so tired as you did at Friday night's ball," he commented. "Are you beginning to adjust to Town hours?"

Her expression had been solemn, but now she smiled. "Yes, I believe I am. Still, I don't really feel equal to more dancing tonight."

He suspected it was not the dancing she wished to avoid, however. "A ballroom can be much like a battlefield—or a chess board—I find. Campaigns are waged by matchmaking mamas and determined bachelors, by fortune hunters and aspiring peeresses, each with their own distinctive strategies."

"Precisely," she agreed. "As well as some campaigns far more subtle than those you have listed. The strategizing can be as wearying as the dancing, I find."

They were nearly to the stairway now, and she paused to look earnestly up at him. "I fear I may make a false move, as some of the pieces appear to be hidden. It is worse than when I played without my spectacles."

Her wide gray eyes pleaded with him for information—and for something else. Or was he imagining that? He led her toward a small alcove near the foot of the stairs, where they would be less likely to be seen by any chance passerby.

"Please believe that I don't wish to hide anything from you, Rowena, and would not if I did not have to. Soon—"

"Yes, so you said. Perhaps within days. But meanwhile . . ." Her voice trailed off with a sigh and he felt something inside him give way.

Reaching the alcove, he covered the small hand that rested on his arm with his own, and turned to face her. "Rowena, I—"

He could not even wait to finish his thought,

wasn't even certain what that thought was. Her near-ness overwhelmed his reason, his senses, and he found himself kissing her—and found her responding eagerly.

With stunning force, the feelings he had experi-enced last night came rushing back and it was as though she were naked in his arms again, ready for the taking he so desperately wanted. Noel, who had always prided himself on his ability to sublimate emo-tion to cool reason, felt like a ravening beast with only one way to feed his hunger.

Rowena seemed to sense his urgency, his need—perhaps even to share it. Her arms came about him, pulling him more tightly against her until his arousal pressed against the firm softness of her belly.

Summoning his last vestige of reason and every ounce of his self-control, he broke away from her to stare, panting, into her eyes. She appeared as shocked as he, her soft lips parted, swollen with the ferocity of that kiss. Her breasts rose and fell rapidly as she stared at him, one hand to her flushed cheek.

"I—I didn't think—"

"Nor did I," he said, managing a half-smile. Raw passion still simmered just beneath the surface. "In fact, I have a difficult time thinking at all when I'm with you, Rowena."

Her helpless nod told him he affected her similarly. She reached toward him with one small hand, and he took it instinctively, though he now knew the risk he ran in doing so.

If he went up those stairs with her tonight, they would not stop until she was his completely, and he hers. He knew it with the same certainty that he knew the sun would rise tomorrow. His whole body tightened in anticipation and he took a step forward.

"There you are!" Lady Hardwyck's voice shattered the private world of passion they had woven together. As one, they swung around to face her.

Her eyebrows rose as she looked from Rowena to Noel. "Well. It appears I may have found you just in time, from the look of things. Rowena, I believe you'd best go up to bed. We'll talk later."

Noel tried to convey both apology and longing in his glance, but Rowena only met his eyes for an instant before turning away—too brief an instant for him to decipher the mix of emotions he saw there. "Good night, Miss Riverstone," he said softly.

She paused, but did not turn around. "Good night," she whispered. He watched her mount the stairs, unable to take his eyes from her, memorizing the curve of her shoulder, her waist, one glimpse of ankle—remembering what lay beneath those skirts.

"Mr. Paxton."

With a start, he remembered Lady Hardwyck's presence. "My lady?"

"Perhaps I should talk with you, as well as with Rowena. However, it is my husband who wishes to speak with you now. He and Lord Marcus are in the library."

Her blue eyes were filled with concern for her friend. He wished he could reassure her, tell her that he meant to make Rowena an offer in form, but until this business with the Black Bishop was concluded, he dared not—any more than he dared tell Rowena plainly that he loved her.

The next few days would be as dangerous as any he

had faced, and it would be wrong to bind Rowena to him unless he could promise her a future together. But had Lady Hardwyck not arrived when she did, he realized, he would have done just that.

"Thank you," he said, meaning more than her message. He suspected, from the look she gave him before turning back to the ballroom, that she understood.

Luke and Marcus both turned to greet him when he entered the study a moment later.

"I thought it was time all three Saints put our heads together to solve a persistent problem," Luke said. "You've both mentioned wanting to do something about that blackguard Twitchell. Earlier today a lad from his flash house was found, beaten unconscious. If Stilt hadn't found him, he'd no doubt be dead now."

"Twitchell beat him?" Noel asked.

At the same moment, Marcus said, "Who was it?"

"Tig," Luke replied, nodding in response to Noel's question. "He roused enough to tell Stilt that Twitchell caught him holding back part of his takings—money that I, in fact, had given him so that he wouldn't have to steal."

Noel felt a cold rage edging out his earlier, warmer feelings. Tig was the lad who had been his go-between, bringing messages from Stilt via Squint, the footman. A plucky, cocky lad with delusions of grandeur—and no more than ten years old.

"That bastard!" Marcus exclaimed, his voice low with a similar rage. "Where is Tig now?"

"Here in this house, in the servants' wing. I've already had a physician attend him, and it appears he will recover." Luke looked at each of them. "Then we are in agreement that it's time Twitchell was removed?"

They both nodded, but Noel said, "Or perhaps replaced? With Twitchell gone, will not the remaining lads simply move to Ickle's flash house—or an even worse one?"

He had recruited a lad or two from Ickle's group when trailing Lord Marcus as Saint earlier this summer, and knew those boys received their share of hard knocks from their master as well.

"My thought exactly, Noel," Luke said with an approving nod. "And I believe I have just the fellow. You may remember Flute, my erstwhile valet? I believe you were rather anxious to have a word with him at one time."

Noel chuckled. He'd been certain that young man would be the key to proving Luke was the Saint—and he might well have been, had Noel's own agenda not changed drastically upon learning that Luke was not the traitor he really sought. "He should be safe enough in Town now," Noel agreed.

"Which is why I've sent for him from Knoll Grange, one of my smaller properties, not far from London. He should arrive tomorrow. I'll brief him on the situation, and assuming Flute is willing to shepherd the boys, I'll confront Twitchell and give him a choice—between the gibbet and the colonies."

"And you'll want us to watch your back, I presume?" Marcus asked.

Luke nodded. "It seems prudent. And Noel, perhaps you can convince someone at Bow Street to ensure for us that he takes ship."

"That should present no problem." Noel thought

for a moment, weighing his other plans, then said, "I have a favor to ask of you, as well."

"Of course." Luke waited for him to proceed, which he did after another long pause.

"I will be engaged tomorrow, and perhaps the next day, conducting some necessary research on that matter I told you about."

"And what matter is this?" Marcus asked curiously.

Noel had not previously mentioned the Bishop to Marcus, on the theory that the fewer people who knew, the fewer would be at risk. Now, however, he quickly outlined the traitor's career, then added his suspicion that Mr. Richards might be the man he sought.

"I need proof, however. I discovered today that Richards' father lives in the country a few hours from Town, an invalid. I plan to question him as soon as possible."

"So you want us to keep an eye on Richards while you are away?" Luke asked.

Noel nodded. "If he suspects that I am on to him, he may attempt to leave Town—or do something desperate. I, ah, would particularly like you to keep him away from Miss Riverstone, if possible. She may be at some risk from him."

Both men stared, and Noel felt his neck heating with embarrassment. "It's not what you think," he explained. "Yes, he has behaved as though he has a romantic interest in her, and I won't deny that I do myself. But certain things he has said, and done, indicate a darker purpose. Already she is dazzled by his highflown revolutionary rhetoric and . . . she believes he is the Saint of Seven Dials."

At this, both men started to laugh. "How that must rankle!" Marcus said with a grin. "To have her admiring another man for *your* daring exploits. I believe I can sympathize."

"If Richards is the traitor you seek, he may attempt to inveigle Miss Riverstone into some scheme, or use her as a hostage against your moving against him," Luke said, sobering. "As she is a guest in my home, I feel honor-bound to prevent him doing so."

"Thank you." And Noel meant it from the bottom of his heart. Without that assurance, he would have to remain close enough to protect her himself—something he recognized as a risky proposition after tonight. It might be said that he himself posed a substantial risk to Rowena's future, if not her life. He *had* to conclude this case, and quickly.

"What explanation do you intend to give Miss Riverstone for your absence?" Marcus asked then. "We would not want to inadvertently contradict it."

Noel frowned. He knew it would be safest not to see her again—not yet. "Can you simply tell her that my duties require me elsewhere?" he asked Luke. "I hope to be able to explain everything soon enough."

"Everything?" both men asked together.

"Your wives both know, do they not?" They nodded. "As it is my hope that once this business is settled I can persuade Miss Riverstone to marry me, it seems only fitting that she know all."

"Then London will need a new Saint—again," Luke commented with a wry grin. "But time enough to think on that later. I recommend an early night, gentlemen. We all have a big day ahead of us tomorrow."

* * *

Rowena stared into the dark, sleep as far away as ever. Noel would not come to her tonight, she knew, not after Pearl had discovered them. He would consider the risk to her reputation too great—though she cared not a fig for that.

She did care about Pearl's good opinion, however. Unwilling to face her best friend's censure until she had sorted out her wildly conflicting feelings, she had feigned sleep when Pearl had peeked into her room half an hour since. There would be time enough for a scold in the morning.

Perhaps she should simply tell Pearl everything, and ask for her advice. From occasional comments between Pearl and Lord Hardwyck, she had the impression that their own courtship had been a rather bumpy one. The need to unburden herself, to get a more objective opinion, was strong.

Not nearly as strong as her need for Noel, however. He was all she really wanted at this moment— his voice, his face, his kisses . . . his body. Was this obsession?

No, she realized, this was love.

Though she had resisted both her feelings and the admission of those feelings to herself, she could no longer deny either. Not only was this love, it was the sort of love that drove the poets to ruin. An all-encompassing and all-too-likely tragic love, given their differences and her betrayal of Noel's mission.

All her life she had both doubted the existence and fantasized about the possible reality of love. Secretly, she had always hoped to find it for herself—to find that one man who would fill the empty spaces in her heart, who was her other half, who could make her whole, even as she made him whole. Now, she knew beyond doubt she had finally found that man.

Rowena cried herself to sleep.

Chapter 18

Noel was up at daybreak, determined to accomplish all that was necessary in time to be in the country by noon. His first order of business was at Bow Street, where he arranged for one of the Runners to make certain Mr. Twitchell boarded a ship for the New World within the week, with orders to arrest the thief-master if he did not leave London in that time.

Sir Nathaniel arrived while Noel was there, so he requested a private conference to explain his own proposed absence over the next day or two, implying that he was close to capturing the Saint but hinting that even more important matters were at stake. It was a measure of Sir Nathaniel's trust in him that he did not require more information than Noel was prepared to share.

By this time, he knew that the office of the *Political Register* would be open, so he went there next, to discover whether any response had yet been received from Mr. R.

"I was hoping you'd be by," the sympathetic clerk greeted him, nervously pushing up his spectacles. The motion reminded Noel sharply of Rowena.

"You have something, then?" he asked, firmly putting such distracting thoughts from his mind.

The clerk nodded. "Came yesterday." He held up a sheet of paper. "He wants us to leave the letters in Green Park, behind a specific rock near the entrance."

"When?"

"Today. He plans to retrieve them this afternoon, he says. I was planning to wrap them in oilskin and put them there myself, later this morning." He handed the note to Noel.

Reading through it, Noel fought to tamp down his sudden excitement. Today! He had not expected results so quickly. The Black Bishop was nearly in his grasp! His trip to question Richards' father would have to wait. In fact, if all went as he hoped, it wouldn't be necessary to go into the country at all.

"Yes, that sounds like a good plan." He handed back the letter. "And thank you. You have done England a great service, Mr. Bell. If all goes well, I'll see that you are recognized for it."

But the clerk shook his head. "I'd just as soon not, thanks, given Mr. Cobbett's politics. Being a hero might be nice, but I'd rather keep my job."

Noel chuckled, his spirits irrepressibly high. "Your choice, of course. But you have my gratitude, nonetheless."

Whistling, he headed for Seven Dials, where he was to meet Luke and Lord Marcus for the bearding of Mr. Twitchell.

* * *

Sunshine often serves to chase away mental as well as physical darkness, as Rowena discovered for herself the next morning. What had seemed hopeless in the dark watches of the night now seemed less so.

Noel had told her he cared for her, and he was nothing if not an honorable man. Now that their indiscretion was no longer secret, he would likely make an offer in form.

And she was very nearly resolved to accept him.

"The periwinkle cambric, Matthilda," she told her maid once she had washed. It was her most flattering day dress, brightening her hair and eyes. She wished to look her best for what might prove to be the most important day of her life.

Marrying Noel Paxton might well mean abandoning active pursuit of her more radical goals, but surely what she would gain in exchange would be worth it. Leisurely discussions of every topic imaginable, long walks, games of chess . . . and the promise of physical pleasures she could scarcely even imagine.

The very thought brought becoming color to her cheeks. She smiled a secret smile at herself in the looking-glass, then turned to allow Matthilda to help her into the gown.

Once married, surely she would be able to persuade Noel more to her way of thinking, she reasoned. He was always willing to listen to her arguments, to give her credit when she was right, though he might dispute her conclusions. Given unlimited time to explain her views, she was sure to bring him around in some areas.

Perhaps this was mere rationalization, making her natural inclination easier to accept, but she didn't care. After a miserable night, she was determined to be happy on this auspiciously sunny day.

"Thank you, Matthilda," she said as the maid put the finishing touches to her hair. Head high, she sailed out of her room and down the stairs, ready to face Pearl's lectures, confident that she could also expect Noel's addresses.

As she had expected, Pearl awaited her in the dining room. Noel was absent, perhaps by Pearl's request. "Rowena, I believe we need to talk," came the anticipated preamble.

"Yes, I suppose we do," Rowena agreed, smiling at her friend's evident surprise at her own cheerfulness. "I'll just get some breakfast and coffee first." She then proceeded to do just that, filling a plate from the sideboard while a footman poured her a steaming cup. "Now," she said, sitting to face Pearl expectantly.

"I'm not certain you are aware of the gravity of your situation," Pearl began once the footman had gone. "It is extremely fortunate that only I saw you and Mr. Paxton last night, in what looked suspiciously like a tryst."

Rowena considered. "Not a tryst, no. He merely escorted me to the stairs, as I was ready to go up to bed. I can't deny that we kissed, however. He is quite good at it." As well as other things, she added to herself.

"Rowena!" Pearl's eyes were wide with shock, though the corners of her lips twitched. "I must say, I never expected—That is, you seem to be treating this very lightly. And just how would you know how Mr. Paxton's kisses compare to any other man's?"

"Well, I don't, actually," Rowena confessed, though for the fun of scandalizing Pearl she was tempted to claim otherwise. "Oh, Pearl, you know I have never been missish. If I enjoy Noel's kisses and he enjoys mine, why should we not please ourselves?"

"So it is Noel now, is it? I suppose that is as well, considering. But I thought you were always opposed to the idea of marriage, likening it to slavery for a woman. Following this course with a man like Mr. Paxton is likely to end in a wedding. You must know that."

Rowena nodded, but slowly. Having Pearl put it into words like that was sobering, despite her earlier resolve. "I have thought of that, yes. But Noel respects my intelligence as no other man ever has. If I am to marry at all, I doubt I could do better."

"But—" Pearl waved a helpless hand.

Rowena looked her friend in the eye, all amusement gone. "Besides," she said simply, "I love him."

Pearl sighed. "I feared it might be so. I have watched how your eyes follow him—and how he watches you, as well."

"Why 'feared'?" Rowena asked in surprise. "I thought you would be pleased."

Her friend looked at her with a sympathy that set off warnings in Rowena's head.

"Where *is* Noel?" she demanded, feeling a sudden dark premonition despite the bright sunshine.

"He is gone," Pearl said. "I don't know where. He left very early this morning."

Rowena half-rose from her chair. "You sent him away, because of what you saw last night? But I told you—"

But Pearl was shaking her head. "No, I did not

send him away, nor did Luke. It was his own decision to leave."

"He has gone back to his lodgings, then?" That's what he'd done before, when he didn't trust himself to be near her. A prudent course, perhaps, but frustrating.

Pearl shook her head again, however. "I fear not. Luke tells me he is gone into the country, and may not return for some days."

Swallowing painfully around the lump that had suddenly appeared in her throat, Rowena stared at her friend. "But why?" she whispered. "Where has he gone?"

"I . . . I do not know. Luke seemed disinclined to discuss it, so I did not press for details."

Rowena's earlier euphoria turned to ashes and dread. He had implied that he was very close to catching the Saint. Might his absence be connected to that? But the Saint operated here in London. Was Noel so eager to avoid her that he had abandoned his quest and returned to his estate—perhaps never to return?

"A few days, did you say?" she asked, grasping at straws.

"Luke did not actually say how long he would be gone," Pearl confessed, "just that he had business to attend to in the country. Perhaps he will return tomorrow."

Rowena averted her gaze from her friend's pitying expression, which told her far more than her words did. *Had* she read more into Noel's words and actions than he had intended? But he had told her he cared for her, and she believed him to be honest, even if she frequently disagreed with him.

"I suppose I will simply have to wait until he returns, then," she said with an effort, pinning a smile back to her lips. Though her appetite had fled, she forced herself to take a bite of smoked ham.

"Of course." Pearl spoke bracingly, which was nearly as hard to take as her pity. "That's the spirit. Now eat up, do, before our morning callers arrive. You have more admirers than Mr. Paxton, after all."

But none who made her heart race and her insides turn to jelly, thought Rowena despondently. If Noel did not return, she saw little point to remaining in London. She thought of her causes, of the plight of the common man, of the heroic charity of the Saint of Seven Dials, but even those could not fire her now.

It was as though Noel had taken the fire that fueled her passions with him.

"Then it's settled," Luke was saying to a sullen Mr. Twitchell. "You can make a fresh start in New York—unless you would prefer Botany Bay, in Australia?"

The burly thief-master glared at him. "Nay, New York'll do. Haven't you growed all high and mighty, now you're a lord and all? I recollect when you wasn't no better'n Skeet, here. Quite the pickpocket you were, once upon a time."

Luke smiled. "I like to think any of these boys has the ability to rise above his circumstances, just as I have. With you gone, they'll have a better chance to do so."

Twitchell snorted his disbelief. "Half these lads would be dead now without me. Gave 'em a trade, didn't I?"

"Thieving is scarcely a trade. In any event, now they'll have a choice."

Noel watched the exchange from the shadows of a nearby alley, his pistol at the ready. He and Lord Marcus were to show themselves only if the situation grew dangerous—which it now appeared it would not. Luke had been adamant that Twitchell have no opportunity to link either of them to the Saint of Seven Dials.

In a few moments the business was concluded and Twitchell on his way to the docks, shadowed by the Runner Noel had engaged earlier that day. He and Marcus retreated to the prearranged meeting spot, two streets away.

"That went more smoothly than I expected it to," Luke said when he joined them. "I suspect Twitchell has more laid by than he's admitting to, and expects to set himself up nicely on the other side of the Atlantic."

"Where he'll be the Americans' problem and not ours," said Marcus with a grin. "I'd say this calls for a small celebration."

"It does," Noel agreed, "but I fear you'll have to count me out. I need to attend to that other matter I mentioned." He saw no point in explaining his change of plans, as he'd be heading to the country soon enough if his quarry didn't show this afternoon.

Noel left them then, stopping at the coaching inn where Kemp awaited him to delay their departure, but cautioning him to be ready to leave on short notice later on. He would go to Green Park alone, the better to stay concealed while he watched for the mysterious Mr. R.

With Richards safely in custody, Noel would be free to court Rowena properly. The thought of retiring to Tidebourne with her as his bride had him smiling again as he headed for Green Park, despite the dark clouds gathering on the western horizon.

Rowena had managed to cling to her smile through nearly two hours of callers, and even to enter into their conversations of gossip and flirtation, but it was most wearisome. All she really wanted to do right now was escape to her chamber until it was time to slip across the street to Green Park and her letters.

Those, she reasoned, should do nicely to help her pass the time until Noel returned.

For he *would* return. Even when they had been so at odds that they were scarcely speaking, knowing that he was hearing the same silly conversations and sharing her opinion of them had helped her to endure the shallow prattle of people like Fanny Mountheath. Now, however . . .

"Yes, if Lord Edgemont is wealthier than Lord Harrowby, that might make him seem a better catch, to some," she said, stifling a yawn. Miss Mountheath had been comparing the relative fortunes of every bachelor in England, it seemed, for the past twenty minutes. "Surely other factors should be considered, however."

"Oh, of course," her tormentor agreed. "I would never want to marry a man who was truly ill-favored, or older than Papa. I am only discussing *eligible* gentlemen. Don't you agree, Lucy?" She and her sister tittered together, while Rowena racked her brain for some plausible excuse to leave the parlor.

To her relief, the butler chose that moment to announce Mr. Richards. Finally, a chance for some rational conversation! So eager was she to escape the Mountheath sisters that she greeted him more effusively than she might otherwise have done.

"How delightful to see you again so soon, Mr. Richards," she exclaimed.

He moved at once to sit by her, after only the briefest acknowledgment of the other ladies present. "I am happy to hear you say so," he said. "Especially as I was able to spend so little time in your presence last night."

"Yes, Mama was saying earlier how amazed she was that you have become so popular so quickly, Miss Riverstone," Lucy Mountheath volunteered. "But of course, being Lady Hardwyck's friend and protégée must have its benefits."

Rowena did not allow the young lady's spiteful comment to sting. She knew by now that neither of the Mountheath sisters—nor their mother—ever had a kind word to say for anyone unless it served their own interests, and seldom even then.

"Pearl has been very kind to me," she replied blandly. Miss Mountheath only sniffed and turned to her sister, freeing Rowena to speak privately with Mr. Richards. "I do apologize for leaving the ball so early last night. I was quite tired by suppertime, however."

"Quite understandable," he said with a most flattering smile. "All of your admirers kept you dancing constantly, to my loss."

She recalled what he had said about dancing last night, but had no wish to argue with him now. "It is more exercise than I have been accustomed to, certainly. And enjoyable as it can be, I confess I prefer chess and conversation to galloping about a ballroom."

For the barest instant a frown crossed his brow—perhaps at her mention of chess, which she instantly regretted. Now, however, he smiled again. "That goes to prove your intelligence—as do the opinions you have shared with me on certain matters. Mr. Spence's proposals, for example."

Rowena's interest quickened and she was pleased to discover that she did still care about such issues after all. "I believe that some of his ideas might be quite workable," she said earnestly. "Certainly, I agree that land should benefit those who work it."

Mr. Richards leaned closer to her and lowered his voice. "Would you care to learn what some of his adherents hope to do, to help bring such a change about?"

Her eyes widened. "Certainly. I had feared Mr. Spence's plans might have died with him, kept alive only in writings. Do you mean that there are yet people actively working toward his ideals?"

"Not so loud," he said, even more softly. "There are those in government who believe anything which might threaten the current system of power to be seditious. But yes, a group of forward-thinking men carry on Spence's dream of a utopia where men are no longer sacrificed as beasts."

The Mountheath sisters rose to take their leave just then, requiring Rowena's response to their farewells. Pearl then asked her a question pertaining to her conversation with Lady Norville on the changes on the Continent since the Congress of Vienna. As Rowena had read extensively on the issue, she spent some time discussing it with them. By the time she was able to turn her attention back to Mr. Richards, he was rising to leave.

"I have exceeded my quarter hour," he said, taking her hand, "and don't wish to outstay my welcome. Before I go, however, I'd like to extend you an invitation."

Rowena looked up at him in surprise, to find him watching her intently, his expression serious. It occurred to her that she had never heard Mr. Richards laugh. "An invitation, sir?"

He bent over her hand, bringing his lips close to her ear. "Come driving with me tomorrow, and I will tell you about those forward-thinking men I mentioned. I believe you will learn much that will interest you."

Though she was undeniably curious, something about his manner bothered her. "I'll have to ask Lady Hardwyck—" she began, glancing over at Pearl, who was still talking with Lady Norville.

"I thought you were your own person, needing no one's permission for your actions?" he reminded her softly.

"Of . . . of course." She had been looking for ways to fill her thoughts and time until Noel returned, had she not? Along with her letters, discovering all there was to know about the Spenceans should fill that role admirably. "What time?"

He smiled, but it was a humorless smile, she thought with a tiny shiver. "I will call for you by five o'clock, the fashionable hour for a drive in the park."

Though an uneasy instinct warned her that she might be agreeing to more than a simple drive, she nodded. "As long as I can be back here by six, that should be fine."

"Of course," he said smoothly. "We can return whenever you wish. Until tomorrow, then." Releasing her hand, he turned to make his farewells to Pearl, and then left the parlor.

Rowena frowned after him, but then shrugged. How much trouble could she possibly get into in an hour? It would give her excellent material for future essays—and for future arguments with Noel. This would be one topic on which he could scarcely claim to be more expert than she was!

When the last callers left a few minutes later, Rowena headed upstairs. She would change into one of her nondescript gowns and conceal her hair before making her foray to Green Park, to reduce the risk that she might be recognized.

Who would have guessed that life would suddenly become so interesting? she wondered with a spurt of amusement. She, who had led such a completely dull existence for twenty-one years. It appeared she was now making up for it with a vengeance.

The most exciting adventure of all, though, was the one she had found in Noel's arms. She only hoped that he would return soon, so that she could experience his kisses and caresses again.

Noel shifted his weight from his right leg to his left, trying to keep his limbs from going numb after standing motionless for so long. Though he was fairly well concealed behind a pair of birch trees, any movement might serve to warn his quarry—not that he'd seen any sign of him yet.

Green Park had been fairly active earlier, with young families and a few couples strolling the paths, enjoying the balmy sunshine. Now that clouds had rolled in and a fresh breeze had sprung up, however, the park was nearly deserted. With a careful glance around, Noel pulled out his pocket watch. He'd been here almost two hours.

And he would wait past midnight and into tomorrow, if necessary, to finally catch the elusive traitor.

He could see the oilskin packet from here, nestled at the base of the black and gray mottled rock. Might he have been spotted? Could one of the apparently innocent pedestrians actually have been a confederate of the Black Bishop—or even the Bishop himself, if Noel were mistaken about Richards?

A few large drops of rain rattled the leaves around him, and he shifted his weight again. All he could do was wait.

The last few stragglers now hurried toward the park gates, clearly anxious to get indoors before the rain began in earnest. A low roll of thunder sounded in the distance. Noel cursed silently and turned up the collar of his coat, then stilled abruptly as a cloaked and hooded figure entered the gates, in defiance of the threatening weather.

Noel narrowed his eyes as the figure approached. Too short and slight to be Richards. Had the man hired a boy off the streets for this errand? All too likely. If so, Noel would have to somehow induce the lad to lead him to whoever had paid him—a gold sovereign should do it.

Now the figure slowed, glancing about as he approached the rock. Yes, he was clearly here for the letters, whoever he was. The hood was pulled close about the face against the intensifying storm—and against detection—but Noel caught a quick glimpse of a small hand and an almost girlish nose. Definitely not a grown man, he thought, not even a short one.

Could it possibly be a woman? That would be awkward, but it would not dissuade him from his goal. Not when he was this close.

Whoever it was had now reached the rock. Stooping, he—or she—groped about the base, found the packet of letters, and tucked it inside the cloak. It was time for Noel to make his move.

He waited just long enough for the person—he was almost sure it was female now—to turn back toward the gates, then followed, quickly but quietly, the now heavy rain masking his footfalls. Even before his quarry had reached the path, he closed the gap between them.

Noel realized now that he was a full head taller than his opponent. Subduing her—him?—should be no problem. When he grasped a cloaked shoulder, the figure gasped, flinched violently, then spun to face him.

His heart seemed to stop as he found himself staring down into Rowena Riverstone's terrified face.

Chapter 19

Rowena turned, one hand upraised, ready in her panic to fight off her attacker, only to find herself face to face with the last person she expected to see. Her heart was already pounding from being so badly startled, but now it began a happier staccato—until Noel's shocked frown penetrated her sudden euphoria.

"Rowena! How—What are you doing here?" he demanded. He sounded angry rather than pleased to see her.

It took her a moment to summon enough breath for a reply after her fright. "Me? What are *you* doing here?" Her voice sounded high and breathless to her own ears. Forcing herself to look him directly in the eye, deliberately strengthening her voice, she asked, "Have you been following me?"

His eyes widened, then narrowed, taking on his strategizing expression. "Rowena, listen to me. This is important. Who sent you here to retrieve those letters?"

He knew! That's why he was here. Still she tried to delay the inevitable. Shrugging, evading his eye, she said, "Letters? What letters?"

"The letters you have inside your cloak." Roughly, he jerked open her gray cloak and grabbed the packet she had tucked into an inside pocket. The back of his hand brushed her breast in the process, but he seemed not to notice the contact.

"Give me those!" she exclaimed, genuinely alarmed now. "They're mine." Vainly, she tried to snatch the letters back, but he held the oilskin package out of her reach.

"Yours?" he asked mockingly. "Do you even know what these letters are, or anything about the person they are addressed to? What were you promised as a reward for fetching them?"

Keeping an iron grip on her upper arm, he opened the packet with his teeth and free hand while she struggled against him, still trying to reach the letters. It was no use. His reach, his strength, far exceeded hers. She gave it up.

"Of course I know what they are," she said, her voice flat with defeat. "They are letters sent to the *Political Register* for the essayist MRR. And I think I can safely say that I know everything there is to know about that essayist. Now give them to me."

"You haven't told me what Richards promised you," he said harshly, a flash of pain in his eyes. That pain startled her again.

"Richards? Lester Richards?" she asked, now thoroughly confused. "What has he to do with anything?"

Noel's grip on her arm loosened somewhat, and he

suddenly looked as startled as she felt. "You were fetching these letters for him, were you not?"

She shook her head. "I told you, they're mine." Was it possible he really hadn't figured it out yet?

"If not Richards, then who?" he asked. "Your brother, perhaps?"

"Nelson has no more to do with this than Mr. Richards." No matter how it might risk her reputation, risk any hope of a future with Noel, she would not implicate anyone else to shield herself.

Noel stared at her, and she could almost see his mind working, trying to make sense of all the evidence. She couldn't suppress a slight smile.

"I thought you more intelligent than this, given your skill at the chessboard," she said patiently, anticipation of his surprise the only thing keeping worry at bay. "The answer should be obvious by now, though I still don't know why it is so important to you."

"And the answer is?" he ground out, clearly stung by her amusement.

Prolonging this was only making things worse. "MRR stands for Miss Rowena Riverstone," she explained, watching as understanding broke across his face. "*I* am the anonymous essayist you've been so curious about."

Noel had felt his heart die within him when faced with what seemed conclusive proof that Rowena was in league with Richards. It presented him with a terrible choice, for if Rowena was helping a traitor, she would share his fate, were she arrested. But now she said Richards was not involved at all. Surely *she* could not be the traitor he sought?

"You?" he asked, still stunned and confused. She must still be trying to protect Richards, as she'd done when she invited Noel to her room—to her bed—two nights since. Now she was claiming authorship of those essays rather than let him be brought to justice.

"How can it be you?" he asked again, more harshly, when she did not respond. "The handwriting, the turns of phrase—it can't be you, Rowena."

"I disguised my handwriting, of course," she told him matter-of-factly. "I knew the essays would never be printed if they were written in a feminine hand."

He continued to stare at her, trying to read her emotions, to detect any trace of a lie, but he saw none. What he did notice was that her cloak was wet through, making her shiver.

"Perhaps we can continue this inquisition indoors?" she suggested through chattering teeth.

He blinked, trying to disentangle his thoughts from the convoluted paths they'd been following. "Of course. My apologies." He spoke automatically, still unable to process this new information. "Shall I return you to Hardwyck Hall?"

Rowena glanced at the mansion across the street. "I suppose so, but we'll need to go in through the back. That's how I left, and no one knows I'm gone, or so I hope. This has taken a bit longer than I'd planned, thanks to you."

Unwilling to let her guess the depth of his conflict, he nodded curtly and extended an arm for her. The letters, at least, were still safe inside his coat.

"Will you not tell me why you were so determined

to discover MRR's identity?" she asked as they exited Green Park. "I assumed before that you believed MRR and the Saint to be one, but I don't know why you came to that conclusion."

So she knew nothing of Richards' treason, after all. Was it really possible she *had* written those essays? Certainly, that would explain her agitation when he had brought up the subject shortly after meeting her. He had assumed at the time that Mr. R—or, rather, MRR—must be her brother, for her to react so strongly—so personally.

With growing relief, he recalled that she had met Richards for the first time only the night before that discussion, and in his presence. She and Richards hadn't had so much as a private conversation at that point. Though she clearly admired the man's writings, she would have had no personal stake in those essays, had he written them.

She must be telling the truth, then. Which meant he was no closer to catching the Black Bishop than he had been weeks ago. Or was he? She was better acquainted with Richards now. Perhaps she could still help him.

He glanced at her to find her staring up at him quizzically. He had never answered her question.

"Why are you so disappointed to discover that I wrote those essays?" she asked now. "What do they mean to you?"

He made a sudden decision—one his superiors would no doubt condemn. "I've been investigating something far more important—and dangerous—than the Saint of Seven Dials," he told her. "MRR was my best lead, but now it appears to have been a false one."

She frowned into the rain as they started across the street. "So you didn't believe Mr. Richards was the Saint after all? You suspected him of something else? Something . . . worse?"

He didn't answer until they gained the other side of Picadilly. After helping her over the swirling mud in the gutter, he turned her to face him, gripping her by both shoulders. He held her eyes with his own and when he spoke, his voice was low and fierce, to underscore the importance of what he would ask.

"Will you promise to say nothing, not even the merest hint, to anyone—especially to Richards?"

Despite her confusion, despite the way he'd frightened her, she couldn't help trusting this man. The driving rain had turned his auburn curls dark, plastering them against his head, making him look oddly vulnerable, though his hazel eyes bored into her own as though he would read her very thoughts.

Mutely, she nodded.

"I have reason to believe Richards is a traitor," he said. "If I am right, he is a very dangerous man, one who has killed more than once over the years to keep his identity secret."

"Over the years?" she echoed faintly. Mr. Richards, a traitor? A killer? "During . . . during the war, do you mean?"

He nodded. "He acted as a double agent, betraying British secrets to the French. Though I know of only three men he deliberately had murdered, his actions indirectly caused the deaths of countless more. Until recently, we believed the traitor had died at Waterloo. Now we know that was not the case, that he is operating here in London."

She couldn't seem to grasp what he was saying. *We?* What had Noel really done during the war? What had he really been doing here in London? Clearly not pursuing the Saint of Seven Dials, as she had believed.

"But what has this to do with my essays? Why did you think MRR might be the traitor? My writings may be controversial, but they are hardly treasonous."

"Let's get indoors, and I'll try to explain." He took her hand, to lead her around to the back of Hardwyck Hall.

Though her world had been tilted on its axis, Rowena could not ignore the thrill that went through her at his touch. She threaded her fingers through his, and felt his grip tighten. Together, they skirted the side garden and took the gravel path to the garden door, to the very spot where he had first kissed her.

"No one saw me leave," she said as they approached, pushing away that memory. "I'd just as soon no one saw me return. Pearl would ask dozens of questions, and I'd be hard pressed to answer without betraying your confidence—or my identity as MRR."

Noel nodded. Holding a finger to his lips, he stepped to the door and pressed an ear against it. "I hear voices. If we enter here, we'll certainly be seen. Perhaps the terrace doors."

She followed him up the broad stairs to the double French doors that led into the ballroom. He tried the handle, but found it locked. Rowena bit her lip in disappointment, glancing about for another way of entry, but he released her hand and knelt in front of the doors.

As she watched in growing amazement, he pulled a wire of some sort from inside his coat and fitted it into the lock, turned the handle, and opened the door easily. "Quietly, now," he whispered.

She stared, but said nothing, following him across the wide ballroom. Someone was bound to notice the wet trail they were leaving, but there seemed nothing they could do about that just now. At the far side of the ballroom, he paused to listen, then led her out into the hallway, toward the main staircase.

This was the riskiest part, she knew, when they were most likely to be discovered by a passing servant or even Pearl herself. Their luck held, however, and they gained the upper hallway without encountering anyone.

"Your room or mine?" he asked softly, his eyes holding the first hint of softness she had seen since that unexpected meeting in the park.

She swallowed. "I, ah, sent my maid out earlier, but she may be back at any time, if she has not returned already."

"You need dry clothing, in any event. If your maid is there, she can help you to change and we can talk afterward. If not—"

"Just a moment," she whispered, suddenly nervous. She went to the door of her chamber, and he retreated further down the hall without finishing his sentence.

Her room was empty, so she removed her cloak, hanging it to dry, then gathered up a complete change of clothing. Afraid that he might disappear if she tarried, she stepped back into the hallway, telling herself that she didn't want to give him a chance to avoid telling her how MRR fit into his investigation.

He was still standing outside his own chamber door. "She's still gone," she said softly.

"But might return momentarily?"

She nodded.

"Then I suggest we talk in my room, as Kemp will be out until this evening." He opened the door as he spoke.

Rowena hesitated, glancing down at the gown and underthings in her arms.

"You can change behind the screen," he said, apparently divining her thoughts. "I promise not to peek."

Feeling foolish for her sudden attack of missishness, Rowena preceded him into the room. It was nearly identical to her own, though decorated in beige and brown, while hers was in green and white. The screen shielding the dressing area from the rest of the room was in the same corner. Before retreating behind it, however, she turned again to face him.

"Tell me, do others believe my essays to be the work of a traitor?" Noel had said "we" earlier, so others must be involved in his investigation.

He shook his head, smiling reassuringly. "I have spoken of that suspicion only to one other person, my superior at the Foreign Office, and he was skeptical. You need not fear you will be in trouble with the authorities for your writings."

"But why—?" she began.

"You should change first," he said, taking her hand in his again. "Your fingers are like ice."

"So are yours," she pointed out, staring down at their joined hands. "You must have been out in the rain longer than I was, if you were lying in wait for your traitor." She covered his fingers with her other hand, gently chafing them.

In response, he brought his other hand up to encase hers. "We could warm each other," he murmured, his voice suddenly low and rough.

Glancing up in surprise, she found his eyes smoldering, his expression hungry. It awakened an answering hunger within her, the one she had tried to keep at bay for two long days. "Yes," she whispered, "I suppose we could."

The knowledge that he hadn't truly been trying to deprive London's poor of the Saint of Seven Dials stripped away the last of her defenses against this man who already affected her so profoundly. She tilted her face up for his kiss, needing that reassurance that he still found her desirable.

He gave it to her, covering her lips with his own, first gently, then urgently. Releasing her hands, he gathered her to him, but their clothing squelched between them.

"We still need to change," she said with a shaky laugh. "I, ah, may need help with the hooks in the back of this gown."

"Of course." His eyes still burning into hers, he smiled—a smile that held a promise that took her breath away. "Turn around."

As though in a daze, she did so. Gently but deftly, he undid the row of tiny hooks fastening her dress, starting at the nape of her neck and working his way down. The air caressing her damp skin made her

shiver, and he pulled her against him to kiss the back
of her neck.

"I said I would warm you, didn't I?" he asked
softly.

The warmth of his kiss, his touch, chased away the
chill most effectively. She turned in his arms so that he
could capture her lips again. He did so tenderly, his
hands moving inexorably down her back as he continued to unfasten her dress.

This time, she could not fool herself that she was in
his arms for some noble purpose, to save the Saint or
the poor. No, she was here because she wanted him,
needed him, to fill that aching void she had never
known she possessed before meeting him.

She stroked his wet curls, then tried to remove his
sodden coat, even as he was removing her gown. The
soaked wool resisted her efforts, clinging heavily until
he released her long enough to divest himself of it.

Her eyes widened at the unmistakable sight of a
pistol tucked into his waistband. Instead of comment-
ing, however, she turned away, taking the opportunity
to strip off her dress, letting it fall to the floor in a
soggy gray heap.

Now clad only in her damp chemise and stockings,
she shivered again. At once, his arms surrounded her,
enfolding her against the warmth of his body, only
separated from hers by the thin cotton of his shirt
and her chemise. The pistol, she noted, had disappeared.

"Would you prefer a blanket?" he murmured, his
lips against her temple.

"No," she whispered, nuzzling his throat. "I trust
you to keep me warm."

He leaned his head back far enough to look at her. "Only to keep you warm?"

She shook her head. "I trust you completely." As she said it, she realized it was true, and how important it was that he know that. "You are the only one in the world who knows my secret."

"I will guard it with my life." His eyes, his voice, made it a vow. "As I will guard you with my life."

Rowena's thrill of pleasure was marred by a tiny thread of fear. "Am I in danger, then?" If Noel was willing to risk himself to safeguard her . . . "Are you?" she added, before he could answer. She would rather die herself than have him die protecting her.

He rubbed his hands up and down her bare arms, warming them, before answering. "I have trusted you with my secret as well, Rowena—a dangerous secret. As long as no one knows that you are in my confidence, you should be safe enough."

"You didn't answer my second question." She reached up to caress the clean line of his jaw, enjoying the roughness of his faint shadow of beard.

"I don't know. I hope not," he replied, but now his expression was guarded.

"The truth. You said that you trusted me," she reminded him.

He nodded, meeting her eyes again. "I can't deny that I'm pursuing a very dangerous man, one who won't hesitate to kill me if he thinks that will help him escape justice. I simply have to make certain not to give him that opportunity."

Though it chilled her heart, she preferred knowing. It firmed her resolve to have all of him she could have now, that she might at least have that memory, that part of him to keep, should the unthinkable happen.

"Thank you," she said. "Now that I know what is at stake, I will be that much more careful." Her voice caught. "I . . . I would not put you at risk for the world."

It was almost a declaration of her feelings, and when his hands stilled their rubbing, she wondered if she had been too bold. Perhaps—

But then he crushed her against him, burying his face in her hair. "Rowena, my sweet. You can't imagine how much that means to me." His voice was muffled, the emotion in it warming her even more than his embrace.

Noel felt that if the Black Bishop burst upon them right then and struck him dead, he would die the happiest of men. Rowena cared for him, trusted him completely. He knew now that he loved her more deeply than he had known it was possible to love. The very thought of putting her in danger was insupportable.

That she felt the same both elated and humbled him. He kissed her again, trying to convey all he felt with his lips, his hands, skimming down her back and up again. She was still chilled—he could feel the gooseflesh on her arms.

"Just a moment." Releasing her, he pulled a blanket from the foot of the bed and threw it around her shoulders, pulling her to him again with the ends. "That's better. I'd be a poor sort of protector to betray your trust already."

Sliding her arms around him, she seized the ends of the blanket and wrapped them around his back until they were both covered. "I've made a commitment here as well," she said lightly, but with an undertone of meaning.

"Have you, Rowena?" He gazed into her eyes, trying to divine the depth of that meaning.

Though she blushed, she did not look away as she nodded.

Noel felt an urgent, overwhelming need to make her his completely, to forge a bond with her that nothing, not even death, could break. "I love you, Rowena. Will you be mine?" he asked, startled by the ragged edge to his voice. "Completely mine?"

"Yes," she whispered, gazing up at him with such trust and adoration that he felt suddenly invincible—and thoroughly aroused. "Please."

"How can I deny such a courteous request?" He tried to speak lightly, if only to disguise the depth of his feeling, which almost frightened him. Keeping the blanket about both of their shoulders, he led her to the bed. "First, let's get rid of the rest of these wet things."

Sitting on the edge of the bed, he yanked off his ruined boots, glad that Kemp was not one of those fastidious valets who would fly into the boughs over them. Then he turned back to Rowena, sitting beside him.

"Your shoes are wet as well—and your stockings," he pointed out. "Allow me."

He knelt at her feet to pull off first one shoe, then the other—sturdy walking shoes rather than thin ballroom slippers, but wet through nonetheless. He cradled one stockinged foot in his hands, marveling at how small and delicate it was—and how cold.

"Now your stockings," he said, his blood quickening in anticipation.

Her eyes widened, but she made no protest as he slid his hands up her calves, to find her garters just above her knees. Slowly, he peeled away the damp stockings, reveling in the smoothness of her flesh. Watching her face as he moved his hands over her legs, he saw her swallow, her breasts rising and falling with her quickened breathing.

Again he lifted one of her feet, now bare, and gently chafed her toes to warm them. She twitched and he grinned up at her. "Ticklish?"

"A little," she confessed, blushing, it appeared, even more deeply.

Releasing her foot without taking his eyes from her, he unbuttoned his shirt and then his trousers. Rising, he quickly stripped them off, then sat beside her on the bed again. She still had the blanket draped about her, so he reached beneath it to untie the ribbons of her chemise.

"I'm glad you're not wearing a corset," he commented, enjoying her softness beneath the thin cotton. He cupped one well-rounded breast, marveling at its perfection.

She gave a little gasp, then said, "I . . . I only thought to be wearing that gown for half an hour, so it seemed unnecessary. But . . . I'm glad, too." Her voice was breathless, but without fear or reserve.

He undid the last tie, then slid his hands up to her shoulders, to push the chemise down over her arms. She wriggled a bit to help him, and the small motion nearly drove him mad with desire. He wanted her now, this instant, but he knew he would have to control himself if he was not to frighten or hurt her. He had had women before, of course, but none had been virgin. This promised to be a very different—and very special—experience.

Finally her chemise joined all of their other wet garments on the floor. As he had done two nights ago, he feasted his eyes on her lovely, voluptuous body, still not quite believing that she was willing to share it with him. He felt honored and awed—and as eager as a ram in rutting season.

The blanket had fallen from her shoulders to the bed behind her, and now he gently pushed her down atop it. "I will try not to hurt you," he said, knowing that some pain might be inevitable.

"I trust you," she replied, her wide gray eyes as open to him as her body.

"And I trust you to tell me if you wish me to stop," he said, hoping he would not be put to that test.

She smiled, an incredibly seductive smile for one so innocent. "I won't, but I promise."

Determined to make this as special for her as he knew it would be for him, he set about pleasuring her. Stretching out beside her on the bed, he kissed her lingeringly on the lips while lightly running one hand from her shoulder, down her side, barely brushing her dark curls, then back up her belly and between her breasts.

She pressed her whole length against him, silently demanding more, and he gave it to her. He stroked her from collarbone to thigh, pausing only slightly at her cleft and breasts, teasing her, making her want him the way he so desperately wanted her. She clutched at him, pulling him closer, urging him on as she arched against him.

Now he brought his lips into play, trailing kisses down the side of her throat, down her chest, and finally capturing the tip of one breast to tease the nipple with his tongue. With a little squeak of pleasure she squirmed, and the feel of her softness against his arousal was almost more than he could bear.

Sliding one hand down her belly, he buried his fingers in her curls, finding and exploring her most sensitive spot until she gasped, pleading incoherently for the same release he craved. Shifting his weight to his arms, he moved above her, again capturing her lips with his as his straining arousal brushed the juncture of her thighs.

"I'm claiming you for my own, Rowena," he murmured. "My own forever. If you've any objection, now is the time to tell me."

Chapter 20

Rowena was sure that if he denied her the fulfillment she craved another moment, she would fly into pieces. She had never imagined such intense longing, such burning *need* was possible.

"No . . . no objections," she panted. "Oh, Noel, *please!*"

In response, he began to move above her, the length of his shaft stroking the spot that cried out most strongly for his touch. She arched her back, trying to increase the contact between them. Every place his body touched hers, chest against breasts, thighs against thighs, lips against lips, sizzled with sensation.

She wanted more.

Wrapping her arms around his back, she pulled him down until he lay atop her, reveling in the hard maleness of his body. His arousal had almost frightened her with its size at first sight, but now she wanted it against her—inside her. He moved again, brushing her thighs, brushing the sensitive juncture between them.

Instinctively, she spread her legs to give him access, then when he seemed to hesitate, she drew them up and around him, pulling him to her as she did with her arms. Her whole body seemed to throb with her need for him, for completion.

With a guttural groan, he slid the tip of his shaft inside her, then withdrew it. She heard herself whimper, then pressed him back down with her legs. This time he penetrated more deeply, but not deeply enough, before withdrawing again. Over and over, each time only an agonizingly tiny bit deeper, he moved into her, then away. She tried to hurry him, but he was stronger than she and took his time.

Her breathing, her heart accelerated, as though she were running a race, straining toward a finish line that hovered tantalizingly out of reach. "Now, Noel, now," she whispered against his lips.

"I don't want to hurt you," he replied with heart-wrenching tenderness. "I want this to be special for you."

She would have laughed if she hadn't been so desperate for him. Special? "What could possibly be more special than this?"

She felt his lips curve into a smile against hers. "I'll show you."

Sliding a hand between them, he stroked her even as he continued to enter her and withdraw, driving her desire higher yet, higher than seemed possible. She felt herself expanding, bursting into flame. Catching his rhythm, she rocked with him, each motion causing new buds of pleasure to bloom.

Just as she felt herself reaching a final crest, the one she was sure would kill her, he drove himself into her, filling her completely. She barely noticed the brief, stretching pain, for an instant later she raced over the top of the mountain of sensation she'd been climbing and exploded into a thousand pieces.

He stifled her cry of triumphant ecstasy with his kiss, absorbing it into himself. Again and again he thrust into her, prolonging her disintegration into pleasure. His arms trembling, he drove into her one last time, and this time she took his groan—almost a shout—into her mouth.

Slowly, slowly, she felt herself descending from the dizzying height she had achieved—that they had achieved together. She had never felt so complete, so satisfied. If this was what married couples did, it was no wonder Pearl always seemed so happy.

"I had no idea," she breathed, when she could speak again, gazing up at him—at her Noel—in wonder.

He smiled down at her with a tenderness that made her heart turn over. "Nor did I."

"You . . . you didn't?" His skill told her she couldn't have been his first. "But surely—"

As he did so often, he seemed to read her thoughts. "I've bedded women before, yes. But this is the first time I've made love to one—and had her make love to me. Believe me, it is an entirely different experience."

Hearing the word "love" on his lips made her almost giddy with delight. "I'm glad," she whispered.

"So am I," he said, then kissed her, a serious kiss that sealed the bond they had just forged between them.

The words "plighted troth" flashed into Rowena's mind. A week ago, the idea of binding herself to a man for life, putting her person and her future under his control, would have been anathema to her. Now it seemed the right and natural thing to do. Noel, she knew, would never abuse any privilege she gave him.

Still, there was much she didn't know about him. As passion ebbed, her natural curiosity reasserted itself. He seemed to sense the change, for he shifted his weight off of her, though he still gazed at her lovingly.

"There is more where that came from," he said teasingly, caressing her as he smiled.

Though his touch intoxicated her, Rowena kept enough of her reason to realize they could not remain undiscovered here forever. "My maid will have returned by now," she said with a sigh.

"Do you want to return to your room, then?"

Smiling, she shook her head. She never wanted to leave him again, though she knew she must. First, though, she needed to know more—enough to help him in any way she could. "You still haven't told me why you lay in wait for me in the park."

With obvious reluctance, he released her. "You're right. Come, let's get dressed, so we can talk without any other . . . distractions." His grin made her want to fling herself back into his arms, but she restrained herself.

While he pulled dry clothing from his clothespress, Rowena slipped her fresh chemise over her head, then pulled on dry stockings. They exchanged more than one heated glance while they dressed, but did not touch each other until Noel offered to do up the hooks of her fresh gown.

With a shiver of anticipation, Rowena turned her back to him.

"Not still cold, are you?" he asked softly, his fingers working quickly up the row of tiny fastenings.

"Not in the least," she assured him. "I don't think I could ever be cold when I'm with you."

His arms went around her to draw her close and he pressed a kiss to the sensitive skin below her ear. Rowena felt passion blossoming again, but forced herself to pull away.

"We need to talk, remember?"

He nodded, though his hazel eyes still smoldered and a smile played about his wonderful lips. "You're right. I'm sorry. Let's sit down."

They moved to the pair of chairs near his writing desk. Rowena clasped her hands in her lap to keep from reaching for him again. "Now, why did you believe the author of my essays was your traitor?"

He sighed. "I have read all of the letters in the possession of the Foreign Office that the Black Bishop sent during the war, as well as two that were intercepted once they knew he was helping the French. There were similarities in phrasing, sentiment, and even handwriting between some of those letters and those sent to the *Political Register* by MRR."

"You read my original, handwritten essays?" she asked. Though it had no real bearing on the matter, she was curious. "How?"

"I, ah, befriended one of the clerks there, once I suspected a link. What I can't understand is how I could have been so mistaken." His eyes were frankly questioning, though not condemning.

She thought hard, trying to piece together everything she knew as she would consider all of the pieces on a chessboard. "You said that you believe Mr. Richards to be this traitor, apart from the essays?"

He nodded. "Everything I have been able to discover about him fits: people he has been seen with, his political leanings, the recent death of a government official who had been linked to Richards—whom he might have been attempting to blackmail."

"Oh!" Rowena felt a sudden shock of fear as another piece of the puzzle fell into place. "Nelson," she said in answer to Noel's questioning glance. "Mr. Richards was demanding information from the Home Office in repayment of his debt."

"I suspected as much," Noel said. "He'll be looking for other sources now that you have settled that debt for your brother." He shot her a grin. "You did a service to more than Sir Nelson when you won that chess game, you realize."

She returned his grin, but quickly became serious again. "Will Nelson be in danger now, as that other man was?"

"It's possible, if he has any reason to believe your brother is suspicious of him."

"I doubt that he is, actually. Nelson is not the most perceptive of men," she admitted.

Noel smiled again. "I had gathered that. Let us hope Richards has, as well. It is your brother's only safeguard."

She nodded, then returned to her probing. "If you have so much evidence against Mr. Richards, why is he still free?"

"The evidence is purely circumstantial, thus far," he told her. "What I lack is any sort of proof that might hold up in a tribunal. I had hoped proving that he was MRR might provide that."

"But—" Similarity of phrasing, sentiments and handwriting, he had said. Suddenly embarrassed, Rowena bit her lip. "I, ah, think I understand now why you believed what you did."

Still there was no accusation in his expression, only curiosity—and tenderness. "Oh?"

"Last winter, after reading Mr. Richards' treatise on Spence's theory of natural law, I . . . wrote to him, expressing my appreciation of his views," she confessed, realizing now that she had acted like a moonstruck schoolgirl. "He responded, I wrote him again, and he sent another letter."

Noel frowned, now looking concerned. "So you have been corresponding with him for the better part of a year?"

"No, just those two letters," she hastened to assure him. "His second letter implied that he had more important things to do, so I dared not write again. However, I . . . I kept those two letters, rereading them frequently until I had all but committed them to memory."

"So your own writings drew heavily from his letters?"

She nodded. It was mortifying to admit to her hero-worship of Richards, and even more mortifying that she had sublimated her own opinions to his, but she was determined to help Noel in any way she could. "I fear I even used his handwriting as a sort of model when I began writing my essays."

"Ah." His brow cleared, though he still seemed

lost in thought. "Do you have his letters here, by any chance?"

"Why, yes. They are in my chamber," she said, blushing at this admission of how she'd cherished the things. "You may have them, of course."

He reached out and took her hand. "Thank you. And thank you for telling me this. Those letters may be even stronger proof than the essays could have been. He signed them, I presume?"

"Yes. So if they match those of the traitor, will that be enough to convict him?" She felt as though she should be worried about her longtime idol, but instead her only concern was for Noel.

"It might well be. That, plus certain information I'm hoping to obtain tonight or tomorrow." He stood. "I need to leave Town, Rowena, but only briefly. I should be back by tomorrow afternoon, and with luck this will all be behind us by the following day."

"Where are you going?" she asked, alarmed by the grim resolve on his face.

Though his smile was no doubt meant to reassure her, the very fact that he felt the need to do so only increased her fear. "I plan to pay a visit to Richards' father, in Hertfordshire. I'm hoping he can be induced to tell me about his son's whereabouts during the war—and perhaps more. The rumor is that they are not on good terms."

Abruptly, Rowena remembered her promise to go driving with Mr. Richards tomorrow. She opened her mouth to tell Noel, but then hesitated. Perhaps she would be able to learn something from Mr. Richards that would prove his guilt beyond doubt, lessening Noel's danger—as long as Noel did not forbid her to try.

"I will fetch you the letters now," she said instead, "so that you can return—safely—as soon as possible." She stood and turned toward the door, but he put a restraining hand on her arm.

"No, keep them for the moment. The letters must stay safe. I would rather leave them in your care until I can take them myself to the Foreign Office with what I hope will be additional evidence. If I should not return—"

"No! I won't even consider that," she said. "But should you somehow be . . . delayed, I will make certain the letters are delivered. Who is to receive them?"

He went to the writing desk and scribbled a name on a slip of paper, then handed it to her, along with the oilskin-wrapped package he had confiscated earlier.

"These are yours, I believe," he said with a smile.

She took it without replying, without glancing at it, her eyes only for Noel.

"You will see me again, Rowena. Nothing can keep me away," he assured her. "I love you. I have to return, to hold you to your commitment—to be my wife."

Though his words made her giddy, she searched his face, trying to divine any thoughts he might be keeping from her. He met her gaze frankly.

"I love you too, Noel. And . . . I believe you." Then, on sudden impulse, she threw her arms around him. "Oh, Noel, promise me you will be careful! Carry a pistol and keep an eye on the road behind you."

"I always do," he assured her, then gathered her in for a kiss.

Reassured, even, while she was startled to discover that the pistol he had carried today was no anomaly, Rowena returned his kiss, trying to put all that she had left unsaid into her embrace. Then, with a single, longing glance, she went to the door, listened for any sounds without, and stepped into the hallway.

When she opened her chamber door a moment later, Matthilda greeted her with wide eyes. "Oh, miss, you're back! I was beside myself, not knowing where you might be. Lady Hardwyck asked for you, and I told her you were having a lie-down."

"I'm fine," she said, keeping her packet of letters behind her. "I'll speak with Lady Hardwyck shortly."

Her maid's expression was still concerned. "Then it was not . . . not your voice I heard in another room a few minutes since?"

The wonder of her new understanding with Noel, temporarily overshadowed by the seriousness of his investigation, returned full force. "Matthilda, if I tell you something, will you promise to keep it a secret until I can inform my brother and Lady Hardwyck?"

The maid nodded, round-eyed.

"Mr. Paxton and I are to be married." Saying it aloud made it even more amazing.

"Oh, miss!" Matthilda ran forward to embrace her mistress. "I've been hoping for just that. A body with half an eye can see how he feels about you—and you, him."

That startled Rowena, but could not dim her happiness. "Then you approve?"

Matthilda nodded, fervently, her eyes shining. "I do love a happy ending," she exclaimed.

"So do I."

But Rowena knew that her happy ending had not yet come—and could not, until Noel succeeded in his quest. She prayed that he might do so quickly and, even more importantly, safely.

For a long moment, Noel stood watching the door through which Rowena had disappeared. This morning, he would never have imagined that his life could have been so completely changed over the course of a few hours. Rowena had given him a gift beyond anything he could possibly deserve—the gift of her love and trust.

Even the incredible experience of making love to her paled in comparison to the future she promised him. A smile still on his lips, he turned back to the writing desk to pen a note to Kemp, then rang for a footman to deliver it. It was absolutely imperative now that he put this business of the Black Bishop to rest once and for all. He would have to move carefully, however, despite his impatience.

Yesterday, he had believed that no sacrifice he could make would be too great if it brought the Bishop to justice. Today, he had much more to live for—and much more to lose.

Donning a cloak against the still-falling rain, he again tucked his pistol inside his coat. Picking up his hat, he headed out to meet Kemp at the coaching inn. There would have to be another slight change in plans.

"I want you to stay here in town." When Kemp would have protested, Noel raised a hand to silence him. "I have a task for you to do here—a vitally important task."

The two men sat at a small corner table in the

smoke-filled taproom of the Brindled Bull, a small coaching inn near Bow Street. The coach was horsed and ready for the journey to Hertfordshire, and Kemp already dressed in coachman's livery to drive it there.

"I can hire a coachman from the inn," Noel said. "If it weren't raining, I'd ride, but as it's a simple two-hour drive each way, anyone minimally skilled with the ribbons can handle it. I need your special talents here in London."

Kemp nodded reluctantly. "I was talking earlier with one of the drivers, a fellow name of Johnny. He'd do right enough. But what if something goes wrong? What if there's an ambush?"

Noel shook his head. "Unlikely in the extreme. No one knows where I'm going, save Lord Hardwyck and Lord Marcus." And Rowena, but he knew she would tell no one. "There's no reason my brief trip should arouse any suspicions."

"Then what is it you want me to do while you're away?"

"This has been a day of discoveries," Noel said with a wry smile at his confederate. "I now know who the mysterious Mr. R is."

Kemp's eyes widened. "I knew you'd catch him. But why do you even need to make this trip, then?"

"Because Mr. R is not the Bishop after all. It is Miss Riverstone."

"Never! That Quakerish girl at Hardwyck Hall?" Kemp was frankly disbelieving.

Noel couldn't help grinning. "You haven't seen her lately. There's nothing Quakerish about her now, I assure you. But yes, she was the one in Oakshire penning those essays."

"Then you're back where you started?"

"Not quite," Noel reassured him. "She has letters from Richards that I'm confident will provide the proof I need, even if this journey should prove fruitless. Still, the more evidence I can amass, the better. I refuse to allow him any leeway to wriggle off the hook, once I have him."

Kemp nodded. "Aye, it's time and more he was stopped. Myself, I won't be happy till I see him swinging at the end of a rope."

"That's my goal, as well. I want you to keep an eye on Richards while I'm gone. If he suspects anything, he may attempt to use Miss Riverstone to block my next move."

"I'll watch 'em both. You want I should stop him from going near her?" He patted the pocket where he kept his pistol.

"No, for he's likely to call on her even if he suspects nothing. We don't dare tip our hand too soon, or he may go into hiding. Just keep watch, and inform me of his movements when I return." With Kemp watching Richards while Luke and Marcus watched Rowena, Noel could feel confident she would be safe.

"Now, where is this Johnny you spoke of? I'll need to have a word with him."

Kemp went to fetch the driver, and Noel spoke briefly with him, explaining what he needed. He seemed an alert enough young man, but not particularly curious—which was just as well.

"I'll just nip around back to let the 'ostler know I'll be gone, and then we can be off," he said.

Noel nodded. He considered asking Johnny not to

tell the 'ostler their destination, then decided that would raise more suspicion than a simple trip to Hertfordshire would do.

"Very well, but don't be long. I'd like to be there by nightfall, if possible."

He would try to arrange an audience with the elder Mr. Richards this very night. Then he could be back in Town early enough tomorrow to prevent Richards from so much as calling on Rowena before he could be arrested.

Lester Richards dropped two gold coins into Johnny's outstretched hand. "Well done, my good chap. This man Paxton is dangerous, but by knowing where he is, I'll be able to prevent him causing any more harm."

"Dangerous?" The young man's eyes grew round. "Mayhap another driver—" He glanced around the stable yard at the bustling crowd of grooms, coaches and horseflesh.

"No, no, you should be at no risk," Richards assured him quickly. "He's a danger to the crown, not to you personally. With him out of Town, I can counteract his plans, and perhaps even prevent his return."

Though it was clear the fellow had no idea what Richards was talking about, he nodded. "My helping would make me a sort of hero, then, wouldn't it?"

"It would indeed. Now hurry on. You don't want him to become suspicious."

Richards watched as the man hurried away, a frown twisting his face. So, Paxton was going to visit his father, was he? There was no telling what the old fool might say to him. Nothing to Richards' benefit, that was certain.

His own investigations had pointed to a link between Paxton and the Foreign Office, though just what that link was, he wasn't yet sure. What was clear was that Paxton was digging for information about him—information that could conceivably identify him as the Black Bishop.

His first instinct was to leave Town before Paxton could return. But no—he had not come this far by letting emotion rule his head. His influence among the Spenceans in London had grown to the point that he was almost ready to fire them into action. They had the numbers and the drive to achieve what he could never do alone, now that France had lost the war. He couldn't abandon that plan now, when it was so close to succeeding.

No, what he needed was some sort of insurance against anything Paxton might attempt, or, better, a way to dispose of the man entirely.

Richards began to smile. The noose might seem to be closing about his neck, but he still had a valuable card or two to play and a few favors to call in. If all went well, Paxton would be in his power by this time tomorrow.

Rowena Riverstone would serve as both insurance and bait to lure Paxton to his doom should Richards' henchman fail. That way, he could rid himself of two problems at one blow, for it was clear Miss Riverstone was far too perceptive.

And she was expecting him to take her driving tomorrow.

Chapter 21

Rowena had never known time to pass so slowly. Dinner, and particularly the time afterward in the parlor, was a trial. She was dying to tell Pearl her happy news. She was certain her friend suspected something, for she kept sending her quizzical looks, but she was discreet enough not to pry, instead suggesting a game of chess.

Lord Hardwyck joined them only a few minutes into the game, and Rowena, anxious to be alone with her thoughts, quickly checkmated Pearl.

"I do believe that was a record," her friend said with a sigh. "However *do* you do it? Matching wits with Mr. Paxton appears to have improved your game—not that it needed improving."

"Can I interest you ladies in some three-handed whist?" Lord Hardwyck suggested, placing a sympathetic hand on his wife's shoulder.

Rowena stood. "Actually, I find myself unusually fatigued. I believe I will go up to bed."

Once upstairs, she waited with barely concealed impatience for Matthilda to finish her ministrations. The moment the maid left her, she pulled out her packet of letters and opened it. Perhaps they would serve to distract her from obsessing about Noel's dangerous mission.

One by one she opened and read them, both startled and amused by the variety of opinions they contained. Nearly all, even those which vehemently disagreed with her essays, praised her writing, which produced a glow of pride despite her gnawing worry.

Tomorrow she would answer every one, she decided, setting aside two, from well-known members of Parliament, for special attention. That project should occupy her until Noel's return.

As she climbed into bed, she sent up a small prayer for his safety, as well as a wish that he might return before five o'clock.

Earlier, when her courage had been high, she had felt more than willing to match wits with Mr. Richards, learning whatever she could for Noel's sake. The sooner he was brought to justice, the sooner Noel would be out of danger, after all.

With nightfall—and Noel's absence—her confidence wavered. Though she would never risk Noel's life or even his mission by refusing, she rather hoped she would not have to fulfill her promise to drive out with Mr. Richards after all.

"Mr. Richards will see you now."

Noel barely restrained himself from saying *finally* aloud.

Last night, he had been informed by the haughty butler that the elder Mr. Richards retired early and was already abed. Today, after returning at ten o'clock, as instructed, he had been kept cooling his heels in an anteroom of the crumbling country manor house for nearly two hours. His mood was definitely the worse for wear as he followed the butler through dim corridors to a cluttered study.

For a moment the room appeared to be empty, and he wondered if he would be expected to wait here for another interminable period. But then a movement caught his eye and he turned to see a slight, stooped man rising from an enormous wing-backed chair.

"So, my son sends his friends now rather than coming himself to demand money of me?" the old man asked querulously. "You can tell Lester to go to hell."

Noel stepped over a pile of books to extend his hand. "Thank you for seeing me, Mr. Richards. I fear you are under a misapprehension, however. Your son did not send me."

The old man snorted and sat back down, ignoring Noel's hand. "So you say. He's used every pretext you can imagine over the years, sirrah. None will work— not anymore. He won't have another groat from me before I die."

Though more encouraged than discouraged by the man's venom, Noel realized he would have to proceed carefully. "Perhaps, then, it will not surprise you to learn that your son may have run afoul of the law?"

The wheezing that emanated from the chair alarmed Noel until he realized it was laughter. "Surprise me? I'd be more surprised if he hadn't. Lester is a snake, never cared for anyone but himself—though to hear him talk, you'd think he was trying to save the world. Pah!" The old man spat.

"May I?" Noel gestured to a small, rickety chair next to the big wing-back. When the man made no objection, he seated himself and leaned forward, so that he had a good view of the man's face. "What do you know of your son's plans, sir?"

The old man fixed him with a keen glance from his watery blue eyes. "More than I'd like, though nothing recent. He hasn't been here in six months. So, are you here to help him, or to sink him?"

Noel hesitated, realizing his answer might well determine the outcome of this case. The man's animosity seemed sincere, so he gambled with the truth. "I'm hoping to prevent him from harming anyone else—ever."

"Found out what he did to me on his last visit, did you? Beat me so badly I couldn't walk for a week, when I refused him money. Surgeon blabbed, did he?"

"Something like that." It was news to Noel, and while it strengthened his position here, it also worried him. If Richards would abuse his own father, what might he do to Rowena if he suspected she was helping Noel?

"Mr. Richards, can you tell me where your son was during the war with France? Did he serve in the military?"

Another snort. "Military? Him? More like he was helping the Frenchies. Always did take their part. Too much like his mother, though I tried to beat that out of him."

"His mother was French?" That alone did not convict Richards, of course, as Noel's own mother was French. But this interview was proving far more valuable already than he had dared hope.

"Aye, pretty thing, before she turned shrewish. Lester blamed me for her death, but she was sickly for years, despite what the doctors did. Didn't have a sturdy English constitution, of course."

For the first time, Noel began to understand what might have originally turned Richards to his treasonous path—not that it excused him in any way. He still had no firm evidence, however.

"The war," he prompted. "Was your son here, or did he go abroad?"

"He left England after his mother died in '09," Mr. Richards said. "I didn't hear from him for three years, but then he showed up asking for money. I gave it to him. Thought he might stay, you see, and it was lonely here. Thought we could mend our fences. But as soon as he had the money and a good meal, he was off again."

"That would have been in 1812?" Noel asked. That fit perfectly with what he knew of the Bishop's movements. "Did you hear from him again after that?"

"Not until last summer. He showed up on my doorstep, again with no warning. He was injured, and all in rags. I took him in, called the surgeon, made sure he received the best care. But you already know how he repaid me, six months later."

Last summer. "When exactly did he arrive that time—when he was injured?"

"About mid-July it was, as I recall."

Shortly after Waterloo. "And that's when he started pressuring you for money again?"

The old man nodded. "Got more and more insistent with each passing month. Said he needed it to set England on the right path. Came himself up until that last time when he beat me. I had him thrown out of the house, and he's only written since then."

"But you gave him nothing?"

"Nay, I've no fault to find with England as it is. Corrupted by the Frenchies, Lester is, that's my thinking. He'd have another bloody terror here if he could. Used to read everything he could find about it, even though I thrashed him when I caught him at it. Got his mother to teach him French early on, behind my back—he can speak it like a frog, you know."

"Yes, I know." Noel had absolutely no doubt now that Richards was the Black Bishop. "Would you happen to have any of his letters? Might I see them?"

The old man rose with an effort. "I burned most of 'em, but I still have one or two from earlier on— before he turned vicious. But blood will out, they say."

Noel suspected Richards had learned his viciousness at his father's knee rather than inheriting it from his mother, but of course did not say so. He waited while the elder Mr. Richards rummaged through a large pile of papers on one of the desks. Finally, he found what he was seeking and shuffled back across the room.

"Here you are."

Taking the proferred letter, Noel scanned it carefully. Yes, the writing was identical to that of the Black Bishop's missives. Combined with what he now knew of Richards' whereabouts during the war, he had the proof he needed.

"You say he's written to you recently?"

"Got a letter from him just yesterday, but I've already burned it. Sounded more desperate for money than usual, but he always had a persuasive way with words. That's why I burn his letters."

Whereas Rowena had cherished them, Noel thought with a sudden pang. Not that she would anymore, of course.

"Did he say anything else in his last letter?" he asked. "Anything about what he might be planning to do?"

But the old man shook his head. "Just a lot of high-flown language about destiny and the future of England depending on him. Always did have an inflated sense of his own importance, no matter what I said or did to convince him otherwise."

Noel rose. "Thank you, Mr. Richards. You've been very helpful. I don't think your son will trouble you further. May I keep this letter?"

"You're welcome to anything that'll help give Lester what he deserves, the blackguard. Just make sure everyone knows his character flaws aren't my fault. It's all in the blood—that damned French blood."

"Of course." Noel was more than ready to take his leave of this bitter and bigoted old man. "Good day, sir."

Tucking the letter into his breast pocket, he retrieved his hat and went out to the waiting carriage.

"We'll make a quick stop at the inn for a bite, then be on our way," he told the young coachman. The lowering clouds promised more rain, which would slow his return, but he should still reach London early this evening.

With luck, the Black Bishop would be in custody by nightfall.

Answering her letters was not proving quite the distraction Rowena had hoped. For one thing, she was too tired to concentrate properly, having spent a nearly sleepless night imagining every possible thing that could go wrong for Noel. Suppose Mr. Richards had followed him, attacked him? Might he even now be lying in a ditch somewhere?

With daylight her fears had receded somewhat, but not her agitation. As he had described his mission, it should have taken little time. Shouldn't he be back by now? She set down her pen and glanced at the clock above the fireplace in her chamber. Four o'clock.

The rest of the letters could wait, she decided, rising. She would go downstairs and find Pearl. Perhaps she or Lord Hardwyck would have news of Noel.

As she neared the parlor, she heard voices and her heart quickened. She listened, hoping against hope to discern Noel's voice among them, but before she could do so, the door opened wide.

"Here you are, Rowena," Pearl exclaimed. "I was just going to send a maid upstairs for you. Won't you join us?"

"I'd love to. I was growing weary of my own company, I confess." Trying not to look too eager, she peered past Pearl to see who else was present. She saw three or four ladies she had previously met, but not Noel. Even as her heart sank with disappointment, a male figure moved into her line of sight.

Lester Richards.

"Well met, Miss Riverstone," he said, bowing

smoothly. "I know we agreed to drive out at five o'clock, but with the uncertain weather, I had hoped I might persuade you to leave early, while the rain is in abeyance."

Rowena struggled mightily to allow none of the sudden panic she felt to show in her expression. "Of . . . of course," she stammered, mentally chastising herself for such a show of nervousness. "Let me run up to my chamber to fetch my parasol."

He bowed again, and she fled—though she hoped it did not look like a flight to anyone else. She desperately needed a moment alone to think. Hurrying up the stairs and into her room, she shut the door behind her.

Whatever should she do? If she refused to go driving with Mr. Richards, he might well suspect that she knew the truth. He was a very clever man. He might even realize that Noel was the source of her new knowledge.

If he figured out that Noel was on to him, what then? He had murdered before, Noel had told her, though it had seemed incredible at the time. If he felt Noel was a danger to him, he might try to eliminate that danger.

No, she could not put Noel at such an additional risk.

But what of her? Sternly calming herself, she tried to think. They would go for a drive, and she would listen to all that he had to tell her of the Spenceans. She would ask questions, drawing him out. Perhaps he would slip and tell her more than he intended of his plans—plans she could share with Noel when he returned.

Yes, that would be best. Mr. Richards would

scarcely attempt to harm her in an open carriage—
especially when it was known she had left with him.

And whether he would attempt it or not, she owed
it to Noel to do all she could to avoid arousing his suspicions. If she was successful, she should be in no danger whatsoever. Her decision made, she picked up her
parasol and left her room.

As she went down the stairs, her alarm began to
subside. Whatever secrets he held, Mr. Richards was
still the same man she had talked with and played
chess with. As her rational mind took over, the idea of
him doing her violence seemed unlikely in the extreme.

By the time she reached the parlor again, she was
able to greet him with perfect calm. "I am ready, sir.
Shall we go?"

As Noel had feared, so much rain had made the
roads a morass of mud. The coach seemed to crawl
toward London despite his eagerness to put this
whole sordid business behind him and embark on his
future with Rowena. Irritably, he shifted in his seat
and pulled Richards' letters to his father out to read
them through again.

Though he did not have any of the Black Bishop's
letters here for comparison, he was certain the handwriting was the same. Surely his superiors—

A sudden sharp report interrupted his analysis—
the all-too-familiar sound of a pistol shot. The coach
swayed to a stop as the horses sidled in alarm. High-
waymen? Unlikely.

Swiftly, Noel tucked the letters back into his breast

pocket and checked his own pistols, tucking one into the pocket of his coat. Then he crouched on the floor of the coach, his other pistol leveled at the door. He heard shouting, and then the door was wrenched open to reveal a masked figure.

Noel did not hesitate for an instant, but discharged his pistol before his assailant could react. Impossible to miss at such close range, the man fell backward into the mud, a bloodstain spreading across his shoulder. He lay still, apparently unconscious.

Dropping his now useless pistol, Noel pulled the other from his pocket and listened for any other sounds outside the coach. When he heard none, he cautiously emerged.

" 'Ere, now!" came the coachman's voice. "What've you done?"

Though Noel suspected this was no random attack, he saw no point in alarming Johnny unduly. "I've shot a highwayman, of course," he said. "I'll search him for any clues to his identity, and then we can be on our way. We'll alert the authorities when we reach the next village."

He knelt to examine the unconscious man on the ground.

"Nay, I don't think so," Johnny said behind him. "Just get back in the coach calm like, and we'll wait here a bit."

Startled, Noel turned to find the young man pointing an ancient blunderbuss at him with shaking hands. "I allus keep this by me, just in case," he said, his voice now shaking as badly as his hands. "I'd rather not use it if I don't have to, though."

Noel's confusion lasted only an instant. "You are in Lester Richards' pay." It was a statement, not a question.

"He didn't tell me his name, but he paid me handsome. Said you were a traitor to the crown, but he could use this journey to keep you from doing whatever it is you plan. I mean to help him, money or no."

"Richards is the traitor, not I," Noel said, keeping his voice calm and rational, even while he marveled at Richards' cleverness. "You would serve England by helping me, not him, I promise you."

Now doubt clouded the young coachman's eyes. "That might be just what a traitor would say, begging your pardon, sir. How do I know which one of you is telling the truth?"

"I suppose you don't. Nor do I have time to debate the matter, if Richards knows of my errand. I'm sorry to do this, Johnny."

With a swift, fluid motion, he brought up his pistol and fired, knocking the blunderbuss out of the young man's hands but only grazing his arm. While Johnny clutched his arm and shook his head in dazed confusion, Noel leapt up to the box and pulled him down.

"I'll drive the rest of the way. You and Richards' other cohort can sit inside."

Noel picked up a coil of rope he had noted earlier without divining its intended purpose—which must have been to tie him up for delivery to Richards. He tied Johnny's hands behind him, pushed him into the coach, then bound his feet. He then bound the unconscious masked man hand and foot and heaved him into the coach as well.

Before closing the door of the coach, he pulled off his assailant's mask. He didn't know the man, but he looked vaguely familiar. Searching his memory, he realized he had been at the gaming hell on Jermyn Street when he was questioning Willie last week. Clearly, Richards had more spies than he had realized.

Which meant that he might know about Noel's meeting with Rowena in Green Park yesterday. Even if he didn't, he certainly knew of Noel's attraction to her, which made her a potential weapon—and put her in considerable danger.

Vaulting back onto the box, he picked up the reins and urged the horses forward through the thick mud, cursing the sticky miles that still lay between him and Rowena.

"Where are we going?" Rowena asked as Mr. Richards drove the slightly battered curricle past the gates of Hyde Park, heading north on Park Lane.

"You said yesterday that you wished to know more about current efforts to make Thomas Spence's dream come true. I am taking you to meet some of his adherents." His voice was calm and unruffled, but Rowena felt a flare of alarm.

"I see," she said, careful to keep her own voice light and unconcerned. "That should be most interesting. Where is the meeting to be?"

He slanted an enigmatic look at her and her apprehension increased. "A place we have secured for this purpose, a short distance east of Mayfair. Why?"

She shrugged, looking past him at the passing scenery, fearing what he might read in her eyes. "I was simply curious. I did tell Lady Hardwyck I would be gone only an hour."

"And she will—what? Send you to bed without supper, if you are late?"

Rowena managed a laugh, but it sounded forced to her own ears. "Of course not. I do not wish to worry her, however, or arouse her curiosity, since I presume you would not want me to tell her about this meeting."

"Of course." His voice was bland but pleasant, and she could tell nothing from it.

She summoned her courage with an effort. "You were going to tell me about the Spenceans and their plans, were you not?"

"I believe I will let you see for yourself, instead," he replied. "You will find it all most fascinating, I am certain."

They drove in silence then, turning east along Oxford Street, then continuing on for a mile or more, following the curve to High Holborn. Rowena was growing increasingly nervous, but dared not question him again, for fear of arousing his suspicions. She tried to convince herself that he could have nothing to gain by harming her, and much, possibly, to lose.

Finally, Mr. Richards turned the curricle north again, along a narrow street Rowena had never seen before, unfamiliar as she was with any of London outside of Mayfair. "We're almost there now," he said reassuringly.

But she felt anything but reassured. The street grew even narrower, and more and more dirty as they moved away from High Holborn. They passed a group of huddled children dressed in rags who pointed, laughed and scattered at their approach. A beggar in a doorway rattled a cup at them, his sightless eyes covered by a filthy strip of red cloth that matched his ragged uniform.

"Is . . . is this area entirely safe?" Rowena couldn't help asking, not much caring now how nervous she sounded. Any rational person would be nervous in such surroundings, she was sure.

"For those who know it well," Mr. Richards replied. "For those who don't belong here, however—" He pulled the curricle to a stop, leaving his unfinished sentence hanging ominously in the air between them. "Come, I'll escort you inside."

Rowena hesitated. "I . . . I'm not really sure—"

"It makes no difference whether you are sure or not." His voice was no longer bland, but hard and commanding. "Come."

When she still hung back, he seized her arm and roughly pulled her to her feet, forcing her out of the curricle. Thoroughly frightened now, Rowena cried out and tried to pull away from him, but he was far stronger than he looked. Inexorably, he led her to the door of one of the crumbling buildings that hung over the alleyway.

Taking a key from his pocket, he unlocked the door and pushed her inside. Releasing her, he then shut the door again, plunging them both into darkness.

"There is no meeting, is there?" she whispered.

"Not yet." She heard a scraping sound, and then a candle flared to life, lit by the tinderbox he held. "Others will join us shortly, however."

Why had she ever agreed to go with him, knowing what he was? *Because of Noel,* an inner voice reminded her. The thought strengthened her somewhat.

"What others?" she managed to ask. "The Spenceans?"

His face looked weirdly evil in the light of the candle he held between them. "One of them is a Spencean, yes. The others have helped my cause without knowing precisely what it is. I've found gold does an admirable job of silencing awkward questions."

Rowena swallowed. Was she to be silenced as well, in a far less pleasant manner? "What . . . what are you going to do with me?"

He smiled, a distinctly unpleasant smile. "That depends on what my informants tell me when they come. For now, we wait."

Chapter 22

It was past five when Noel finally reached London. His first stop was by necessity the Foreign Office, where he relieved himself of the two men in the coach.

"The younger one seems to have no real knowledge of this business," he told Under-Secretary Hamilton as the two men were conveyed to a secure room for questioning. "Richards paid and duped him. The other, however, may yield something useful."

"We'll have to have a surgeon take a look at that shoulder first," Hamilton replied with a stern glance at Noel. "You still believe Richards is the Bishop, then? Have you any more proof than you offered me before?"

"I have this." Noel pulled the letter Richards' father had given him from his breast pocket. "I have also discovered that Richards' movements during the war dovetail remarkably well with those of the Bishop."

"Then he is your mysterious essayist after all?"

Noel shook his head. "No, but following that trail led me to him anyway, via a more circuitous route."

"But—"

"Please, sir, I must go now, to see to the safety of someone who has helped me, and who may be in danger at Richards' hands. I will return as soon as possible."

The Under-Secretary sighed and nodded. "Very well, I won't detain you. Lord Castlereagh will expect a full accounting when you return, however."

"Of course." Noel hoped he could satisfy his superiors without bringing Rowena's name into the business. But more important was ensuring her physical safety.

Leaving the muddy, driverless coach at the Foreign Office, he hailed a hackney to take him from Whitehall to Hardwyck Hall.

He had barely given his name to the butler when Lady Hardwyck rushed down the stairs to greet him, her violet eyes wide with distress.

"Oh, Mr. Paxton, thank heaven you are here!" she exclaimed before he could utter a word. "I knew that note we received must be false. Luke is quite cross with me, but if he had only *explained* everything, I should never have let her leave with him."

Noel put up a hand to stem the outpouring, though what little he understood of her words caused him a deep foreboding. "Calmly, please, Lady Hardwyck. Do you mean to say that Miss Riverstone is gone?"

She nodded. "She went for a drive with Mr. Richards. They were to have returned within an hour, but it has been a good deal longer than that now. Then Luke returned home and said that Mr. Richards might be *dangerous*. If I had only known—"

"It is not your fault, my lady," Noel assured her, though his anxiety was increasing. "Is Lord Hardwyck here? Is there somewhere we may be private?" He glanced around at the alarmed faces of the footman and butler in the hall.

"Oh, of course. I'm so distracted I'm not thinking clearly. Poor Rowena! To think—But come, Luke is in the library."

Noel reached the door before she did and opened it for her. Luke was standing near the fireplace, talking to a pair of boys Noel recognized as Skeet and the footman Steven, formerly known as Squint.

"Then Stilt should be back soon with word?" Luke was asking the pair, who responded with nods.

"He took over at Oxford Street when I couldn't keep up," Skeet said. "Traffic was heavy, so he most likely won't have lost 'em."

Noel stepped forward. "What's this? Did Stilt follow Richards and Miss Riverstone?"

"Aye," said Steven. "Lord Hardwyck said as how I should keep an eye out for the rotter, 'specially if he came sniffing 'round Miss Riverstone, so when she left with him, I set Skeet after them and ran to get Stilt, as he's the biggest."

Lady Hardwyck rounded on her husband. "You told these boys, but didn't tell me?"

"I'm truly sorry, Pearl," he said, and looked it. "I thought I had. I've been so busy, it must have slipped my mind."

"What time did they leave?" Noel asked, pulling them back to the matter at hand.

Luke turned to him. "Don't look like that, man. I'm sure she will be all right."

Noel realized he must look as stricken as he felt, and made an effort to tame his features. "What time?" he repeated.

"Four o'clock, perhaps a bit later," Lady Hardwyck replied, her hands tightly clasped before her. "He said he was taking her driving in the park."

"Nay, drove right past it, he did," Skeet said. "She didn't look all that upset, neither, though I was a fair bit behind by then. It was a good job I saw Stilt when I did."

Noel frowned. "Then you think she never intended to go to the park either?"

The boy shrugged. "I can't rightly say. She was talkin' to him, but I couldn't hear nothing. She didn't seem put out, though."

Surely, Rowena couldn't have—"You mentioned a note?" Noel said abruptly to Lady Hardwyck.

"Yes. Yes, here." She handed him a folded slip of paper.

Dear Pearl, it read in a stilted feminine hand, *I have eloped with Noel Paxton, with the aid of Mr. Richards. Please do not be angry with me. Your friend, Rowena Riverstone.*

"It doesn't sound at all like her," Lady Hardwyck said as Noel frowned over the scrap. "Though it looks rather like her hand."

"Does it?" He had never seen Rowena's undisguised hand, he realized. This could well be Richards' writing, however, cleverly disguised. That would be ironic, considering how many times Rowena had disguised her own hand to look like Richards'. "When did you receive this?"

"I found it, actually, about half an hour since," Lady Hardwyck replied. "It was set at the base of the urn near the front door."

"To dissuade us from following, of course," Luke said brusquely, shooting a sympathetic glance at Noel. "I'm sure Richards planted it."

"Of course." Noel could not believe otherwise. He would not. "If you will excuse me a moment, I need to see whether my own man left any sort of message for me. I asked him to keep an eye on Mr. Richards as well."

Turning on his heel, he headed for the stairs. Surely, Kemp could not also have failed him? What he couldn't understand, the thing that gnawed at him most, was why Rowena had agreed to go with Richards in the first place. She couldn't possibly still have any sympathy for him, knowing what he was, what a risk he posed.

Could she?

What they had shared yesterday had been real, heart-wrenchingly real. He knew that with every instinct, every feeling, every bit of his reason. Emotion could never have clouded his judgment that completely.

He took the stairs two at a time and burst into his chamber—the chamber where he had shared such an incredible experience with Rowena only yesterday. It seemed eons ago, now. Scanning the room, his eyes lighted on a sheet of paper on the writing desk that he had not left there. He snatched it up and read what Kemp had written in a hasty scrawl.

Miss R gone in old brown curricle, chestnut pair, with BB. Following on horseback, will send word.

Thrusting the note into his pocket, Noel headed back downstairs. Kemp gave no clue as to whether Rowena had gone willingly or not, but at least she had someone beyond a street urchin watching out for her now.

"Has no other message come?" he asked the assembled group as he reentered the library. "My man followed them as well."

Four heads shook as one. "How—?" Lady Hardwyck began, when they were interrupted by a pounding on the front door. Disregarding all dignity, they hurried from the library *en masse* in time to see the butler, Woodruff, opening the door to a panting Stilt.

"Mr. . . . Mr. Paxton," he gasped, staggering into the hall when Woodruff, after a questioning look at Luke, let him past. "I have a . . . a message from . . . Mr. Kemp."

"What do you mean he never returned?"

Rowena, stiff from two hours on the one spindly chair her gloomy prison afforded, now listened to everything Mr. Richards and his unkempt confederate said, in hopes of learning something useful.

"Just what I said," the unsavory-looking older

man repeated. "Eddie never reported back, so I dunno if he done the job or not."

Mr. Richards cursed, first in English, then in fluent French. "I'll have to keep the girl until we know," he finally muttered. "If Paxton escaped, he'll be looking for her—and we can use her to lure him in."

It was all Rowena could do not to gasp aloud, but she dared not let Mr. Richards know she had heard. He had tried to have Noel killed—might even have succeeded! And her own life was apparently forfeit either way, though somehow she found herself worrying less about that than about Noel.

If he had survived, she would not allow herself to be used as bait to draw him to his doom, she was determined. She would contrive to kill herself first, if that was the only thing that could prevent it. Life would not be worth living without Noel, in any case. Living with the knowledge that she had caused his death would be far worse.

"We have lookouts posted about Lunnon. If Paxton returns to Town, we'll know it."

Mr. Richards snorted. "You and your cronies have not instilled in me a great faith in your abilities, Thirk. I should have handled the job myself."

The other man shrugged. "Mayhap you should. But mayhap you wouldn'ta had the stomach for it, neither."

"Fool!" Mr. Richards spat at him. "I've had more experience at—" He glanced at Rowena, who kept her eyes on the floor in apparent dejection, then lowered his voice so that she had to strain to hear it. "I've killed more men than you've picked pockets. One hundred times as many, if you count those the French managed for me during the war. Don't talk to me about 'stomach.' "

The ragged man Thirk backed away, apparently shaken. "Well, all ri' then. I'll, ah, just see if any of our lads have anything to report." He moved to the door.

Mr. Richards turned away from him with a sneer. "As you will. Miss Riverstone, why so glum? Did you not once express to me a desire for adventure?"

Rowena looked up, trying to keep both fear and loathing from her face. "I did, though I had hoped to be an active participant in it. Can I not help in whatever you are planning?"

He narrowed his eyes at her through the gloom. "Do you really have no idea? Has Paxton said nothing to you?"

"Paxton?" she repeated with what she thought credible-sounding surprise. "Noel Paxton? What has he to do with this?"

"What indeed." A grim smile twisted his mouth. "If I believed—" He broke off at the sound of voices at the door. "Yes, what is it?"

"Blind beggar says he's heard something," Thirk replied, coming back into the room. "Someone telling someone else to take a message to Mr. Paxton."

Mr. Richards rounded on the other man at the door, the beggar Rowena had noticed earlier, in his tattered infantry uniform and day's growth of beard, the dirty red cloth bound across his eyes. "What did they say?" he demanded. "Their exact words."

The blind man cringed away at Mr. Richards' tone, but Thirk seized his arm to prevent him from leaving. "Just you up and answer," he told him.

"It . . . it was a man and a lad," he finally said in a weak, quavering voice that spoke of long illness. "The man did most o' the talkin.'"

"And what did he say?" Mr. Richards bit out each word.

"Lessee . . . 'Get you to Hardwyck Hall,' he said, 'and tell Mr. Paxton where they are. I'll go meself to Bow Street.' I'm guessin' he means to fetch the Runners," the old man added.

Mr. Richards cursed. "How long ago was this?"

The beggar shrugged his stooped shoulders. "Mayhap an hour? Mebbe less."

"Then we don't have much time. Even if Paxton was dispatched, the Runners could arrive at any moment. Come along, Miss Riverstone."

Rowena had been watching the blind beggar closely as he gave his account. Something, she was not sure what, seemed slightly off about him. At Mr. Richards' command, she rose and moved closer, covertly studying the old man.

His hands she realized with a shock as she drew level with him. He twisted them together, and they were disguised by a thick layer of dirt, but they were not the wasted hands of an old man. Instead, they looked strong and smooth. She glanced up at his scruffy face and saw a wisp of chestnut hair peeping from beneath his knitted cap. Surely, it couldn't be—?

Quickly, she turned back to Mr. Richards. "Where will we go now? Have the Spenceans another meeting place, one the Runners won't find? We don't dare let them stop us now. Too many people stand to benefit by your success."

"Precisely," he agreed, giving her a speculative

glance and a slight smile. "If no one is here when they arrive, they will have no evidence beyond a serving man's word. Which means you'll have to come with us, old man," he said to the beggar.

The old man shuffled forward most convincingly, barking his toes on the door frame, even though Rowena was fairly certain he was no more blind than he was old. "But how will I find my way back?" he whined.

"That's none of my concern. Thirk, turn the horses around."

While the other man did as he was bid, Mr. Richards grasped Rowena's arm with one hand and the beggar's arm with the other and led them both from the room. Thirk made a difficult business of turning the curricle around in the narrow alley, while Mr. Richards looked on in growing impatience.

"Here, here, let me do it," he finally exclaimed. "You watch these two."

Thirk jumped down and Mr. Richards released his two prisoners. Rowena, alert for any move the false beggar might make, was ready when he acted. The moment his arm was released, he turned swiftly. Catching him totally by surprise, he knocked Mr. Richards to the ground. Rowena dove to the side, evading Thirk's lunge in her direction.

" 'Ere, now, none o' that!" Thirk cried, reaching inside his coat as Mr. Richards struggled to his feet. At the same time, the "beggar" tore the bandage from his eyes and pulled a pistol from beneath his rags.

Mr. Richards stared. "Paxton! How—?"

Before he could finish his question, Thirk pulled out his own pistol, leveling it at Noel—who fired without hesitation. Thirk crumpled to the ground. Richards lunged for Noel, but Rowena snapped out of her shock at the violence she had just witnessed and shoved him from behind.

"Good girl," said Noel in his normal voice, pulling a second pistol from his tattered coat. "You've just helped to apprehend the Black Bishop, one of the most dangerous men in Europe."

Mr. Richards glared up at him. "You've no proof. I made sure of that."

Noel raised a brow. "I believe I have more proof than I need, actually. Your man Eddie is in the custody of the Foreign Office even now, along with that poor coachman you duped. Unfortunately for you, he seems a patriotic sort. And then there are your letters, to your father and to Miss Riverstone. Remember, we have several you sent during the war, when you were pretending to work for England."

"And there was his plot to kill you, as well," Rowena added. "I heard him discussing it with Thirk, here."

Richards shot her a venomous glance. "I should have known better than to believe for a moment you were sympathetic to my cause. Women can't be trusted, especially women who fancy themselves clever."

"In Miss Riverstone's case, I'd say it's a good deal more than fancy," Noel said with a smile for her that set her heart racing, despite the grime and stubble marring his face. "She's the most intelligent woman I've ever known. Indeed, one of the most intelligent persons I've known, of either sex."

"There's plenty you don't know," Mr. Richards

spat. "I have friends, supporters. Your life won't be worth a fig if you kill me."

Noel shrugged. "Oh, I don't plan to kill you myself. Kemp should be arriving momentarily with a contingent from the Foreign Office. I rather doubt you'll escape the noose, however. As for friends, you've killed several of mine. I consider myself finally avenged."

"Several?" Mr. Richards looked genuinely curious, though not at all repentant. "I heard you knew Geraint—"

"And Burroughs and Thompson—perhaps better known to you as Graywolf and the Red Boar." Noel's expression was grimmer than Rowena had ever seen it, his eyes bleak with remembered grief.

Sudden understanding broke across Richards' face. "Puss in Boots!" he exclaimed. "I should have guessed it."

Noel sketched a cynical bow. "At your service. Or, rather, at my country's. Ah, here they come now." He turned to greet his manservant Kemp, who rounded the corner just then with six sturdy, uniformed men behind him.

"All's well," Noel told them. "Take these two in and I'll join you once I've had a chance to get Miss Riverstone safely home and clean myself up."

He supervised the binding and bundling of Richards and Thirk into the curricle, then turned to Rowena.

"Are you certain you are all right?"

"I'm fine," she replied, staring at him with wonder. "You . . . you were a spy during the war?"

He nodded, meeting her eyes with a crooked grin.

"And never set foot in Canada, I fear. I apologize for the falsehoods I told you."

"It seems they were justified." She could not stop staring at him as she fit all the pieces together in her mind. She remembered how deftly he had unlocked the ballroom door yesterday—was it only yesterday?—and another suspicion formed.

Lowering her voice, she asked, "Might you also be the Saint of Seven Dials?"

"I did say you were the most intelligent woman I've ever known." His grin widened.

Now it all made sense—his evasiveness about the investigation, the return of her mother's jewels, Noel's irritation when she had praised Mr. Richards for his daring as the Saint.

"So I can now give credit where credit is due," she said, smiling back at him. "It appears I have a debt of gratitude to repay."

He leaned down to brush her lips with his. "And I believe I know just what payment I will demand. But first, let's get you back to Hardwyck Hall. We both have some explaining to do—and an announcement to make."

Epilogue

Rowena wondered whether anyone had ever been happier than she was today—her wedding day. Noel's estate of Tidebourne was charming, similar in size to River Chase, but far more welcoming, in her opinion. When they had arrived at the rambling manor house yesterday, she had instantly fallen in love with it.

Now, less than an hour before the wedding, she was attempting to give a truncated version of the events of two weeks ago to Noel's twin sister Holly, who had traveled from Yorkshire with her husband, the Marquess of Vandover, to attend her brother's nuptials.

"So when Noel arrived, Kemp had already persuaded a blind beggar to exchange clothing with Noel. His impersonation was flawless—I did not recognize him myself for a full five minutes, though I was in the same room with him."

Holly, a handsome black-haired woman, laughed.

"Yes, Noel always loved disguises, even as a boy—we both did, actually. I believe it's the main reason he was so determined to become a spy during the war. So now this traitor is under arrest?"

Rowena nodded. "He will stand trial soon. Had I known the full measure of his crimes, I confess I would never have been so foolish to go driving with him that day—though I suppose that helped to speed his capture."

Just then a curly-headed toddler ran up. "Mama! Mama! Come see puppies!"

Holly knelt down with some difficulty, as she was in the latter stages of pregnancy. "Yes, Cliff, we'll go see them as soon as the wedding is over." She ruffled her son's hair.

Rowena watched with a lump—a happy lump!—in her throat. Three-year-old Clifton looked remarkably like his uncle Noel—like a child of her own might look one day. They had not yet spoken of children, but she was certain Noel would be a wonderful father, after seeing him play with his nephew last night.

Noel's mother and older sister, Blanche, bustled in then, along with Pearl, to help with Rowena's final preparations. Mrs. Paxton chattered in French-accented English with the occasional French phrase thrown in, while Blanche devoted herself to little Clifton, cuddling and cooing to him.

"You will wish to leave off the spectacles, *non?*" Mrs. Paxton asked as Pearl adjusted Rowena's veil.

She shook her head. "No, I promised Noel I would not. He says he likes them."

Mrs. Paxton clucked her tongue, but Pearl gave Rowena a quick hug. "You are a very lucky woman, you know," Pearl said. "You have found a man who loves you for yourself, and who will not attempt to change you into something you are not."

"Yes," Rowena said with a smile, "I know." Nor would she attempt to change Noel, as she had once thought to do.

It seemed but a moment later that she was entering the little village church where she and Noel were to be married by special license. He had not been willing to wait the extra week for banns to be read—and, in truth, neither had she.

Noel stood by the altar at the front, looking outrageously handsome in his tailored deep blue coat and breeches, his chestnut hair curling roguishly about his ears. His eyes met hers and he smiled, a smile of such infinite promise that it was all Rowena could do not to run down the aisle to him. Her stately procession seemed almost painfully slow, so eager was she to join him.

They repeated their vows steadily, gazing into each other's eyes throughout the brief service. The moment they were pronounced man and wife, Noel gathered her into his arms and kissed her, right there in the church, in full view of the assembly.

Rowena melted against him, but finally the tittering behind them pulled her to her senses. "Later," she whispered.

He answered with a suggestive wink. "I'll take that as a promise. You still owe me, you know."

"And I plan to pay you in full, in only a few hours." Anticipation made her giddy, and she knew she was smiling like a fool as she proceeded back down the aisle on his arm.

She didn't care. The one man whose opinion she valued considered her the most intelligent of women. What others thought of her mattered not at all.

Once out on the lawn under the warm September sunshine, they were surrounded by family and friends. Sir Nelson came forward to embrace his sister, while Noel was congratulated by Lord Hardwyck, Lord Marcus, Lord Peter and Harry Thatcher.

"You're a lucky man," Lord Peter said, clapping Noel on the shoulder. "Now it only remains for Harry and me to find our perfect mates."

Mr. Thatcher laughed. "You know my feelings about matrimony. I've no plans to marry, ever—whatever the inducement. And as for you, I can't imagine any woman living up to your exacting standards."

"Perfection or nothing," Lord Peter agreed with a grin.

"Then you're in no more danger than I."

"If you will excuse us, gentlemen?" Noel put an arm around Rowena's waist and led her away from the throng, toward the carriage waiting to take them back to Tidebourne. "Harry and Peter ought not to tempt fate like that," he said to her with a chuckle.

"Why?" she asked. "Did you once say something similar?"

He smiled down into her eyes and her heart turned over. "If I did, I was speaking from profound ignorance. Of course, how could I know I *would* meet the perfect woman, one who combines intelligence and passion in one beautiful package?"

"Passion?" she asked, grinning up at him.

"Mm. Were you not passionate about all of the causes you espoused? You certainly sounded so."

"Perhaps," she agreed. "But I was still very innocent then. Now I intend to turn my passions to other things."

"Dare I hope I might be one of those things?" he asked, his hazel eyes darkening with desire.

"Indeed," she said, letting all the love she felt for him shine from her own eyes. "I plan to adopt you as my pet cause."

"I believe I like the sound of that," he said, pulling her to him for a kiss that promised years of passion to come.